Black Tiger

Black Tiger

A Novel of Slightly Alternate History

Brian J. Smith

ISBN (E-book): 978-1-7338913-3-2
ISBN (Paperback): 978-1-7338913-2-5
Centauri-Evergreen Publishing

Dedicated to the memory of

Lieutenant Thomas R. Francis, USN

Taken from us far too soon.
You are never forgotten, my friend.

Other books by Brian J. Smith

Singularity Point

Forward

I began the first draft of this novel back in 2008, two short years after the F-14 Tomcat was retired from service and there was still a healthy debate going on concerning the merits of that choice. The first draft was centered around a lot of technical information gleaned from articles written at the time, mostly comparing the flight characteristics and payload/range between the F-14D and its proposed follow-ons versus the (then) relatively new F/A-18E/F Super Hornet. Ultimately I didn't like what I came up with, and shelved the project indefinitely—one of the advantages of writing as a hobby rather than a profession.

I was still intrigued by the argument, and as it happened, the RTS computer game *Command: Modern Air / Naval Operations* (rebranded in recent years to *Command: Modern Operations*) contained several 'concept' platforms in its usable database, including variations on the proposed F-14E. I created a series of five missions with the same title and roughly the same plot as this novel. (That was done under my internet gaming handle, jmarso.) It's been a few years since I looked, but I think those missions are still available to play as part of the community mission pack. Part of the problem when writing the first draft and designing the game missions was finding a way to make Iran a credible military threat in a scenario where the vast weight of U.S. military power was brought to bear against it. The other problem was finding a way to introduce the F-14E Advanced Super Tomcat long after the Tomcat was retired and the existing airframes destroyed. The solution I found was to re-write modern history.

Fast forward to 2020, when Covid had us all stuck indoors and looking for things to do. I dusted off the old manuscript, gave it a read, and started a second draft. It turned out I didn't care for that one either, but the third time was the charm. Although some of the old technical comparisons remain, I have tried to make this a story-driven, fast-paced, adventurous tale that is fun to read rather than a technical treatise over long-settled arguments. The fictional advanced Tomcats in this story derive their data from none other than the *Command: Modern Operations* database I used to create the Black Tiger mission pack all those years ago. Players of *Digital Combat Simulator* (DCS) may also recognize a couple of the scenarios that show up in this story, also derived from user-made missions I've created for that game. All other technological innovations that appear are sourced from internet articles I've stumbled across over the years, and may not bear any resemblance to actual, existing technologies. That is another advantage of writing an alternate timeline story—the allowance for elements that might border on sci-fi.

In a similar vein, readers knowledgeable about the Navy's units and callsigns will recognize some real world units mixed in with fictional units that either don't exist, or whose names and unit types don't match their real-world counterparts. That is simply a case of dramatic license on my part.

If you are reading this, thanks for making the purchase and I sincerely hope you enjoy the ride. Feedback, good or bad, is always appreciated on the sites where the book was found. If it is well received, I may explore a little further down this imaginary timeline, giving Fargo and his shipmates the opportunity for new adventures.

Acronyms/Abbreviations

ACLS	Automatic Carrier Landing System
AESA	Active Electronically Scanned Array
AIO	Aviation Intelligence Officer
APU	Auxiliary Power Unit
AWACS	Airborne Warning and Control System
BARCAP	Barrier Combat Air Patrol
BDA	Battle Damage Assessment
BRAA	Bearing, Range, Altitude, Aspect
BUPERS	Bureau of Naval Personnel
CAG	Carrier Air Wing (Group) Commander
CAP	Combat Air Patrol
CDC	Combat Direction Center
CHOP	Change of Operational Control
CIWS	Close-in Weapons System
CNO	Chief of Naval Operations
CSG	Carrier Strike Group
CVIC	Carrier Intelligence Center
CVBG	Carrier Battle Group
CVW	Carrier Air Wing
DARPA	Defense Advanced Research Projects Agency
DCAG	Deputy Carrier Air Wing Commander
DCNO	Deputy Chief of Naval Operations
DESRON	Destroyer Squadron
ECMO	Electronic Countermeasures Officer
ELINT	Intelligence data derived from an electronic source
EMCON	Emissions Control
ESM	Electronic Surveillance Measures
ESSM	Evolved Sea-Sparrow Missile
ETA	Estimated Time of Arrival
EW	Electronic (or Electromagnetic) Warfare
FLIR	Forward Looking Infrared
FOD	Foreign Object Damage
HAQ	House Arrest, in Quarters

HUD	Head's Up Display
HUMINT	Intelligence data derived from a human source.
ICS	Intercom System
IFF	Identification Friend or Foe
IFT	In-Flight Technician
IRGC	Iranian Revolutionary Guard Corps
IRIAF	Islamic Republic of Iran Air Force
IRST	Infrared Search and Track
ISR	Intelligence, Surveillance, Reconnaissance
JCS	Joint Chiefs of Staff
KIA	Killed in Action
NATO	North Atlantic Treaty Organization
NATOPS	Naval Aviation Training and Operational Procedures Standardization
NCA	National Command Authority
NCO	Non-commissioned Officer
NFO	Naval Flight Officer
NSA	National Security Advisor
NSAWC	Naval Strike Air Warfare Center
NSC	National Security Council
OOD	Officer of the Deck
OPSEC	Operational Security Measures
OSINT	Intelligence data derived from open (publicly available) sources.
PLAAF	People's Liberation Army Air Force
PLAN	People's Liberation Army, Navy
PRC	People's Republic of China
RESCAP	Rescue Combat Air Patrol
RFP	Request for Proposal
ROE	Rules of Engagement
RIO	Radar Intercept Officer
RWR	Radar Warning Receiver
SAM	Surface-to-Air Missile
SDO	Squadron Duty Officer
SEAD	Suppression of Enemy Air Defenses
seaRAM	Rolling Airframe Missile System

SFTI	Strike Fighter Tactics Instructor
SIGINT	Intelligence data derived from communications.
SITREP	Situation Report
SUCAP	Surface Combat Air Patrol
SVTOL	Short / Vertical Takeoff and Landing
TAO	Tactical Action Officer
TACCO	Tactical Coordinator
TAD	Temporary Assigned Duty
TARCAP	(Over) Target Combat Air Patrol
USAF	United States Air Force
USN	United States Navy
WSO	Weapons Systems Officer

Alternate History

1989: John Lehman is confirmed as U.S. Secretary of Defense after the failure of Senator John Tower's confirmation hearing. Congressman Dick Cheney is considered for the position but deemed unsuitable due to health issues. Lehman, a reserve naval flight officer, is one of the architects of the 1980's Maritime Strategy and a strong proponent of naval aviation.

1990: Saddam Hussein invades and occupies neighboring Kuwait.

1991: The United States leads an international coalition to liberate Kuwait from Iraqi occupation. Iraq's armed forces are decimated during the short war.

The A-12 Avenger program is canceled. The F/A-18E/F Super Hornet is proposed as an advanced, low-cost replacement for the A-6 Intruder.

The Soviet Union officially dissolves, with Boris Yeltsin serving as President of the Russian Federation. A long-term economic downturn begins in Russia.

1992: The Naval Advanced Tactical Fighter program is cancelled. The Secretary of Defense calls for an increase in F-14D production beyond 1992 as a stop-gap while a study is conducted to address the future make-up of the navy's carrier air wings. McLaren Aircraft claims its Super Hornet program fills the gap, while Ironworks Aerospace proposes a next-generation version of the F-14 Tomcat. The Defense Department orders a competition and fly-off between prototype aircraft, to take place in 1995.

William J. Clinton is elected the 42nd President of the United States.

1995: A fly-off is conducted between the prototype YF-18E and YF-14E. The 'Advanced Super Tomcat' far exceeds the capabilities of the 'Super Hornet' in every category except cost per unit and cost per flight hour. However, the Super Hornet program has a strong lobby on Capitol Hill, and the Clinton-era drawdown is fully underway. The proposed Super Hornet will result in a consolidation of aircraft fleets, supply chains, and reduced flight hour costs. The contract is awarded to McLaren Aircraft despite stiff opposition from the naval aviation establishment.

1996: China embarks on a two decade modernization and buildup of their armed forces, especially their navy, following the Taiwan Strait Crisis.

An internal Navy program to give the F-14 a ground-strike capability proves remarkably successful. 'Bombcats' serve as all-weather strike aircraft and airborne forward-air-controllers over Bosnia, matching and sometimes exceeding the capabilities of the legacy F/A-18 Hornet and the F-15E Strike Eagle.

1999: McLaren Aircraft wins the Joint Strike Fighter competition and is awarded the contract to put the F-35 into production. Three variants are planned: two conventional versions for the USN and USAF, and a Short/Vertical Takeoff and Landing version for the USMC and some foreign buyers.

The F/A-18E/F Super Hornet enters service with the U.S. Navy.

2001: After the closest and most contentious election in United States history, the Supreme Court rules in favor of Albert A. Gore, who is sworn in as the 43rd President of the United States.

On September 11th, Middle Eastern terrorists hijack several commercial airliners and fly them into the twin towers of the World Trade Center, and the Pentagon. President Gore promises a full investigation, and a strong response when those responsible are identified.

Six weeks after the attacks of September 11th, the United States submits a list of demands to Al-Qaeda and the Taliban regime in Afghanistan, demanding the surrender of Osama Bin Laden and the ringleaders of the 9/11 attacks. These demands are refused outright, and the United States launches a massive Tomahawk missile strike into various parts of Afghanistan. This strike is viewed as the weakest possible response to the situation, and there is significant public outrage. The Gore administration yields to public pressure and promises that further retribution is on the table.

2002: In February, U.S. troops invade Afghanistan. Carrier-based strike fighters are the only assets capable of sustained combat operations in support of Operation Just Riposte, the first phase of the war in Afghanistan. The F-14 Tomcat is the only naval aircraft with the payload/range capacity to operate in the far northern reaches of Afghanistan without over-taxing available tanker resources.

No connection is proven between Saddam Hussein's Ba'ath regime and Al-Qaeda, so there is no planned invasion of Iraq. U.S. focus shifts almost completely from the Persian Gulf to Afghanistan, and by late April the U.S. backed Northern Alliance has defeated the Taliban. A democratic government is placed in power.

In May, a large battle is fought at the Tora Bora cave complex in eastern Afghanistan. Although the battle is a crushing defeat for Al Qaeda and terrorist forces, Osama bin Laden escapes into the tribal areas of Pakistan and remains at large. The Gore administration faces fresh criticism for its handling of the military situation in Afghanistan, and is blamed for allowing bin Laden to escape.

Relations between the United States and Saudi Arabia are strained to the breaking point when the identities of the 9/11 hijackers are made public. The U.S. begins a phased withdrawal of its forces from the kingdom, maintaining only a light presence in Qatar and the United Arab Emirates. Operation Southern Watch, the enforcement of the no-fly zone over southern Iraq, is ended in favor of supporting operations in Afghanistan. This period marks the beginning of a reduced U.S. presence in the Persian Gulf, most notably the cessation of aircraft carrier deployments, which do not resume for a decade.

With the U.S. focus shifting away from the Persian Gulf, Iran covertly arms and equips Shiite Arab militias in southern Iraq as a proxy force to facilitate the overthrow of Saddam Hussein. Iran also supplies weapons and support to the northern Kurdish tribes. Iranian mullahs begin moving among the Shia majority population in southeastern Iraq, building closer ties with Tehran. Weakened and impoverished after years of western sanctions and the loss of most of its military, Iraq begins to destabilize.

2003: Iran launches a surgical invasion into southeastern Iraq, capitalizing on low U.S. force levels in the Persian Gulf and the perceived weakness of the Gore administration. The Gulf States and western allies denounce this move, but it has the welcoming effect of firmly tying down two troublesome regimes. Iran's objective is limited to seizing the oil-rich southeastern border provinces where the majority Shia population is friendly to them. Several weeks after Iran invades, the northern Kurds declare their independence and announce the formation of a Kurdish state in northern Iraq. The Kurds request recognition and aid from the Gulf States and allied western nations, but the Turkish government staunchly opposes such action; it is faced with a secessionist movement from its own tribal Kurds in eastern Turkey. Russia provides covert aid to the Iraqi Kurds, knowing this will be a thorn in Turkey's side and therefore a distraction for NATO. Meanwhile, Iran provides diplomatic assurances that it has no intention of violating Saudi or Kuwaiti sovereignty, or interfering with the flow of oil through the Persian Gulf.

2004: Running on a platform of competency in international and military affairs, former JCS chairman Colin Powell announces his bid to run in the '04 presidential election. Powell is seen as a moderate, perhaps even a centrist, and is immensely popular. He wins the general election in a landslide, becoming the nation's first African-American president-elect.

Problems in the form of engineering flaws, cost overruns, and delays plague the JSF program. Initial production and deployment of the F-35 is facing a years-long delay. International partners express concern over rising costs, and some withdraw their partnership.

2005: Colin Powell is sworn in as the 44th President of the United States with Jack Kemp as his VP. Both men are considered right-leaning moderates, and Powell's popularity is firmly bipartisan. Condoleezza Rice is confirmed by the Senate to the post of Secretary of State.

By mid-year, Iran has conquered southeastern Iraq and absorbed it into Iran. These gains give Iran access to over two million barrels of Iraqi oil *per day*, a windfall which Iran uses for a staunch military buildup and modernization. The additional revenue is also used to consolidate its territorial gains, exert increased influence over Gulf waters, and accelerate its nuclear weapons program.

2006: The Powell administration cancels the F-35 JSF program, citing cost overruns, ongoing engineering problems, and several security breaches resulting in data-thefts by China. The Senate Armed Services committee calls for an overhaul of military-industrial procurement practices, and much stricter oversight. The cancellation of this program creates a dilemma over the replacement of aging aircraft fleets, and the Defense Department puts out two new requests for proposal: one for a conventional replacement for the legacy F/A-18 and F-16, and one for a separate design to replace the AV-8B Harrier.

The F-14 Tomcat is retired from service. Despite concerns over a black-market supply chain of parts going to Iran, the fleet is placed in the Boneyard in Arizona rather than being destroyed. Ironworks keeps several airframes for use as test-and-evaluation aircraft, as the cancellation of the F-35 program sparks fresh interest in the new development of next-generation designs.

2007: Pacific Aerospace presents a design to replace the AV-8B Harrier: the X-36. It is a substantial redesign of the X-32 prototype which originally lost to the F-35. Both the USMC and Royal Navy feel this design corrects the X-32's shortcomings. No other companies have expressed an interest in this RFP, and Pacific Aerospace is awarded the contract. Work begins on the future AV-36 Shark.

McLaren Aircraft and Ironworks both present proposals for conventional next-generation aircraft. McLaren's is a clean sheet design: the YF-25. It can be produced either single or dual cockpit, with or without dual flight controls. For land based versions, unnecessary naval components will simply be removed or modified as needed, resulting in lighter weight and increased payload/range. The YF-25 exceeds the RFP requirements, pushing the middle ground in the concept of the technological low end of a high/low-mix air force. However, with the repeated reductions in F-22 procurement numbers, the USAF feels this design is the perfect stopgap. The Ironworks proposal is even more expansive: "Flight Deck 21", Fifth Generation replacements for both the Super Hornet and the EA-6B Prowler. The concept involves redesigned, upgraded versions of the F-14 and EA-6B, along with a tanker version of the Prowler airframe. Flight Deck 21 would almost double an aircraft carrier's strike footprint when compared to McClaren's 'all-Super Hornet' flight deck, heralding a return to deep interdiction and standoff capabilities that have degraded steadily since the Vietnam era. The Defense Department takes an unusual step: it awards McLaren Aircraft the contract for the JSF replacement, but also contracts with Ironworks to continue research and development on Flight Deck 21 in partnership with DARPA.

2008: U.S. intelligence services locate Osama bin Laden in Pakistan. Operation Neptune Spear is carried out after several weeks of intensive planning, resulting in his death. The United States begins an immediate phased withdrawal from Afghanistan, planned to be completed by 2011. U.S. relations with Pakistan sour after learning that Pakistani officials knew Osama bin Laden was sheltering there.

The U.S. housing market collapses, marking the beginning of a deep recession in the U.S. economy.

U.S. President Colin Powell is re-elected for a second term.

Following years of back-and-forth negotiations, Ukraine and Georgia are denied admission to NATO at the Bucharest Summit. Russia subsequently conducts an invasion and occupation of Georgia, calling it a "Peace Enforcement" operation. This goes relatively unchallenged by the Powell administration, which is fully engaged in the ongoing withdrawal from Afghanistan.

2009: Vice President Jack Kemp succumbs to cancer. Condoleezza Rice is sworn in as Vice President of the United States following his death.

2011: Iran has fully integrated its gains in Iraq. Most maps recognize new borders which show the former southeastern Iraq as part of a larger Iran, with Iraq being a smaller, landlocked country with no port access to the Persian Gulf. What remains of Iraq is enflamed in a full-blown civil war between Iranian proxy Shia militias, northern Kurds, and the Ba'ath regime. Saddam Hussein is besieged, struggling to remain in power.

Condoleezza Rice announces her candidacy for the 2012 presidential election and is immediately endorsed by President Powell. Former Governor Gary Johnson announces his candidacy as a third-party independent candidate, threatening to be an election spoiler. While the Powell administration has demonstrated a strong foreign policy, a deep, lingering economic recession has weakened the administration domestically.

Operation Just Riposte comes to an official end on the tenth anniversary of 9/11, following a three-year phased withdrawal from Afghanistan. Within months, civil war wracks Afghanistan as resurgent Taliban elements seek to re-establish control over the country. The Powell administration implements Operation Mountain Watch, a limited effort to aid the Afghan government with UAV assets, intelligence, and materiel. Although U.S. intelligence agencies and the Afghan government covertly employ U.S. contractors, no standing U.S. military force remains in the country.

2012: After a long hiatus, The United States deploys a carrier strike group into the Persian Gulf, re-establishing a strong naval presence in the region.

Iran continues taking arms deliveries from China, Russia, and Pakistan. These include the components of an advanced integrated air defense system, modern fighters, and airborne early warning aircraft. In addition, Russian and Chinese contractors arrive in Iran and begin the covert formation of the Russian and Chinese volunteer groups.

Former state governor James Marsden unexpectedly wins the three-way 2012 presidential race, defeating Condoleezza Rice and Gary Johnson. Although he takes only 44% of the popular vote, he wins the electoral college.

2013: James Marsden is sworn in as the 45th President of the United States. Elected on promises to restore America's ailing economy, he is regarded as a foreign policy neophyte. International adversaries see his fledgling administration as an opportunity to further their own agendas.

Gulf Region
2012

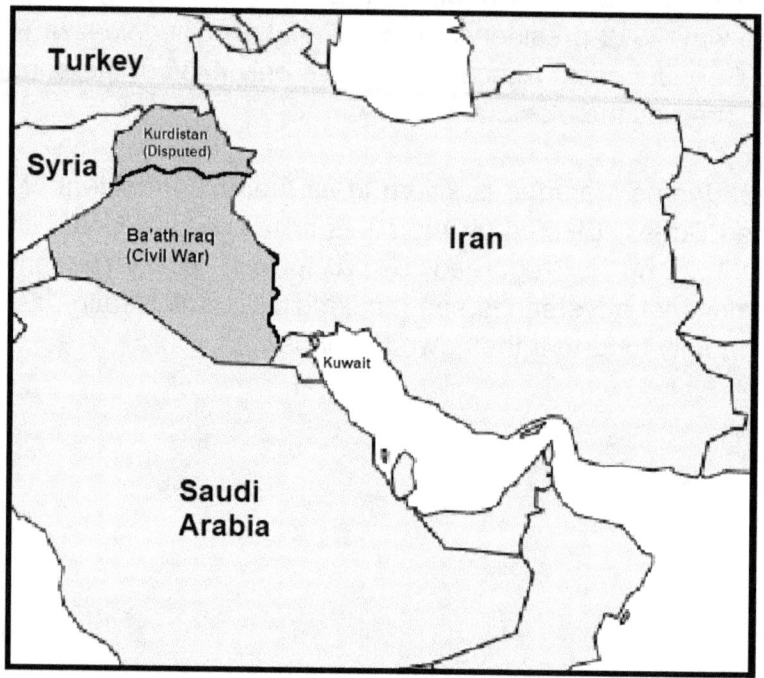

Prologue

2012
Islamic Republic of Iran

Arkady Kovalev, formerly *Polkovnik* (Colonel) of the Russian Air Force, mentally tuned out the lecturing voice of his new Iranian liaison as he took in the surroundings of the man's office. It was somewhat more opulent than he'd expected to find here, featuring wood-lined walls decorated with Persian trappings and written works in Farsi, a language he didn't understand. Even the aroma of the room was somewhat exotic, smelling slightly of some form of spice or incense. It was far different from his past life in the 159th Aviation Regiment at Besovets, near the Finnish border. It was also a far cry from his native home in Pskov. He absently wondered if he'd ever see home again, and wondered even more at his general apathy on the subject. He had volunteered for this assignment because he wanted a change; because he was sick and tired of poor pay and bad food, and sick of freezing his balls off in Besovets.

Now that he was here, he wasn't sure he wanted to be here, either.

"Colonel Kovalev?"

"Eh? My apologies, *Agha*, can you repeat that?" Kovalev replied in Russian, using a Persian honorific.

"I asked if your accommodations are acceptable."

Acceptable? Kovalev thought, forcing himself not to laugh. "*Da*, they are acceptable," he said stoically. As acceptable as they could be, in a country run by religious fanatics, that banned alcohol entirely, and made their women cover themselves from head to toe. *Why in the hell did I volunteer for this? What was I thinking?* He asked himself, then answered: *You were thinking that the flying would be good, and the money as well.* If nothing else, at least he'd get paid on time here. If not, he'd be headed home very soon. That was the advantage of being a mercenary rather than a Russian military officer: mercenaries got *paid.* He sat up a little straighter in his seat. "They are acceptable," he repeated.

The man sitting across from him was Brigadier General Hamed Abdi of the Iranian Air Force. Abdi also made it plain from the start that he also held rank in the Iranian Revolutionary Guard Corps, the regime's praetorian guard, and the ones who *really* called the shots here. Kovalev had to admit that General Abdi was more than just a stuffed shirt; he'd racked up an impressive trio of air to air kills against the Iraqi Air Force during the first Iran-Iraq war. That was three more planes than Kovalev had ever shot down, and that was one of his hopes for this new chapter in life: that a lifetime's worth of training and experience might finally count for something in the air. The recruiters had hinted that this job held the promise of action along with monetary reward.

"Although this was explained to you before," Abdi went on, "I want to make it clear: The unit you are joining is not here to train our pilots, although you will sometimes train *with* them. There are plans in motion designed to benefit your country, mine, and our allies. These plans will involve risk and bloodshed, but the rewards will be . . . substantial. The Iranian government recognizes that you are here as a foreign volunteer. Because of that, certain . . . *allowances* will be made, so long as you do not publicly flout our laws and customs. Do you understand?"

Kovalev glanced sideways at the man sitting next to him, former Russian Air Force Brigadier General Toma Baranov. Baranov was a tall, thickset man with round, ruddy cheeks pocked with acne scars, a shock of unruly red hair, and an outlandish handlebar mustache. He saw Kovalev's inquiring look, smiled slightly, and gave him a curt nod. Kovalev looked back to Abdi. "*Da,* general. I understand."

"Serve this unit well, and you will be treated well. Superior performance will be met with superior rewards. We understand that you are not Muslim, and that you hold no personal loyalty to the Islamic Republic. Still, our relationship can be mutually beneficial. Do you have any questions for me?"

"*Nyet*," Kovalev replied. He'd ask his questions of Baranov, not this man. Abdi rose from behind his desk, signaling that the meeting was over. Both Russian men to came to their feet and handshakes were exchanged.

"Welcome to the *Krasnyye Kogti*," Abdi said with finality: the *Red Talons*. Kovalev nodded in approval.

***

A short time later, the two Russians drove slowly down a military flight line, where Kovalev got his first look at the fighters. The Iranians had taken delivery of more than a hundred modern aircraft over the past three years composed of a mix of Russian, Chinese, and Pakistani models. Half were older jets, a mix of Russian and Chinese MiG-21 and MiG-29 castoffs, a handful of older MiG-31 interceptors, and early-model SU-27s. Those jets were integrated straight into the IRIAF to be flown by the Iranians. The cream of the new deliveries was a trio of topline AWACS aircraft, three squadrons of JF-17 Thunders obtained from China and Pakistan, and two dozen modern Flanker and Fulcrum variants.

The latter were the planes they looked at now, designated for use exclusively by the volunteer group of Russian mercenary expats. These jets were single-seat MiG-29Ms, originally earmarked for Syria, but undelivered due to the civil war there. They didn't carry the mottled green and brown camouflage schemes of the IRIAF, or the solid olive green sometimes seen on IRGC units. These were painted in a dark gray and black camouflage that would have looked normal on any Russian air base, except for the Iranian roundels on the wings and fuselage, and the small Iranian flag on the tails. The wingtips were painted blood red, and each vertical tail was decorated with a trio of blood red claw marks making a bold, diagonal slash. Tied down and unattended except for armed guards, the fighters looked sleek and lethal, poised to slay on command.

It wasn't lost on Kovalev that no expense had been spared here. These were new, top-line export fighters, among the first off the production lines. He turned slightly toward Baranov, feeling a mixed sense of thrill and trepidation. "What are we *really* doing here?" he asked.

"Not here, *tovarich*," Baranov said quietly, gesturing subtly at their Iranian driver. Although nothing further was said, Kovalev understood the implications: that the driver understood Russian, and that trust in their Iranian masters went only so far.

After completing the tour of the flight line and hangar facilities, the driver delivered them to their quarters. The building was a square-wraparound, with an open center courtyard featuring a mosaic-tiled swimming pool. The style was distinctly Persian, with Abbasid architecture and an arch in front of the entryway formed by a sculpture of twelve-foot high scimitars. The grounds around the complex were well kept, and the building was large enough for each pilot to have his own room. Larger rooms at the diagonal corners of each floor were converted to a gymnasium, reading room, common area, and a lounge with a discreet bar, respectively. The latter had a sign on the door in Farsi prohibiting entry to all non-authorized personnel, including the janitorial staff. The lounge was empty when the Russians entered. Baranov made for the bar without hesitation, reaching blindly behind it to pull out two glasses and a bottle of good Russian vodka.

Baranov grinned slightly as he charged both glasses, handing one to Kovalev. "To the fallen," he said. Both men raised their glasses and tossed off the contents. Baranov repeated the process twice more, toasting the *Rodina,* and wives and sweethearts in turn. After the third swift round, Kovalev was finally smiling.

"I sensed your doubt when meeting with General Abdi," Baranov said. "It's understandable. I felt the same way when I first arrived. This place . . . it's not like home," he added, a slight shadow crossing his features. It made Kovalev wonder what compelled General Baranov to retire early and volunteer for this. He'd known the man only by reputation until now, a reputation sullied by rumors of corruption and black marketeering. In modern Russia, however, such things were accepted as normal by those in power—it was just the way of things. One could even argue that Baranov simply followed the example set by his own superiors.

This whole operation was, in part, a clandestine action of the Russian government. Certain Russian air force units were recently visited by recruiters, extolling an opportunity to fly as fighter pilots in Asia-minor. Further, these were well-paying mercenary positions, and volunteering would not be seen as a black mark or sign of disloyalty to the *Rodina*. Kovalev, Baranov, and others had signed on, either resigning or retiring their commissions to come here. Kovalev had been a late joiner, picked up in the very last round of recruitment. They had wanted a few more senior officers, and he was the highest ranking Russian officer to volunteer except for Baranov.

Which raised a question.

"Are you going to be flying?" Kovalev asked. To put it delicately, Toma Baranov was well past his prime. Arguably Kovalev was as well, but he'd come from an active line unit and was in excellent physical condition.

"Maybe occasionally, but I was recruited to command our volunteers and liaise with the Iranians. There are two groups of volunteers: Russian, and Chinese. The Chinese are led by a former general as well: a man named Cheng Ye. Although his status is technically the same as mine, I have a distinct feeling that he still holds his active rank in the PLAAF. This whole operation was China's idea, presented in secret to the leaders of the Iranian Revolutionary Guard Corps, and they agreed to it. Our government was brought in as a willing partner."

"This Cheng Ye. . . is he a fighter pilot?"

"A pilot, and much more, I think," Baranov confided. "You'll meet him soon enough. He's a hard one, my friend, possibly a true psychopath, and completely committed to his government's cause." He paused, adding after a moment's somber reflection: "I think that Cheng Ye might be the most dangerous man in Iran."

"What will the Chinese be flying?"

"We'll fly the fighters you just saw, and a second group of Russian volunteers will fly and operate the A-50 AWACS planes. The Chinese will fly a squadron of advanced two-seat Flankers, and one squadron of the JF-17's. The remainder of the JF-17's will be flown by the Revolutionary Guard Corps. Our presence will be kept secret for as long as possible, but eventually the west will learn of it."

"To what purpose, though?" Kovalev asked. "Who are we to fight? The Iraqis? The Saudis?"

"If needed," Baranov smiled darkly, giving him a skeptical look.

"The Americans?"

"We are mercenaries, Arkady Davidovich. We'll fight who we are told to fight. Iran wants control over the Persian Gulf, and they want to destroy Israel. They also benefit greatly when the price of oil goes up, and so does the *Rodina.*"

"What do the Chinese gain?"

"That is unclear to me, but they want *something.* They've never forgiven the Americans for backing them down over Taiwan in 1996. It was an unacceptable loss of face, which they will never forget or forgive. They play a long game, and as I said, this entire operation was their idea." Baranov topped off their glasses, nodding sagely as he did. "It's ironic," he added, looking briefly into his glass before tossing off the contents in one swallow. "The Ayatollah's regime has proven expert at using proxies, yet it cannot see when it is being used as one itself. Or perhaps it does see, and feels the tradeoff is worth it."

Kovalev's head was slightly abuzz with strong drink. "So, we use one another for our own ends."

"You have just defined all international relations," Baranov chuckled. "'Borrow a sword to kill another' is an Asian proverb of war. I think the Chinese want the Americans tied down here, distracted, and engaged while they continue to build and modernize their forces. American naval experts have talked about a 'pivot to the Pacific' now that the war in Afghanistan has ended. The Chinese would prefer to avoid increased U.S. attention and presence in what they feel is their territory. The Chinese will use this country to bleed the Americans and sap their confidence, while Russian participation masks their own complicity. Our Chinese friends don't care if Iran is smashed to pieces in the process, but that won't happen. The Iranian people are more resilient than that, and the Americans haven't won a war since they defeated Japan. No, *tovarich*, we've seen over and over how it plays for the Americans: when they've bled enough, when we've made it painful enough for them to be here, they'll spin it into some ridiculous claim of victory and leave."

"So ultimately, we are tools in the hands of the Chinese communist party, then?" Kovalev asked. "Are our lives to be so casually spent?"

"That is the traditional fate of mercenaries, is it not?" Baranov replied rhetorically. He turned a hard, frank gaze on Kovalev. "The trick, *tovarich*, is to survive *long enough*."

"Long enough for *what?*"

"Long enough to go home with a fat bank account, and no need to ever work again. To be famous among our people and respected by our enemies. To have status. To *matter*."

Baranov watched Kovalev, saw the mental wheels turning as he reached out and filled the glass of the other pilot, and then his own. Finally, the younger man nodded slowly, making his decision. He would commit to this mercenary life, and wherever it took him. He raised his glass.

"To *long enough*," Arkady Davidovich Kovalev said thickly. Baranov raised his glass in return, and they drank to it.

Part I
Gray Wolf

I

FEB 2013
The Persian Gulf

Silver moonlight washed the wings of the F/A-18F Super Hornet as it cut through the night air over the waters of the Persian Gulf. In the fighter's front cockpit, LCDR Mike 'Fargo' Thorsen relaxed in the soft red glow of the muted instrument lighting beyond his helmet visor. When he turned his head slightly to the left, the helmet mounted display drew a small green box around the position of his flight lead, marking his position for easy reference. He could see the other aircraft as a dark silhouette accentuated by the dim green strips of its formation lights, sitting squarely within the designation box.

Fargo's eyes briefly scanned inside, checking their position on one of his displays. They were approaching their designated CAP station, and he established himself on lead's port side just before they hit their pattern entry point. As pre-briefed, he saw the lead aircraft double-flash its formation lights to signal it was throttling back. Fargo pulled power as they turned northwest, entering a holding track with twenty mile legs straddling either side of the CAP waypoint. His placement on lead's port side kept him looking toward the threat axis rather than away from it. When they reversed direction to the southeast, he would set up on lead's starboard side. Rinse and repeat for the next couple of hours, barring the unforeseen.

All airborne units were trying to stay off the radios as much as possible; the Iranians had monitored Fifth Fleet communications over the entire deployment, and had the frequencies well-mapped. Lately, any time the Iranians overheard calls between aircraft, particularly naval units, they would clobber the frequency with loud chatter in Farsi, shrill audio-recordings of the Muslim call to prayer, or whatever annoying forms of interference they could transmit short of actual electronic jamming. Frequency hopping radios mitigated the issue, but it was better to keep Iranians guessing about which frequencies were in use. Tonight, in true military fashion, someone had either failed to get the word, or chosen to ignore it out of sheer apathy or boredom.

"Lobo 1-1, Spyglass. Show you on station," called the young, female voice of a distant E-3 Sentry AWACS controller. The Air Force had the night shift for overwatch tonight; the last of the carrier's E-2C Hawkeyes had recovered on the prior event, and they were done for the day. The USAF asset talking to them was based out of either the United Arab Emirates or Qatar; Fargo wasn't sure which.

"Lobo 1-1," came the curt reply from the WSO seat of the lead fighter. The voice belonged to the squadron executive officer, CDR Ron 'Lurch' Leaper; 'Lurch' because he was 6'3" and about 170 lbs. soaking wet. Fargo felt a twinge of pity for the XO; Lurch was a little high strung even on his relaxed days, and the added stress of having the air wing commander in his front seat wasn't helping. Referred to as "CAG", the air wing commander wasn't a bad guy at all, but he *was* still CAG. When the squadron commanding officer rolled out in a few months and Lurch fleeted up to command the Gray Wolves of VFA-12, CAG would be his immediate boss and the author of his fitness reports. This much face time could be a double edged sword, depending on how things went tonight.

Fargo's own WSO (pronounced *wizzo*) voiced his own displeasure over the intercom. "Way to go, *Chair* Force," LTJG John 'Dexter' Wong said derisively from the jet's back seat. There was a moment's pause before he added: "She *did* sound like a fox, though."

Up front, Fargo grinned slightly under his oxygen mask. "Oh, it's a trap, y'know?" That was the joke, at least—that the prettier she sounded on the radio, the likelier it was that she was uglier than sin.

"Okay, so riddle me this, Batman," Dexter moved on, "whose brilliant idea was it for us to shut off our radars tonight? There are only two types of strikers on the Boat: Hornets, and Rhinos. It's not like we're fooling anyone, here."

"No point in giving the gomers any more info than we have to," Fargo countered. "Without an ESM line off us, they'll have to paint us with a radar to even know we're here." He knew Dexter was just venting; without the radar to fiddle with, the WSO was more bored back there than Fargo was up front.

Dexter grunted and then fell silent after that, leaving Fargo alone with his thoughts. Their assigned CAP station was about 45 NM southwest of Kharg Island, almost right in the center of the Gulf on a rough line between Bushehr and Kuwait City. This was slightly northwest of the area in which the *Boxer* carrier strike group was operating. There wasn't much sea room to be had anywhere within the confines of the Persian Gulf, and even less when factoring in a twenty-mile standoff from all foreign shorelines whether they were friendly or not. Higher authority wanted a strong presence at this end of the Gulf, to monitor the new status-quo in what used to be southeastern Iraq. For better or worse, that territory and those oil fields were now part of Iran.

The question on everyone's mind tonight was whether the Iranians were going to continue their harassment of the *Boxer* strike group. The Iranians were reluctant night-flyers in past years, but that had apparently changed. As they modernized and expanded their military they were showing a new appetite for night operations, along with increased proficiency. The reason for this late event was that the Iranians were sending up fighters almost nightly to make provocative, high speed runs at the strike group. It was dangerous behavior, but since the runs were conducted in international airspace at ships sailing in international waters, the U.S. had no official cause to protest. Still, the message being sent from Iran was clear: *We know where you are, we don't want you here, and we can hit you any time we choose.*

It was the sort of thing that gave admirals ulcers, which in turn drove up their operational tempo, wearing down personnel and equipment. The night-time harassment was a few weeks old now, and the air wing had adjusted its flying to compensate. The optempo was almost around the clock now, with some exceptions on nights when they opted for a ready alert instead of airborne CAP stations. Five months into a planned six-month deployment, personnel were already tired and short tempered, and maintenance requirements were starting to suffer. The Air Force was relatively uninterested in doing a lot of night flying for Navy force protection; wrestling a few AWACS events per week out of them was the extent of their cooperation. The Navy hadn't complained—nobody in the chain of command wanted to give the impression that a carrier strike group needed help to defend itself. The commander of the U.S. Fifth Fleet in Bahrain also didn't want to show weakness to Iran by pulling the strike group back into the Gulf of Oman.

So here they were.

"Hey Fargo, do you have the datalink page active up there?" Dexter asked after a half hour of silence. Fargo grunted a negative, reaching out to switch his lower display over to the Situational Awareness (SA) page. He spotted the ESM line coming from over Iran, where someone was looking in their direction with an active radar. The fighter's ESM suite gave a bearing line towards the source, and shared that information through the datalink.

Given the growing consternation over Iranian harassment of the strike group, RADM Brandt and his staff were getting trickier themselves. Two of the air wing's EA-6B Prowlers were up tonight, with all their ELINT sniffing pods and antennas out, and there was an EP-3E Aries flying out of Bahrain as well, quietly loitering around the northwest end of the Gulf and eavesdropping for signals, communications, or any other forms of electronic intelligence. All these assets, including the fighters on two separate CAP stations and the strike group's surface ships, were sharing information in a single datalink. That allowed the multiple ESM bearing lines to be cross-referenced into a position fix and correlated with the corresponding E-3 radar track. Usually, the activation of radars was a pre-cursor to a night-time game of chicken between Iranian fighters and the strike group, so everyone on the event perked up. The Iranians typically used ground-based radar stations to control their fighters, or occasionally they'd fly one of their old F-14 Tomcats and use its powerful, American-made AWG-9 radar system as a makeshift AWACS.

Tonight, they were seeing something completely new.

Fargo did a quick double-take at the SA page and had to remind himself to look outside and maintain position on CAG. What he'd glimpsed was interesting to say the least—interesting enough for Lurch to break their self-imposed radio silence.

"Dexter, you see that?" the XO asked.

"Affirm," Dexter replied. Everyone tuned into the datalink saw same thing: about 40 NM southeast of Shiraz, they were picking up the radar off an A-50 Mainstay AWACS aircraft, the Russian equivalent of their own E-3 Sentry. The operators in the back of that aircraft would have a clear radar plot of all air and sea targets over the entire northern part of the Gulf. This was completely unexpected, since Iran didn't have any Mainstays, or at least not until now. That prompted two immediate questions: *who* did the aircraft really belong to, and *why* was it flying over Iran at night?

The second question was indirectly answered by the next radio call from the E-3. "Lobo 1-1, Spyglass. New group, Bullseye 100 for 90, medium, flanking. Designate Group-1. Group-1 is heading for the coast and accelerating. Reset and be ready to commit."

"Lobo, wilco," Lurch replied over the radio, sounding animated. Fargo was now wide awake as well, all sense of lethargy gone. With the order to reset, CAG immediately turned northwest, back towards their CAP waypoint. He turned left, making it easier on Fargo, who simply executed a left turn at the same rate, crossing directly behind CAG as they passed through ninety degrees of heading change. When they rolled out in the opposite direction, he was in combat spread back on CAG's port side without having to cross under. "Talk to me, Dex," he grunted under the sudden 5G turn, eyeballs outside and concentrating on flying the jet. There was a nice gibbous moon tonight, but it was still a black hole out there over the Gulf waters.

Dexter strained to talk until the G came off. "Bullseye is Kharg Island, so the bogeys are probably off the airfield at Shiraz. Link shows 'em on a direct line from there to the strike group. I'm not getting any ESM lines off them, but that makes sense: they can stay radar-silent with the Mainstay giving them vectors."

"How many?"

"Looks like a two-ship, unless they're pretending to be Blue Angels tonight."

"Two ship, then," Fargo opined out loud, taking odds against Iranian flyers wanting to bunch up in a tight formation at night. "Break out the weapons checklist," he added, knowing that CAG and Lurch were doing the same thing. Dexter ran through the checklist with him, and they prepped the jet for war. Fargo switched from cruise to air-to-air mode up front and selected an AMRAAM. The only step they skipped for now was turning the master arm switch on, and the radar remained in standby for the time being. In all other respects, they were combat-ready.

They heard Strike call one of the airborne Prowlers, and order it to direct frequency jammers at the Mainstay and the bogeys. Technically speaking that was a hostile act on the part of the Americans, but apparently the bosses had had about enough of these nocturnal jabs at the strike group. Fargo silently nodded approval: he knew what would happen next. Once contact between the Mainstay and fighters was disrupted, the latter would likely switch on their radars and give away their aircraft-type.

The tactic worked. "Ho, racket! I've got a line on 'em!" Dexter called from the back, rattling off the nomenclature of a Chinese-made radar.

Fargo strained his brain, reaching for the professional knowledge that went with his job. "Bogeys are . . . JF-17's, then . . . what the hell?" he said uncertainly. *That* didn't compute. That model of fighter was made in Pakistan, and under license to China as well. Like the Mainstay, the Iranians weren't known to have any.

"Sweater Boy's been preaching that the Iranians bought some," Dexter replied, using the derogatory nickname appended to their squadron's Air Intelligence Officer. "I think this is the first anyone's seen them, though."

"Nice to know we can jam those hosers, anyway," Fargo casually reflected.

"Lobo 1-1, Spyglass. Your vector 010, take Angels 30."

"Lobo, wilco," Lurch replied. Fargo programmed a climb and plugged burner, staying with CAG as the lead Super Hornet leapt skyward, accelerating slightly in the climb. Fargo grimaced; he'd begun his career as a fighter pilot flying B and D-model Tomcats, and he missed them terribly. While the Rhino did have a few digital virtues, it lacked acceleration, sustained turning performance, and top-end speed when compared to the retired Tomcat, or in fact just about any other modern fighter. *But what fighter guy ever cared about* those *things?* he often snarked. The "Rhino" nickname for the Super Hornet was aptly chosen, as far as he was concerned.

"She's setting us up for a flanking intercept," Dex informed him, knowing his pilot's attention was all outside right now. Fargo had a firm grasp of the tactical picture without looking at the scope but appreciated the calls by his WSO.

CAG's voice suddenly crackled over the radio. "I'm blind on you, Fargo. Still with me?"

"Right with you, CAG. At your eight o'clock with a bit of stepdown."

"Ahh…roger. Tally."

"He doesn't fly enough at night," Dexter opined from the back seat. "He should've let us fly lead."

"*Says the fuckin' nugget WSO*," Fargo retorted sharply, putting an abrupt end to that line of conversation. He knew Dexter was acting the salty fleet veteran, parroting what he'd heard others say, and he didn't like it.

The cockpit was quiet for a few minutes after that, until the next set of calls came from Spyglass. The first one reported that the bogeys were going feet wet; the second ordered the pair of Super Hornets to turn southeast and 'Gate', meaning to use their afterburners for maximum speed. Lobo flight complied. The bogeys were crossing ahead of them now, some 45 NM off their nose, and also accelerating to supersonic speed. This was the same stunt they'd seen before, with the Iranians running straight

7

at the carrier strike group on a potential attack-profile, only to turn away before things got *too* tense. After a short run in burner, Fargo eyed his fuel gauges and saw that they were going to have to hit the tanker for some gas before recovery. Payload/range was another one of his beefs with the Rhino, when compared to the retired Tomcat.

"Lobo flight, Spyglass. Go active and lock them up. Call radar contact."

"Dash one going active," Lurch called. "I've got the leader, Dex. You take the trailer."

"Wilco. Two's active," Dexter added, bringing up the radar. Each Super Hornet actively locked a bogey in the fire control mode guaranteed to set off the Iranian pilots' radar warning receivers.

"Spyglass, Lobo 1-1, radar contact," Lurch called. He called 'Judy' as well, taking control of the intercept from the E-3, who would continue to monitor. "Lobo flight committed on Group-1. Strike, Lobo 1-1, Declare."

"Neutral. Weapons tight," an older, mature sounding voice replied immediately. With that reply, the two Super Hornets were denied permission to fire unless one of the bogeys fired a weapon either at them or one of the ships of the strike group. They heard 'Alpha Whiskey', the strike group's anti-air warfare commander, use the international Guard frequency to warn the Iranian fighters that they were standing into danger.

"That first call, was that the admiral?" Dexter asked.

"Maybe. I thought it sounded like him," Fargo replied. He didn't doubt for a minute that RADM Brandt was taking a direct hand in matters at this point. "Can you get the bogeys on IR?"

"I've got 'em but there's no definition at this range. They're just small blobs."

Fargo could see the target designator boxes around the bogeys in the HUD, although they were invisible to the naked eye at this range and in the dark. He noticed that the left-to-right drift of the boxes in his display stopped and started to reverse itself. At the same time, Lurch called that the bogeys were turning east, nose-cold to both the strike group and the flanking

Super Hornets. In less than a minute the bogeys were pointed north, back towards Iranian airspace, and had slowed to subsonic speed.

Another false alarm.

"Break radar lock," Lurch called.

"Two," Dexter replied, complying with the order. The Iranian RWRs would go silent now that they were no longer being spiked. Lurch was, in effect, rewarding them for turning away. Within minutes, the Prowlers were ordered to shut down their jammers, and the Super Hornets placed their radars back in standby. Spyglass directed them to reset to their CAP station, and things quieted down again. The bogeys turned southeast and eventually made another sprint at the strike group. The second round played out identically to the first, only it was the second CAP station vectored onto the intercept. Both bogeys and the Mainstay finally shut down their radars and headed for home, eventually disappearing off the datalink.

For the Iranians, it was another successful night poking the Sleeping Giant.

When they were ordered off station to recover, Fargo was fighting a crick in his neck from looking sideways at his lead all night, his eyes were burning slightly with fatigue, and he was feeling the onset of a headache. It was past midnight now, and he'd been up since about 0600 the previous morning. His workload as the squadron's maintenance officer, or "MO", didn't allow for niceties like crew rest unless he wanted the XO living in his ass. Thanks to the mystery appearance of the A-50 and JF-17s, the debrief was going to be a doozy as well. He figured he'd be lucky to finish that by 0200, if not later, and then he'd be right back at it again, bright and early. He realized that he hadn't even seen tomorrow's flight schedule yet, so there might be another late night to look forward to as well. Hopefully the Skeds-O had shown a little mercy, but he wasn't banking on it. He reached under his visor and knuckled his eyes, trying not to dwell on the night trap in his immediate future—that was by far the most terrifying, energy draining thing he'd do today, and required a level of precision that made the rest of it look easy, including the air-to-air refueling in the dark.

Thank God for FLIR and a nice, bright moon, he thought to himself. That, and the Persian Gulf's benign seas states: there was rarely a pitching deck to worry about in Gulf waters.

"How are you doing up there?" Dexter asked, tapping some of that mental symbiosis between pilot and WSO.

"Hanging in there," Fargo replied with more stoicism than he felt.

"Gawd, my ass is completely numb and I'm starving. We've already missed midrats, too."

"My heart bleeds for you. Y'know, back in Afghanistan we used to fly *nine-hour* strike missions in the Tomcat. We're talking multiple-cycle events and having to tank four or five times."

"I'm sure it was uphill, in the snow, both ways, too," Dexter yawned. "So, you gonna fly this one tired or use the ACLS?" Dexter asked, referring to the automatic carrier landing system.

Fargo sighed. "Didn't you read the maintenance logbook during preflight, Dex? It's griped." Their ACLS was down due to an electrical glitch the maintainers hadn't isolated yet.

Dexter deftly avoided the question. "Well, it was mighty nice of you to give CAG and the XO the full up jet, I'm sure they appreciate it. Although, seeing as though you *are* the MO, not sucking up your own department's slack would have been a bad look."

Given their disparity in rank and experience, it was a testament to Fargo's 'no rank in the cockpit' philosophy that Dexter felt comfortable busting his balls like that. Still, there were times (like right now when he was tired and cranky) that it felt like his nugget WSO was pushing the boundaries.

"I didn't give 'em the jet, maintenance control did," Fargo retorted.

Dexter snorted again from the back seat. "And maintenance control works for *who?* I rest my case," he said smugly.

The pre-recovery aerial refueling with an S-3 Viking tanker went normally. Fargo wondered what was going to happen in a year or two when the Viking fleet retired from service. The Super

Hornet had a buddy-tanking capability, but using strikers as tankers was just one more way to knock down an air wing's punching-weight, in his opinion. There was a fight in progress between two aerospace giants over the issue of jammers and tankers, with each having their respective 'camp' within the defense establishment. One was promoting the EA-18G "Growler" as part of the "all Hornet" flight deck, while the other was flying prototypes for EA-6E Advanced Prowlers, which also included plans for a tanker-variant reminiscent of the old KA-6D. Nobody was certain which way it was going to go, but Fargo had his own sour suspicions.

When they departed the marshal stack sometime later, CAG coupled his autopilot to the ACLS and enjoyed a hands-off approach to a perfect 3-wire trap. Dead tired, Fargo hand-flew a Fair pass to a 2-wire and was just thankful to get aboard on his first attempt. When they were shut down on deck and Dexter opened the canopy, Fargo peeled off his helmet, leaned back in the ejection seat, and wearily draped his arms over the canopy rails. It was an old ritual of his after a night-trap: just taking a moment to let the heart rate come down and decompress slightly from the always-harrowing experience. He took a deep breath, letting the humid night air refresh lungs that felt bone-dry from sucking oxygen through a rubber mask for the past two hours. The wind blew over him at thirty knots as a Prowler slammed onto the deck somewhere behind him, engines screaming temporarily as they fought against the arresting cable that brought it to an abrupt stop.

A young face appeared over the canopy rail as the sound of the Prowler's engines wound down behind them. Although it was too dark to make out facial features under the cranial and goggles, Fargo recognized his plane captain.

"How was the flight, sir?" the plane captain shouted over the din of wind and jet engines.

"Awesome!" Fargo yelled back with a tired grin. "I can't believe they pay me to do this!"

At that moment, he truly meant it.

***

The next morning, Fargo looked up from a plate loaded with bacon, hashbrowns, and toast as LCDR Ned 'Stinky' Mullen, the squadron operations officer, approached with tray in hand. "Pull up a seat, shipmate," Fargo said amiably, gesturing to the spot beside him. Across the table, Dexter was slowly working his way through a bowl of mixed fruit and berries with a small bowl of oatmeal, a single half-slice of wheat toast, and iced tea. While most navy officers hydrated themselves with coffee, Dexter was a tea drinker, either iced (unsweet) or hot, depending on what was available. The slender WSO looked down his nose at the plate of biscuits and gravy topped with bacon that the Ops-O was tucking into, wrinkling his nose in slight distaste.

"You hinges are going to die of heart attacks before your fortieth birthdays," he opined, using the derogatory term junior officers reserved for lieutenant commanders. In the minds of their juniors, O-4's had hinges installed on their necks upon their promotion to facilitate all their 'yes-men' nodding at higher authority.

"Bite me, nugget," Stinky fired back with a derisive grin.

"For a skinny little runt, you sure have a big mouth," Fargo added. "I grew up on the farm, son, where the three-thousand calorie breakfast was a mark of manhood."

"What happened to you, then, sir?" quipped LT Deidre "Deedee" Danforth, who took a seat at the table right after Stinky. She reached out in the spirit of junior officer solidarity for a high-five from Dexter. They were having breakfast in Wardroom One, also known as the 'Dirty Shirt', where flight suits, deck jerseys, and soiled uniforms were authorized, and all the meals were served cafeteria style. Wardroom Two was more formal and required a more presentable appearance. Most of the air wingers and flight deck personnel took their meals in the Dirty Shirt, while the officers assigned to the ship's company tended to gravitate to Wardroom Two. Wardroom One was located forward, on the O-3 level of the ship.

"Jeez, Fargo," Deedee added, "you look like you were shot at and missed, then shit at and hit."

Fargo was going on about three hours sleep, but he wasn't going to whine about it. He shrugged instead. "Ma always said I needed more beauty sleep than I get."

"Clearly she was smarter than you look. I heard you guys had a long night," she added, segueing into the real topic. Stinky paused in the act of stoking himself with chow as they looked expectantly between Fargo and Dexter. Stinky and Deedee were paired together as a crew; she was a pilot, and the Ops-O a WSO. Fargo ate while Dexter gave them the quick rundown of the prior night's events. The other two listened intently and exchanged a glance between them as the tale wound down. Stinky leaned in a little conspiratorially.

"Did you guys know that DCAG was flying on that event last night too?" he asked, referring to the deputy air-wing commander.

Fargo nodded. "Not at the time, but we saw him later during the debrief."

"You hardly ever see CAG and DCAG flying during the same event, and *never* at night," Deedee observed.

"CAG flies his share of night flights," Fargo said flatly, feeling irritated that this was coming up again. "So does DCAG, for that matter."

"Well, CAG maintains his night currency—*barely*—and he gets a lot of gouge pinkie hops. And DCAG is an ECMO," Deedee reminded them. ECMO stood for 'electronic countermeasures officer,' a naval flight officer who flew in Prowlers the same way WSOs back seated the F-model Super Hornets. For NFOs, day or night didn't matter nearly as much as for the pilots doing the flying. The coveted 'pinkie' hops she referred to were flights that counted as night traps, but usually ended during nautical twilight before it got dark enough for the horizon to completely vanish. Deedee was the Skeds-O, responsible for putting out the squadron flight schedule, so she was familiar with CAG's flying habits. CAG split most of his flying between the two Super Hornet squadrons, although he was also qualified on Prowlers and legacy Hornets. Every so often he even took a hop with one of the rotary squadrons and got some stick time flying helicopters, although always during the day and with a squadron instructor in the other seat. It was one of the top benefits of commanding an air wing—getting to fly multiple aircraft types.

Fargo felt stupid over his urge to defend CAG; usually there was more satisfaction in ripping on senior leadership, but unlike DCAG, who had a volcanic temper and a socially crippling Napoleon complex, Captain VanNortwick was a stand-up guy with minimal careerist character flaws. Fargo looked sternly between the two junior officers, careful to keep his voice even and level in the crowded wardroom. "Deedee, how old are you?"

She batted her eyes at him. "Why commander, don't you know it's impolite to ask a lady her age?"

Fargo shot her a toothy grin. "I'll remember that—*the next time I'm speaking to one*. C'mon, Double-D, fess up. how old? Twenty-seven? Twenty-eight?"

Deedee smiled sourly. "Well, I guess I walked right into that one. Okay, twenty-six."

"And Dex, you're a year or two younger. Let me tell you something: CAG was flying these waters when he was your age, *at night*, back during the Gulf War. That's the *first* Gulf War, kids—not Afghanistan—when you two were getting ready to hit pre-school."

"Cool story, sir. What's your point?"

"The point," Stinky cut in firmly, "is that we don't talk that trash. Not in the ready room, or any other public spaces. This is your first sea tour, and you've been blessed in your leadership so far, whether you realize it or not. Think about how fun it'll be next go-round after DCAG fleets up," he added pointedly. "We can't dictate what you bullshit about in your staterooms behind closed doors, but if you want to badmouth your seniors, keep it there. Kay?"

"What's the first rule we taught you youngsters?" Fargo asked, pointing at Dex.

His WSO sighed. "If you can't be quiet, don't be new," he said, as if reciting it for the class.

"And the second?" Stinky added, pointing at his pilot.

"Never pass up an opportunity to shut the fuck up."

Stinky grinned, leaning back and spreading his arms wide. "See? Who says mentorship is dead?"

"Okay, okay, point taken," Deedee conceded. "Back to the matter at hand, though. We had CAG, DCAG, our XO, the Merlin's XO, and Brand X's skipper all airborne during this event last night. Does it seem like someone upstairs might have had an inkling that some mystery Iranian assets were going to show up?"

Fargo shrugged. "Probably. That many oak leaves and eagles in the air at night *is* a rare occurrence, and I'm positive the admiral's intel team is better informed than Sweater Boy. But he has been saying this entire cruise that we were going to see some strangeness from Iran."

"Heh. Speak of the Devil, and he shall appear," Stinky said, elbowing Fargo. The four of them looked up and saw one LTJG Aston Chadwick II, looking inspection ready in a fresh pair of pressed wash khakis, shined black shoes, and a blue-knit sweater of the same type favored by Surface Warfare Officers. He was a bit of an enigma as far as Air Intelligence Officers (AIOs) went. Many were prospective pilots or NFOs that washed out of flight school but retained that link to the naval aviation community—they tended to wear aviator gear and talk the talk. "Sweater Boy" Chadwick was cast from a different mold: one that oozed northeastern blue blood, old-money, and good old-fashioned, snooty elitism. Rumor had it that he was an Ivy Leaguer, although nobody had ever cared enough to ask where he went to school. Rather than a custom Gray Wolves squadron nametag on the breast of his sweater, his was generic black leather with nothing but his name and rank embossed on it, along with assignment and unit: AIO, VFA-12.

"Mind if I join you?" he asked in his normal, somewhat-haughty-without-trying tone.

"Sit down," Fargo said, as they scootched their chairs to make room. Chadwick looked around briefly and cadged a free chair from an adjacent table, which he sat on in reverse, his arms folded across the top of the backrest. He looked between the four of them from behind a pair of navy-issue Clark Kent birth-control glasses. "Well?" he said almost expectantly. "I told you this was going to happen, didn't I?"

"You betcha," Fargo replied for all of them, noticing the AIO was empty-handed. "You gonna eat something?"

"I ate earlier, in Wardroom Two," Chadwick replied, glancing in slight distaste at the food choices on the plates of the two department heads.

"Missed you at the debrief after the last event last night," Fargo went on. "I'd have thought you'd want to be there, to see all your hard work and predictions vindicated."

Sweater Boy sniffed slightly. "There wasn't any need. I knew this was going to happen, and I read the reports on it first thing this morning."

"So, what does it mean?" Deedee asked. "Break it down for us."

Chadwick glanced around. This wasn't a secure space, and they could tell he was mentally gauging what was okay to say here. "The Iranians have been taking better than two million barrels of oil *per day* on average from what used to be southern Iraq—that much is old news by now. They don't have the refinery capacity to do much with it, but it's worth a ton of money sold as crude and shipped out of the Gulf, right? I'll give you two guesses who their biggest customers are right now, too."

"China and Russia?" Deedee guessed.

"—Wro—" Chadwick started to reply.

"—China and North Korea," Dex cut in. The AIO looked irritated that Dexter had stolen his thunder, but it was no surprise. Dexter might be a first-cruise nugget, but he already had a reputation as a walking database on threat platforms, capabilities, and he had a farsighted grasp of socio-political issues. That was the source of his callsign: "Dexter" was the name of the child-genius from the cartoon "Dexter's Laboratory."

At this stage of the deployment, it was fair to say he was past the 'New Guy' stage, but he wasn't considered a salty cruise veteran quite yet. Dexter graduated at the top of his training class, was sharp as a tack, and one of the few NFO's they'd ever run across whose *first* choice was to be a back seater instead of a pilot. After flying with him for most of the cruise, Fargo had few complaints.

"Correct," Chadwick confirmed with a polite nod at Dexter. "That's over thirty-six billion-with-a-*B* dollars per year with crude at fifty dollars a barrel, and more than that when oil prices are running higher. Anyhow, we've had reports for over a year now that Iran is using that money to buy modern weapons and materiel from China and Russia, and after last night we've confirmed jets from Pakistan as well. Or at least indirectly through the Chinese, if not directly from Pakistani factories. Right now, Big Intel is trying to figure that one out, and exactly how many the Iranians have."

For all that they ripped on Sweater Boy for the ultimate crime of not fitting in, he had their full attention now. Last night had been a wake-up call for everyone—*nobody* had expected to see an A-50 flying over Iran. Fargo looked serious and concerned at the same time. "What exactly do they have?" he asked.

Chadwick glanced around again, taking stock of who was within earshot of the table. "We can't talk about numbers in here, but let's just say they've built up a nice, modern high-low mix consisting of stuff like you saw last night, Fulcrums, some Flanker variants, and some...uh, *advanced* Flanker variants. Plus, all the dangerous stuff that hangs under the wings."

Stinky frowned. "Unless they plan on dumping all their old planes, they don't currently have the manpower to fleet up a whole new air force within a year or two."

"And then there's that," Chadwick agreed, as if he was holding the missing piece of a puzzle. His eyes were strangely intense. "Bear in mind, this all started several years ago, when we were tied up in Afghanistan and not paying so much attention to the Gulf. Last night marked, how shall we say it? The end of the beginning?"

"C'mon, *Sweater Boy*, enough with the Winston Churchill," Deedee needled him.

"Yah, give us the straight gouge, dude," Fargo urged.

"I can't say anymore in here. Let me bring up a little history though, about some of the experiences our pilots had in Korea and Vietnam. Some of them joked that they'd never understood how so many Asian pilots had round eyes and blond hair creeping out from under their helmets. Ponder that."

"Interesting," Dexter commented, the four aviators sharing glances between them. "Is that confirmed?"

"Not yet," Chadwick allowed.

Just then another Gray Wolves pilot, LT John "Bender" Riley, paused in passing at their table. "Hey y'all, spread the word. All officers meeting in the ready room at 0900."

"Why is it, as operations officer, I get to find these things out second hand?" Stinky vented to the universe at large. He made a mental note to fang the duty officer when he got back to the ready room.

"What's it about?" Deedee asked him.

Bender shrugged. "Hell if I know. I'd stay and chat, but I need to hit the chow line before they shut down. See y'all later."

"It's gotta be about last night, right?" Dexter asked.

Fargo glanced at his watch, thankful that Deedee had somehow missed him for the flight schedule today. Aside from popup annoyances like this AOM, he'd be able to get some work done and maybe grab some much needed shuteye later. "We'll find out, I s'pose. Anyone who needs me, I'll be hip deep in paperwork for a bit. Enlisted evals don't write themselves."

"As if proofing what the shop chiefs write counts as 'writing'," Deedee snorted.

"Well, none of you Div-O's catch the grammar mistakes or smooth out the verbiage, so *someone* has to make sure the troops have a shot at advancement," Fargo growled. It was a valid enough criticism sometimes, although he was painting with a pretty broad brush—lack of sleep was making him prickly.

Deedee smiled. "If I worked in maintenance instead of ops, you wouldn't have to re-write the ones I sent up," she riposted.

"Liar," Stinky chuckled, as he stood up to leave. "Look at all the ink I have to bleed on every schedule you write."

"It must be hell, all that lofty rank and power not living up to the hype," Dexter quipped.

Stinky fired a Parthian shot as he departed. "Didn't I tell you to *bite me*, nugget?"

***

Fargo stepped into the ready room a few minutes before 0900, to find the usual crowd of officers milling about, jaw-jacking, grabbing coffee, and checking their email on the two community computers before finding their way to their personal chairs. The deck of the large compartment was tiled in blue linoleum, and the chairs were covered in two-toned blue and gray Naugahyde, with nametags like the ones they wore on their jackets and flight suits velcroed to the tops of the head rests. One bulkhead was painted with an oversized version of the Gray Wolves squadron patch: a snarling black wolf's head with sharp fangs and angry red eyes, against a gray background. The opposite bulkhead was painted with the blue and gold insignia of the ship. It consisted of a slightly caricaturized picture of a stocky pugilist with thinning hair, slight jowls, and round spectacles. He bore an uncanny resemblance to Theodore Roosevelt, and that was probably by design. Underneath the ship's name, her hull number was painted boldly: CVN-71. Back in the day, some bright-eyed swamp dwellers in Foggy Bottom had wanted to start naming aircraft carriers after dead presidents and service secretaries. That was firmly nipped in the bud by the navy establishment and some senators with a sense of history, and aside from the lead ship of this class carrying the hallowed surname of Chester Nimitz, modern carriers bore proud, traditional aircraft carrier names.

Every time Fargo glanced at the ship's insignia, he wondered how strange it would have seemed if this ship had been named after Teddy Roosevelt.

He wandered over to where their personalized coffee mugs hung on their pegs, grabbed his own, and charged it with coffee. He cast a sidelong glance at the computers, where Stinky was quickly reading the latest email from his wife and kids. Fargo's lips pressed in a thin line, feeling a dull numbness inside as he tried to recall what it was like to get an email or letter from a sweetheart. He'd married a girl from college back in flight school, but it hadn't lasted beyond his first tour. The way it ended had soured him on relationships, with the one good thing coming out of it being a somewhat singular focus on his career. Still, Stinky's career was going just as well as his—and with a family to boot.

The department heads all had seats in the front row of the ready room. Fargo was getting comfortable when Stinky slid into the seat next to his, holding a rough copy of the next day's flight schedule. The two quickly compared notes, talking about which jets were up, which were down for maintenance, and the couple that might come up if placed on the schedule for maintenance check flights. "Y'know," Stinky added, "one of these days we need to take a break from the JOPA crowd and fly together."

JOPA was short for 'junior officer protection association', basically the informal junior officer mafia. JOPA even had its own patch, which officers ranked O-3 and under wore proudly. Once someone promoted to O-4, they were duly expelled and their JOPA patch came off forever—probably the same time as their hinge was installed, according to legend.

"I'm game, whenever you want to throw it on the schedule," Fargo nodded. There was sometimes tension between O-4's due to the stiff competition at that career stage, but fortunately Fargo and Stinky were past that. Operations and Maintenance were the two plum department head jobs in every aviation squadron, and their prospects for further advancement were good. The fact that they were friends was good for operational synergy as well.

"Attention on deck!" barked the squadron duty officer. All conversation immediately ceased, and the assembled officers came to their feet. The skipper strolled up to the front of the ready room with the XO in tow.

"Carry on," the skipper said with a slight smile, and there was a temporary low murmur as everyone took their seats. CDR Calvin 'Chill' Jefferson was a black officer with a deceptively easy-going demeanor. That was not the source of his callsign, although it was an easy assumption he did nothing to dispel. Those with a longer history in the strike fighter community knew that "Chill" had started out as "CHHL", a lucky verbal play on 'Cannot Hold His Liquor.' That stemmed from a couple unfortunate club nights during his days as a west coast RAG student at Miramar. Fortunately, both his liver and his career had survived those youthful indiscretions. Jefferson was solidly competent, a mediocre dogfighter but a great ball-flyer, and he had a steel trap mind with a thirst for details that drove subordinates crazy. Given the XO's bouts of uptightness, it was not a command pairing made in heaven, but it could have been a lot worse. Chill Jefferson was relaxed and easygoing, *provided* you showed up with the minutiae he demanded. He was the kind of skipper the enlisted troops loved: they found him relatable, a sports-fan who could recite endless statistics, quick with a smile and a joke, and his near-eidetic recall meant he never forgot a name, or any piece of information about a sailor's record or family life once he learned about it. Jefferson was on the fast track to a bright future: one that held nuclear power school, command of an aircraft carrier, and eventually flag rank.

The skipper made a few brief remarks, outlining the events of the night before for those who either hadn't heard, or were going on rumor alone. Then he called up Neo, their Strike Fighter Tactics Instructor, to give them a refresher briefing on the capabilities of the A-50, the relatively new JF-17 Thunder, and the various Fulcrum and Flanker variants. Fargo found himself comparing this information with the hints Sweater Boy had dropped at breakfast. *Did Iran really have all this new hardware?* If so, they could potentially slam the door shut on the Strait of Hormuz if they decided to do it. The Persian Gulf was not the easiest place to operate a carrier strike group—the headaches involved in their day to day operations had proven that. The Iranians possessed large numbers of shore based Silkworm anti-ship missiles, along with some higher-end supersonic missiles as well. The Russians, and later the Chinese had been developing these missile systems for decades *specifically* to target U.S. aircraft carriers and surface units.

Fargo knew first-hand that the myth of American military invulnerability was just that—a myth. As Lord Admiral Nelson once said in the 18th Century, a ship was a fool to fight a fort. Within the confines of the Persian Gulf or especially the Strait of Hormuz, that was exactly the prospect they faced daily. No navy on the planet stood a chance against shore batteries firing swarms of anti-ship missiles from a mere twenty to thirty miles away. If the Iranians timed a mass attack when a force was trapped by the confines of the strait, reaction time would be next to nothing. That was before one factored in scouting data from AWACS style assets, unmanned drones, or even a fishing boat with a radio, loyal to the other side. Missile salvo calculations written years before distilled the problem down to cold equations: if enough missiles came all at once, the result was grim.

Then there was the brand-new administration on Capitol Hill. America and its military had done well under the two terms of President Powell. His administration was marked by rare competence, largely correcting the mis-steps of the preceding Gore Administration. They had bagged Osama bin Laden and brought the troops home from Afghanistan under his watch. The Marsden Administration had come as a surprise—it was something unexpected. Early election polls tagged Condi Rice as a shoo-in. Her election would have meant back-to-back minority presidents and the first female president as well. Frankly, Fargo was still amazed that she'd lost. James Marsden was a big unknown, with less than a month in office. In fact, President Marsden hadn't even filled all his cabinet positions yet. The early indication was that the foreign policy pendulum was about to swing sharply to the left, which often meant hard times for the military establishment. Unfriendly regimes were notorious for testing new presidents; Iran's nightly provocations were just that sort of thing.

When the meeting wound down, the skipper called Stinky and Fargo to a sidebar with the XO. "We picked up a tasker from CAG this morning, gents," the CO informed them. "Fargo, what did you say during the debrief last night?"

"Well sir, I just mentioned that we might troll some jets along the coastline just outside Iranian airspace, to see what happens. There's the new Mainstays, but also some intel pointing to the Iranians putting in an integrated air defense system. If we could get them to turn some radars on, we could start mapping the whole thing out and get a better look at what they've got."

"Well, DCAG thought it was a hell of an idea. He's got the wing staff planning the whole caper, and he's going to Honcho it from the ECMO seat of his Prowler. Guess what you're doing tomorrow?"

Fargo grinned. "Using myself as bait for some SAM radars?"

Chill pretended to shudder. "You just named your own poison, son. Better you than me! Ops-O, CAG and DCAG wanted Fargo specifically for this—don't ask me why. Make sure he and Dexter are on that event."

"Aye aye, sir," Stinky replied.

"Eat your heart out, Brand-X!" Lurch chuckled, pleased to one-up their rival Super Hornet squadron—last night's ride with CAG was paying dividends after all.

When the front office wandered off and left the two department heads standing alone, the Ops-O turned to Fargo. "Look at my lucky roommate, the butt kisser!"

"Look into my eye, hoser," Fargo retorted, pointing to his left eye with his middle finger. Then he suggested: "Come fly this one with me! Weren't we just talking about it?"

Stinky looked thoughtful. "The skipper said to put Dex on it, so I'd better not. You know how he gets about details like that. I might put Deedee and myself on as Dash-2, though. It sounds more fun than boring holes on a CAP station for another double-cycle. Brand-X is gonna be a little wrapped when they hear about this."

"Hell with 'em. Breaks of navy air, y'know?"

"You betcha," Stinky replied, doing his best imitation of Fargo.

II

The Persian Gulf

Fargo flexed his shoulders in the straps and watched the catapult officer, also known as the 'shooter', pass him the signal to power up as the catapult went into tension. He pushed the throttles forward with his gloved hands, taking the engines up to full military power. His eyes scanned over the instruments one last time and he wiped out the flight controls; he and Dexter looked outside and checked that the control surfaces were moving normally. Outside the aircraft, two safety checkers conducted their final check of Lobo 205, watching the flight controls move, checking panels, looking for leaks, and conducting a last visual check of the weapons to ensure their safety pins were removed. They rolled out from under the plane and assumed their safe positions slightly behind and out to one side, holding out their hands with thumbs up to signify everything was okay.

Fargo and Dexter were sitting on the starboard bow catapult with their wingman, Lobo 202, sitting back on one of the waist cats. This was a section launch, coordinated to send both airplanes into the air together. Fargo asked Dex if he was ready, then fired off a thumbs-up and a salute to the shooter. The shooter made his own final safety check before lowering his arm, touching the deck, and pointing at the bow. There was an eyeblink's delay, and then Fargo was jammed back in his seat as the jet went from zero to one-hundred-fifty knots in less than three seconds. He felt the G from the stroke fall off as the plane came off the bow and he instinctively took the controls, reaching to bring the gear handle up as he executed his right clearing turn. This took them right of the ship's path in the event something catastrophic happened and they had to eject. An ejection was survivable—getting run over by an aircraft carrier generally wasn't.

"They're with us," Dex called over ICS; after looking back to make sure their wingman was airborne behind them.

"Rog," Fargo replied. He leveled them off at 500 FT and headed straight out along the ship's course. 102 executed a running rendezvous and formed up on his left side in loose cruise. At seven miles and clear of the carrier's traffic pattern they commenced a visual climb up to their transit altitude—this was a standard Case I departure. It was a bright, sunny day, and there was hardly a cloud in the sky. Dexter checked them in with Strike, and they were on their way to their first mission waypoint about sixteen miles off the Iranian coast.

Fargo felt his stress and troubles fade away now that he was in his element. This was what it was all about: nothing but a fast jet, clear skies, and turning taxpayer money into noise and jet fumes for the next couple hours. Both jets carried their standard CAP weapons load: external fuel tanks, four AMRAAM missiles, and two wingtip Sidewinders. A pure anti-air load and tons of gas: it was a fighter pilot's dream.

Fargo eased over onto the first heading of their planned track. The plan was for them to fly down towards Lavan Island, approximately two hundred miles away from their current position, and then track back to the northwest about fifteen to twenty miles off the Iranian coastline. It was close enough for the Iranians to take notice, but well within international airspace. Flying at 20,000 FT, they kept their radars turned on to highlight their presence and see what developed. There hadn't been any Mainstay sightings since the first one two nights ago, so in addition to mapping some new SAM radars, they were hoping to draw one out. Either way it was a nice morning for flying, and they were going to get to do something 'real-world' besides racetracks on a CAP station, or a made-up training mission. A pair of Prowlers with ELINT and SIGINT pods were hawking them on this event, ready to capture any data worth having, or supplying a little electronic interference to test the capabilities of the Iranians. DCAG was the mission commander, but there wouldn't be any radio contact between them unless necessary—all the fighters had to do was fly their mission profile.

Fargo leaned back, relaxed, and contemplated whether these moments were worth the long months spent living on the big gray

Boat, a broken marriage, and all the other daily stressors. From his current vantage point, the answer was *yes*. Dexter was still engrossed in his radar and other electronic gadgetry; it was going to be a quiet cockpit until his WSO got bored and wanted to chat.

***

The P-3 Orion maritime patrol aircraft entered fleet service back during the early 1960's, seeing action during the Cuban Missile Crisis when newly commissioned P-3 units participated in the naval blockade of Cuban waters. The Orion was designed primarily to localize, track, and destroy threat submarines, but it was also used for extensive maritime surface surveillance, and in times of war could carry a broad arsenal of weapons. During the Bosnia conflict, P-3 units conducted standoff cruise missile attacks against fixed land targets. The venerable Orion had served in the air arms of no fewer than fifteen countries aside from the United States, including, ironically enough, Iran. The aircraft's replacement, the brand-new P-8A Poseidon, was just entering service but had not yet deployed.

The Canadian variant of the Orion was designated the CP-140 Aurora. The Canadian Forces often deployed their Auroras to work in concert with U.S. P-3's, and this morning an Aurora flying out of Masirah was on station in Gulf waters. Their mission was in support of maritime security operations, performing an overwatch of shipping traffic moving through the Gulf, and verifying that certain 'contacts of interest' matched the electronic identities they were transmitting to the world at large. The Aurora was unable to datalink with the *Boxer* strike group, a disadvantage that was a source of irritation for everyone involved, but there was little to be done about it. Information could be passed, but it was a slower process requiring voice communication and manual data inputs on both ends.

The Aurora's non-acoustic sensor operator suddenly sat up at his station, watching the ESM screen with sudden interest. He called the tactical coordinator (TACCO) and reported detection of an AWG-9 air-to-air radar somewhere north of their position.

"We know the Iranians are still flying a handful of their old F-14's," the TACCO replied. "They must have one foot in the grave, though, eh? They use the Tomcat as a mini-AWACS sometimes because the radar is so good. What's the signal strength?"

"Pretty high. He holds contact on us, I'm sure."

The TACCO was also the Aurora's mission commander, and ordered a report to the *Boxer* group's Sea Combat Commander, code-named 'Alpha Sierra.' The answering controller told them to stand by, and the channel was silent for a few minutes before he came back and advised them that Strike held the contact on the datalink: an Iranian F-14 about 85 NM north of the Aurora, well within Iranian airspace.

The Aurora acknowledged and went about its business.

***

Several hundred miles away in the *Boxer*'s combat direction center (CDC), the Strike controller nervously bit his lip as he looked at the display, which showed the Canadian Aurora. What he also saw was a second Iranian air contact near the reported F-14. There were no Mainstays radiating right now, which meant the Iranians were probably using their 'Persian Cat' in the AWACS role. He suspected that the second contact was another fighter, probably a section of two flying close formation and painting as a single contact. It was tagged India Alpha 15, and it was starting an oh-so-casual drift down towards the area being worked by the Aurora. He looked at the display again and saw that Lobo flight was also headed in that general direction, getting close to the end-point of their planned route before turning back to the northwest. He thought about it for a moment, and then got on the net. "Lobo 2-1, this is Strike. Do you hold air track India Alpha 15 on the link?"

There was only a slight pause before he got an answer back. "Strike, Lobo 2-1, negative radar contact but we do hold him on datalink."

"Lobo flight, cancel prior tasking. New tasking follows: your vector 165, signal Buster. Provide top cover for a Pelican working surface to Angels 2, link-track Charlie-Alpha 31. Tanker assets will be vectored as necessary. Go radar silent and be ready for a commit."

"Lobo, wilco!" came the excited reply from a rather young sounding voice.

"Closeout, Strike," the controller called the airborne Hawkeye AWACs bird. "Are you monitoring this?"

"Strike, Closeout copies re-task of Lobo 2," the AWACS controller sent over the net. "Assuming tactical control for intercepts. We hold all players in primary radar contact."

"Closeout, Strike copies," the AWACS controller replied. In the *Boxer*'s CDC, the Strike controller picked up the handset at his station, a direct line to the tactical action officer. "TAO? This is Strike control. I need you over here right now. Better see if we can scare up CAG, too," he sighed.

***

"Radar is in standby," Dexter called from the back seat. "It's all link data now, baby." Dex turned sideways and exchanged some hand signals with Stinky in the other jet, confirming that their wingman had also ceased radar emissions. The two Super Hornets could be detected on radar, but only if the scanning beam of the radar was pointed at them. With their own radars shut down, they weren't generating any telltale bearings on Iranian ESM receivers. The lack of an ESM line from the Iranian F-14 meant that its radar was directed away from them, tracking the Aurora to their southeast. The second contact moving south toward the Aurora was the one causing this sudden change in plans.

Fargo got Deedee's attention and passed her some hand signals to let her know what he wanted. She nodded and broke off smartly, assuming a loose combat spread on his right beam with about a mile separation. From there, the two crews could visually clear each other's tails. He began hawking the fuel gauges now that they were off their planned profile. If things got exciting they could find themselves on fumes before they knew it—they were a relatively long way from the ship and heading farther away still.

"Dang," Dexter remarked over ICS, "we aren't going to make cycle, are we?"

"For a dumb nugget, you're smarter than you look," Fargo chuckled.

"So, we tank and score a double, eh? Yay, us. Another one."

"You bitchin' about bagging more flight time? What's the matter, you got a hot date back on deck?"

"Only with a slider in the Dirty Shirt."

"We're gonna miss lunch, dude. You'd better eat your pogey bait if you need a sugar hit. I saw you stash that Snickers in your ankle pocket, Mister Health Nut."

"You want half?" Dexter offered.

"No thanks, bro. I'm good," Fargo smiled. "Benefits of a farm-style breakfast."

Once the initial excitement passed, things settled down again as they drove farther to the southeast, watching everything unfold on the datalink feed they were still receiving. Closeout wasn't talking to them yet; there really wasn't any need, so long as Fargo was making good decisions, and he was. They were at a point where the less they all had to say on the radio, the stealthier they would be during any intercept. After some time, their bogey picked up speed and was on a clear course to intercept the Canadian patrol plane.

"That bogey is going to beat us there by a bit," Dex remarked from the back. "Should we tap burner?"

Fargo spared a glance at their fuel state. "We could, but I don't like where that would put us fuel wise. The timing ought to work out okay. We'll be getting there right around the time the bogey does, and still on his beam. If Iran wanted to shoot themselves a P-3, the Tomcat could have come south and taken the shot from within his own airspace. I'm guessing this is going to be a little harassment, or even a thump. Either way, we'll be in a good position to spring a surprise of our own, you betcha."

A 'thump' was when a fighter snuck up behind a slower moving transport or a helicopter and executed a sudden pull-up right in front of it. It usually surprised and startled the pilot on the receiving end, and it could cause damage as the victim flew through the jetwash of the offender. Thumping was considered an unfriendly act, reminiscent of the sort of games the United States used to play with the Soviets during the Cold War, but it wasn't really a shooting offense unless it caused a mishap. Given the games the Iranians had been playing recently, this was a potentially dangerous escalation. If fighters started hassling each other in a merged environment, the odds of someone taking a shot went up drastically.

"Looks like the bogey is headed down," Dex remarked.

A moment later they got their first call from AWACS. "Lobo 2-1, Closeout. Your current vector looks good. The farther north you can keep it, the later the Persian Cat will paint you on radar. Take Angels 10."

"Closeout, declare on India Alpha 15," Dexter called. They had already run the weapons checklist, the jet was in air-to-air combat mode, and all they needed to fire was to switch the master arm switch on and bring up the radar.

"India Alpha 15 is *Bogey.* Air Warning Yellow, Weapons Tight." The latter meant that they were only permitted to fire in response to a hostile act or in self-defense.

Dexter acknowledged the ROE as Fargo initiated their own descent, taking them down toward 10,000 FT. Dex was looking over his charts and scopes in the back. "Cheat left about five degrees, boss. We've got some wiggle room on this side of Iranian airspace."

"Copy," Fargo replied, easing them left. He leveled off at 10,000 FT, just as the ESM chirped tentatively for the first time. "Does the Tomcat have us?" he asked.

"Not just yet," Dex replied. "We're picking up some radar lobing, that's all. At this angle-off we're very low doppler, and we'll be outside his antenna sweep for a bit longer. Can you see the P-3 yet?" he asked. Fargo was looking, but there was nothing visible in the designator box on his visor display. They were big planes whose four Allison engines left highly visible smoke trails, but like any distant air target they could still be hard to spot visually. Dexter was working the ATFLIR pod in back, and he found them with his gadgetry before Fargo ever saw them with the good old Mark I eyeball.

"Got the Aurora," Dex muttered. "I'm going to work back to pick up the bogey. Should have him pretty qui—whoa! MiG 29's! There's two of them flying tight!"

"Can the Tomcat see us?" Fargo asked tensely, his pulse suddenly shooting up.

Dex studied his scopes. "He just turned nose cold, to the northeast. He's blind."

That was unfortunate timing for the Iranians, and Fargo grinned like a shark. "Better lucky than good, I always say."

***

Aboard the Canadian Aurora the crew had forgotten all about surface contacts for the moment. Alpha Sierra called them with a warning about an incoming bogey but assured them that they were under fighter protection. Not for the first time, the TACCO wished he could see the whole picture on a proper datalink. Now he felt like a worm on a hook, and he didn't much like it. "Navigator, tune up the frequency for Strike. I want to hear what's going on."

"Roger," the NAV/COMM replied.

"Sensor 3, TACCO. Any ESM on friendly fighters?"

"Negative. I've lost the ESM line off the Iranian but still have our own AWACS, and that's it."

"We've got Strike up on UHF-2, but nobody's talking," the NAV/COMM reported.

"Are we *sure* we've got fighter cover?" the plane commander called from the flight deck.

"We're spiked at our six o'clock!" Sensor 3 called suddenly. "We've got a MiG behind us!"

"What type?" the plane commander called, sounding frazzled.

"Never mind," the TACCO said calmly, looking out his large, round window. "Flight, look off your left wing, eh?"

The pilot did so and saw the olive green paint scheme adorning an Iranian MiG-29 Fulcrum. The pilot was holding position off his wing, and his wingman, based on ESM, was somewhere behind them at their six o'clock.

"Holy shit, that's *cool*," the in-flight technician called over ICS. He was acting as an aft observer right now, seated at the port galley window and using binoculars to conduct visual surface searches. He had a pretty good rear-quarter view of the fighter. "Is that actually an Iranian Air Force plane?" he asked a moment later. "The coloring is weird."

The plane commander's observation was more pragmatic: "He's armed. Four air-to-air missiles."

"Probably a Revolutionary Guard plane, but still Iranian," the TACCO said, replying to the in-flight tech. "IFT, get up here with the rigging camera. Let's see if we can get some shots of this guy before he pisses off."

"On the way," the IFT replied.

"Nav, call in the air contact report."

"Copy."

"TACCO, Sensor 3. Still no ESM on the Persian Cat. They've either gone radar-silent or turned away from us."

"Well, they already found us, eh?" the TACCO retorted dryly. "Job's done."

"True enough."

The IFT arrived in the cockpit with a large, high-resolution digital camera that they used to take pictures of surface contacts. The IFT turned the camera on and centered it in the large, round observation window right behind the left pilot's seat. He began snapping pictures, one after another, as fast as he could take them. The Iranian pilot didn't notice right away, but as soon as he did the MiG dropped down and slid back, executing a snappy aileron roll before breaking away to port and rapidly vanishing from sight.

"Well, that's one way to get rid of the little hoser," the pilot remarked.

***

"Are we recording all this?" Fargo asked, watching the beautiful image of the MiG centered in their FLIR's field of view. The picture was so clear they could count the missiles under the wings: it looked like two radar-guided missiles and two heat-seekers, like their own loadouts. Fairly standard, but bad news if they were fired in anger.

"Oh yeah, we are," Dexter replied, his excitement shining through in his voice. This was the kind of stuff you lived for on deployment, along with good port calls. Short of pulling the trigger, this was as real as it got. Unfortunately, it looked like it might be about to get just a little more real. The lead MiG peeled away from the Aurora, but the one behind dropped down suddenly and started to accelerate. "He's gonna thump him!" Dex half-shouted.

"Aww, Jeez," Fargo grumbled. "Don't make me lock you up, you stupid sumbitch!" He broke radio silence. "Deedee, you got the cold bogey?"

"Tally."

"I'm gonna run off Thumper. Cover my six."

"Always."

"Lobo 2, Closeout, merged plot. Give us a SITREP," the AWACS controller called.

"Lobo, going active," Dexter replied. He added a 'Judy' call as soon as he had radar contact, and that was that.

***

The Aurora crew was half expecting it to happen, but it still made them jump when the MiG-29 flashed under the patrol plane's nose and pulled up hard, climbing like a rocket. The fighter was in full afterburner, using raw power to affect the maneuver from a relatively low starting speed. The plane commander gripped the control yoke and held the patrol plane steady as it flew through the fighter's jet wash at about 200 knots. The pass wasn't close enough to do any damage or crack the outer pane of the Aurora's thick cockpit windscreen, but it rattled them and made them furious. The plane commander shouted some particularly vile epithets after the offending MiG, but harsh language was all he had to counter with.

Suddenly, a female voice broke over the radio on the Strike channel. "Charlie Alpha 31, this is Lobo 2-2, a flight of two navy fighters. We've got your six. Vector 160 until advised. We'll clear these bozos out."

The plane commander beat the NAV/COMM to the radio. *"Thank you!"*

***

Fargo saw the MiG pull into the vertical on the thump, then rapidly roll ninety degrees and pitch back, essentially a vector roll that evolved into a diving turn: a 180-degree reversal that would allow him to rejoin his flight lead or re-engage for a second pass. Fargo rolled inverted from above and pulled through at about the same time the MiG rolled in the vertical, selecting afterburner and tearing down from above with several thousand feet of altitude advantage. The beauty of it was that Fargo was now looking at the belly of the MiG: they were on his blind side. "Lock him up," Fargo snapped tersely.

Dexter's initial urge to whoop as the world turned upside down was dashed by the sudden, cold realization that they were committing on a pair of MiG-29's in what amounted to a visual range 2V2. The MiG-29 was one of the world's top-rated visual-range dogfighters; the F/A-18F was *not*. Still, it was a poor craftsman that blamed his tools. He'd trained for years for this moment, and now it was here. Besides, wasn't his pilot a former SFTI with two combat deployments in Afghanistan? If any pilot in the squadron could handle this, it was Fargo. Training took over, and he brought the radar active. Almost as an afterthought he called: "Verify master arm switch on."

"It's on," Fargo replied. "Good call, dude. He selected Sidewinder and switched the radar to boresight acquisition. A low, growling sidetone almost instantly went high-pitch as the IR seeker on the missile locked onto the MiG, and Fargo flew the bogey into the dashed circle on his HUD, watching the symbology change as the radar locked the MiG and set off its radar warning receiver. The shoot cue appeared above the target designator box in his display. "Gotcha, bitch!" Fargo snarled. He had both a radar and infrared lock; if he chose to fire, the MiG was dog meat. Even more so than Dexter, he was aware of the precariousness of their position if this situation dragged out, given the various strengths and weaknesses of his jet versus his opponent's. The temptation to fire and remove the danger was *overwhelming.* His warrior blood was up—every nerve, every instinct in his fighter-pilot hindbrain was screaming at him: *Shoot!*

Thumping a patrol plane is not a capital offense, Fargo reminded himself. Not only that, but the current ROE forbade it. He held his fire.

The MiG pilot was obviously startled by the warning tone of his threat warning receiver, telling him that someone behind him had a firing solution on him. He reacted in a pretty predictable manner: after a frantic 'Linda Blair' turned up nothing visual in his aft quarter, he reversed hard and executed a minimum radius turn, hoping to either force an overshoot of a close-in adversary or at least get nose to nose with a more distant threat. The MiG was still in full burner and accelerating as it went into the turn. Fargo was closing fast with a significant airspeed advantage at the start, so he popped up with perfect timing and rolled in the vertical to keep his quarry in sight, turning some airspeed back into altitude and bringing his nose over the top as he pulled into a lag pursuit. That prevented the overshoot and kept the MiG out in front of him, where it belonged. Fargo figured the MiG pilot would catch sight of him and reverse again, pull up, and try to drag him into a rolling scissors—the Fulcrum had enough thrust to accelerate straight up, so that would pose a problem for the Super Hornet.

Fortunately, that didn't happen. The MiG stayed in a level turn, and Fargo realized the Iranian hadn't spotted him. The opposing pilot was probably looking back into the plane of his own turn instead of scanning his entire rear quarter, where he *should* be looking. Or maybe he thought the threat was beyond visual range, but the abruptly broken radar lock on the reversal should have clued him that he was in a knife fight. Either the Iranian was stupid, or Fargo had scared him stupid, which was even better: a rattled opponent on the defensive was prone to mistakes.

With a smile splitting his face, Fargo eased his pull and let the jet slide back to the outside of the MiG's turn, back to its blind side. The old saying was never truer than right now: *Lose sight, lose the fight*. He put the radar in vertical acquisition now, scanning up and down along the jet's lift-vector, and within a moment he re-established radar lock. From the moment Fargo selected a missile, they'd never lost a good firing solution with their all-aspect Sidewinder and off-boresight targeting capability. "Deedee, you still got the leader?" Fargo called.

"Yeah, he's flailing around, trying to figure out why he's locked up. I think he lost sight of his wingman when he jinked, and he sure as hell doesn't see me. These guys have lost SA completely."

"They never had it to begin with—their overwatch in the Persian Cat never saw us coming. My guy's a hamburger, I've already simulated shooting him twice," Fargo added, watching with his senses on hair trigger. As soon as the MiG's wings rocked back, signaling another reversal, Fargo popped up hard and rolled away in the opposite direction over the top, then completed the barrel roll and pulled back into lag pursuit on the MiG's six, still hugging his blind side. Once again the MiG pilot had a chance to pick him up visually but missed it. They locked him up for a third time, and the MiG abruptly rolled out on a heading directly for Iranian airspace, went to full burner, and dove for the deck—he'd had enough. Fargo leveled out and let the Fulcrum go, watching it accelerate away. Chasing the guy would only waste gas and prove embarrassing; below 10,000 FT with tanks and stores, a Super Hornet in full afterburner had a hard time breaking Mach-1. The MiG was already way faster than that as it ran for home.

"MiG-2 is extending—he's bugging out," he called.

"MiG-1 is disengaging," Deedee replied. "Fargo, I'm at your three o'clock high," she called. Fargo's head snapped around, and he saw Deedee's jet rolling out of a steep dive and levelling off about a thousand feet above him and half a mile to his right. Her quarry was two rapidly dwindling dots of fire as the other MiG rocketed northward in full afterburner.

More than 200 NM away, the AWACS controllers in the Hawkeye regained a clear picture once all the fighters had some separation. "Lobo 2, Closeout. I show bogeys running supersonic, heading 020 for the airspace boundary, nose cold. Disengage. Your green vector 220."

"Copy disengage," Fargo called. "Knock it off." He eased back on the throttles and broke left, taking his nose off the retreating MiGs and breaking radar lock. He called for Deedee to form up as she echoed his 'knock it off' call. She followed him into his turn and was already closing the distance to rejoin.

"Lobo 2, Closeout. Reset, take Angels 20. Alert fighters are en-route to provide top cover. Resume previous tasking."

"Copy, Closeout," Fargo replied, waiting for a steer from Dexter and initiating a climb. Deedee stayed glued to his wing, and he felt a rush of exhilaration burst through him. *What a great day this turned out to be!*

Captain VanNortwick's voice suddenly came over the radio. "Lobo 2 and flight, this is Strike Actual," he said. "Alpha Bravo passes BZ!" *A verbal 'attaboy' from CAG and the admiral himself, eh?* Fargo thought. *Nice!*

"Thanks, with our respects," Dexter replied for them all. They listened as Strike cleared the Aurora back into its operating area and turned them back over to their primary controller.

"Now we're cooking with oil!" Fargo grinned. "How are you doing back there?" he asked. He'd put some heavy G on them during the maneuvering, and it was tougher on the WSO, who didn't always know when it was coming.

"I feel *great!*" Dexter replied. A few minutes later it started feeling a little anti-climactic. "Now what?" he added.

Fargo chuckled. "Now we finish our original route, so DCAG doesn't feel cheated—God help us if that happens, right? Then we find a tanker, land this puppy, and celebrate with sliders and autodog tonight. Just a fleet average day, bro." Sliders and autodog were slang for burgers and soft-serve ice cream—both staples of the Dirty Shirt wardroom.

"*Out-standing!*" Dexter whooped. Fargo's face split into a big grin. Dexter was showing the earmarks of a proper 'warrior' junior officer. The remainder of the flight was fueled by pure adrenalin.

***

Tehran, Islamic Republic of Iran

Major General Weh Heng was an officer of the PLA, the People's Liberation Army of the Communist Party of China. He'd had a long, successful career, and was well connected within the party. His own son, a rising star in the PLA, was married to a relative of the Chinese president. His current posting was military attaché to the Chinese Embassy in Iran. His joss had been exceptional for his entire life; he enjoyed good health and relative wealth, wanted for nothing, and feared nothing except failing his Party and his country.

The man sitting on the other side of his desk absolutely terrified him.

Brigadier General Cheng Ye of the Chinese People's Liberation Army Air Force (PLAAF) was rather unremarkable at first glance. He was 5'7", slender but with an athletic strength about him, with close-cropped, jet-black hair, and black eyes. Weh Heng decided it was the eyes that caused a chill fear to permeate any room he was in. They were cold and soulless, as if Ye cared for nothing in the world, including himself. When he spoke to General Weh, those eyes locked intensely onto the attaché's, unblinking and predatorial. Ye's eyes had darted about quickly upon entering the office, almost like a raptor's, cataloging every detail, then discarding most of them as irrelevant. In his world, there were things that mattered and things that didn't; the latter were summarily ignored, never to be acknowledged or bothered with again. Cheng Ye put off an aura of darkness—Weh felt that Ye was the only person he'd ever met in whom he could sense *evil* like a tangible thing. Weh Heng was a good communist; his god was the State, but Cheng Ye almost made him believe in the Devil.

"Our first attempt to lure the Americans into a hostile act has failed," Cheng Ye reported. "It might have succeeded had my own people or the Russians executed it, but General Abdi was insistent that it be carried out by the Revolutionary Guard. We are planning a second operation, which will be carried out soon."

Weh Heng was the superior officer between the two of them, but there was nothing in Cheng Ye's attitude or demeanor to suggest he was anything other than the one in authority. Just the force of his personality in the confines of this office had the attaché back on his mental heels, although he was quite capable of disguising that fact. A man must have three hearts: one he showed the world, one reserved for his inner circle of friends and family, and one known only to himself. The innermost heart was where true ambition lived, held secret in a culture where nobody—not even friends and family—could ever be trusted completely. His inner heart quailed under the gaze of Cheng Ye, but his outer heart was a stoic, impassive mask. Face had to be maintained, *always*.

"I've seen the report, and your proposal," General Weh confirmed. "As a tripwire to set a chain of events in motion, it will be effective. Beijing is concerned, however, at how it will be received among the rank and file of the IRIAF. If they are given the perception that their lives are being wasted on foolhardy games whose purpose is unclear to them, it might set them at odds with their Revolutionary Guard overseers."

"It is true, some of them lack the courage of their commitment to their great Islamic Revolution," Cheng Ye stated without any apparent rancor. "They will be the ones sacrificed first, but I

Brian J. Smith

understand the Party's concerns. You have my assurance that I will see to this matter myself. I *guarantee* the success of the next operation."

Despite his discomfort, General Weh couldn't help but make the veiled threat. It was the Party way, and ingrained in his nature as a PLA officer. "Failure will not be tolerated, general. How can you personally guarantee success?"

Cheng Ye smiled, and General Weh had to physically force himself not to shudder at the sight of it. "You may relay to our Party leaders in Beijing that it will succeed, or I will be dead. Is that guarantee enough, general?"

"One could ask for no more," General Weh replied graciously. *Psychopath!*

"Then I must return to my unit," Cheng Ye said. Both men came to their feet but didn't shake hands. General Weh sketched the slightest of bows, which General Cheng acknowledged with the barest of nods. Both were dressed in mufti, and neither man saluted the other. A moment later Cheng Ye was gone, and the room seemed to brighten as if the sun had appeared from behind a cloud.

General Weh's secretary, a beautiful young Chinese woman and his occasional mistress, immediately appeared in the doorway looking slightly pale and troubled. Cheng Ye hadn't spared her a single word or glance on his way out, and despite the potential loss of face over being summarily ignored, she had never been more thankful for it. She bowed slightly.

"Is everything alright, sir?" she asked. Under any other set of circumstances, the question would have seemed ridiculous. In that moment it seemed totally appropriate, yet face had to be maintained. General Weh gave a hearty laugh that was totally faked.

"Everything's fine!" he assured her robustly. "A little more tea, perhaps."

"Right away, general," she said, bowing slightly and leaving him to contemplate the maelstrom soon to be unleashed in the waters of the Gulf.

The Persian Gulf

Copies of the HUD tapes from the two Super Hornets circulated through the various squadron ready rooms, and for a short time the four aviators from the Gray Wolves enjoyed a minor celebrity status within the air wing. It would wear off quickly; Fargo had seen this sort of thing before and frankly, among the combat blooded among them it wasn't a very big deal. Still, it was the first time in many years that Iranian and American fighters had hassled one another in the air, and the first time it had ever happened as payback for a 'thumping'.

Fargo got together with Neo, the Gray Wolves' SFTI, or Strike Fighter Tactics Instructor, for a more detailed debrief and breakdown of the event. Fargo was a pilot while Neo was a WSO, but their career tracks had been similar. Both had attended the nine-week power projection course at NSAWC, the Naval Strike Air Warfare Center, in Fallon, Nevada following their first squadron tours. Still known in navy circles as TOPGUN, the power projection course was a graduate level program designed to create tactics instructors who would return to the fleet to pass on what they had learned.

Neo was a senior lieutenant on a 'Super JO' tour; he'd spent his first shore rotation attending NSAWC, then teaching in the Super Hornet fleet replacement squadron before coming to the Gray Wolves for a second fleet tour in the SFTI role. He was responsible for all squadron tactical training, including qualifying crews as section, division, and strike leaders. It was the same job Fargo had held in his last squadron before promoting to O-4 and transferring to the Gray Wolves as a department head. Likewise, when this deployment ended, Neo would be promoted to O-4 and roll to another squadron for his own tour as a department head. It was a coveted career track—not everyone got to attend NSAWC, or get a second tour as a junior officer in a fleet squadron. Most aviators had to go to sea at least once in a non-flying billet, either on a staff of some kind, or as 'ship's company' in a billet like assistant navigator, catapult officer, or elsewhere in the air operations department.

Rumor had it that NSAWC was about to undergo another name change, and that the power projection course was going to be expanded to thirteen weeks. The entire program had already been cloned by the early warning, electronic warfare, and helicopter communities. Every branch of naval aviation had its own version of TOPGUN these days, and part of their collective job involved training entire air wings prior to their deployments.

Neo's debriefs with the two air crews involved breaking down the encounter, analyzing what had happened, and talking about what they could have done differently or better. This was how they learned and got better at their jobs, even though no two aerial engagements were alike. Fargo was pleased at the outcome, but he was aware of how it could have gotten ugly fast. If the Iranian pilots were more experienced, less startled at being jumped, or their Tomcat spotter had picked up Lobo flight on radar, the tables might have been turned quickly. What haunted Fargo was the possibility that after sparing the MiGs, the MiGs might have turned the tables on the Super Hornets and shot them. That would have been the sorriest of epitaphs, and it left a bad mental aftertaste. Despite the shitstorm it would have caused, there was a small part of Fargo that regretted not taking the shot when he had it. He had to satisfy himself that his decision had at least been ethically and legally correct, even if tactically risky.

Fargo passed through the ready room a couple days after the thumping incident, hunting coffee, when a flash of dark blue caught his eye. It was Sweater Boy, sitting in his seldom-used chair and poring over some imagery with a loupe magnifier. Their AIO didn't spend much time in the ready room unless he wanted to use one of the computers, or catch the evening movie after the last event. Curious, Fargo looked over his shoulder.

"You're in my light," Chadwick snarked, then looked up and saw the maintenance officer. "Sir."

"What do you have there?" Fargo asked.

"Some satellite imagery of Iran."

Fargo frowned. "Isn't that stuff classified? Shouldn't you be looking at it in CVIC?"

Sweater Boy shook his head. "Not this stuff, sir. It's OSINT."

"You lost me," Fargo replied.

"Open source Intelligence. I downloaded these off Google Earth. I do that sometimes, and if I find anything interesting, I kick it up the food chain for a look from a real reconnaissance satellite."

"So? What have you got?"

"Well, a flight line full of Flankers with a weird camo scheme. Neither the Iranian Air Force nor the Revolutionary Guard uses it. Here, look," he added, handing over a color print. Fargo took the sheet, squinting at the slightly blurry image. Fargo held out his hand for the magnifier and ran it over the pictures, but the resolution wasn't good enough to make much out of it. The Flankers were a two-seat variant, but there were so many variants that it was hard to keep track of them all, and impossible to determine what these were using a low resolution internet photo.

"That does look off," Fargo admitted. "It almost looks like Chinese camo."

"I thought so too. We're sending this stuff to the office of naval intelligence and Langley for evaluation, and hoping to get back some imagery with better resolution."

"You aren't suggesting the jet isn't Iranian, are you?"

"No sir," Sweater Boy replied, a little hesitantly. "No, nothing like that," he added more firmly. "It could be they just haven't re-painted them yet. Some of these acquisitions of theirs are new."

"How many are there?" Fargo asked. "And what about variant types?"

"I'm working on it, sir," Sweater Boy replied through a tight-lipped smile.

Fargo sighed, handing back the picture and the magnifier. "That'd be good information to have, y'know?"

"I'm working on it," Sweater Boy repeated. "So are a lot of other people."

"It would be nice to have it before we're on our way home from deployment, y'know?" Fargo quipped.

"Speaking of which, did you hear that our relief is transiting the Suez Canal right now?" Sweater Boy asked. Fargo hadn't heard that. In fact, he wasn't even sure they were going to be relieved. This was the first carrier deployment into the Persian Gulf since early 2002, and it didn't seem like they had accomplished a whole lot other than to stir up Iran. After the pivot away from Iraq after 9/11, there hadn't been much reason to be here. This deployment had been quiet up until the past few weeks. Fargo asked which strike group was on its way to take over.

"It's not a carrier strike group," Sweater Boy informed him. "It's an expeditionary strike group. USS *Nassau*, with two other amphibs and a destroyer squadron in company. How many jets does a ship like *Nassau* carry, anyway?"

Fargo shrugged. "Depends on how she's fitted out. A half dozen Harriers or so, and mostly helicopters. They're probably better suited for maritime security operations than we are, but a lot more vulnerable as well," he said thoughtfully, wondering who in D.C. was making these decisions. The thought of an Iranian Air Force equipped with Fulcrums, Flankers, and AWACS stacked against a half-dozen ancient Harrier jump-jets gave him the willies. He added: "If I was in charge at Fifth Fleet, I'd probably sit 'em in the Gulf of Oman for a while, given what's been happening to us every night."

Sweater Boy shook his head slightly. "That would make them operationally worthless for anything on this side of Hormuz, if all they really have is helicopters. I see your point though," he added. "Hopefully we don't get extended out here," he added.

Fargo felt a different sort of dread at those words—the deployment fun-meter had hit zero some time back, and they were all ready to go *home*. "You didn't hear anything, did you?" he asked apprehensively. "Gawd, that's all we need, is for something to screw up our port call in Rota on the way back!"

"Nothing yet," Sweater Boy replied, "but if the Iranians get any jumpier than they've been, all bets are off. You know how it goes better than I do."

"Yah," Fargo replied, feeling a little hollow inside. He made his excuses about needing to get back to work, and headed out. His conversation with the AIO cast a pall on his mood, like a storm cloud on the horizon. As soon as people started talking about deployment being extended, it was like a Chinese curse and Murphy's Law being baked into the cosmos: perception would become reality, like a jinx.

BOHICA, Fargo mentally sighed, feeling eternally trapped by the gray bulkheads of the Boat. *Bend over, here it comes again!*

III

MAR 2013
The Persian Gulf

As dawn broke over a solid overcast in the northwestern Gulf, a lone Flanker crossed the Iranian coastline and descended to a mere fifty feet over the water. This aircraft was Cheng Ye's personal fighter. Unlike the other Flankers flown by the Chinese pilots of the *Feilong*, the 'Flying Dragons,' this jet was a single seat prototype and carried a unique paint scheme. Rather than a broken camouflage pattern in shades of blue and gray, it was painted a solid robin's-egg blue, with the form of a sinuous, oriental-style dragon painted in darker blue and gray over large portions of the top and bottom planforms of the jet. Like the Russian Red Talons, the *Feilong* squadrons carried Iranian markings. The other standout feature of the jets flown by the Chinese volunteers was that their names were stenciled below the cockpit rails in Chinese *kanji* characters, and the characters for *Feilong*, 飞龙, were painted boldly on either side of the nose in red.

Cheng Ye found it satisfying that the idea of state-sanctioned mercenary aviators flying for a foreign ally was another case of intellectual theft from the Americans. It arguably began with the Lafayette Escadrille of World War I, but the real comparison was the American Volunteer Group formed in 1940. Known by its more popular name, the Flying Tigers, the AVG recruited active duty military aviators from America and paid them to fly for China against the Japanese. The Flying Tigers racked up an impressive kill ratio in just a few months of operations, using tactics that played to the strengths of their older aircraft against their newer, nimbler Japanese opponents. After Pearl Harbor was attacked and the United States formally entered the war, the AVG was absorbed back into the U.S. Army Air Corps, with its personnel returning to regular, active duty status. That model had been copied here, with Cheng Ye acting as a modern day Claire Chennault. The only difference was that Chennault didn't fly combat missions with the AVG, while Cheng Ye led from the front.

It was the perfect morning for what he intended to do. There was a solid, 5000 FT overcast over the Gulf this morning, and the Americans were just preparing for the day's first flight operations, which hadn't begun yet. There were no AWACS aircraft currently airborne anywhere in the Gulf, American or Iranian. The cueing data he had on the position of the American aircraft carrier came from spies in simple commercial watercraft that were never far from where the Yankees were operating. These craft used an Iranian-made laser-semaphore system to pass information to the coast. It was an asymmetric method using simple equipment adapted from laser rangefinders, and only needed an unbroken line of sight to the next craft or station in the relay chain. Given the volume of sea traffic in the Gulf, it worked well when the Americans conducted operations inside one of their predictable 'carrier boxes.' A similar system was in place along the coastline of Iran and its islands, allowing secure, line-of-sight visual communications without radio transmissions.

What he was about to do was dangerous, so dangerous that he might not survive it. However, he had not embarked on his mission without a plan of action in mind. The original plan had called for an IRIAF pilot flying an antiquated, expendable F-4 Phantom to conduct the mission, but the Iranian squadron commander handed the task had immediately protested to his superiors, arguing that it was a suicide mission with no military value. That wasn't true, although the IRIAF commander had no way of knowing that. In any case, this was the first opportunity for Cheng Ye to prove his worthiness and establish the bona fides of the Flying Dragons with its Persian employer, so he had opted to take it on himself. Besides, it was clear that the provocations up to this point were not achieving the desired effect; even the thumping of a maritime patrol plane a few days prior hadn't resulted in shots fired. Cheng Ye was determined to move their strategy forward—today would be the day.

Cheng Ye's jet wasn't just unique in its looks. It was heavily upgraded, boasting the latest engines taken from a technology demonstrator prototype. Cheng Ye's ship featured vectored thrust nozzles and the ability to super cruise—the only aircraft in the Flying Dragons that could do so. He pushed his throttles up to full military power, and with its light missile load the jet accelerated to just under the speed of sound. He was too low to achieve super cruise in this regime; the air was too thick, and he was burdened with a pair of underwing drop tanks—he was going to need every drop of the fuel they carried.

When he came over the horizon, he began seeing the ESM lines from the American AEGIS radar systems emanating from the carrier's escort ships. He knew the ranges inside the Persian Gulf were short enough, and the American radar systems good enough that they would detect him almost immediately. He advanced his throttles into afterburner, and the Flanker pressed forward, rapidly going supersonic. He eased the jet up to an altitude of 500 FT, knowing they had certainly detected him by now. He was trusting to short reaction times, confusion, uncertainty, and requests for orders up and down the American chain of command to give him the precious minute or two he needed. More than anything else, he was hoping to trade on the innate American reluctance to use deadly force in situations like this. The idea was to act quickly, decisively, inside the decision loop of the enemy commanders. The OODA loop (observe, orient, decide, act) concept was studied extensively by Chinese strategists. Ironically, it was formulated by an American air force officer in the 1980's.

Cheng Ye smiled coldly—a mirthless, emotionless smile. He could see the carrier on the horizon now, rapidly growing larger as the water passed underneath him in a supersonic blur. It was an incredible rush of speed, but it evoked no thrill or emotion in Cheng Ye. He was a machine now, singular minded in his purpose, with ice water flowing through his veins.

***

Two Gray Wolves Super Hornets sat just behind the two bow jet-blast deflectors, standing the ready alert. The lead aircraft was crewed by Chill and Neo, with LT Cole 'Bender' Riley and LT Patrick 'Boner' McGhee in the pilot and WSO seats of Dash-2, respectively. Given their last names and call signs, this crew pairing was often referred to around the ready room as the "Irish brothers" or the "Bender and Boner show." They'd spent the past few hours fitfully dozing, thumbing through magazines, or listening to music as they suffered through another ready alert. Most squadron commanders didn't get saddled 'bad deals' like this, but the past couple weeks had seen the entire roster of air crews leveraged to the maximum extent of their endurance. The skipper's presence on this alert was a necessity to meet the requirements of the flight schedule, and he'd taken the early morning Ready-5 as the means to free himself from flying duties for the rest of the day afterward.

The voice of the Air Boss suddenly boomed across the flight deck, amplified to godlike, ear-splitting volume over the 5MC. "NOW ON THE FLIGHT DECK! FLIGHT QUARTERS, FLIGHT QUARTERS! LAUNCH THE ALERT FIVE AIRCRAFT!"

Controlled pandemonium immediately broke out in and around the two Super Hornets and the bow catapults. Chill looked over at Bender and rapidly shook two fingers in the air, confirming the Air Boss's order to start 'em up. In less than a minute helmets were donned, canopies closed, checklists completed, and the whine of jet engines broke the still morning air as USS *Boxer* heeled slightly, making as swift a turn into the wind as a ship that size could make. Behind them, the ship's wake frothed a furious white, showing a graceful arc in the turn as the carrier's nuclear-powered screws drove her up to launch speed.

Both Super Hornets taxied onto the catapults and the jet blast deflectors came up behind them. As the pilots went through the process of extending their wings and lowering their launch bars for hook-up, they were multi-tasking with their WSOs as they pressed through the takeoff checklist with a speed borne of long familiarity.

In the back of the lead Super Hornet, Neo was multitasking even a little more. He tuned up Strike frequency as soon as they had power on the jet and he could switch on the radios, trying to figure out what was going on. It was rare to launch an alert like this, so something was up. He listened to a few frantic radio calls going back and forth between Strike and Alpha Whiskey, and that cued him where to look next.

"Holy shit!" he breathed, looking out low over the horizon at his nine o'clock, out to the port side of the ship. A black dot was coming at them at incredible speed, low over the water, swiftly resolving into the shape of an airplane. "Skipper, nine o'clock on the horizon! Look!" In almost the same motion, he switched over and slewed the FLIR pod that way, and it immediately locked onto the incoming plane. He'd get just a few seconds of footage before the wings and upper fuselage of the Super Hornet masked the pod and it lost lock. It was a head's-up move given everything else that was happening.

"Wow. Someone's gonna get fired," Chill remarked with amazing casualness.

Neo's attention was forced back inside as they prepared to launch. The skipper ran the power up to full MIL, wiped the controls, and smartly saluted the shooter. To their left on the other catapult, Bender was doing the same. Neo let his fingers play over the top of the lower ejection ring—a subconscious thing on his part—and braced himself for the stroke. And he waited . . . and waited . . . nothing. He looked outside and saw the shooter giving the signal to suspend the launch. A short time later Chill throttled down the engines.

"What in the *fuck*?!" Skipper Jefferson's voice erupted over the ICS. "Boss, this is 208," his voice crackled on the radio a moment later. "SITREP?"

"Problem with the cat. Stand by," the Air Boss's voice came right back. "Stand by . . ." he repeated a moment later, distracted, obviously juggling chainsaws on his end.

Neo looked out to his left again, just in time to see a Sukhoi Flanker punch off its external fuel tanks just shy of the carrier as it overflew them in full afterburner at supersonic speed. A thunderous clap rocked the flight deck, and several of the windows lining the bridge and flag bridge cracked and shattered, raining broken glass on the flight deck around the ship's island. Some of it was picked up by the wind and whipped aft, hitting parked aircraft, causing a couple superficial cuts to flight deck personnel. One of the Air Boss's windows up in PRIFLY blew out as well, adding to the mayhem. Neo felt his stomach tighten—it occurred to him that he knew what he was seeing when the fuel tanks came off the Flanker. The inexperienced 19 year old bridge lookouts, hopped up on excitement and adrenalin, probably thought they saw something else entirely.

"Okay!" The Air Boss's voice thundered over the 5MC, loud enough to drown out the sound of four Super Hornet engines. He was obviously too busy to be perturbed by what just happened. "We're launching 211 solo! Get her in the air!" he barked.

The Irish brothers were sitting ready the entire time, engines run up, watching, and waiting. The shooter had simply stood there with his hand in the air, and now he finally dropped to one knee and touched the deck, before pointing forward. The catapult fired, hurling 211 off the deck and into the air.

Neo, with nothing better to do for a few seconds, jumped on the radio. "Boss, 208. Be advised that the bogey jettisoned his tanks right before going over us. The bridge might be thinking he just tried to bomb us. Those were fuel tanks—just a head's up."

Up in PRIFLY, the Air Boss couldn't be bothered by Neo's call—he had bigger fish to fry as he prepared to order an immediate combat FOD walk down of the flight deck. They had to get the broken glass, and any other debris picked up before the first event, or half the jets on deck would ingest it on startup and ruin their motors. "What? Okay, thanks," Boss replied over the radio, gesturing impatiently to his assistant to deal with it. The assistant Air Boss picked up the direct line to the bridge.

"Captain? Mini-Boss. Relay from 208: If anyone up there saw it, those were fuel tanks that came off the bogey, not weapons. Uhm . . . no sir, I'm not sure how he knows. Uhm . . . no sir, I'm not sure if he's sure. I can call him back . . . ?" Mini-boss held the phone away from his head as the ship's captain went high-order in his ear. *Jesus, what the hell did I do?* Mini-boss asked himself.

***

Cheng Ye used his own IRST system to watch what was happening on the flight deck of the carrier as he made his overflight. He saw the deck crew scurrying like ants around the two fighters, preparing to launch, and noted that they were Super Hornets. By the time they launched, he'd have had such a head start and speed advantage that they'd never catch him, and even their ARMAAM missiles would be hard pressed to hit him by the time they were in any position to fire. The real threat was from the surface ships, but fortunately they hadn't fired at him yet.

He knew his joss was extraordinary to make it to this point. He could have been killed by any number of defensive systems: standard missiles from the cruisers or destroyers, evolved sea-sparrow or rolling airframe point defense missiles, or even an old-fashioned CIWS cannon. Low and supersonic, his plane would look like a fat cruise missile to any of those if they were placed in an automatic firing mode. As he'd hoped, he'd caught the Americans asleep at the switch, or at least surprised them enough to make it this far.

He punched off his fuel tanks as he passed over the ship— he needed as little drag as possible now, and he'd almost run them dry. He had a full internal fuel load, speed, two IR missiles, and his wits to escape with. His IRST system remained padlocked on the carrier's flight deck as he passed over; the picture immediately started to recede as he pulled away, still in full afterburner. According to his airspeed indicator he was accelerating through Mach 1.4 now that the external tanks were gone; he hoped to push her up to 1.6 in the thick air. He began a gradual, shallow arcing turn back to the north, towards safety.

Behind him, he saw just one of the Super Hornets launch and immediately turn on an intercept heading. He knew his IRST would be masked in moments, but for the moment he had decent situational awareness. Why wasn't the second Super Hornet launched? And why had they launched any aircraft at all when they could have just shot him down with missiles from one of the ships? Cheng Ye didn't have the answers to those riddles, but as he looked over his right shoulder and visually padlocked the one airborne Super Hornet, he mentally flipped through his pre-prepared options and decided on a course of action. His original plan was to simply run from a pair of Super Hornets, but a single American plane was another matter entirely. Even better, he was safe from the SAM threat while the American plane was nearby. Without looking away from the target behind him, he thumbed a switch on his stick, selecting one of his two R-73M IR missiles.

***

"Lobo 1-2, Departure, hot vector 340. Out of your turn Bandit will be at your 12 o'clock, nose cold and rapidly opening. Strike passes you are cleared to commit, weapons free. Splash the bandit."

"Roger copy, Lobo 1-2, commit on the bandit," Boner replied. Up front, Bender was busy getting the jet cleaned up, and accelerating. They had about 150 knots coming off the cat—the bandit had an enormous speed advantage. Catching him was going to be problematic, but they'd do their best.

"I'm in air to air, master arm on," Bender called. "Punch the tanks, boyo."

"Tanks coming off," Boner replied as the jet surged forward. As soon as he could select the stations and hit the jettison button, the Super Hornet ditched several thousand pounds of gas it wasn't going to need and a lot of drag along with it. Bender selected max afterburner, and sighed as the jet pushed sluggishly against the thick air. Boner locked the Flanker up with both the FLIR and radar. They had a clear picture of the bandit on both infrared and regular television. All they had to do now was generate some closure or get closer before a missile could catch a supersonic target this low. "C'mon, baby . . . c'mon, baby," Boner chanted, mentally urging the Rhino to go *faster*. The distance between the two jets began to stabilize as the Super Hornet accelerated and the Flanker inexplicably began slowing down.

Bender was fully charged with adrenalin up front, and nervously ad-libbing a lyric from Smokey and the Bandit, the ready room movie from the night before: "*You can run like you're on fire, but you're gonna die real tired . . . we're northbound, now watch that bandit run!*"

"He's wings level and out of burner," Boner called excitedly. "He's slowing down . . . We're closing now . . . I don't think he sees us!" In the heat of the moment, he didn't consider the fact that there was only one reason for the Flanker to give up its massive speed advantage.

"This will work out perfectly," Bender replied. "I'm going to put an AMRAAM right up his ass. We finally get to break one of their new toys," he growled in satisfaction.

***

Cheng Ye made his play. Decelerating rapidly to subsonic speed, he pitched up and let the Flanker pass into the overcast. Once he knew he was momentarily out of sight, he pulled power to idle, popped his speed brake, and went high-Alpha. The R-73M missiles he carried had a 60-degree off-boresight capability, with helmet-mounted cueing. All he had to do was look at the enemy, and that would tell the missile seeker where to look. He fed in some thrust vectoring and executed a beautiful pirouette, twisting his fighter off axis in a varsity display of airmanship. Sun Tzu spoke clearly about using the terrain to one's advantage in warfare. In this case, the terrain was a solid, two-thousand foot thick overcast that hid him from sight just long enough. The growl of the uncaged IR seeker in his ear grew louder as it sniffed the hot afterburners of the pursuing Super Hornet emerging from the cool morning cloud deck.

The American jet appeared a moment later, a bit closer than he anticipated and not-quite supersonic in the climb. Cheng Ye's eyes widened a fraction as a missile came off the Super Hornet, dropping off the left wing and igniting almost immediately. He didn't hesitate; he squeezed the trigger at the same time the IR warble in his ear changed pitch, indicating it had locked the enemy. His own missile came off the rail and made an immediate, sharp turn to the right, at almost point blank range.

***

Bender was so focused on being able to fire that he missed the sudden jump in closure rate displayed on his HUD as the bandit pitched up abruptly and disappeared into the overcast. "Blind," he called immediately, although they still had radar and infrared lock. The IR picture blurred slightly for a moment as it sought to resolve the sudden change in outside conditions. When high-resolution was restored an instant later, they saw that the other aircraft appeared to be going vertical—at least that was how it looked to them. *Go up to blow up,* Bender snickered to himself. When the Super Hornet burst out of the cloud tops and Bender suddenly realized the other jet was practically suspended mid-air in front of them, it was too late. Of all the things they expected to face from Iran, a super-maneuvering fighter with thrust-vectoring was *not* one of them.

Several things happened almost simultaneously. Bender already had an AMRAAM selected, a good shoot cue, and he pulled the trigger. In the same instant, there was a thin white trail of smoke as a missile came off the bandit and made a hard turn straight at them. Bender didn't even have time to curse before the missile struck the nose of the jet and detonated. The explosion of the warhead, coupled with the kinetic energy imparted by a transonic target and the shockwaves generated by a shredded airframe, resulted in a thunderous fireball that consumed the fighter completely.

***

Cheng Ye couldn't believe his joss as the AMRAAM blew past him without locking on. It was past him almost before he mentally registered it; even before he could thumb chaff and flares. The range was too short when it was fired, the closure too fast. If the Super Hornet's pilot had selected an IR missile instead of the

AMRAAM, they would have killed each other. Expectation bias—the surety that his adversary was simply trying to run away as fast as possible—had doomed the American.

These were the thoughts that passed coldly and analytically through Cheng Ye's mind as he worked to save himself—he wasn't out of danger yet. He finished the maneuver that had put him into firing position, letting the nose swing gracefully below the horizon as if he was an airshow performer. He retracted his speed brake, rolled out on his escape heading, powered back into afterburner, and dove for the deck. All these tasks were performed without conscious effort; they were merely the act of flying, performed by a veteran fighter pilot. Within seconds he was supersonic again, fifty feet over the water, running for home.

As he planned beforehand he switched his radar over to sea-search mode and located the nearby supertanker he'd marked as part of his preflight planning. Larger than an aircraft carrier, the massive, oil-laden ship was plodding eastward through the Gulf waters, making her way towards the Strait of Hormuz and blissfully ignorant of the action happening in the skies nearby. He eased in a slight turn towards it, planning to pass slightly behind it and then put it between himself and the American carrier task force. When it was far enough behind him, he'd look for the next ship to mask himself with. It might be enough to break any radar tracking they held on him. If not, the Americans still ran the risk of hitting a neutral target if they fired at him.

The hardest, most dangerous part of his mission was over. All he had to do now was get back over land and he'd not only be safe, but a living legend among his men. Flying this mission, surviving it, and scoring a kill against a peer opponent would give him *tremendous* face.

More importantly, his strategic goal was surely well achieved.

***

Alpha Whiskey was the callsign for the strike group's Anti-Air Warfare commander, the officer responsible for defending the force from airborne threats. This job typically fell to the senior officer commanding one of the AEGIS-equipped surface escorts. In this case, it was the captain of the sole *Ticonderoga* Class cruiser in the strike group. The captain had been enjoying a quiet breakfast in his private mess when the bogey first popped on their radar screens. Now he was in the ship's combat direction center, trying to get a handle on this debacle and contemplating the sudden ruination of a two decade naval career.

"What do you mean, you *lost* the Super Hornet?" he asked with quiet intensity.

The TAO looked like he was about to be sick. "It's gone, sir. It just went off the scope. No IFF, and it never entered the datalink. The plot was merged for a few seconds—they might have been shot down."

"The bandit?"

"350 for 18, nose cold, and right on the deck," the enlisted controller reported. "He's running away fast, but we can still get him. Standing by to engage with birds," she added, referring to their stable of SM-2 Standard missiles.

"Where's the Super Hornet's wingman?" Alpha Whiskey asked.

"There never was a wingman, just the one," the TAO supplied. "Alpha Bravo called weapons free on the bandit," he added.

"Splash the bandit," Alpha Whiskey ordered.

The TAO gave the order, then picked up a handset and made a call over the Strike net. "99 Alpha Bravo, this is Alpha Whiskey. We are taking track India Alpha-1 with birds. Alpha Whiskey out."

"Alpha Whiskey, Alpha Bravo Actual. Belay that order. Weapons hold," the radio crackled with the unmistakable voice of the admiral. At almost the same time, they all felt the ship shudder slightly as an SM-2 missile left the tube, streaking skyward in hot pursuit of the offending bandit.

"*Jesus H. Roosevelt Christ!*" the captain snarled, looking up at the overhead in supplication.

The TAO scrambled some more, and less than a minute later the shot was aborted, with a two-and-a-half million dollar missile added to the morning's bill.

"Picture?" Alpha Whiskey asked.

"Sir, I hold one track, India Alpha-1 at 352 for 24, low and cold. We're starting to lose him in the surface clutter; there's a lot of ships out there. Other than that, clean air picture other than a couple slow movers in the commercial corridors."

The captain turned to the TAO, who was one of the ship's senior lieutenants. "Mister Webster, call your relief. Start putting together the report on whatever it was that just happened here."

"Aye aye, sir," replied the ashen-faced lieutenant.

The captain picked up a handset. "OOD, this is the captain. Call Smokey and tell him to prep for flight quarters. Break the helo out of the hangar and get her ready to go."

Just then, the radio crackled again. "Alpha Whiskey from Alpha Bravo. We're sending a helo over to you right now. You are directed to bring your TAO and report to Alpha Bravo Actual on the double. Awaiting acknowledgement."

What little color the TAO had left drained from his face. The ship's captain eyeballed him like a specimen under glass as he amended his orders. "OOD, belay the helo. Just stand by for flight quarters, we've got one inbound. Relay to the exec that I'm headed over to flag country for a come-around with the admiral." He hung up the handset. "You gonna answer that radio call, mister?"

The TAO acknowledged the call. His relief showed up in record time, prompted by the tell-tale rock-and-roll of a missile launch, when the ship wasn't even at General Quarters. After an extremely hasty watch turnover, the captain was waiting for him in the corridor outside the CDC for a quick sidebar. "Get your facts together quick, then get aft to meet the helo. The admiral is going to want answers."

"Sorry about dropping the ball, captain—it all went down fast, from the moment we caught the track on radar until it was on top of us. We're about to get fanged pretty good, aren't we?"

The captain laughed bitterly. "Son, this is a little more serious than a 'dropped ball'. I'm about to be loudly and publicly relieved of command. And you'd better start dusting off your resume—it's my sad duty to inform you that you've reached your terminal rank in this man's navy."

***

RADM (Upper Half) James Brandt, commander of the *Boxer* strike group, was on a three-way video conference call with the admiral commanding the Fifth Fleet in Bahrain, and the Secretary of the Navy in Washington D.C.

"So, both the pilots are dead?" SECNAV asked.

"Yes sir," Brandt replied. "There's not much data to go on. Both aircraft were above a cloud deck and out of visual contact, there is no datalink information, and all we have is the radar plot from the surface units. Our plane chased the Iranian, the plot merged for a few seconds, and then the Iranian was the only contact. We know what type of jet the Iranian was flying and how it was armed, thanks to some quick thinking by one of the aircrews on deck before the launch. We conducted an extensive SAR effort in the vicinity of the incident and there were no survivors or even any debris that we could find. Given the speeds involved, my air wing commander is of the opinion that the Super Hornet blew up either as the result of some massive internal failure, or . . ."

"Or they were shot down," SECNAV finished grimly. "Let's not be naïve here, we know which it was." He sighed. "I don't need to tell you how bad this looks for us," he added. Both flag officers stood mute—they knew how it looked better than SECNAV did. "There's more bad news, I'm afraid. It hasn't hit the news wires yet, but it will later this morning. Iran has arrested two Americans in Tehran, one archaeologist and one independent journalist, on charges of espionage. It's all trumped up garbage, but Iran's leadership has issued a statement that they are to be tried, and if found guilty, either imprisoned or executed."

VADM Cash was the commander of the Fifth Fleet. "Why do American citizens keep going to places like Iran against State Department guidelines?" he asked wearily.

"Do you think Iran would actually execute U.S. nationals?" Brandt added.

"Whether they would or not, tensions are escalating," SECNAV replied. "This is a measured provocation on the part of

Tehran. We're a new administration, and they're testing our resolve. I've just come from a meeting of the national security council, and we'll be meeting again in a few hours. What steps have been taken to identify how this happened, and ensuring it never happens again?"

"My investigation is ongoing, but I've already identified and corrected a couple of links in the error chain," Brandt offered without being too specific. "The main problem is the ambiguity in our rules of engagement. Under the prior administration, force commanders had more leeway in this matters." *Meaning I could have had standing orders in place to shoot the asshole down before he got anywhere near us! All this would have been avoided!*

"This isn't the prior administration," SECNAV said sharply. He was a political appointee, a very new one at that, and there was no mistaking the hint of warning in his tone. "Now I have orders straight from the NCA, which I will relay to you now: Under no circumstances are U.S. military forces to retaliate against the Iranians or take any hostile action in response to this incident except in direct self-defense. Is that understood?"

"That's understood clearly, mister secretary," Cash replied.

"Good. And there's to be no more nonsense like there was last week between our fighters and the Iranians. You know what I'm talking about? The incident with the patrol plane?"

"Yes sir," Cash replied again. Brandt was starting to flush under his collar, his temper rising dangerously, but he knew to open his mouth now was to invite being relieved himself—he was on thin ice as it was. Still, even Cash couldn't just let SECNAV's unilateral decree go by without comment "You understand of course that the incident with the patrol plane was instigated by the Iranians?"

"I understand that, but we need to avoid such incidents in the future," he said. "Now—"

"—Excuse me, mister secretary, but how can such incidents be avoided if they are instigated by the other side? It's a fact of life: the enemy gets a vote."

"Iran is not an *enemy* nation," SECNAV growled. "I realize we can't control them, but we can manage situations! I repeat, gentlemen, do your best to see that such incidents are avoided in the future! Now, I need your recommendations. How should we handle this going forward?"

The two admirals had discussed options before conferencing with the SECNAV, and VADM Cash laid them out now. "First, we can move the strike group over into the Gulf of Oman until the *Nassau* group arrives on station. It gives us some sea room and reduces tensions inside the Persian Gulf. Option two is leaving them in place—in that case I'd like to keep the *Nassau* group in the Gulf of Oman and peel off a couple of her escorts to bolster the *Boxer* Group inside the Persian Gulf. Option three is maintaining the status quo. My first choice is to hold both groups on the eastern side of the Strait of Hormuz, in the Gulf of Oman."

"What about logistical support in that area?" SECNAV asked.

"We can handle it from Masirah," Cash replied.

"I'll present all your options, but I can tell you right now that President Marsden isn't going to like your first choice. I don't either—it makes us look weak after what just happened. We can't afford to look like we're running scared from the Iranians. Especially not when they're holding two of our citizens as virtual hostages."

RADM Brandt couldn't hold back any longer. "Mister secretary, we should not expect these provocations to stop," he said firmly. "If anything, they're going to get worse. What happened this morning is only going to embolden them. If the administration is worried about looking weak, then sitting here letting them prod us may not be the best course of action."

"I've already said that our forces retain the right of self-defense. Was that not clear?" SECNAV asked, looking frankly at him on the screen over the rims of his reading glasses. It was clear that the two flag officers were beginning to strain his patience.

This guy's a clueless bureaucrat and he doesn't understand jack shit about any of this, Brandt fumed to himself. "It's clear, sir," Brandt replied, showing his poker face, and noting the casual glance of warning from Cash.

"I'll keep your recommendations in mind, gentleman. I need your public affairs people to send us the information on the downed pilots ASAP. There will be an official statement from the White House press office following notification of their next of kin. I'm going to sign off on this end. Thank you for your time."

SECNAV dropped out of the call, leaving just the flag officers. They waited to say anything until the communications center in Bahrain was *sure* that Washington D.C. was no longer conferenced in.

Brandt felt the need to tread carefully with his own boss. The same chain of authority and responsibility that doomed his Air Warfare commander could doom him the same way. Regardless of who screwed up, the captain of a ship was responsible for everything that happened under his command. By the same logic, Brandt was equally responsible to his superiors as the strike group commander. From that perspective he had put his own boss in a very bad position. He waited for Cash to speak first.

"Well, that wasn't much help to us," Cash sighed, stating the obvious. "For now, we'll mix things up just a bit. Move your group to operating area two off Qatar. If we get the okay, I'll move you even farther east, back towards the strait. I'm also going to curtail the EP-3 flights for a week or so."

"Aye aye, sir. If you're worried about the ELINT flights being exposed, the air force could cover them out of Al Dhafra. Don't they complain about under-utilization?"

Fifth Fleet's reply was noncommittal. "I'll have my staff look into that." Brandt suspected that Cash didn't want to infer to his CENTCOM superiors that the strike group couldn't provide cover to the ELINT missions, but *Boxer*'s air wing was already showing the strain from dealing with nightly Iranian harassment.

"Sir," Brandt said, "about this deal with the Iranians feinting at us every night—I'm worried that we're getting too used to it. If we let this become a regular thing, it dulls our edge. The controllers eventually accept it as normal, get a little numb to it, and then it can bite us in the ass when it suddenly turns into the real thing. That may have been part of the issue this morning."

"I understand the concern, but let's keep our perspective, here," Cash said. "There's a difference between gamesmanship and a true attack in force."

"The gamesmanship alone has killed two of my people, sir," Brandt said behind clenched teeth.

Cash's face darkened. "You're right. And I'm eager to see the official report on that, *admiral*. If you are worried about complacency among your people, *correct it!" Or I'll find someone who will*—that was the unspoken threat.

"Yes sir. Buzzing the carrier was an unfriendly act, but shooting down one of our jets was something else. An act of war should be treated like what it is."

Gerald Cash made a show of wearily removing his spectacles and rubbing at the bridge of his nose with pinched fingers. "Look, Jim, we're on the same side here. We've dealt with these issues in the Gulf for decades, now. I was a Div-O on deployment out here back in '88 when we accidentally splashed that Iranian airliner, and I saw the whole Tanker War from the deck of a destroyer. The bottom line is that we don't make policy—it gets passed down from 1600 Pennsylvania Avenue and we're responsible for executing it. The shootdown of your jet was an escalation, so the issue of force protection becomes more open to interpretation. They fired before, so that increases the likelihood that they might fire again, right? Now, I can't countermand an order from the NCA, but I trust you to *do the right thing*," he emphasized, leaving Brandt to read between the lines. The strike group commander didn't like it, but he understood it. One didn't rise to flag rank in any branch of the U.S. military without being an astute, budding politician. Cash was tacitly giving him permission to safeguard his command, and the rope to hang himself at the same time. *If it works you're a hero, if it fails you're a bum.*

"Any word from higher up about the presence of the Mainstays or the newer fighters?" Brandt asked. "The Mainstays in particular are a real headache."

Cash slowly shook his head. "Negative. We keep making inquiries, and they keep saying they're 'working on it.' Over-reliance on non-human intelligence sources has its limits, and we're paying for it now. If my staff finds out anything new, you'll be the first to know."

"Thank you, sir," Brandt replied. Then, the million-dollar question: "Are we going to be extended?"

"I can't answer that yet, but with the arrests of two civilians, don't be surprised if it happens." *BOHICA it is, then,* Brandt thought sourly. His family would be upset when he missed his son's upcoming wedding. Another missed milestone in a career full of them—the story of his life, writ new.

The call ended on that note. Brandt's chief of staff had sat in, listening the entire time. CAPT Pat Moreno was a surface warfare officer, but after almost a year in the job he had developed a decent grasp of the complexities surrounding carrier air operations. Brandt had to choose between sending him to replace the captain he'd relieved earlier in the day, or ship's exec. He'd gone with the latter, and tapped one of the destroyer captains as his new Anti-Air Warfare Commander. He didn't like scrambling his command like this, but it was necessary. He hadn't even kept the fired captain on staff; he was already on his way to the beach.

"What do you think, COS?" Brandt asked, using the typical wordplay on 'chief of staff.'

"I think we need to do something other than just sit and take it, sir," Moreno growled. "Boiled down, all SECNAV really did was order us not to embarrass the administration while maintaining the status quo."

"Suggestions?"

"Well sir, you're absolutely right about the Mainstays being the source of a lot of our pain. What if we simply jammed them whenever they're airborne?"

Brandt thought about it. "Blanket jamming is too aggressive, given the circumstances, but it's a different story when they assume a possible attack posture. In that case, we can argue force protection. Let's do this: *any* time they run fighters at us, we jam 'em hard. I mean *really* jam them—the kind that'll dim the lights and scramble TV sets in Bandar Abbas. It'll screw with their civil air traffic, as well. Then, when they break off, we let up."

"I'll investigate our Prowler availability. What we're talking about is 'on call' electronic warfare coverage going forward."

"Tell CAG to figure it out."

"Aye aye, sir."

"And Pat? One more thing."

"Yes sir?"

"Hear me clear as a fucking bell: *there will be no repeats of today.* You put the word out to CAG and the other warfare commanders, and make sure the airborne controllers understand it as well: The next Iranian fighter that breaks a twenty mile standoff from this ship gets splashed, and I don't give a good god damn if they hang me later. Is that clear?"

"Aye aye, sir."

"That's all, then."

***

The atmosphere in the Gray Wolves ready room was as subdued as Fargo had ever seen it. There was none of the usual jovial banter and ball-busting going on, and the little cliques of friends that tended to powwow in different quarters of the compartment were absent. In fact, there wasn't much of a presence at all, right now. The SDO sat behind the duty desk in his wash khakis, his chin resting glumly on one hand while the other doodled on the already graffiti-plastered desk blotter. Deedee and Stinky were getting ready to brief an event with another crew, and a few others were sitting spaced out in their individual seats, each in their own little introspective worlds. Neither the skipper nor XO was around right now. The squadron's overall mood was dark, bitter, and angry.

No fighter squadron was a stranger to loss. Mishaps were part of life in naval aviation, and anyone who had been around a few years had lost either a friend, a former classmate, or someone they knew. It was like any other loss, in a way. People cycled through the various stages of grief and pressed on. This was different though; this time there wasn't just grief, but rage. Fargo felt it himself. Right after the memorial service for the Irish brothers that morning, Dexter coldly commented that he wished they'd smoked the MiGs they'd encountered when they had the chance. Fargo knew he'd made the correct call at the time, but his heart couldn't disagree. He hadn't said anything, just walked away wrapped in his own thoughts. He was reminded of some old wisdom from Nietzsche about taking care to avoid becoming the monsters you were fighting, but Fargo wanted payback.

He pulled down his mug and charged it with coffee, nodding to his roommate as Stinky came over to pass him the latest scuttlebutt. "Well," The Ops-O said in a low voice, "I found out why we were an hour late getting the memorial service started."

"Yah? What happened?"

"Apparently the Iranians flogged one of their decrepit P-3's into the air and did a flyover of the strike group. Probably taking some pictures of us, trying to find out what their little stunt accomplished. The admiral decided his new 'twenty mile rule' doesn't apply to forty-year old patrol planes, so we let it happen."

"We intercepted it though, right?" Fargo asked.

"Oh, sure. They had a section of Hornets on them, Blue Angel tight the entire time. Once they were away from the strike group and headed home, a jet from Brand-X rolled off his CAP station and thumped them good. Payback's a bitch, right?"

"Any come-arounds as a result?"

"Rumor has it that CAG took a big blast from flag country. DCAG lost his shit and went high-order on their skipper, but that's just expected, y'know?"

"Sounds like DCAG, you betcha," Fargo shrugged. "Who was it that thumped the Iranian?"

"I don't know his name, but it was that short Italian guy who talks like he's on The Sopranos."

"Guido," Fargo chuckled. "That asshole," he added with almost a hint of fondness. "God love him."

"Well, he's in HAQ for a while, but it was probably worth it. I gotta brief this event," Stinky added, raising his mug in a casual salute. Fargo nodded and watched him go join the others.

***

Islamic Republic of Iran

Cheng Ye looked at 'marinetraffic.com' on his computer screen, a website presenting a real time maritime plot of the various commercial vessels plying the waters in the vicinity of the Iranian coastline. Both General Abdi and Toma Baranov sat in chairs in his spartanly appointed office.

"Nobody can argue that you did your part," Baranov said with a healthy dose of respect, "but the Americans have not risen to the bait as we had hoped."

"The Americans are cowards, led by a coward, Abdi fairly spat. He was in a rare mood today, clearly feeling emboldened by the success of Cheng Ye's mission and the bonus destruction of one of the vaunted American warplanes. His eyes were ablaze with the revolutionary fire, which was just what Cheng Ye wanted to see.

"Then we must increase the stakes," Cheng Ye said, turning cold, black eyes on the Iranian. "My plan is approved, then?"

"It is," Abdi replied, "we just need a suitable target in the right time and place to execute it."

"I have one," Cheng Ye replied, turning the monitor so the other two could see. "This cargo ship, the *Orgullo de Carino.* By midnight tomorrow she'll be in a perfect position, about 30 miles from Lavan Island. The Americans have moved their carrier group off Qatar, putting them in the perfect place to respond. It gives us a full day to brief, prepare, and shift assets as needed."

Baranov leaned in, reading the outlined data box on the cargo ship. "That ship left an Iranian port, carrying Iranian trade goods. She sails under a Spanish flag. Are you sure?"

Abdi nodded eagerly. "Cheng Ye is right, this one is perfect. Because she's been trading in Iran, it will make our claim of an attack by independent jihadists even more plausible. Spain is also a member of NATO—the Americans will feel an obligation to help on that basis."

Baranov shook his head. "You won't be fooling anyone if you follow through with the air plan as it's written."

"We won't be fooling the *Americans*," Abdi corrected him, "but we can sew misinformation and uncertainty elsewhere, especially among the Gulf States. To the rest of the world, the air battle will be the result of a terrible misunderstanding, fed by an American cowboy desire to avenge the recent loss of their airmen. The western media these past years has proven more an ally than enemy. They can almost certainly be trusted to muddy the waters and sew dissension amongst our foes. With luck and the vocal condemnation of the United States by your respective countries, it will lend credibility to the actions we take afterward."

Baranov shrugged casually. "Naturally, we will do our part."

"You will have a part in this operation, but not a combat role." Abdi informed him. "The fighting will be carried out by certain, troublesome elements of the IRIAF. They will prove more useful as martyrs than as heroes."

"As you wish," Baranov replied with a shrug.

***

The Persian Gulf

Two nights later, a pair of *Feilong* Flankers passed feet wet just south of Kushkonar, heading in a southerly direction 500 FT over the water. The lead aircraft was Cheng Ye's single seat fighter, while his wingman flew the two-seat variant and carried a single Chinese-made C-701 anti-ship missile. This was a smaller weapon, roughly the equivalent of an American Maverick, and chosen specifically for this mission in which the goal was to wound, not kill. Their target was the *Orgullo de Carino*, and this weapon by itself didn't carry a large enough warhead to sink her. Not immediately, anyway.

At the same time, the U.S. carrier task force was busy intercepting two sections of Red Talon Fulcrums that were harassing them at high speed to the south, directed by the Russian Volunteer Group A-50 AWACS aircraft that was up and flying tonight. The Americans were employing heavy jamming in response—a tactic they had resorted to since the day after the overflight of their carrier and shootdown of their fighter. Cheng Ye was counting on the heavy jamming working in his favor, masking his own mission, while their Russian volunteer counterparts provided a distraction to the Americans. Although Kovalev's flight was taking care not to get close enough to prompt being fired upon, they were being far more innovative in their approach patterns and using twice as many aircraft as normal. Cheng Ye could just imagine the American carrier commander frothing at the mouth, his hands tied behind his back by his own weak-willed political leadership.

There was no radio communication between the Chinese volunteers, nor was any necessary. Cheng Ye was flying tonight as an observer, although he was armed with a full anti-air load just in case his wingman needed cover.

The second Flanker closed on the expected position of the Spanish freighter. Their sea search radars were fully jammed by the Americans in response to Kovalev's flight, but their IRST systems were unaffected, and the older 701 missile they carried also employed an infrared seeker. They found the Spanish ship easily enough, given that Iranian forces had maintained tracking on it since selecting it as the bait ship for this operation. It was a commercial ship, unarmed, and completely unsuspecting.

Cheng Ye's wingman fired from twelve nautical miles away, then watched the missile track in and hit the port side of the freighter. The explosion was impressive and looked to be non-lethal. Ablaze with fire on one side, the ship slowed and went dead in the water, taking on a slight list. Frantic Mayday calls went out on Channel 16, the international maritime common channel. Thanks to the broadband American jamming, those calls for help would go unheard until Kovalev's flight turned back into Iran and the jamming stopped.

Cheng Ye smiled coldly. When your enemy acted in predictable ways, it was easy to turn their actions to your own advantage. The Chinese fighters turned back toward the coast and headed inland, flying low to mask their presence with the terrain. Defying the effectiveness of American jamming and foiling their electronic spying was easy: they simply overflew the Revolutionary Guard speedboat docks at the south end of Nayband National Park. The sound of the jets passing over at low altitude within a certain time window was the pre-arranged signal for the boats to finalize their preparations and put to sea. No radio communications were made, so nothing was overheard.

IV

The aviators sat poised with pens over their kneeboard cards when their own AIO appeared on the ready room's closed-circuit television, wearing his blue SWO-sweater. This was the event CVIC brief, and it promised to be an interesting one. "Good morning," the AIO addressed them in black-and-white, like something out of a bygone era. "This is Lieutenant J.G. Aston Chadwick II," he paused, smiled, and pushed his Clark Kent nerd glasses farther up the bridge of his nose, "also known as 'The Sweater Boy.' This is the Event Two briefing."

Deedee let out a shriek of delight. "Ohmigod, he's *owning* it!" she howled.

"Shut up, goddammit!" Stinky growled at her.

Sweater Boy rustled the papers he held in front of him like he was Walter Cronkite. "Strike Group Two is currently located west of Qatar, where this morning we will be assisting a naval surface action group and U.S. Coast Guard assets conducting maritime rescue operations southwest of Lavan Island. Last night, sometime between midnight and 0200, a Spanish cargo vessel reported being attacked, and that she was on fire, listing, and dead in the water. It is unclear at this time whether she was hit by hostile fire or struck a sea mine, but she is in distress and requires assistance. All sorties on this event will be in support of that effort." He went on to provide the standard information, which included the weather briefing, local airspace and standoff requirements, nearest land, suitable diverts, and so on. Since this event would also include a larger-than-usual amount of communication with surface units, he called special attention to those callsigns and frequencies on their communications 'card of the day.'

When he was finished with the administrative details, he returned to the meat of the brief. "USS *Thach* and USS *Halyburton* have detached from this strike group to form Task Force 50.5, which will join the U.S. Coast Guard Cutter *Butler Island* to render aid and assistance to the stricken freighter. The commanding officer of USS *Thach* has assumed duties as Kilo Bravo, the surface action group commander. Air units from Event Two will be providing top cover and support to Task Force 50.5. One E-2C Hawkeye, callsign Closeout, is already airborne and monitoring the air and surface picture. Multiple surface contacts have been detected between the stricken freighter and Lavan Island. They have not yet been positively identified.

"One division of Super Hornets from the Gray Wolves will assume RESCAP over the operation. Your mission is air defense but be prepared to provide additional support as tasked. One section of Hornets from the Redhawks, armed for anti-surface action, will stand by on an Alert-15 status. Tankers and jammers will be airborne on this event, held between the strike group and the rescue operation.

"Crews are cautioned that the stricken vessel is relatively close to Lavan Island and the coast of Iran, although well outside its territorial waters. ESM lines indicating the presence of SA-11 and SA-6 surface-to-air missile batteries on Lavan Island have been detected. The buffer between the edge of the SAM envelope and the location of the rescue operation is only thirteen miles, so use extreme caution maneuvering to the northeast of your CAP waypoint. The twenty mile standoff from Lavan Island has been waived for this operation, but all units are to remain outside the twelve mile territorial limit. There is an Iranian AWACS aircraft airborne this morning, but no fighter activity has been observed."

Sweater Boy looked up from his paperwork, directly into the camera. He smiled, and casually removed his glasses. He was a handsome fellow without them, polished and clean-cut in his Ivy-League frat-boy sort of way. "That is all. Good luck and let's fly safe out there." Deedee fell out of her chair, clutching her sides and no longer able to contain herself as she was wracked with laughter. Dexter was grinning and shaking his head.

Stinky spared a sharp look at his pilot. "Hey there, stick-monkey. You wanna get with the program here? This is some serious shit." He reached over and grabbed her notecard, checking what she'd written. She hadn't missed anything important that he could see.

"I'm dialed in, sir, don't worry," Deedee assured him, picking herself up and taking her card back. "That just kills me, though. If Sweater Boy keeps that up he's going to be his own little cult of personality."

"Okay, enough about Sweater Boy. Let's get down to business," Fargo said firmly. He was the division leader for this event, and the other seven pilots and WSOs gave him their full attention. He broke out his pocket NATOPS checklist. "Alright, there's a lot to cover on this one. Let's get'r done so we can get topside…"

***

All mirth had vanished a couple hours later when Lobo flight checked in with Closeout and assumed their CAP station. Fargo directed his second section to a pattern 1000 FT above his own so they could stay out of each other's way as they made racetracks. They'd passed over the two frigates that were closing on the position of the stricken ship; they were only a few miles away at this point. USCGC *Butler Island* was already on scene, moored against the *Orgullo de Carino*'s undamaged starboard side. The fires were out, but a thick column of greasy smoke still rose skyward from the freighter, carried away and scattered by the light surface winds. Dexter had the two vessels locked with the FLIR; they were watching the events below them in real-time on high-resolution infrared and video.

It was quiet in the jet from the moment they caught sight of the two *Perry* Class frigates, which drove home the seriousness of the situation. Fargo was normally comfortable with silence, but after several minutes he called back to see how his WSO was doing. To his surprise, Dexter sounded unusually grim. "She was hit by a missile," his WSO said flatly.

"What makes you say that?"

"The Iranians wouldn't mine their own coastal waters. Why the hell would they? And look closely as we circle back around her to port side. It's hard to see because of the smoke, but the damage is mostly above the waterline. I also think any sea mine would have packed enough wallop to sink her. No, someone definitely took a shot at her."

"I wonder who, and why," Fargo reflected. "Doesn't make a lot of sense for, say, a pirate to pot shot her and then vanish . . ."

"Yeah, exactly," Dexter went on, "there's really only one way it makes sense."

"There is? What's that, then?"

"She's a decoy, or bait, meant to pull us in close to the Iranian coast. My hackles are up, sir. I think we'd better stay frosty here."

"You aren't giving me a warm fuzzy, here, y'know. And quit calling me 'sir.'"

"Yes *sir*. Riddle me this, Batman," Dexter added a moment later, slewing the pod to lock onto the Coast Guard Cutter *Butler Island*. "I totally grok why a Coastie is the best platform to lead a rescue op in a situation like this, but how is it that *any* of our Coast Guard ships are assigned halfway around the world, in the Persian Gulf?"

"It has to do with maritime security operations," Fargo explained. "Boarding, search, and seizure kind of stuff. Coast Guardsmen have law enforcement powers, like the ability to make arrests. The Navy doesn't, and it's as simple as that. So, the Coasties get to hang out in the fun Gulf right along with us."

A moment later the radio crackled. "Lobo 1-1, Closeout. Contact Kilo Sierra on channel Blue-1. Lobo 1-3, your section is to remain with me."

"Lobo 1-1 copies," Dexter replied.

"Lobo 1-3 copies," Dash-3 answered in turn. Dexter exchanged a couple hand-signals with Stinky and the two jets switched their primary radios over to the surface group's tactical net. Dexter guessed they were talking to the TAO on one of the two frigates, probably the lead one.

"Kilo Sierra, Lobo 1-1, flight of two Super Hornets, checking in."

"Lobo, Kilo Sierra. Hey, we know you are tasked as high cover, but can you guys point your noses toward Lavan and see if you can get some imagery on that gaggle of small surface contacts? They've been working slowly towards us for the past forty minutes, picking up a little speed, and we're getting suspicious. I could send our helo over, but that'll take time, and the captain wants them identified soonest."

"Can do, stand by," Dexter replied. Fargo glanced over at Deedee, who gave him a thumbs up. He rolled the Super Hornet into a turn to the northeast while Dexter worked his magic with the radar in sea-search mode, coupled to the FLIR pod.

"Watch the SAM envelope, boss," Deedee prompted them over their squadron frequency. They'd gotten a couple of intermittent ESM hits already, as an Iranian SA-11 search radar swept over them periodically. They could detect the radar, and it could see them, but the navy fighters were beyond the range of the battery's missiles if they maintained their standoff from Lavan Island. So far, the Iranians hadn't locked them with any fire control radars. Given the current bad-blood, that might have merited calling in a SEAD strike and claiming self-defense. Fargo throttled back in response to Deedee's warning, giving them a little buffer before they needed to turn away.

"Contact," Stinky called. Dexter had it as well: a loose grouping of fifteen surface contacts, all moving in the same direction: directly toward the rescue operation. When he locked up one of the contacts and went to high magnification on the FLIR, Dexter's suspicions were confirmed. He cycled rapidly from contact to contact, pausing momentarily to look them over before moving on to the next one.

"I've got to turn us back," Fargo told him—they were pressing into the edge of the SAM envelope.

"Okay," Dexter replied, sounding distracted. Fargo turned the section back to the southwest, and once the turn was completed Deedee wordlessly slid out into a combat spread.

Dexter was back on the radio. "Kilo Sierra, Lobo. Okay, your skunks are fifteen armed speed boats, all mounting twin fifty caliber machine guns. No missile tubes spotted on the first look. Contacts are on course 235, speed 8 knots. They are headed in your direction."

"Kilo Sierra copies. 99 Kilo Bravo, this is Kilo Sierra. Surface Warning Red, weapons tight. All units in Kilo Bravo set Condition I and prepare for surface action starboard. Break. Lobo from Kilo Sierra, can you give us a couple more looks? We really need to know if any of them are rigged with mines or missiles."

"Can do," Dexter replied. "Recommend you contact Alpha Bravo and request on-call SUCAP support."

"I will pass your recommendation to Kilo Bravo. Kilo Sierra out."

"Can we get a little lower?" Dexter asked. "If they've got MANPADS, we should still be good at or above twelve thousand, and outside of five miles."

"You betcha," Fargo replied, mentally agreeing with the WSO's threat assessment. He called Deedee and dropped them down from 20,000 FT to 12,000 FT. They turned back in to give the targeting pod another look at the surface contacts. There were still no missile mounts to be seen. Stinky commented on the radio that these boats looked too small to carry any sort of sea-launched anti-ship missiles, but man-portable SAMs could not be ruled out. During their third orbit, the speed boats suddenly picked up speed, accelerating to twenty-five knots. Dexter called it in.

"Lobo, Kilo Sierra," came the reply. "Requesting show of force. See if you can scare them off."

"Stinky, what do you think?" Fargo asked the senior WSO in the other jet over their squadron frequency.

"One of us can take high perch and cover the other's six during the flyover. I recommend looping around them and flying a sneak pass from behind, supersonic. No advanced noise to cue them, and hopefully the boom startles them enough to forget about shooting any MANPADs until we're out of range."

"Concur." Fargo wanted to fly it himself, but he was still division leader and responsible for the entire CAP. As Stinky once said, delegation was an art-form. "Deedee, they're all yours. Give 'em a wake-up call." Deedee rogered him and he watched his wingman suddenly drop towards the ocean, hooking north and passing under him to fly a wide arc and come back up along the wake of the speedboats. He checked their position and made sure she was going to stay clear of the Lavan SAM envelope.

"We need to make a three-sixty ourselves for the SAM envelope," Dexter informed him. He jumped on the radio. "Stinky, call your turn back our way,"

"Wilco," the other WSO replied, sounding excited. Dexter reported to the surface units that they were commencing the show-of-force run. Fargo reefed them into a 6G turn, tapping the burners to keep their energy up as he reversed course yet again, away from the speed boats and back towards the rescue operation. In the other jet, Deedee and Stinky ran their weapons checklist and selected their master arm switch to on so they could dispense countermeasures if required.

"We're behind them. Dash-2's in the turn to the northwest, in burner," Stinky called. "We're blowing our tanks," he added a little hesitantly. Fargo knew why—the Rhino needed the lowered drag count, or they were going to have trouble getting supersonic at sea level.

"Copy," Dexter replied. Fargo continued his own turn, programming maximum rate to get the FLIR pod back into gimbal on the speed boats as fast as possible. Dexter worked the radar and pod with speed and intensity, finding their wingman and tracking them, then scaling out so he had a better view of the area around them. Although they were several miles away, Fargo was straining his eyeballs, looking for any telltale danger signs the old fashioned way. The radar warning receiver suddenly went off in his ear, informing him that they were locked by an SA-11 fire-control radar. "Ignore it," Dexter said quickly. "We're outside of their firing envelope. Music coming on, though," he added, switching on the Super Hornet's electronic countermeasure systems.

"Deedee, I'm ground spiked," Fargo called. Dexter was reporting the same thing to Kilo Sierra, for relay to Closeout.

Deedee and Stinky blew over the speed boat flotilla a few seconds later at Mach 1.1 and a mere 300 FT over the water. A loud sonic boom cracked over the speedboats, powerful enough to rock them crazily from side to side as they drove forward through the calm seas. Deedee came out of burner just as she went over to reduce the Super Hornet's IR signature. The Iranians weren't as surprised as the Super Hornet crews had hoped. First one, and then two smoke trails blistered into the sky a few seconds after the flyover, tracking after the jet.

Dexter saw the missile trails on infrared. "Smoke in the air!" he called. "Flares!" Stinky mashed the button in his back seat and executed the countermeasures program he'd dialed in. A string of white-hot flares and several bursts of chaff blossomed behind the Super Hornet as Deedee unloaded in a slight pushover and hugged the deck even closer, judging that she was too fast for an effective break turn. Neither of the hand-held SAMs got close; both zeroed in on the hotter, closer flares. "You're good . . . you're good!" Dexter told them a moment later. Deedee passed out of MANPAD range quickly.

Fargo executed a hard right turn away from the speed boats and Lavan Island. "Deedee, rejoin. Call your tally."

"Blind."

Fargo reached up, flipped the master arm switch on, and popped a single flare. "Look high and right, one o'clock."

"Tally. Rejoining," she called. "Woo-hoo!"

"Kilo Sierra, Lobo, show of force complete. We were fired on by the surface contacts and ground spiked by Lavan Island SAMs. Declare surface tracks hostile."

"Kilo Sierra copies. Target track numbers are being assigned now in the datalink," he advised. "99 Kilo Bravo, this is Kilo Sierra. Surface Warning Red, Weapons free on tracks Sierra India one through Sierra India fifteen inclusive. Lobo, Closeout needs you back on their net. You are cleared to switch. Bravo Zulu and thanks." Dexter acknowledged the call as the Super Hornets climbed back towards their CAP waypoint.

"Shit's getting real," Dexter commented from the back a minute later.

Fargo nodded in agreement, adding: "Yah, you betcha."

***

It got even more real almost as soon as they were back on the Strike net. *Boxer* had launched the Alert-15 SUCAP, so another section of fighters was headed in their direction with a mixed anti-air / anti-surface loadout. The eight Maverick missiles carried by Redhawk flight would knock out half the speed boats in a single salvo once they were in range. These were legacy Hornets, older F/A-18Cs that claimed kinship to their larger Super Hornet cousins.

It wasn't long before things got more interesting still. Closeout called with a popup group of four fighters launching from the airstrip on Lavan Island. According to their intelligence, Iran didn't normally stage fighters there. Coincidentally, there just happened to be some today. Closeout immediately vectored the CAP to the southwest, giving them the airspace buffer they would need to stay out of the Lavan SAM envelope if they had to turn nose-on for an engagement. The bogeys weren't radiating their radars, which meant they were almost certainly taking vectors from the distant A-50. Fargo fairly salivated at the thought of what he could do to the Iranian AWACS if only he was flying an F-14 with some Phoenix missiles, but that was not the case today.

It didn't mean there was *nothing* to be done, however. "Strike, Lobo 1-1. Request Music support from Merlin." That was a request for jamming from their airborne Prowler.

"Merlin 1-1, Strike. Music authorized."

"Merlin," came the abbreviated reply. Jammers were activated, and the ECMOs in the back seats of the Prowlers worked their electronic voodoo. Shortly thereafter, the flight off Lavan Island was forced to activate its own radars when data from their AWACS could no longer get through. That gave them an immediate ID on the bogeys, which had formed up and were heading directly at them now.

"Bogeys are F-5s," Dexter reported. "Strike, declare on bogey group."

"Stand by," Strike responded. A moment later, Closeout vectored them back towards Lavan Island and the bogeys.

"Strike, Lobo," Stinky called. "We were ground spiked by Lavan Island. Bogeys are off Lavan Island. Declare!"

"Stand by!" the Strike controller replied, sounding irritated this time.

"Lobo, Closeout," the Hawkeye called. "New gorilla group at your 030 for 50, medium, hot. Designate Group-2. Group-2 is Bogey." The 'gorilla' designation meant that the group was composed of multiple targets. They could see on the datalink that the second group was headed for them as well, and accelerating.

Fargo got on the radio. "Strike, Lobo. We may need a re-task of Redhawk flight."

"Strike copies. Stand by."

"This is getting stupid," Dexter remarked from the back. Fargo couldn't disagree. "Can someone make a fuckin' decision, please?"

In Dash-2, Stinky was done 'standing by.' "Closeout, this is Lobo. Judy," he called. "Fargo, recommend we pincer Group-1."

"Agreed," Fargo replied. "Reaper, take your section right. Deedee, we go left. Now!" he called. The two pairs of fighters broke in opposite directions, one headed north, the other south. On radar and datalink, they saw the entire F-5 group turn south towards Reaper's section.

Dexter was the best chess player in the squadron, and he was pretty good at the Chinese game of go, as well. "Clever," he remarked. "They're trying to draw us off the second gorilla group. Those are the guys we need to be worried about."

"Two can play at that game," Fargo replied. "Reaper, keep your turn in. Pull them back to the southwest." Reaper acknowledged with a quick mic-flash on the radio.

"Strike, this is Lobo lead. Listen up—we don't have the time or gas to dick around here. If the northern group is a raid, the Lavan group is a decoy and we're getting caught between them. I need a declaration on these groups, and I need Redhawk chopped over to me, right now!"

Someone in charge finally made a decision. "99 Alpha Bravo, air warning red, weapons tight. Group-1 is Bandit. Group-2 is

Bogey. Lobo, commit on Group-1. Redhawk, stay on present tasking. Closeout, monitor Group-2."

"Redhawk."

"Closeout."

"Lobo, commit!" Fargo ordered. He turned south; he and Deedee were now flanking the F-5 group that was in loose pursuit of his second section. "Sort 'em!" he almost snarled. "Reaper, turn northwest and Gate," he ordered, signaling Reaper and his wingman to light their afterburners and haul ass. He wanted a nice, clean line of fire.

"Stinky?" Dexter called.

"Good sort," the other WSO replied.

"Go ahead and engage, Deedee," Fargo ordered. Both Super Hornets were targeting a pair of Iranian F-5's each. "Fox-3! Fox-3 again!" Fargo called, squeezing the trigger twice in succession. Deedee mirrored him as she called her shots. A total of four AMRAAM missiles left the rails of the two Super Hornets. These were active missiles fired with the controlling radars in a track-while-scan mode; they wouldn't set off the Iranians' radar warning receivers until the missile radars went active in their terminal phase. In short, the Iranians would get very little warning before the missiles arrived.

"Lobo-4 is spiked! I'm defensive!" Reaper's wingman called. One of the F-5s had just fired at him.

"Reaper's turning to engage," Dash-3 called.

Out ahead of them, Fargo saw three black smears appear in the sky one after the other, showing steepening vertical arcs as aircraft wreckage fell towards the ocean. "Dash-2 has two good kills," Stinky reported, sounding excited.

"Lead has one good kill," Dexter reported.

"Reaper is tally on one bandit, bugging northeast," Dash-3 called. "I've got a shot."

"He's all yours," Fargo called immediately.

"Fox-3!" Reaper called, followed soon thereafter by cry of: "Good kill! Splash one!"

Fargo felt himself calming down a little bit. "Lobo, rejoin. Rackhound, you still with us?" he called Dash-4.

"Four is clean, rejoining," Rackhound replied.

"Now we're cooking with oil, you betcha!" Fargo quipped to his WSO. "Closeout, Logo for bogey dope."

"Lobo, closeout. Group-2 is at your 025 for 27, medium going low, supersonic. They're passing feet wet and on profile to engage surface units. Group-2 is declared hostile. Snap 025 and commit immediately!"

"Lobo, commit," Fargo replied, feeling a sinking feeling in his stomach. They had ESM on the second group now: they were F-4 Phantoms, six of them, each capable of carrying a hefty load of weapons. The two frigates were currently engaged in a surface battle, and neither was AEGIS equipped; a dozen or more anti-ship missiles were going to overwhelm them in their present circumstances. Their best hope was that the intense jamming from the Prowler was going to buy them the time they needed.

Once again, Dexter was thinking ahead. "Redhawk, Lobo, are you up on Strike?"

"Affirm," came the immediate reply.

"Request you radar-lock Group-2 in single-track. If you can set off their threat boxes, you might spook them into ditching their stores and going defensive."

Redhawk 1, wilco. Two, you take the eastern half. I'll work the western half."

"Two, wilco."

"That's beautiful, Dex," Fargo said appreciatively. A few seconds later the Gray Wolves had their targets sorted, and another salvo of AMRAAMs was in the air. By using the Redhawk Hornets for his scare-tactic, it left the Super Hornets free to engage multiple targets with their own radars in a different mode. Even before the missiles began reaching their targets, they could see that Dexter's gambit was paying some dividends. Four of the six Phantoms broke off their attacks to go defensive, spooked by their radar warning receivers. Of the two that remained, one was hit before it could fire. The lead aircraft doggedly pressed home its attack. Dexter had it on FLIR, and they saw two anti-ship missiles drop off the wings and ignite their motors, instantly disappearing off the screen.

"Vampire! Vampire! Vampire!" Fargo called. "Two Vampires inbound from Group-2!" A moment later he involuntarily jumped in his seat as the Phantom violently blew apart as it started a defensive break; the FLIR imagery was stark and spectacular.

"Holy shit! Splash the lead Phantom!" Dexter called from the back.

Over the next several seconds, the raid was cleanly broken up. Four of the six Iranian Phantoms went down in the first salvo, one bugged out and got away, and Redhawk-1 fired his lone AMRAAM and batted cleanup, scoring a single kill. For all practical purposes the entire engagement was beyond visual range, or 'BVR.' Nobody merged with a bandit, and no heat-seekers were fired.

Of the two anti-ship missiles launched by the lead Iranian Phantom, one was destroyed by the lead frigate's Phalanx CIWS cannon. The other was spoofed by countermeasures and electronic warfare from the Prowler and the frigates; it went 'stupid' and plunged into the sea, missing all the ships.

Closeout reported a clean air picture, and Fargo ordered his division to report their fuel state. All of them were low on fuel, but Deedee was almost at Bingo; the show of force run in afterburner had put her behind the rest of the pack. Fargo called and requested permission to head south for the tanker track. Closeout informed them that relief fighters were en-route to assume the CAP, and they were cleared off station.

Fargo wished he felt better about the engagement as they drove south to tank; he always figured he'd be exhilarated after his first air battle, but maybe that would come later. Right now, he was just thinking about those surface ships he was sent out here to protect, and was grateful as hell none of them had taken a hit. He knew there was going to be plenty to debrief on this one, and plenty of room for improvement. On the 'management' side of the house, indecision had almost cost them dearly. "How are you doing back there?" he asked his WSO.

"Good," Dexter replied.

"How many did we get?" Fargo asked.

"Two for sure. The rest will come out in the replay," he replied. "We just shot down nine Iranian jets and didn't lose a single one of ours."

"I'm just glad none of the ships were hit."

"We were lucky," Dexter went on. "This whole thing was a setup—a trap."

"Come again, now?"

"I'm serious, Fargo. The whole surface action was a sideshow. Those speed boats were never going to do any serious damage—I doubt they even got close. What the hell is going on here, anyway? Five months of peace and quiet, and suddenly we're at war?"

Fargo blew out a sigh, peeling off his oxygen mask and letting it hang from the side of his helmet. He was drenched in sweat, like he'd showered in his flight suit. "I don't know, Dex," he said. "Maybe Sweater Boy can tell us. You sure did a helluva job, though, you betcha. That gambit with the radars might have saved the day for the surface ships."

"That's why I'm back here," the WSO replied.

***

U.S Forces clash with Iran during rescue mission, resulting in 'significant' Iranian losses.

-Washington Post

U.S. attacks Iranian rescue mission! Was this retaliation for recent Iranian shootdown of U.S. warplane?

-L.A. Times

PAYBACK! Navy fighters go 9-0 against Iranian air force!

-N.Y. Post

Russia calls emergency meeting of UN Security Council! Russian ambassador to the UN demands censure of the U.S. over hostilities in the Persian Gulf.

-N.Y. Times

Iran claims the damaged freighter sailed from Iranian port, stating that U.S. warplanes fired on a local rescue effort.
-Atlanta Journal Constitution

Washington D.C.

President James Marsden angrily threw the newspaper onto the Resolute Desk in the Oval Office. The USA Today headline seemed deliberately aimed at mocking his administration in bold, black print:

War in the Persian Gulf? U.S. Navy fights air and sea battle against Iran.

"So, what you're telling me," Marsden shouted at his Secretary of Defense, "is that we actually *did* fire first? Is that what I'm hearing here?"

"No, sir, not exactly—"

"—What do you mean, *not exactly?* We either fired first or we goddamn well didn't! Which is it?"

"The first shots were fired by the speed boats shooting at our aircraft. We can't say for sure, but we think the speed boats may have been responsible for the attack initial attack on the *Orgullo de Carino*."

"The . . . wait, the what?" the president asked, confused.

"The cargo ship that was attacked," the national security advisor explained.

"Oh," Marsden replied, glancing at the NSA in irritation. The man looked like he hadn't slept in a week. "Are you alright, Gary? You look a little peaked."

"I'm fine, Mr. President, just tired. Thanks for asking."

The president looked at the Chief of Naval Operations, ADM Kirkwood. He was a submariner, with a limited grasp of carrier operations and air warfare. He'd been summoned here almost as fast as the news had broken, without time for a proper briefing and breakdown by his own people. He didn't think that Fifth Fleet had even had time to file an official report to CENTCOM yet, just some FLASH message traffic giving a brief outline of events. There was still a lot to unpack about what had happened, and his feeling was that this entire meeting was a premature, presidential knee-jerk.

"Well, what do you have to say?" the president barked.

Unlike the NSA, ADM Kirkwood had dealt with a few 'screamers' in his day. Marsden did not intimidate or impress him. *The Accidental President* was how Pentagon staffers covertly referred to him in private meetings. Marsden was elected with less than half the popular vote, and after two terms of the airtight competency of the prior administration, the next four years looked to be a struggle on multiple fronts. "Nothing concrete as of yet, Mister President," Kirkwood answered. "The incident is hours old and we're still analyzing what happened. Iran is making a lot of claims that don't hold up even under cursory scrutiny—"

"—*Look at this shit!*" Marsden bellowed, brandishing the newspaper like a club before slamming it back onto his desk. "The media sure as hell thinks *they* know what happened!"

"They always do, sir," Kirkwood said placatingly, mentally adding: *Take that up with your idiot press secretary!* He kept his expression neutral as he continued. "We'll present the real facts in short order." He went on to clarify a couple of points for the commander in chief; things they *did* know for sure. The two big questions revolved around Iranian claims that the speed boats were simple jihadists or pirates, and that the Iranian aircraft were entering the area to engage the speedboats, coming to the aid of an ongoing Iranian rescue effort. According to them, the Americans had acted carelessly and recklessly, committing unprovoked hostile acts. They also claimed that the U.S. aggression was a hair-trigger response to the prior 'accidental' shootdown of an American warplane, a claim that U.S. detractors were eager to latch onto. Everyone in the room understood these were fabricated falsehoods, but they were cleverly spun in a media-environment that thrived on the ignorance of its consumers.

President Marsden's reaction seemed overly temperamental, if not petulant. As far was he was concerned, he'd given orders that the Navy 'keep things quiet' in the Persian Gulf, and that was that. His initial reaction was as if the naval establishment had openly defied him. ADM Kirkwood was still confused on the details himself—his knowledge of air engagements was spurious at best. He'd be getting a briefing from the Atlantic Fleet air boss later that day, and hopefully his own questions would be answered.

The national security advisor sniffed and cleared his throat, and all eyes turned to him. "Can I make a suggestion, Mr. President?"

"Please, by all means," Marsden snapped sarcastically. "That's why you're here, isn't it?"

The NSA nodded blandly. "The news headlines are irresponsible and infuriating, but we'll have a response very soon. Can I suggest that we adjourn for the moment, allow for a gathering of facts, and reconvene in conference with the security council? Our response will be easier to formulate when we have a clear picture of what happened."

Marsden glanced around the room, to be met with confirming nods by the Secretary of Defense, CNO, and the White House Chief of Staff. "Okay then, let's do it that way," he agreed, seeming to lose some of his bluster. "I don't need to attend the full NSC meeting. Get your fucking facts straight, and then then Gary can conduct an NSA briefing for me, and I'll decide how we proceed moving forward."

"Yes, Mister President," his chief of staff replied. Everyone stood up and ushered out of the office.

Just outside the Oval Office, SECDEF paused and turned on the CNO. "What the hell is happening out there in the Gulf, admiral?" he asked.

Kirkwood frowned. "Iran is making some strange moves, sir. Militarily speaking we've seen a spike in Iran's capability and the acquisition of advanced hardware, but nothing to account for this new hostility."

"Acquisitions paid for with stolen Iraqi oil," SECDEF growled.

Kirkwood shrugged. "The prior administration was not inclined to do anything about that. I think the State Department needs to jump on this, and really try to find out what is driving these aggressions. They're deliberately pushing our buttons, and we don't really know why."

"What do you make of the reports that the Spanish ship was sailing from an Iranian port, with Iranian trade goods?"

"Almost certainly true, and irrelevant. The IRGC doesn't give two shits about foreign-flagged cargo ships, and they'd have sent her straight to Davy Jones if they saw an advantage in it. In this case, the ship that was hit lends credibility to their false claims—it helps with the information war."

"Recommendations? Should we get the hell out of the Gulf?"

"I'll reserve my recommendations until we have facts in hand, Mister Secretary. As to our presence in the Gulf, that is a political decision, not a military one."

"We need to decide soon. This country still hasn't completely recovered from the housing bubble collapse. As of this morning oil is up twelve bucks a barrel, and pump prices are thirty cents higher than yesterday."

"Yes sir," Kirkwood agreed. "That's worth an extra twenty-four million dollars *per day* to Iran, just based on what's coming out of those stolen Iraqi oil fields. Maybe our questions about motive can be answered by just following the money."

***

Islamic Republic of Iran

Cheng Ye sat across from Weh Heng in his own office. This time, the military attaché had come to him, rather than vice-versa. It gave Cheng Ye great face, and reduced that of his political rival, even if only by a small amount.

"Beijing is pleased with your progress," Weh Heng informed him after the usual formal niceties had been observed. He paused as an Iranian youth, perhaps barely into his teens, entered the office with a tray bearing a fresh pot of tea. The young man was dusky and handsome, and Weh Heng noted with interest that Cheng Ye's soulless eyes, which ignored everything that was irrelevant to him, lingered momentarily on the youth. The youth, in turn, looked reserved, even cowed, sparing Cheng Ye a fearful glance as he set the tray down and bowed slightly before making a quick and silent exit.

Interesting, Weh Heng thought, mentally filing that away.

"Our hosts, in turn, are pleased with our support on the international stage. The Americans will be outnumbered when the security council votes to censure them, and their own media will help turn American public opinion against its own government. Our strategy—"

"—*My* strategy," Cheng Ye interrupted softly, but his tone carried danger.

"—*The* strategy," Weh Heng continued without missing a beat, "is working well. What do you see as our next move?"

Cheng Ye sat very still, giving nothing away with his body language, which others tended to find unnatural. "We wait and see how the Americans react. The Iranian claims in the world press are certain to anger them, especially when they conduct their own analysis of the battle. There are two possible outcomes: they will retaliate as a show of strength and frustration, or again attempt to let matters lie. At this point, I think the Americans will respond. It is their way to 'punch bullies in the nose,' as they like to phrase it, and Marsden, by all accounts, is a man ruled by his emotions. He has already shown a fear of appearing weak."

"So sorry, but how do you draw this conclusion?" Weh Heng asked.

"By his actions. The prior administration put a carrier group into the Gulf as a show of strength and resolve over events in Iraq, after years of comparative neglect. Marsden was advised to withdraw it shortly after taking office, and he refused."

"And you believe the Americans will respond aggressively now?"

"I say it is *likely*. When that happens, it opens the door to the final part of this phase of our overall plans: the expulsion of the Americans from the Gulf, and their inevitable violent response. At this point, I believe the arms and equipment we have provided our allies have emboldened them to new heights. In time, we may even be able to walk back our own participation, further masking our aims."

"This matter of expelling the Americans? How does Iran accomplish that with its inferior force structure? Even with the new aircraft and missile systems, they are far outmatched."

"Asymmetric warfare. Have you ever read about Millennium Challenge 2002?"

"I have not."

"It is an enlightening read. It was an exercise put on by the Americans that year, a wargame conducted partially by computer simulation, but still involving great numbers of personnel, ships, and aircraft. It cost the Americans almost a quarter billion dollars. A retired American flag officer, a member of their Marine Corps, was recruited to lead the opposition force and assigned virtual assets and capabilities on par with Iran at the time. It was supposed to be an honest test and evaluation of evolving American tactics and capabilities."

"And?"

Cheng Ye's dark smile sent chills down Weh Heng's back. "It was a disaster for them. The opposing force sank the entire Yankee fleet in the opening moves of the wargame, on the first day. This was done through use of asymmetric tactics, maximizing the advantages of a Yankee fleet placed too close to a hostile shore, and restrictions imposed on the Americans by the presence of neutral units. In short, the very conditions they face today."

Weh Heng laughed. "What was the reaction of their leadership?"

"Denial," Cheng Ye replied. "The results didn't conform to their expectations, or justify the billions spent by their military industrial complex. They are the ultimate masters at self-deception. They reset the exercise, placing so many constraints on the opposition force that the result was no longer a true test, but a scripted exercise. The officer leading the opposition force resigned in protest before it was halfway over."

"That was a decade ago," Weh Heng warned him. "American capabilities have advanced significantly in that time and will undergo another leap by the end of this decade. They must have taken *some* of the lessons to heart."

"Perhaps. Our allies have treated it as a case study in how the Americans might be defeated. Many of the asymmetric methods utilized in the simulation have been studied, adopted, and even improved upon by General Abdi's people. The Iranian laser-semaphore system is an example of secure, near real-time communications that cannot be intercepted or overheard. It is reserved for those communications which *must* remain secret, while they allow the enemy's satellites and eavesdropping sensors to overhear routine communications, some of which are deliberate deceptions. They are also willing to make a sacrifice of either willing martyrs or their politically untrustworthy. For example, one of the Phantom pilots killed in the air battle was the squadron commander who refused the overflight mission that I carried out. Our allies have learned their lessons well, and patiently bided their time. Furthermore, lack of resources has made them quite innovative. I am curious," Cheng Ye added, "what have we learned about their nuclear program?"

"Those matters are beyond your security clearance," Weh Heng reminded him, attempting to assert his own authority and regain some of his lost face.

Cheng Ye's smile was devoid of warmth. *You have no clearance for that information either then,* he thought, seeing through the response. "I merely ask because there are possibilities for the asymmetric use of an Iranian-made nuclear weapon, when they finally have one."

Even Weh Heng wasn't prepared to contemplate that level of devilry—not yet. The belief was that Iran wanted a nuclear capability primarily for the deterrence value it provided, with

North Korea being the classic example of a modern success story in that regard. The entire world, especially the United States, was forced to treat North Korea differently once it became a nuclear power. Of course, the Iranians also wanted nuclear weapons as a tool to destroy tiny Israel. He shuddered slightly to think on how Cheng Ye might make use of one, especially if acting from the shadows. It wouldn't be a simple or direct usage, he was sure.

"Ah, so," Cheng Ye continued when Weh didn't respond, "in any case, with this latest engagement, we have achieved the result we desired. General Abdi and his leaders feel that the time has come to put their careful preparations in play," Cheng Ye continued. "With a fledgling, weak administration in Washington D.C., coupled with the direct support of the Party of Mao and the Russian government on the Iranian side, I have convinced General Abdi that the timing may never be better."

"Beijing looks forward to seeing the results," Weh Heng said.

V

U.S. censured in the UN Security Council. United States abstains from the vote in protest, calling the entire process 'a sham.'

-The New York Times

Iran's Expanding Modern Arsenal—Is Iran putting an advanced integrated air-defense system in place?

-Defense News Weekly

Female aviator is the navy's new Top Gun! Two decades after gender integration, Deidre Danforth shoots down the gender divide.

-USA Today

Defense Department debunks Iranian claims, releasing combat footage showing missile attack on U.S. ships.

-Washington Post

The Persian Gulf

The assembled officers of the Gray Wolves occupied their ready room chairs, waiting for the skipper to arrive and the all-officers meeting to begin. In the meantime, they were watching repeating news footage of recent American action in the Gulf, released to the press to counter the claims of victimhood being made by the Iranians. Fargo watched for the umpteenth time as FLIR footage from an orbiting helicopter showed the two U.S. frigates engaging the speed boat swarm with their Mark 38 machine gun systems. Set to burst fire, the weapons sent streams of 25 mm shells at the advancing swarm, cutting long white swatches into the water where the rounds struck. Where one of those lines intersected a speed boat, the boat would vanish, torn apart by the burst and occasionally punctuated by a small secondary explosion. The Mark 38 system was designed specifically for small, fast targets such as the frigates faced here. The video soon cut away to another piece of footage, this time the CIWS mount on USS *Thach* putting a virtual wall of lead into the air, blowing apart an incoming anti-ship missile approximately 800 yards from the ship. It was high-octane stuff—naval combat for real. Fargo figured that whoever was running the FLIR pod on the helicopter had a bright future in broadcast news.

"Hey!" someone yelled at the squadron duty officer behind his desk. "Change the news channel! The big-titty blond is about to come on!"

"Which one?" someone else guffawed. Fargo grinned. The malaise that briefly fell over the ready room after losing the Irish brothers was gone now, burned away by the heat of combat. The Gray Wolves were back in proper form.

"Seriously, screw Traitor News!" someone else called. That was their favorite burn for TNN: just substitute the word 'Traitor' for the 'T'.

"Change the channel!"

"All right, all right, y'all keep your pants on!" the SDO growled back, thumbing the remote. A cheer went up when the channel changed, and they were treated to a fresh viewing of their favorite replay of all: Dexter's pod footage of Deedee and Stinky outrunning shoulder-fired SAMs during their show of force over the speed boat swarm. Those few seconds had made Deidre Danforth famous in the space of a few days, not just because of the footage of her evading enemy fire, but the fact that she had scored three kills in the air battle that followed. Post-mission analysis had confirmed her score: she'd shot down two F-5's and an F-4. Ironically they were all American-made airplanes, sold to the Shaw's air force prior to the events of 1979.

Given the media explosion that ensued, Deedee's biggest worry now was being grounded to protect her from harm as a media darling and recruiting tool, or worse still, being detached and sent home for a public affairs tour. As the ready room hooted and hollered at the television screen, Deedee blushed a bright red and turtled even further into her high-backed chair. Who knew that being a famous aerial killer could be so embarrassing?

Stinky was stoically tolerant of the fact that the media spotlight had missed him completely. Judging by the single-minded focus on Deedee, one would have thought she was flying a single-seat E-model.

Fargo slept badly the first night after the battle, but he'd been fine since then. Their pod footage clearly showed their Phantom kill exploding midair, with no chutes. He wasn't sure about the single F-5 they'd hit first, and he wasn't dwelling on it. He'd never *wanted* to kill another person, but anyone strapping on a fighter had better be prepared for the eventuality, or go sell insurance instead. The Iranian pilots had been armed, aware, and engaged—he had no regrets, and now he was one of the few pilots in the U.S. Armed Forces with even a single air-to-air kill.

Dexter seemed to be fine as well; he took the praise in stride, knowing it was deserved. He hadn't let it go to his head—when asked, he was prone to repeat how lucky they were to have gotten away without a single loss. His new demeanor was harder, more serious, and nobody called him 'nugget' anymore.

"Attention on deck!" the SDO called, bringing all conversation to a halt.

"Carry on," Chill said, prompting them to retake their seats. He cut to the chase without any warmup. "Some of you may have heard the scuttlebutt by now that we're planning a strike in retaliation for the events of the other day. The rumors are true. This will be a one-off, a show of force to remind the Iranians that our patience out here has its limits. The target will be Lavan Island since its SAM batteries spiked our people during the rescue operation."

"I'm surprised Marsden had the balls to go for this," Stinky whispered in Fargo's ear. The latter nodded but said nothing.

"Without further ado, I'm going to turn it over to everyone's favorite AIO for an updated threat briefing." The skipper clapped once, then pointed into the crowd. Aston Chadwick II, in clean-pressed khakis, SWO-sweater, and Clark Kents, stood up and moved to the front of the room.

Someone began a chant. "Sweat-er-boy! Sweat-er-boy! Sweat-er-boy!" Everyone took it up, and Sweater Boy grinned hugely as he took center stage, nodding and holding out his hands like a comedian pandering to the crowd. As Deedee had predicted, the cult of personality had taken hold. Even the other squadrons in the air wing knew 'Sweater Boy' Chadwick by now. He was undoubtedly the most well-known AIO in the history of USS *Boxer*. The junior officers all had sheets of paper wadded up and ready, and they showered him with a salvo of paper snowballs.

Then they got down to serious business.

***

Islamic Republic of Iran

Hamed Abdi watched as the dirt-streaked Antonov transport aircraft touched down on the runway at Rafsanjan Airport. It was an older, weathered looking An-12 Cub, a high-wing transport with four turboprop engines, looking like it had seen better days. Airplanes like it flew in and out of this airport on a semi-regular basis, so the appearance of this one drew no special attention. If anything, it was even a little rattier looking than the usual assortment of planes that passed through. Nobody looking at it would care to fly on it as a passenger, that much was certain. The fact that the plane was exceptionally well-maintained and flown by a highly experienced crew was easily disguised.

The aircraft taxied onto the single, square-shaped tarmac north of the runway, where it was waved into a parking spot and shut down. The pilots were picked up and transported to their lodging in the nearby city, and the plane itself was left unattended, or so it appeared. That was also a misdirection; there was a well-armed security force not far away, and the aircraft was kept under close observation until nightfall. A few vehicles arrived after dark to unload the cargo: a single large metal container embedded in a slightly larger wooden crate. The entire package was approximately three meters square. It was craned into the back of a large, covered flatbed truck under the close supervision of several Iranians in plain clothes, including Hamed Abdi.

Abdi knew what the crate contained, and what it portended. Not even Toma Baranov or Cheng Ye knew about this part of Iran's plan going forward; this had been negotiated and carried out between the Iranian and Russian governments in complete secrecy.

The Russians were old masters of the *maskirovka,* or game of misdirection. In the early days of the Cold War, after Stalin died and Nikita Khrushchev became General Secretary of the Soviet Union, there was a large disparity in the number of nuclear weapons between the United States and Soviet Union— far larger than was suspected in the West. The U.S. stockpile of nuclear warheads outnumbered the Soviets' by more than a hundred-to-one, and was far more versatile. Khrushchev feared the appearance of weakness and embarked on a campaign of pure misdirection, feeding on the nuclear fears begun during the Eisenhower years, and convincing the western world that Soviet Russia possessed a far larger nuclear arsenal than it did. One of Khrushchev's famous claims (and totally untrue) was that the Soviets could 'produce missiles like sausages.' It wasn't until the late 1960's and 1970's under Leonid Brezhnev that Soviet stockpiles of nuclear warheads caught up with (and eventually surpassed) U.S. numbers.

Once a nation became a nuclear power, it achieved a different status on the world stage. The United States and Soviet Union were first, followed closely by Britain, France, China, and then others. Nuclear powers in the modern world included NATO, Pakistan, Israel, India, most recently North Korea. The international change in attitude towards a nuclear North Korea was significant: it had an immediate chilling effect, proving a deterrent to foreign aggression or even the wanton imposition of economic sanctions.

Iran's nuclear program was progressing slowly but steadily. Still, it might be a decade or more before Iran made its first home-grown nuclear weapons and could begin building a stockpile. Their Russian allies had quietly proposed the idea that they trick the world into believing they had achieved nuclear status much sooner, using deception: a Khrushchev-style *maskirovka*.

Months before, specific amounts of raw uranium ore taken from Iranian mining operations in the Saghand and Khorasson regions were sent north to a facility in Russia, where it was expertly enriched to weapons grade in a facility designed to mimic what was known of Iranian enrichment facilities. It was then built into a warhead designed by Iranians (but built in Russia) for a low-yield atomic explosion, and now the warhead was returning to Iran. It wasn't possible to achieve the deception by having Russia supply the warhead; nuclear forensics was a very real science, and it was possible to examine residue or fallout after a nuclear blast and determine where the materials in the device had originated. Sometimes, important details about the weapon's construction could even be discerned. There was no question that western scientists would eventually obtain such residue. When the time came, it was vital for them to believe that the weapon was produced in Iran, with natively mined and enriched uranium.

The weapon now in Iranian possession wasn't meant to be used against their enemies, but just to scare their enemies into believing that Iran could produce more of them. There were risks involved with such a bluff, but the Russians convinced them that the rewards far outweighed the risks. In the end, the Iranian leadership hadn't needed much convincing. As the world's largest state sponsor of terrorism and proxy terrorist organizations, any method to sew confusion, turmoil, and fear amongst their hated enemies was a golden opportunity. Abdi and his superiors considered the possibilities, and concluded that Iranian domination of the entire Persian Gulf might be well within their grasp.

It was an old trick to hide something important by leaving it in plain sight, usually amid some form of 'natural' background—like leaving an envelope full of cash sitting in the open on a cluttered desk, or maybe in a stack of unopened mail. The way to draw unwanted attention to something important was to *treat it as important,* so the exact opposite of that was done here. There was no fanfare, no use of military aircraft, no fighter escorts, large military ground escorts, or anything of the sort. The crate could have contained anything and was treated casually, as if its contents were of little to no value at all. Western intelligence services and their satellites would see nothing here that flagged as interesting or out of the ordinary, prompting a closer look. Communications were handled strictly by human couriers, with no use of land lines or radios that might be intercepted.

The cargo was loaded onto its truck and unceremoniously driven away, unescorted, towards a secret location in the desert, in the sparsely populated South Khorosan Province. There were others waiting for it there, and when the final preparations were complete the real *maskirovka* would begin.

***

The Persian Gulf

The marshal stack was almost cleared out by the time Chill and Neo reported overhead with a division of planes in tow, with Fargo and Dexter leading the second section. The strike on Lavan Island was over, and would go down as the strangest, and least-eventful combat operation in the past decade.

To put it plainly, only one side showed up to the fight.

On the U.S. side it was an impressive half-deck strike, utilizing one division of Super Hornets as sweepers, two divisions of legacy Hornet SEAD strikers and bombers, a division of Super Hornets from the Gray Wolves carrying tactical air-launched decoys, two Prowler jammers carrying additional SEAD loadouts, two large Air Force tankers with S-3 tankers serving as hose multipliers, and an E-2C Hawkeye providing AWACS coverage. CAG led the strike himself, flying the lead sweeper and hoping to bag a MiG or two when the IRIAF came up to joust in the defense of its island. Twenty-six aircraft in total participated. None were lost; none were even spiked by an Iranian radar, much less fired at.

Their primary targets, the Iranian SA-11 and SA-6 surface-to-air missile batteries on Lavan Island, were right where they'd been mapped. The Iranians made no intervening attempt to move them, or stage more fighters on Lavan as a ready alert, or to bolster the island's defenses at all. When the strike launched from *Boxer* and began assembling at its rendezvous point to push on the target, the single Iranian Mainstay in the air had shut down its radar and landed. No Iranian fighters launched, and not a single surface-to-air fire control radar was turned on. A single SA-11 search radar swept over the strikers as they approached Lavan, almost acting like a beacon of sorts to entice them in. The Gray Wolves launched over a dozen decoys, which flew over Lavan without being engaged and eventually fell out of the sky after exhausting their fuel. The SEAD strike carried out its one-sided punishment, destroying the two inert SAM batteries, cratering Lavan airport's deserted runways and tarmac, and destroying the airport's control tower.

After launching their decoys, the Gray Wolves orbited slightly off axis from the remainder of the strike with their radars shut down, watching events unfold on datalink.

When the last of the strikers called off target and the whole gaggle moved south to recover, the Gray Wolves found themselves with some extra fuel and a long wait while the ship recovered the strike. Skipper Jefferson opted to turn the wait into an impromptu training event, breaking his division off for some practice intercepts and air combat training with the Hawkeye controllers. At the end, feeling his oats and with Neo in his back seat, he'd challenged Fargo to a guns-only dogfight, *mano-e-mano*.

Fargo took up the gauntlet and beat the pants off his boss. Neo's help was enough to give Chill a fighting chance, but Fargo could tell that there was heavy coaching going on in the way the skipper's best moves always seemed to come just a hair late— the time it took Neo to prompt him. It wasn't in Fargo's nature to 'let the boss win', or anyone else for that matter, when he was exercising the skills of his trade. Nor was Chill the type of guy who would have appreciated it. Fargo wasn't the type who thumped his chest and blustered about 'who was the best fighter pilot' over beers in the club. He was the quiet one who would just smile and nod, then take someone to the schoolhouse when the opportunity came up. When Dexter wondered out loud if maybe they ought to let the skipper get a shot off for pride's sake, he was met with stony silence from up front. Less than a minute later Fargo gunned his commanding officer one last time before the 'knock it off' call for time and fuel.

It was flying around the Boat where Chill had earned his reputation. He'd been Top Hook for the entire air wing over the whole cruise, and the 'greenie board' which tracked pilot landing grades held a near-unbroken string of OK-3's for the Gray Wolves skipper. If getting taken to the woodshed in a dogfight had rattled his cage at all, it didn't show once the controller passed signal 'Charlie' and they broke into the landing pattern. Fargo was on the downwind leg, nearing the '180' from which he'd begin his own approach turn, when he saw the skipper's jet catch a perfect 3-wire on deck below him. There hadn't been a word from Paddles during Chill's entire pass—the skipper flew the ball like the jet was on rails.

Fargo was Dash-3, leading the second section with Deedee on his wing, as usual. Rackdog was the skipper's wingman, and had the slight misfortune of a hook-skip after flying a solid approach; the Super Hornet roared airborne after the bolter and would have to try again. Then it was Fargo's turn, coming around the '90' and into the groove.

"I've got the ball," Fargo reported to his WSO, meaning that he could see the Fresnel lens and use it for glidepath reference.

Dexter made the radio call using their side number, aircraft type, and fuel state measured in thousands of pounds: "202, Rhino, ball, five point five." That information was necessary to ensure the arresting gear was set properly for the aircraft it was about to trap.

Paddles called him slightly fast at the start, and Fargo worked to correct his profile as his scan worked around the Big-3: lineup, ball, angle-of-attack. His counter-correction after getting back on-speed was insubstantial. The jet began to settle ever so slightly, and Paddles gave him one sugar call for power as the ball drifted half a cell low. Fargo corrected again, centering the ball, then keeping it there for the remainder of the pass. The jet flew over the ramp and slammed onto the deck, catching a solid 3-wire in the end.

"Nice job," Dexter complimented him from the back.

"Yah," Fargo replied sourly from the front. He knew the LSO well enough to know he was going to get a 'Fair' grade on that pass. *Serves me right, too, for being off speed at the start.* He taxied out of the landing area and paused while the red shirts safety-pinned their missiles, then moved on into their parking spot as directed for shutdown.

"You flew a lot of green ink in Afghanistan," Dexter observed, referring to Fargo's prior combat missions. In the Navy, combat time was recorded in aircrew logbooks in green ink for ease of reference and accounting. "Is it just me, or was that about the strangest combat mission flown this side of the Twilight Zone?"

"Yah, it was, you betcha," Fargo scowled. *It felt like a grown man beating on a helpless child.*

"So, what the hell?"

"I don't know, Dex. I'm just ready to get the hell out of the Gulf and go home. My fun meter is pegged."

Dexter was quiet for a moment—it wasn't like Fargo to complain about anything, especially to him. He could tell his pilot wasn't happy about any of this. "Why does it feel like we somehow just got suckered again?"

"Well," Fargo sighed, "let's just say this punitive venture, which looked good to someone on paper, is going to go over like a fart in church with the western media."

Dexter thought about that as he unassed the jet.

***

"Well, what the fuck was *that* all about, anyway?" CAG barked at the intelligence officers in the carrier's CVIC. "Were the sites we hit even real, or were they decoys with a single working radar to sucker us in?" He waited expectantly for an answer as the members of the intelligence team looked at each other hesitantly. "You don't have any idea, do you?" he snarled after a moment.

"They weren't fake sites, sir," someone finally said.

"And we know it wasn't a SAM trap," one of the others added. "If it was, they'd have locked and fired on the strike at some point."

"No shit, Dick Tracy!" CAG thundered. "Last I checked, this was CVIC: the *carrier intelligence center.* Does anyone in this room have a single idea, clue, or *even a guess* as to what is going on with Iran?" Nobody replied, and the debriefing team was obviously cowed by CAG's rare blast of temper. It was somewhat routine for DCAG to go into a screaming fit, almost expected, but not Captain VanNortwick. It was disconcerting for everyone, including the aviators who had flown the strike.

"Fuck it," CAG finally said in disgust. "That was a total non-event! There isn't even anything to debrief! I'm heading up to flag country to see if anyone on the admiral's staff has a fucking clue what prompted the most hostile nation in the Gulf *to completely ignore an attack*!" CAG stormed out of the space, leaving a dark cloud behind him.

"Aren't we supposed to be *happy* when we don't get shot at?" Dexter muttered in Fargo's ear.

"I thought so," Fargo whispered back. He figured that CAG was probably lamenting the lost opportunity to score a kill in the air before the sun set on his flying career, but he'd never figured the guy as a glory-hound who went *looking* for a fight. CAG's reaction might also be a result of the strangeness of the mission; Fargo was unsettled and confused himself, and he didn't like the feeling at all.

In CAG's absence, the Gray Wolves CO was the senior officer present. He stepped into the vacuum left by CAG's stormy departure and took charge, to the slight discomfort of the regular debriefers. "Okay people," he said easily, "what happened out there was unexpected, but that was a successful mission given our objectives. Hey, a strike without any return fire is ideal, right?" he grinned. This drew a low chuckle and helped dispel the tension. "There are always *details* we can look at within the bigger picture so that we can refine and improve our strike planning processes . . ."

Aww, jeez. There goes the next hour! Fargo mentally cringed. He resisted the temptation to glance at his watch, and wondered how long it would be before the first person snuck out on the pretense of making a head call and conveniently forgot to come back. He wished he could work that gambit himself, but he wasn't anonymous enough with his own CO to get away with it.

As Skipper Jefferson moderated an excruciating dig into the minutiae of the mission, Dexter's mind wandered down its own path, conducting a broader analysis of his own. Most military officers considered themselves well versed in strategic matters, but what they really understood was their own 'slice of the pie': mostly their own weapons systems, tactics, and the importance of logistics that was baked into U.S. military operators at all levels.

Dexter Wong was a little different. He was born and raised in America, but his parents were Chinese immigrants. He was bilingual, fluent in written and spoken Mandarin, and he tended to think about things from an eastern rather than western perspective. He liked to look at things by taking the long-view, with an eye on both past and future. How had current events been shaped by past events, and how would they shape the future in turn? He'd read and re-read Sun Tzu, Thucydides, Clausewitz, Musashi, and he was an avid lover of games like chess and *go*. Lately, as things got more and more bizarre, he was convinced that they were being subtly manipulated by someone with a hidden purpose.

Starting with the antagonistic nightly feints at the strike groups in the Gulf, nothing that Iran had done over the past couple of months made any real sense. CAG's reaction to this strike was a clear indication that their leadership was frustrated by it. But Dexter knew it made sense to *someone*. He'd replayed the *Orgullo de Carino* scenario repeatedly in his mind. The strike on the cargo ship had prompted a rescue mission, the rescue mission had resulted in a battle, and the battle was being used by Iran to wage a public affairs campaign—*no,* he amended, *an* information warfare *campaign*—aimed at painting the United States as a hostile threat to regional security. Before that, there was the flyover that resulted in the shootdown of the Irish brothers, which had made *Iran* look aggressive.

But what if that hadn't been the intention? As a fighter guy, Dexter could fully appreciate turning the tables on a pursuer and killing him as an act of self-preservation. But what if the Iranian *leadership* had counted on their own fighter being shot down? That's what *would* have happened if the air warfare commander had been on the ball, right? Legally speaking, Iran had the right to overfly any vessel in international waters and within international airspace, including U.S. warships, but there were prudent limits that still had to be observed. The media never cared about details like sonic booms from an aggressive flyover causing damage and injuries; they only cared about their choice of narrative. If the Flanker was shot down before or after the overflight, the Iranians could have spun *that* event as an aggressive over-reaction by the Americans.

But to what end? It was no secret that Iran wanted the United States out of the Gulf, but that was a pipe-dream. The Gulf was too important to energy security, which in turn equated to national security, and no media narrative could budge that fundamental truth. Iran's purchase of modern planes and air defenses was a long-needed upgrade, having little to do with American presence *per se*. Recent Iranian acts seemed aimed at prompting an *increased* U.S. presence rather than diminishing it. *Who would that benefit?*

Certainly not Iran, Dexter reasoned.

Thucydides' *History* spoke of the importance of making and breaking alliances among enemies and allies alike, and the utilization of alternate fronts as diversions to achieve military goals where desired. Sun Tzu also spoke of alliances as the means to attack an enemy by proxy while preserving one's own resources. Who benefited long-term from increased tensions between Iran and the United States?

Dexter ran down a mental list. Iraq, for one. Saddam Hussein was besieged, barely maintaining his hold on power in the middle of a vicious civil-war. Sunni Arabs and Kurds were dying by the thousands and tens of thousands, and the world was barely paying attention. Iran was Saddam's greatest enemy, and open hostilities in the Gulf might present him an opportunity to retake lost territory. None of the Gulf States were culpable; their relationship with the United States was a marriage of money, convenience, and arms sales. That left China, Russia, and North Korea. Of the three, Russia seemed the obvious choice. Tensions between Iran and the U.S. diverted attention and resources away from Crimea and the Baltic States, where Russia plainly had designs. Instability in the Persian Gulf meant higher oil and gas prices, a *definite* benefit to Russia, which was dependent on its energy exports for trade and foreign currency. Furthermore, Russia *had* sold Iran at least some of their new fighters and advanced air defense systems, even if none of them had been in play today. So, was Russia a potential 'man behind the curtain' here? If so, what was the end goal?

Dexter wondered if Sweater Boy ever thought about any of this strategic stuff. Did the admiral or his staff think about it? Did *anyone?* Or did they just react when things happened?

"Dexter! You awake, son?" Skipper Jefferson called. Dexter's mind snapped back to the debrief, and he saw all eyes were on him. Fargo's elbow dug sharply into his side.

"Sorry Skipper, say again?" he asked sheepishly.

The skipper repeated his question on a mundane technicality, adding: "You need to keep your head in the game, there, Dex!"

***

Virginia Class Submarine USS North Carolina
Near the Strait of Hormuz

Up until the late 1990's, the submarine threat to western forces in the Persian Gulf was non-existent. Then Iran purchased three Soviet-era *Kilo* Class submarines, which were capable of firing torpedoes, anti-ship missiles, or laying mines. The Iranians were new to submarine operations and their fledgling program was initially beset by problems. The submarine batteries originally designed for colder waters needed to be refurbished, there were issues with crew proficiency, and the environment itself was not conducive to submarine operations. Gulf waters were shallow, and the Strait of Hormuz subject to strong currents. All these things were serious challenges to Iran's program, and in past decades the Iranian submarine force, which consisted mostly of midget submarines alongside their three larger subs, remained tied up in harbor. The Iranian *Kilo* force had undergone its latest refurbishment in 2012, and since then there was a concerted effort to ramp up their operations and crew proficiency.

The same problems faced by the Iranians in Gulf waters were shared by the United States and Great Britain, who also operated submarines in the Gulf on occasion. The difference was that western submarines were manned by extremely skilled and proficient crews. Nuclear-powered submarines were louder than diesel-electric boats, but the traffic volume and bad acoustic conditions in the Gulf also helped them remain covert when operating there. USS *North Carolina* was tacitly assigned to the *Boxer* carrier group, but she was currently detached to operate on her own in a support role, working as a lone hunter.

Even more advanced than the preceding *Los Angeles* Class boats, the *Virginia* Class attack boats boasted a myriad of capabilities. She was equipped with twelve vertical launch system (VLS) bays capable of firing long-range land attack cruise missiles, photonic masts with multiple cameras and imagers that replaced old–fashioned periscopes, and she hosted a large variety of electronic surveillance, eavesdropping, and communications equipment. The latter included a prototype laser communications system that could pass information at broadband speeds. Her sonar system was the most advanced ever built, with portions extending along the sides of her hull in addition to bow-mounted and towed-tail arrays. Although she was equipped with the standard nine-man lockout trunk, *North Carolina* was also outfitted with a dry deck shelter and SEAL Delivery Vehicle (SDV) to conduct special operations.

One of the special operations they had conducted was a dangerous experiment to attempt a new method of tracking the Iranian Kilos in these waters. The SEALs conducted an undersea infiltration of Bandar Abbas harbor, breached Iranian port security, and attached experimental blue-laser locater beacons to the bottoms of the hulls of all three submarines. These were designed to remain inert, powered by battery packs that only activated when pinged by a discrete ELF radio pulse. When signaled, the unit would switch on and its laser system would attempt to lock on to any nearby receiver, thereby ratting out the position, course, and speed of the target it was riding. This was a modification of the blue-laser technology already used for subsurface communications, but less complicated because no actual communication was necessary—the unit merely had to make itself briefly known to the receiver. The ranges on this system were limited due to constraints of undersea laser systems, but the tracking submarine used unmanned undersea drones to expand her scanning range. The idea was to catch diesel or Air-Independent Propulsion (AIP) submarines coming out of port and track them safely from beyond counter-detection range. The tracking submarine could then engage a target herself or pass cueing data to air or surface-based ASW units.

Nobody was sure how well the system would work or whether it would be discovered by the Iranians. A close inspection of the hull by divers or in a dry-dock would certainly reveal the presence of the device. Although designed for minimal impact on a submarine's hydrodynamics, it would have a very slight effect on flow noise and drag, subtly changing the acoustic and trim characteristics of the sub. The hope was that these effects would be too small to notice, especially by crews as non-proficient as the Iranians. The technology was new and proprietary, and the units themselves contained a small magnesium charge set to slag the internal components if the unit was detached from the hull.

The go-ahead for the operation to plant the devices was given after the last Kilo sortie, during which U.S. forces were unsuccessful in locating or tracking the Iranian submarine using conventional methods. The advantage of diesel-electric submarines like the Kilo was that they were almost silent to passive sonar systems when running submerged on their batteries. In shallow, heavily trafficked environments like the Gulf, passive tracking was a nearly impossible task. Active sonar tracking was still effective, but it gave away the presence of the hunter. It was used sparingly for that reason, and almost never by other submarines.

When the Kilo returned to port, the SEALS made their infiltration and completed their assignment. All that remained was to determine whether the experimental devices worked or not.

For better or worse, the opportunity was upon them. In an almost unprecedented move, multiple Iranian submarines were putting out to sea at once. In *North Carolina*'s control center, things were starting to get busy. The control center was comfortably dim and preternaturally quiet; even though they were practically undetectable themselves, silence was somewhat second nature.

"Sonar, Conn, give me a track update on India Kilo 2," the watch officer said quietly into his headset.

"Conn, Sonar. I hold track India Kilo 2 bearing zero four eight degrees at fourteen thousand yards. Course two zero five, speed six knots, depth eight zero feet. Bearing rate change is holding constant."

"Very well," replied LT Whorley.

The commander of the embarked SEAL team was LT Kevin Reese. He appeared quietly and unobtrusively in the control center, standing out from the submariners in their blue 'poopy-suit' coveralls in a desert khaki flight suit identical to the kind worn by aviators. A simple cloth nametag velcroed to his chest displayed the muted SEAL trident insignia over his name and rank. The picture would not have been complete without the steaming mug of black coffee in the lieutenant's hand, and he nodded cordially to the watch officer before standing in an out of the way spot to watch what was going on. The SEALS weren't generally interested in what they considered the 'bubble-head stuff,' but in this case he was curious as to whether their mission into Bandar Abbas harbor was bearing fruit.

"What's the word?" Lieutenant Reese quietly asked Whorley when he had a minute. The two had gotten to know one another during the SEAL team's stint on board, and they got along well even though their professional worlds were completely different.

"We've gotten good signals off two of the three sets," Whorley informed him. "We're set up so the data goes to the sonar operators, since the lasers are just another form of directional signaling. One boat is headed over to the eastern side of the strait towards the Gulf of Oman, and the other is heading into the Persian Gulf. So far so good—we've got our drones sending an ELF ping about once per hour, and no sign of counter-detection. The third boat either didn't come out, or we just aren't picking her up."

"Excellent," Reese replied, gratified with their success. This deployment was scheduled to end soon, and the team was getting antsy about the prospect of getting off the submarine. A graduate of San Diego State University's NROTC program, Reese had chosen the teams to challenge himself and discover his limits, but life aboard a submarine pushed those limits in different ways. He'd spent a day and a half aboard a sub during summer training as a midshipman, and been bored to tears the entire time. He vowed to never again set foot aboard a submarine when the training ended, and now here he was, trapped aboard a submarine. At least the chow aboard the boat was pretty good—consistently better than the surface navy.

"What about the other thing?" Reese asked. The SEAL mission into Bandar Abbas resulted in an unexpected discovery: the half dozen midget submarines assigned there were missing, replaced by elaborate metal-and-wood decoys meant to make it appear as though those vessels were still in port. Their satellites had obviously been fooled, since the report on the decoys was met with surprise and consternation by their chain of command.

"Well, they changed our ROE this morning," Whorley replied. "We've gone from yellow and hold to yellow and tight, but nobody we're tracking has been declared hostile."

Reese whistled, drawing a couple quick looks from around the control center. "Is that ROE unusual for you guys?"

"For the most part, yes. Iran is making noise about what they are calling an unprovoked attack on Lavan Island, and claiming that U.S. ships may be attacked without warning."

"Think the camel-jocks will try anything?"

"Doubtful," Whorley replied, then added: "It sounds like the usual bluster. But now we've got this sortie of the entire Iranian subsurface force in Bandar Abbas. Things are getting interesting."

"No doubt, dude."

Their conversation was interrupted by the arrival of the captain in the control center. *North Carolina* was commanded by CDR Rick L. Bergstrom III, USN. Scion of an old-money Connecticut family, Bergstrom had attended the U.S. Naval Academy and later picked up a master's degree from Yale. He was a good administrator and submariner, but with a reputation for being a 'ring knocker'. That was an uncomplimentary label applied to Academy graduates with a condescending attitude, or who tended to look down on *anyone* who didn't attend Annapolis.

The submarine captain and SEAL officer were a study in opposites. Bergstrom was tall and thin, with dark hair, fine, aristocratic features, and the aura of academia. Reese was shorter, wore his blonde hair on the long-side of the regulations, coming off like a surfer and fitness buff. Bergstrom's demeanor of slight disdain for the embarked SEALs irritated Reese, but since Bergstrom was the captain there was nothing to do but tolerate it with quiet, professional stoicism. Captain Bergstrom was just one more reason Reese was eager to be off the sub.

"Good afternoon, gentlemen," Bergstrom greeted everyone. "Lieutenant Whorley, SITREP." The watch officer spent the next few minutes giving his CO a complete contact report on the two Iranian submarines they could detect.

Reese excused himself from the control center. He was replaced by the sub's executive officer, LCDR Ron Dubicki. His arrival meant Whorley had to explain the situation for the third time in ten minutes, but he didn't mind. The XO grinned in excitement, and his enthusiasm was infectious. Dubicki's interpersonal skills far exceeded Bergstrom's, and even though he was another Academy man, nobody called Dubicki a 'ring knocker.' Bergstrom monitored the control room in aloof silence while the XO worked from station to station, checking readouts and gauges, asking opinions, and exchanging encouragement or a quiet word here and there with the men manning the consoles. When he was satisfied with the situation he made his way back around to the captain's side.

"You read the morning message boards, XO?" Bergstrom asked.

"Yes sir. Sounds like things are getting twitchier topside," he replied, referring to the situation faced by the surface force. "Just as well we're finally transiting out of here in a few days. I'm surprised we haven't heard a response yet on the midget submarine decoys that Reese's team found in the harbor."

"Well, there was the change in ROE."

"Yes sir, but I figured that was more about Iran's threats than our report."

"I guess we'll see. Our contacts are splitting up. Per our orders to remain in support of the strike group, I'm going to stick with India Sierra-2. If she maintains a straight course we'll ease into her baffles and just tag along behind her. Let's get a contact report out on both targets as well. In the meantime, have weps load a couple torpedoes into the tubes and have them ready to go. If Iran goes hostile on short notice, I want to be in position to kill this guy fast."

"Aye aye, captain."

VI

Iranian spokesman states his nation was 'shocked' at the raw violence of unprovoked strikes on Gulf island facilities.

-L.A. Times

Iranian officials threaten to close the Strait of Hormuz, promising a 'harsh response' to unprovoked U.S. aggression.

-Atlanta Journal Constitution

Oil prices spike in wake of Gulf violence! Prices are up 18% over a two-month period.

-Chicago Sun-Times

U.S economic recovery stagnant, with high energy prices deemed a significant factor.

-San Francisco Chronicle

U.S. attack on Lavan Island was retaliatory in nature. President Marsden confirms: "This was a direct response to previous attacks on U.S. forces".

-N.Y. Post

President Marsden faces tough criticism on Capitol Hill Senate Majority Leader cites 'inexperience', 'incompetence' in foreign policy.

-Washington Post

Russia denounces U.S. strikes as 'naked aggression.' Chinese ambassador states: 'This violence is unnecessary and regrettable.'

-Reuters

Iranian spokesman says its forces stood down during strikes, attempting de-escalation. Pentagon officials respond by saying Iran is trying to conceal 'significant capability gaps.'

-Baltimore Sun

The Persian Gulf

"This briefing is classified Secret," Sweater Boy informed the assembled Gray Wolves ready room. There was simply no way to pack the entire squadron into the CVIC for this briefing, much less the other squadrons in the air wing, who were receiving similar briefs from their own intelligence officers. Both hatches leading into the compartment were secured, with masters-at-arms posted outside to make sure there were no keyhole peepers.

"I know the rumors have been fast and furious, but I've got the straight gouge, both good and bad. The bad news first: we *are* being extended on deployment—" a loud groan went up, forcing Chadwick to raise his voice, "—BUT ONLY TEMPORARILY, a week or two at most."

"Pipe down!" Lurch barked from his seat in the front row, looking back at the room like an angry parent in the front seat of the family station wagon. The loud groans gave way to quieter rumblings of discontent.

Sweater Boy pushed his Clark Kents farther up the bridge of his nose. "The good news is that Carrier Strike Group Five, headed up by USS *Coral Sea,* is transiting eastward across the Med for the Suez Canal, and will relieve us as soon as they arrive. It is unknown at this point whether CENTCOM is going to hold her outside the Gulf or have her transit through the Strait. The *Nassau* group is already here, in the Gulf of Oman, and the decision has been made to put them into the Persian Gulf where they'll be most effective. That will happen tomorrow.

"As you have probably also seen on the news, Iran has declared the Strait of Hormuz closed to inbound U.S. military traffic and stated that any ships attempting to navigate west through the strait may be attacked without warning. According to them, this is in response to escalating U.S. aggression in the region. The State Department has denounced the claim as 'saber rattling' and the White House has stated that the United States will not allow any nation to restrict freedom of navigation in the Persian Gulf or anywhere else. In short, it's business as usual in the war of words. Here on the pointy end, however, you'll notice that we are coordinating continuous AWACS coverage with the Air Force and maintaining round-the-clock ready alerts and CAPs. The Air Force has been helping with that as well for a change, bless their little hearts. There have been some other interesting developments as well. Taken alone they merit caution. Taken together? They are concerning."

Sweater Boy called for the lights, and the ready room darkened. He used a slide projector to begin showing the aviators overhead reconnaissance photographs of various parts of Iran. "First, all of you have been asking about recent Iranian acquisitions. That picture has firmed up some, and I'm able to show you these." He showed them a series of slides detailing the IRIAF air base at Shiraz, where they spied a squadron's worth of gray-black single seat Fulcrums sitting in two neat rows. Some close-up shots showed the blood-red color of the wingtips, but even more interesting was the overhead view of the some of the maintenance personnel servicing the flight line.

"I was about to say that those jets look Russian," Lurch said from the front row, "and I don't think Iranians are natural blondes. Are we looking at what it looks like we're looking at?"

"Yes you are, XO, and it gets even better," Sweater Boy added. He switched to a new set of slides, at a different airbase. The resolution of the images taken by their spy satellites never ceased to amaze them. The joke was that they could read the headlines off a newspaper, but it wasn't really a joke. In this case, the two-seat Flankers with their Chinese-blue camouflage paint schemes, and their canopy rails and noses marked with kanji ideograms were plain to see. "NSA and Langley have confirmed that there are two groups of mercenary pilots augmenting the IRIAF. For now, we think it is only these two units, which are both squadron-strength. We're trying to find out if there are more of them."

"Wait, go back one," Fargo interrupted. Sweater Boy clicked back one slide, and Fargo stood up to point at one end of the westernmost row of jets. "That one there. It's single seat, and the rest are two seaters. Its planform is painted like a dragon, and the rest of it is a solid color. Do you see it?"

"Son of a *bitch!*" Neo swore from somewhere in the audience.

"What?" Skipper Jefferson asked sharply. Neo typically flew as his WSO.

"Yeah, you're right, sir!" Sweater Boy said, leaning in and peering at the slide more closely. "What Commander Thorsen is saying is that the single-seater is the plane that did the supersonic overflight of this ship. It's the one—"

"—The one that killed the Irish brothers?" Chill interrupted flatly.

"Yes sir. It's highly likely."

Jefferson got up out of his chair and faced his squadron, pointing at the slide behind him. "Ya'll burn that image into your heads, ya got me? *Remember it*," he ordered grimly, before taking his seat. Everyone knew what he was implying: *open season.*

"Why just the one single seater? And why the unique paint scheme?" Lurch asked.

"They've got a ringer in the group," Fargo interjected. "That jet is flown by their Richtofen, or something along those lines. Probably the group leader, but in any case someone who warrants special treatment. That's a customized paint scheme, and they aren't afraid to let us see it."

"There's more," Sweater Boy went on. "So far we've identified the base where they are housing at least one squadron of JF-17's. We think there may be one, possibly two more. Our best guess is that the Iranians have sourced the Thunders either directly from China, or indirectly from China through Pakistan. We don't know yet if they are being flown by IRIAF pilots or contractors."

"We're seeing the *what*. Do we know the *why*?" Jefferson asked.

"No sir, although there is some speculation that the contractors are there to help train the IRIAF on their new equipment. If I may," he continued. He switched over to slides showing isolated image-captures of large, tracked vehicles moving mobile launchers in high, rough terrain. Different photos showed a more distant perspective, giving them a grasp of where the sightings had taken place with respect to coastlines. In other areas, heavy equipment was being used to cut fresh roads into mountainous coastal areas.

"They're putting in SAM sites," Lurch said.

"A *lot* of SAM sites," Sweater Boy added. "They've got all the makings of a substantial integrated air defense system. Once in place and operational—"

"—Hold up a tick," the skipper interrupted again. "How old is this data?"

Sweater Boy looked uncomfortable. "Some of the imagery is a month old. It takes a while to analyze the data, make classifications on which systems we're seeing, and then get it disseminated down to us."

"So, what you're saying is that these SAM sites are potentially already in place?"

"Yes sir."

"Jesus!" Stinky mumbled to Fargo. "That could give them solid SAM coverage over the entire northern half of the Gulf!"

"You betcha," Fargo replied grimly. *They might have shot down our entire Lavan Island strike. Why didn't they?*

The XO was thinking along the same lines as Fargo. "Lieutenant Chadwick," Lurch said, "was this assessment made *before* our strike on Lavan Island?"

"No sir," Sweater Boy answered quickly. "It was in work—this is new data to us. However, there is a possibility that the strike was within range of coastal SA-10 envelopes without us knowing it."

"So why on Earth wouldn't they have engaged us? They had a Mainstay up when we were launching the strike. They *knew* we were coming. Now we're hearing that they may have had long-range SAMs in position and just opted not to use them?"

"That's right, sir," Sweater Boy said seriously. "What it probably means is that they don't feel their level of proficiency on the gear is adequate to use just yet."

"Or they are waiting to spring the mother of all surprises on us at a time of their choosing. Are they using contractors for the SAMs as well?" the skipper asked.

"Unknown, sir," Sweater Boy replied flatly. "There hasn't been much SIGINT pertaining to these equipment buys, and as you know, human sources on the ground are practically non-existent these days. All we have are these satellite captures. Langley is beating the bushes in Russia and China to try and find out more about these contractors. All we can say for sure is that they aren't active duty Russian or PRC military."

"Active duty or not, they're still *military*," Fargo interjected with a hint of exasperation. "There aren't any civilian fighter pilots in Russia and China. How you label them is just semantics."

"Yes sir," Sweater Boy agreed. "That's how it shapes up. A hand went up in the back, and the AIO pointed. "Yes?"

"This delay is gonna hose up our port call in Rota, isn't it?"

"Above my paygrade, Chunder. Sorry."

Lurch turned once more and looked daggers at Chunder, ready to fang him, but he was pre-empted by Skipper Jefferson standing up again to face the squadron. "Last word I got from upstairs is that the port call is still on, but y'all know that's written in wet sand."

Cheers this time, subsiding fast under more threatening glares from the XO.

"Last couple of points," Sweater Boy said. "All three Iranian *Kilo* Class subs have sortied from Bandar Abbas. There is no word from flag country on whether we are tracking them or not, I merely bring it up as a data point. The Iranians also have a fleet of midget submarines. Apparently they went to some effort to disguise the fact that those have put to sea as well, utilizing mock-up decoys to make us think they were still in port. How we discovered the deception is classified well above us, so don't ask because even I don't know. The midget submarines are potential minelayers if Iran decides to go that route, or they can lie in wait at a chokepoint, virtually undetectable, and pop off a couple of torpedoes each. That amounts to a decent spread of torpedoes if they are operating together. We all understand that this isn't anything a fighter squadron can do anything about, but the overall point is that we're seeing a mass sortie of almost all Iranian sea assets. There are also signs that Revolutionary Guard speedboats and numerous other small craft are staging in and around Bandar Abbas, Saheli Latidan, and Kooh Mobarak. All three are located along the eastern coast of the chokepoint formed by the strait. Finally, we have imagery indicating that shore-based anti-ship missile batteries have been moved as far south as Kooh Mobarak in the eastern strait, coupled with SAM batteries for self-defense. The bottom line, gentlemen—"

"—And ladies!" Deedee hollered with mock indignation. Sweater Boy blushed slightly, but plowed on: "The bottom line, *people*, is that there are real indications that Iran is serious about its threats. The deployment of submersibles is alarming, given their usual lack of confidence when it comes to submarine operations."

"Any talk of pre-emption? Taking them out before the strike group transits?" someone asked.

"No," Skipper Jefferson replied, taking the question. "The subject came up, but the level of violence involved would be tantamount to declaring open war on Iran. Part of our planning and coordination with the Air Force involves defensive contingencies, but the NCA was burned in the media by Iran's lack of response to our Lavan Island strike. In short, it made us look like schoolyard bullies, and they want to avoid that again at all costs."

"The Iranians are winning the information war," Dexter said to nobody, but loud enough to be heard.

"What was that?" Chill asked. "Come again?"

"It's information warfare, sir. The Iranians have provoked our actions and succeeded in painting us as the aggressor, which in turn is being used to paralyze our willingness to respond. Especially now when the *Nassau* group is about to be put in a vulnerable position."

"What are you, Dexter, some kind of armchair admiral?" Chill grinned, generating a round of subdued laughter. Fargo wasn't laughing, and neither was Stinky or Lurch. "Are you some kind of Horatio Nelson or Raymond Spruance? Are you bucking for a transfer to the admiral's staff?"

Dexter blushed. "No sir."

"Then how about you stay in your lane there, Sun Tzu, and worry about putting warheads on foreheads? Strike groups have been transiting the strait since before you were a gleam in your daddy's eye, and nobody's been sunk yet. Iran knows we'll *end* them if it comes to that. Let the guys with stars on their collars worry about grand strategy. Kay?"

"Yes sir," Dexter replied, slinking slightly into his chair.

Now Lurch stood up. "That brings up a point, though. I hear our intel officer outlining some serious threats, and the questions he gets back are about port calls and going home. In the meantime, we've buried two of our own and the plane captains are painting Iranian flags on some of our jets. Listen and hear me CFB, Wolves—you'd better start conducting yourselves as though we're at war, not like we're on our way to the beach. The time for that will be when we're passing Gibraltar heading west, and even then it's not too late to get turned around and sent back. Get your heads straight! Is everyone picking up what I'm putting down?" There was a low rumble of affirmation, which only made Lurch scowl harder. "I can't *hear* you!"

"*Yes sir!*" the room answered with volume.

"Amen," Stinky whispered in Fargo's ear.

"Last item," Sweater Boy said, taking back the floor as the skipper and XO sat back down. "The plan for now is to have the *Nassau* group transit under the 'right of innocent passage' rules we normally use. That means ships buttoned down, no flight ops, and no major emitters in use during the transit. However, at the first sign of Iranian aggression, that goes out the window. If you are airborne and hear the codeword 'Starlight', it means the entire strike group is going active and setting Condition I."

"What it will really mean is that the balloon has gone up," Lurch called from the front, clarifying things. "If you hear 'Starlight', be ready to start shooting."

"Shit's getting real," Stinky mumbled to Fargo, unknowingly parroting Dexter's words in the jet the day of the big air battle.

Fargo's reply was the same: "Yah, you betcha!"

***

USS *North Carolina*
Southwest of Bandar Abbas

"Sonar, Conn, track update on India Kilo 2," the watch officer said quietly into his headset.

"Conn, Sonar. I hold contact India Kilo 2 bearing 180 degrees at 2500 yards. Course 180, speed 4 knots, depth 110 feet. Bearing rate is holding constant. I currently hold passive sonar contact on her transient," the sonarman added, indicating that he was tracking the Iranian Kilo using the boat's sonar, not the experimental laser-tracking system. The experimental system wasn't needed now, because the Kilo was putting out some sort of mechanical transient that was generating noise. Their sonarmen thought it might be a loose equipment mounting somewhere inside the hull, but they couldn't say for certain. All they knew was that it was causing a vibrating 'rattle', generating a frequency line that could be tracked. LCDR Dubicki had just grinned and commented: "Better lucky than good!" when informed about it.

"Very well," replied LT Whorley. He moved around to check the chart, and confirmed what they already knew: the Iranian submarine was making bare steerageway, in a slow creep towards the *Boxer* strike group which was southwest of them and heading in their direction. Their UUV communications drone was trailing well behind them where the Kilo had no chance of detecting it; every couple hours it would move to mast depth to send and receive updates from the strike group via SATCOM, with the drone using its laser-communications relay to transfer the information to *North Carolina* in real time. Given the way things were going topside, they were expecting to receive orders to engage the Iranian submarine at any time.

The *Nassau* group's planned transit of the Strait of Hormuz was short-lived. USS *Green Bay*, a *San Antonio* Class amphibious dock ship, had struck a mine in the Gulf of Oman, approximately 60 NM south of Bandar Abbas near the entrance to the strait, almost due east of the northern tip of Oman. The bulk of the expeditionary strike group turned south immediately, heading back into the Arabian Sea under orders from COMFIFTHFLT. Two destroyers remained in company with *Green Bay,* one alongside to render firefighting, medical, and damage control assistance, while the other was standing sentry with her AEGIS system fully activated and missiles primed to fly.

Nassau and *Green Bay* were conducting flight operations between the ships, running portable pumps, damage control specialists, and firefighting gear one way, while evacuating dead and wounded personnel the other way, using four MV-22 Osprey tiltrotor aircraft. Some of the severely wounded were being medevac'd directly to the United Arab Emirates. Harriers from the *Nassau* were flying as well, holding a RESCAP south of the stricken ship, where the coastlines were far enough apart for international airspace to exist. CENTCOM and Fifth Fleet had placed a request for diplomatic clearance for U.S. aircraft to operate in Omani airspace, but approval was pending.

Hours after the initial mishap, Iran was making no claims of responsibility, or doing anything to interfere with the rescue effort. Of course, CENTCOM had one suspect and one only for the placement of sea mines in international waters. The problem was *proving* it.

In summary, there was a lot going on topside right now.

LT Reese appeared in the control room, looking for an update from his friend. It was hard for his men to sit idle, standing by, without knowing anything about what was happening. Captain Bergstrom gave him a look that signaled his presence was a nuisance; Reese nodded respectfully to the captain and resolved to keep his visit as brief as possible. XO Dubicki saw him and pulled him aside—LT Whorley was busy and didn't need any distractions.

"Just checking in, sir," Reese said quietly.

"Well, right now we're wondering if the Kilo we let go to the east is the culprit that laid a mine or two in the path of the *Nassau* group. If so, there's a chance the boat we're trailing is going to try the same stunt on the *Boxer* group. We're expecting a shoot order any time before they can get into position."

"Does this mean we're at war with Iran?"

Dubicki grinned. "It probably depends on who you ask. I bet the crew of the *Green Bay* would say 'yes' right about now. Sometimes, though, it's about plausible deniability. Say we quietly put a Mark 48 into an Iranian boat and nobody else was around to see it. Who can say *what* happened, right? We were never here."

"And everyone knows those guys aren't proficient at operating their boats," Reese nodded, seeing the XO's point.

"Exactly. The *Boxer* group is headed in this direction to support the *Nassau* group during their transit, even though that's off for now. They're almost directly between Dubai and Abu Musa island, without much sea room to play with. Captain says that COMFIFTHFLT might use this as an excuse to move them all the way through the strait into the Gulf of Oman on the pretext of rendering aid to the *Green Bay*. It saves some political face and gets us the hell out of this duck pond."

"What about the mines?"

"The prevailing opinion is that there are only a few, and carefully placed in the path of the oncoming strike group. Civil shipping traffic has slowed down and spread out a bit, but nobody else has had any problems. Iran doesn't want to strangle shipping, because they need to move their oil as well. They just want us out of the picture."

"It makes sense, but that's just a guess," Reese said tensely. "What if the prevailing opinion is wrong?"

"Then the whole gulf might be a lake of fire if one of those supertankers hits a mine and spills its load of crude. That would suck, wouldn't it? Except for those who can travel *under* water," Dubicki grinned.

Bubble heads are just plain crazy! Reese thought to himself. "I…uh, see your point, XO."

"Conn, Sonar! Transient, bearing three two zero! It's a ways off, but it sounded like an explosion on the surface."

The tension level in the control center went up palpably.

"Think someone else maybe just hit a mine?" Reese asked the XO.

"It's possible," Dubicki replied, his grin gone. "Better clear out," he added. Reese nodded, but didn't leave the control center completely. He stepped just beyond the open hatchway and listened from there.

"Sonar, Conn. Any read on how far?"

"Negative sir, but it's a long way off. The acoustic line was weak and there's lot of bottom bounce," the sonarman replied. Bottom bounce was an acoustic condition where sound waves in shallow water ricocheted back and forth between the ocean floor and the surface. In effect, the shallow depth formed a natural sound channel, allowing loud noises to carry over long distances. "Conn, Sonar! Possible depth change on contact India Kilo 2! She's holding course but going shallow…I'm getting hull popping noises."

"She must have heard it too," Whorley said. "She's going up to check in."

"Either that or she intends to snorkel and run her diesels," Bergstrom replied. "If she plans on lying in wait for the *Boxer* group, she'll want to do it with a full battery charge. Could be both," he added. "Either way, it suits me. Attention in the control center: captain has the conn," he announced with an annoying hint of self-importance. "Belay your reports."

"Captain has the conn," Whorley echoed.

"Bring her up to mast depth. Slight up angle initially, and then match the Kilo. Try to stay in her baffles as we rise. Signals, extend the ESM mast as well." Things were tense and quiet for the next several minutes as *North Carolina* shallowed out, shadowing her Iranian quarry to the surface. She finally reached the point where her sail was just under water and her masts could broach the open air. Captain Bergstrom ordered them back to two knots to minimize any visible wake or 'white capping' their masts might create on the surface. As soon as the masts were exposed, sensitive receivers began picking up frantic communications on all channels. The feed was piped over the speakers in the control center, and the color drained from Bergstrom's face when he realized what he was hearing.

"Jee-suz!" he breathed. "Down masts! Lieutenant Whorley, sound battle stations!"

"Down masts, aye aye, sir!" He turned to the chief of the boat. "COB, Sound battle stations, torpedo!"

"Sound battle stations torpedo, aye aye!"

"Weps!" Bergstrom called. "Firing point procedures. Update firing solution on India Kilo 2!"

"Aye aye, captain!"

Dubicki saw Reese standing in the hatchway to the control room, looking confused. He moved over to the SEAL officer. "What is it?" Reese asked tensely.

Dubicki looked grimmer than Reese had ever seen him. "All hell's breaking loose up top."

VII

The Persian Gulf

The afternoon's CAP assignment for the Gray Wolves was Fargo and Dexter in Lobo 201 leading the section, with Deedee Danford and Stinky Mullen flying wing in Lobo 209. They were assigned a radial off the ship that put them well out to the northeast—about as near to the mouth of the Strait of Hormuz as they could get and remain within international airspace. It was considered a high threat area for obvious reasons, and the Gray Wolves had sent their best. After the word came down about USS *Green Bay* hitting a mine near the strait, a sense of dark inevitably had settled over the aviators of *Boxer*'s air wing. Nothing was officially declared, but there was no question anymore that they were on the front lines of a war that was coming at any moment.

Boxer was running four CAP stations: two outer stations utilizing Super Hornets, and two inner stations utilizing legacy Hornets. Four more sections of fighters were manned and ready on the flight deck, two sitting Alert-5 on the catapults with two more on Alert-15 behind them. CENTCOM was running another pair of CAP stations farther west, over the open waters between Qatar and the U.A.E. These CAPs were made up of F-15E and F-16C fighters on station, with more on ready alert at Al Dhafra and Al Udeid. A USAF E-3 Sentry was operating south of the Air Force CAP stations, while Boxer had an E-2C Hawkeye airborne to the southwest of the strike group, and south of its western, outer-ring CAP station. The Air Force aircraft were restricted to self-defense due to combat holds placed on them by the governments of their host nations. The Iranians didn't know that, however. The positioning of the Air Force CAP stations did little to help the *Boxer* group; they were mostly an additional show of force.

Due to the increased threat of Iranian SAMs, each Super Hornet on CAP carried two HARM anti-radar missiles, cutting into their anti-air load. The HARMs were designed to home on

SAM radars and destroy them, but that might not help much if the aircraft was already well inside the kill zone of the SAM in question. By the time the HARMs did their job, so would the SAMs. Fargo's flight was already within the engagement zone of any number of threat SAM-types, if they were situated on nearby islands or the southern coast of Iran. Right now, there was no evidence that any of these sites were in play, and no SAM radars of any type had been detected so far.

It wasn't much fun to be in the air today. The Iranians were playing hell with their communications channels, clobbering them with broadcasts in Farsi and spurious attempts at jamming, and forcing them to do a lot of frequency-hopping. Iranian controllers would randomly broadcast on Guard that U.S. planes were violating their airspace, accompanied by vague threats. It was simple harassment, but it raised the workloads of the fighter crews and airborne controllers, shortened tempers, and put everyone on edge. The good news was that the weather wasn't bad: there was a scattered layer at about four thousand feet, and then another scattered layer at about seventeen thousand punctuated by a lot of puffy cumulus clouds. It was a nice day for flying, except for the prospect of a shooting war looming over them like a shadow.

A small reprieve on the airspace restrictions came when they were given diplomatic clearance to fly in portions of Omani airspace. The Hawkeye controllers passed them a new set of reference waypoints, which Dexter feverishly plugged into the navigation system before informing Fargo that they could operate anywhere over water in Oman's airspace, as well as over land in a twenty-mile radius around Khasab on the Omani side, equating to the whole northern part of the Musandam Peninsula. It changed the whole nature of the aerial picture and gave them substantial buffer space to the east and southeast. A few minutes later Strike called them and shifted their CAP station another twenty miles to the northeast, almost over the strait itself. It put their CAP waypoint inside Omani airspace, based on the new clearance, and put them about 70 NM away from *Boxer*.

The clearance to overfly Oman also opened the airspace over the strait to aircraft flying up the Gulf of Oman from Masirah or the USS *Nassau.* The latter shifted her RESCAP station to the north, closer to the stricken *Green Bay* and her surface escorts. The two destroyers escorting USS *Green Bay* temporarily chopped to the operational control of the *Boxer* strike group, linking their combat systems, and seamlessly integrating into the force. The two groups of ships were 110 NM apart and separated by the Musandam Peninsula, but the airborne Hawkeye served as the relay between them. This gave the *Boxer* group a clear air and surface picture stretching over three hundred miles from east to west, covering the whole eastern portion of the Gulf and the southern coast of Iran around the Strait of Hormuz. It was good coverage, but the number of air and surface contacts to be tracked inside it was staggering.

Fargo's flight hadn't been on their revised station for ten minutes before things started happening. It started with communications between Strike and a flight of Marine Corps Harriers off *Nassau* operating nearby. The Harriers, callsign Bulldog, were co-opted off their RESCAP station on the pretense of time-critical tasking and ordered to investigate a surface ship operating just south of the middle of the strait. There was also a P-3C in the vicinity, but Strike ordered it to stand off at medium altitude and continue its electro-optical surveillance of the contact. Dexter informed Fargo that they were closer to the surface contact than the Harriers, but apparently Strike wanted to hold them where they were—the number of airborne contacts over Iran had been slowly building for the past half hour.

The concern over this surface contact was clarified by Strike's follow-on remarks to Bulldog flight. The P-3's optical surveillance had detected objects going into the water off the stern of this contact. The objects had immediately sunk, which implied a possible minelaying operation. Two Seahawks with SEALs were en-route to the contact for a board-and-search operation, and Strike wanted both reconnaissance and a show of force from the Harriers.

"Bulldog 403 holds a skunk at my 320 for 24," replied a grim sounding voice with a distinctive southern drawl.

"That's your track, designate India Sierra 26. Track is declared neutral at this time. Surface warning yellow, weapons tight."

"Bulldog."

"Aww Jeez, that ain't good," Fargo muttered.

"Jeez is right," Dexter remarked. "You think Strike considered the fact that a couple Marines probably don't have the first frickin' clue what a sea-mine looks like? It could be a fishing boat dropping . . . I don't know—"

"—Big metal garbage cans?" Fargo asked with a wry grin under his helmet.

"And here we are with no anti-ship stores," Dex said glumly. "Well, whatever is happening, the Iranians are watching. Check the datalink," he added.

Fargo nodded in the front. "I see it. We got double Mainstay coverage today, east *and* west. They've got superb radar coverage on us right now, as good or better than we have on them. Have you heard of them having two AWACS up at the same time before?"

"Negative," Dexter replied.

Fargo frowned slightly, looking more closely at the link data. "Looks like they've got an assload of fighters airborne too, but they all seem to be content hanging out inside Iranian airspace."

"If they know what's good for them they'd better stay there," Dex muttered darkly from the back. "And there it is," he grunted a moment later. "Looks like I spoke too soon. Check the link."

Stinky called almost at the same time: "Hey Fargo, check the link!" Fargo was already looking: two airborne radar contacts were moving fast on an intercept heading for the flight of Harriers closing on the surface contact. For a moment, Fargo experienced a weird sense of *déjà-vu*. This was starting to remind him of the thumping incident, but uglier. If they tangled with the Iranian air force today, there would be shots fired.

"Lobo 2-1, Strike," the controller called a moment later. "Provide cover for Bulldog 403 and flight while they investigate a surface contact. New threat bearing 010 for 70 miles, on intercept course for Bulldog. Stand by for vectors from Closeout."

"Lobo 2-1, copy," Dexter replied.

"Lobo 2-1, Closeout. Your vector 270, signal Buster. Take Angels 15. Air warning red, weapons tight."

"Lobo 2-1 copies," Dexter replied. Deedee split off into combat spread, and Fargo pushed the throttles up as they temporarily turned away from the bogeys, heading west. Fargo saw it was a vector to set them up for a flanking intercept on the approaching threat, which might convince the Iranians to either head north, or at least turn away from the Harriers to address the threat of the Super Hornets instead.

"Dex, bust out the weapons checklist," Fargo said grimly. His WSO already had it ready to go.

***

Bulldog flight roared down from altitude at high subsonic speed, flying in extended loose trail. Bulldog 412, the wingman, locked up the target with an IR Maverick missile. If the surface contact took a shot at his section leader during his first pass, 412 was prepared to smoke him without further ado. Neither of the Marine pilots were in a particularly merciful mood—there were over 600 of their brothers and sisters aboard the stricken *Green Bay*, and some of them were dead this morning.

Bulldog 403 dropped down to 100 FT over the water and made his first run over the contact at 450 knots. It was a high speed pass that didn't give the pilot much time to see what was going on, but he could make as many follow-up passes as he wanted. The first pass was dedicated to finding out if they were going to shoot at him or not. No tracers or missile smoke trails rose to meet him, and he broke hard right about a half mile beyond the contact, bleeding energy and picking up something approximating a downwind to set up for a second pass. He didn't want to loop back in too close because he knew his wingman was booming along in trail behind him. As he rolled out of his 180 degree turn and began to accelerate again, he looked back and saw his wingman flash past the target as well. From his vantage point it didn't look as though any fire was being directed at his wingman, either. "Hey Swampy," 403 called to his wingman, "you see anything?"

"Didn't see no bullets," came the reply in the form of another deep southern drawl. "There are a few guys on deck, but I went by too fast to see any weapons. What about you?"

"'Bout the same. See anything in the water?"

"Negative. Hell, Bo, I wouldn't know a sea mine if it blew up in my face. Aren't they round with spikes or something like that?"

"Bo" Ritchie chuckled. "Only on Gilligan's Isle, brother. I'm coming around to give 'em another look."

"Roger, I'm set up to cover you."

There was a sudden burst of static on the frequency, and then another voice cut in, speaking heavily accented English. "Attention U.S. aircraft, attention U.S. aircraft, this is the Iranian Revolutionary Guard. Be advised that you have penetrated Iranian airspace! You are required to withdraw to your mother ship and land immediately!"

MAJ "Bo" Ritchie swore under his breath, switching over to his non-encrypted radio and keying it angrily. "Iranian Guard, this is a United States Marine Corps fighter operating outside your airspace. I am well south of the Iranian boundary."

The Iranian sounded a lot more animated now that someone had answered. "American fighters! You are in Iranian airspace! Withdraw immediately or you will be attacked! Acknowledge!" This wasn't unusual—the Iranians commonly tried such intimidation tactics, but U.S. policy was essentially to ignore them. Today was a little different, obviously.

"Iranian Guard, you'd better check your gear, pal. My flight is outside your airspace and any attempt to engage me will be met with deadly force. Y'all have a good one, now." He switched back over to encryption. "Swampy, kick Green-3."

"Two," his wingman replied. Bo reached down by feel and switched the radio over to a different tactical frequency, and a moment later two mic flashes over the radio let him know that Swampy was with him. He watched the horizon turn sideways as he reefed the Harrier into another hard right turn, bringing it back around and preparing for a slower pass that would give him a better look. He'd climbed to 500 FT on his downwind, and the water got closer again in his turn as he let the jet slip back to the lower altitude. Many jet pilots weren't comfortable yanking and banking this close to the water, but the Marines were old hands at operating low, usually in support of Marine infantry under fire. The brackish green blur of the water under the wing and canopy yielded a heady sensation of speed as the Harrier rolled out of its turn and lined up for another run. The second time he overflew the craft he was able to see a lot more: the ship was corvette sized, and he spied something that looked like a mounted machine gun toward the bow of the vessel. There was another located roughly amidships, but both weapons were currently unmanned. There was a knot of men on the stern deck, where they were rapidly trying to cover up a row of metal objects with a large tarpaulin. Whatever the objects were, they were lined up on the starboard side of the stern. It recalled the 50's era war movies featuring tin can destroyers with depth charge racks. Another tarpaulin already covered objects on the port side. The two lines of objects were uneven, suggesting that some had already been dumped overboard.

It looked more than a little incriminating.

"Strike, Bulldog 403. We've conducted two overflights of track India Sierra 26. The craft appears to be a gunboat, currently heading 285 at approximately 5-10 knots. The vessel is mounting two twin fifties, one on the bow and the other on her starboard beam. Her crew is in the process of covering up several metal objects arranged in two rows, port and starboard, on her stern. We can't make out anything in the water. The craft has taken no hostile action against us."

"Strike copies, stand by," came the reply. Swampy completed his second flyby of the target behind Bo, didn't have anything to add, and so he stayed off the radio. Bo brought his jet around a third time, preparing to make a third pass at a different angle. He thought for a moment about the Harrier's pending replacement, the AV-36 Shark, that was rumored to have a 360-degree electro-optical targeting suite—one that would allow him to look over a target like this from a long way off, at a much safer altitude. The Harrier was a fantastic jet, but antiquated.

Bo's musings were interrupted when Strike got back to him: "Bulldog 403, Strike. The Seahawks are 20 minutes out. Maintain observation position over the target and take no further action unless advised. Notify us immediately if they drop anything into the water. Report fuel state."

Bo checked his gauges; he was looking good, and the *Nassau* wasn't all that far away if he could cut across northern Oman on the way back. "Swampy, gas check," he called to his wingman.

"Ahhh, Swampy is tiger," his wingman reported, indicating he was good.

"Strike, Bulldog flight is tiger," he replied.

"Copy, Bulldog. Be advised, you have bogeys on an intercept course. Threat bears 018 for 40, medium, hot. Lobo 2-1 and flight will provide cover. Advise immediately if you are spiked. Air warning red, weapons tight."

Bo didn't like *that* at all. "Strike, request permission to drop the surface contact and assume an air to air posture."

"Negative, you are out of position. Be advised that if you turn nose on to the bogeys you *will* violate Iranian airspace. Maintain visual contact with the surface contact, and Lobo will cover you."

"Strike, from 40 miles they can shoot us *without leaving* Iranian airspace!"

"Strike, Closeout," the Hawkeye controller called.

"Go, Closeout."

"Recommend Bulldog flight vectors 100 and Angels 4. They'll drag the bogeys right into Lobo's envelope, and then you can vector the P-3 back in to watch the surface contact. If the bogeys turn southeast to pick up the P-3, then Lobo and Bulldog have a four ship bracket on the bogeys. That gets everyone on solid footing here."

There was only a slight pause. "Closeout, Strike concurs. Bulldog, stand by for vectors from Closeout." A moment later the Hawkeye controller issued the vectors. The two Harriers broke away from the surface contact, heading easterly. Out to the south, the P-3C slipped back towards the potential minelayer, getting better imagery as they got closer. There was an unintended consequence of the Harriers' departure: the Iranian corvette's crew didn't realize they were still under observation from the distant patrol plane. Once the Harriers were gone, the tarpaulins were immediately removed from the mystery objects on the stern deck, and the deck crew resumed their task.

***

"Wow, good call!" Dex said appreciatively from the back seat. On the datalink, he watched the two Iranian fighters (which still weren't emitting their own radars, so it was impossible to classify them) turn to a southeasterly heading and accelerate briefly, as if to catch the Harriers in a stern chase. That didn't last long, however. Whoever was directing them from the eastern Iranian Mainstay saw the tactical disadvantage the Iranian flight was getting into, and vectored them back to the north, essentially breaking off contact for the moment. Both bogeys decelerated back to subsonic speed after their brief supersonic sprint and retreated into their own airspace. Closeout ordered Lobo to reset to their CAP station, and the Harriers were directed back to the rogue surface contact.

"Hey Fargo, you know what Confucious say?" Dex chortled in his best 'coolie' accent.

"Well, you'd know if anyone would, Wong," he grinned.

"Confucious say that the victorious general wins the battle before it is fought!"

"I think that was Sun Tzu, Dex."

"I know that, you dumb squarehead. Work with me man, I'm starving. How much longer we got out here?"

"A while." He looked back and saw that Deedee was closing in on him, slipping back into a loose parade formation. Behind them, puffy cumuliform clouds whipped past the planes at about 400 knots, with nothing but blue skies above the layer. She saw him looking over and gave him a big thumbs up. Fargo flashed her one in return. Stinky was head down in the back seat of their jet, buried in the link picture. Fargo glanced at it himself and saw that the Iranian bogeys were turning to the west and slowing considerably, paralleling their own course some fifty miles to the north of them, feet dry in their own airspace.

They'd keep a wary eye on each other, for sure. There was a lot of flying left to do this cycle, and the games might not be over with yet. Fargo told himself to stay frosty.

***

Aboard the P-3C monitoring the corvette, the TACCO watched on electro-optics as two men, barely discernable as such at this distance, rolled some sort of large metal canister off the aft end of the boat. It hit the water with a splash and sank from sight almost immediately. "Nav, fix their position," he said calmly, knowing he didn't need to issue the order, but too professional not to.

"Already done," the NAV/COMM replied smugly.

"Sensor 3, TACCO. You see that?"

"Yes sir. The pics are uplinking to Fifth Fleet and the *Boxer* group right now. Hard to say for certain, sir, but that sure as hell looked like a captor mine to me."

"It did, didn't it?" the TACCO replied, feverishly mashing buttons at his station. "Flight, TACCO. I'm sending you a fly-to point. We need to hustle over there and see if anything is visible from the surface."

"That's inside the skunk's MANPAD standoff," the pilot said hesitantly.

"I know. We need to mark that drop, though."

"Roger," the pilot replied. The TACCO felt the pitch of the four Allison turboprops change and the slight press in the seat of his pants as the pilot accelerated them from loiter to approximately 380 knots indicated airspeed. That was 25 knots short of the Orion's top speed at sea level, but about as fast as the old, tired motors would push them in level flight. In the meantime, the TACCO was duty-bound to address what he'd just witnessed.

"Nav, why don't we give him a call and see if he *hablas* the *Ingles*."

From across the center aisle, the NAV/COMM grinned and dialed up Channel 16, also known as maritime common. It was the channel all seagoing vessels were expected to always monitor. "Attention Iranian vessel at—" he added the exact lat-long coordinates, then continued: "This is a United States Navy maritime patrol aircraft. You have been observed releasing objects into a major shipping lane. Please state the nature of your operations in these waters, over." Nobody answered, even after he repeated the call two more times.

The P-3C overflew the datum point two minutes later, releasing a smoke marker and active sonobuoy as they went. They were about a quarter mile astern of the corvette, and the appearance of the patrol plane startled the deck crew into sudden action. The tarpaulins came out again, and the crew moved to cover up the objects on the stern.

"Busted!" the Sensor-3 operator chuckled grimly. It was all showing up in nice, high resolution on the electro-optics.

The TACCO scowled. If those were mines the Iranians were dropping, there was going to be *trouble*—especially after the *Green Bay* had already hit one. He felt some light-G come on as the pilot banked the aircraft away from the Iranian corvette, looking to resume a safe standoff from which they could return to their fuel-conserving loiter profile.

"Aft observers, TACCO, can you see anything in the water near the smoke marker?" Both observers were looking carefully with binoculars and Sensor-3 was scanning the area with the electro-optical camera as well, but nobody saw anything on the surface. Whatever the Iranians had dropped was underwater now. The TACCO instructed Sensor-1, the primary acoustic sensor operator, to send out an active sonar ping from their sonobuoy. They were rewarded immediately with a solid echo off a stationary object nearby, resting at a depth of only twenty feet below the surface. That *had* to be a mine. Realistically speaking, the TACCO didn't see what else it could possibly be.

"Strike, Victor Papa 33," he sent. "I have confirmation of a subsurface object, stationary, depth 20 FT, dropped by track India Sierra 26. I classify the object as a probable mine, confidence level two. Coordinates to follow, but they are being placed just south of the main shipping lane. India Sierra 26 should be declared hostile, and I request permission to engage her. Victor Papa 33 is standing by for orders."

"Victor Papa 33, this is Strike. We have your data and your visual feeds, and be advised Alpha Bravo is monitoring. Stand by one." There was a slight pause, and then an older, harder, more confident voice came onto the radio.

"Victor Papa 33, this is Alpha Bravo Actual. Put the Mission Commander on the radio."

"You've got him, sir," the TACCO replied.

"Listen carefully. We've recorded all your data and imagery, and it's being uplinked to Fifth Fleet and the NCA. Call India Sierra 26 on maritime common and order her to heave to and await boarding: I've got two helos loaded with SEALs a few minutes out. Make it very clear that we'll sink him unless he complies immediately. If he fails to stop, attempts evasive maneuvers, engages you, or puts anything else into the water, your orders are to engage and destroy. Bulldog is back overhead for strike support if needed. Read back your orders." The TACCO complied. "Very good," the admiral went on. "According to our data, we estimate he's seeded approximately four to six mines. Do you concur?"

"Yes sir," the TACCO replied. He and the Sensor-3 agreed on that.

"Okay, we have a track history on her, so we have a bearing line along which we expect the rest of the mines to be. The SEAL team might be able to obtain exact coordinates if they take the boat intact. Execute your orders."

"Aye aye, sir," the TACCO replied. A few moments later he repeated his call to the Iranian ship, ordering her to heave to or be sunk. This time they got a response, but it was a bunch of shouting in Farsi interspersed with a few key snippets of English. The phrases "do not shoot us," and "we are fisherman" figured prominently. Not even a nice try, given the presence of two fifty caliber machine guns mounted to the boat's deck and a distinct lack of fishing equipment. The NAV/COMM repeated the order for the vessel to heave to, and within a minute the ship throttled back and came to a full stop. Nothing else went into the water, and it began to look like the situation might resolve without shooting. The NAV/COMM advised Strike, and they were told to maintain electro-optical contact and await the arrival of the SEAL team.

Two MH-60R Seahawk helicopters eventually hove into view on the horizon, advancing steadily in a loose combat spread as they approached the boat. The Iranians were not expecting helicopters—there was a sudden bustle on deck when they were spotted. The lead helicopter called the ship on Channel 16, ordering them to prepare for boarding and for the entire crew to muster on the stern deck with empty hands.

That was the moment things went to hell.

Rather than complying with the orders from the helicopter, the bustle of activity turned into a frenzy. Four members of the crew raced to man the gun mounts, while two more men produced familiar and deadly-looking tubes which were already being raised to shoulders.

"MANPAD! SCRAM!" the TACCO shouted over the radio. In that one confusing moment nobody was sure who the TACCO was shouting at, so each pilot reacted instinctively. Two Seahawks and the Orion broke sharply away from the ship, all three aircraft spitting flares as two shoulder-fired SA-6 SAMs rocketed into the air, aiming at the helicopters. Fortunately, both missiles were decoyed by flares. The Seahawks were barely off the water, trading what little altitude they had for speed, and were running for a safe standoff distance. The Orion already had a good standoff—the P-3 pilot's reaction was purely instinctive.

The TACCO immediately called for master arm and the weapons checklist, and the crew worked as a well-oiled machine as they transitioned smoothly from surveillance to attack mode. The TACCO sent the pilot a heading to fly, and the crew grunted slightly under a 3G load as the pilots honked the venerable 'war pig' back around to put it nose-on to the hostile ship. As soon as the axis was correct, the TACCO targeted the ship with a pair of Mavericks and fired. The missiles streaked in and struck the corvette dead center, resulting in a spectacular explosion. Two missiles might have been overkill, but one of the offended Seahawks hit the burning hulk again for good measure, even as a full range of secondary explosions lit up the stern of the vessel. When the fireworks ended there wasn't much left but a burning oil slick, some debris, and a few mangled, broken bodies floating on the surface.

There was no way for the P-3 crew to know it, but the explosion of the minelayer was the pre-planned tripwire for everything that followed.

***

"Lobo 2-1, Closeout. Your bogeys are turning back to the southeast; it looks like they are setting up to intercept either the P-3 or Bulldog flight. Vector 275."

"Lobo 2-1, wilco," Dex replied. Fargo snapped off a pair of hand signals to Deedee. The two fighters executed a formation tactical-turn to the west before Deedee slid back out into combat spread. Fargo ran them up to mil power, knowing that the sooner they got the buffer space they needed, the sooner the controller would turn them back for the intercept. In the back, Dexter was looking closely at the big picture on datalink.

"Fargo, check tracks India Alpha 44 and 46," he called. Fargo looked, and saw what looked like another group of Iranian fighters, probably at least a four-ship division, also accelerating south toward the scene of the action. "This is gonna get touchy," Dexter added.

Fargo had to agree. In fact, it looked like a *lot* of Iranian air contacts were starting to move south and accelerate—not just in their little slice of sky, either, but along the entire southeastern coast of Iran. What he saw was a potentially major raid shaping up. He knew the bosses aboard ship were watching and evaluating, deciding what to do. Fargo swallowed, gripping the stick and throttles a bit more tightly. He didn't really want to say it out loud to Dex, but his gut was telling him that they were seeing the opening move of a major battle.

He didn't need to say it, because his WSO saw the same thing he did. "Ho-lee shit," Dexter whistled from the back seat. Others were seeing it too: radio chatter was starting to increase exponentially, and Strike started switching individual flights to ancillary frequencies to facilitate clear communications. The problem with that was that it caused information silos, with units losing situational awareness beyond their own circumstances— the fog of war was rolling in.

Closeout vectored them back to the east; Fargo saw things starting to happen fast. He eyeballed the distances and closure rates, then pushed his throttles into afterburner. Almost in the same moment, a frantic call came from Bulldog flight: "Strike, Bulldog 403! I'm spiked! I'm engaged defensive!"

"99 Alpha Bravo, this is Strike. Starlight! Starlight! Starlight! Air warning red, weapons tight. All India tracks are declared hostile. Repeat, all India tracks are Bandit! Authentication one-romeo-romeo-five!" With that declaration, they were cleared to fire on all tracks in the datalink carrying the 'India' designation, meaning they were Iranian military.

"Authentication confirmed!" Dex called from the back, his voice rising in pitch. "Stinky, sort targets!" Dex added a moment later.

Fargo glanced at his fuel, and eased them out of afterburner; they were currently at Mach 1.2 and decelerating as soon as he throttled back. *Too slow! C'mon, you fucking pig!* Fargo cursed, watching the airspeed drop off. He would have liked to stay in burner, but he had to watch their fuel now. Whatever he burned, Deedee would burn a little more staying in position on him, and their tactical situation sucked.

"Bulldog 412, Fox three!" Swampy called. He'd just loosed an air to air missile at the Iranian bandits. "Fox three again!"

"That was his whole AMRAAM wad," Dex remarked. The Harriers had been carrying Mavericks as well, limiting their air-to-air loads. "I've got racket off the lead group: Oh, man! They're *Tomcats!*"

"This is gonna break my heart, then," Fargo groused.

"Dex, I've locked up the eastern bandit," Stinky called.

"I've got the western guy. Ready to shoot," he called to Fargo.

Fargo watched the target designator box appear in his HUD, with the shoot cue appearing above it. He pulled the nose up slightly and squeezed off an AMRAAM. "Lobo 2-1, Fox-3!"

"Lobo 2-2, Fox-3!" Deedee called a moment later. Two AMRAAM missiles came off the rails of the two Super Hornets, followed by two more a few seconds later with the appropriate calls. They were firing from a flanking position on the bandits; the Persian cats were approximately thirty miles off their nose, heading left to right as they flew south, and Lobo flight flanked them from the west.

The Persian cats executed two supersonic shots apiece from medium altitude with active, then semi-active missiles. One streaked in and struck the P-3 in the vicinity of its number four engine. The Orion was running straight south at about 300 FT above sea level and 390 knots, as fast as they could push it. The missile shredded the right wing flaps, destroyed the outboard engine, and damaged the inboard; fortunately, the old Orions were built like tanks. The right wing stayed on the plane, although shrapnel scythed through the aft part of the fuselage and seriously wounded three crewmembers. The pilots maintained control, and the plane limped out of the combat area on two engines to find cover over Oman. It would survive the day.

Bulldog 403 wasn't so fortunate. The lead Iranian pilot fired two missiles at him, but Bo's threat warning receiver didn't tell him how many, only that there was at least one. He broke hard, attempting to beam the missile and firing off chaff. Bo saw the first missile detonate in a chaff cloud behind him, and turned back to the north to press the engagement, only to be hit by the second missile. In an instant the warhead caused a catastrophic failure of the large engine at the center of the jet, rupturing fuel and hydraulic lines. A secondary explosion blew the airplane apart in a spectacular fireball. Bo Ritchie died without even realizing he'd been hit.

A fourth missile fired by the Iranian Tomcats locked onto the northernmost of the two Seahawks, which couldn't outrun supersonic fighters or missiles. The helicopters were maneuvering at low speed instead, mere feet above the waves, spitting countermeasures and hoping their gyrations would fly any incoming missiles into the water or force them to overshoot. The fourth missile struck the Seahawk's rotors and exploded, shredding them. The saving grace was that the helo only fell about ten feet before hitting the water. The impact was hard, and shrapnel took its toll on the occupants, but it wasn't fatal to everyone. Two of the crew members and a handful of SEALs survived, finding themselves floating in the waters of the Gulf.

Because their second salvo was made up of semi-active missiles, the Iranian Tomcats were forced to stay nose-on to their targets until their shots resolved, limiting their own ability to evade. The AMRAAMs fired by Bulldog 412, aka 'Swampy', arrived first, both hitting the western Tomcat. The old, tired fighter pitched nose down, then tumbled and disintegrated, exploding in a gigantic fireball as fuel vapors ignited. Fargo's two missiles flew straight into the fireball and blew up, but they were wasted shots. Swampy in Bulldog 412 had managed to avenge his own wingman.

The lead Persian cat slowly arced to the east after its missiles hit their targets, supersonic in full afterburner when Deedee's AMRAAMs closed on it. With just a little more separation the Tomcat might have gotten away, but the delayed turn robbed it of sufficient head start. The two missiles blew through the chaff clouds behind the fighter and hit it squarely in the tails, blowing off the aft third of the fighter and causing the rest of it to disintegrate against the Mach 'wall'. Due to the speeds involved when they were hit, neither of the Iranian Tomcat crews survived.

"That's a kill! Splash one!" Stinky called excitedly over the radio.

"Confirmed," Dex called, feeling a little piqued that their kill had been snaked out from under them. It was okay, though: there were plenty more coming at them. "Fargo, we've got racket off the second group. Looks like two Foxhounds, and two Fulcrums." MiG 31's and 29's, respectively. Both pairs were coming south, closing on them at supersonic speed.

"Bulldog 412, Lobo 2-1. Stores check," Fargo sent.

"Bulldog 412, two heaters and guns."

"Bugout southwest. We've got four fresh bandits coming in hot."

"Negatory, Lobos. I'm all in."

"Gung ho, Marine! Bandits at Angels 14. Break off to the northeast and flank 'em. We're turning head to head with them, north of your position at about 20 miles."

"I'll stay clear of your shots. Don't mind me," Swampy called in his now-familiar drawl.

"Jesus, that guy has balls," Dex breathed. Those jarheads *are* crazy."

"Would we be bugging out if Deedee and Stinky just got fragged?"

"Point taken," Dex replied, getting on the radio. "Stinky, sort targets. You take east."

"Wilco," Stinky replied.

Each Super Hornet had two AMRAAMs and two Sidewinders left; the HARMs were useless to them right now. Statistics showed that it generally took two or three AMRAAM shots in a nasty BVR environment to boost the Pk (probability of kill) up above 80%. The bottom line was that they were about to shoot their wad and hope for the best against four bandits. Fargo glanced at the link, thinking about shouting for backup, and saw there wasn't any to be had. All hell was breaking loose, and they were operating well northeast of their originally planned CAP station, and the nearest friendlies were engaged with bandits of their own. At that moment the threat warning receiver went off: a two-toned warble that went from low to high frequency as it detected a missile launch against them. At almost the same moment, a target designator box appeared on his HUD along with the shoot cue.

"Bandits locked," Dex reported.

"Fox three!" Fargo called repeatedly, squeezing the trigger every two seconds until all the AMRAAMs were gone. It was the longest six-count of his life. He was vaguely aware of Deedee calling her shots and remarking in a strangely calm voice that she was spiked by the MiGs and going defensive. Fargo echoed her call, telling Dexter to punch off their external tanks as he jammed the throttles into burner and broke hard right, diving for the deck and mentally urging the Rhino to go *faster.* He began firing off chaff and flares; it was possible that the incoming missiles would have both active radar and infrared terminal guidance. It was only at that moment that he wondered if these latest opponents were Iranian, or foreign expats. There was no way to know.

The irony of their situation was not lost on Fargo—this was the very sort of engagement the F-14 had been designed for. With a section of Tomcats and a full 4-Phoenix / 2-AMRAAM / 2-Sidewinder mix, he and Deedee could have shot all six of these gomers *long* before the bad guys could fire back, and they'd still have enough missiles left over for another round of bandits. The F-14 didn't have AMRAAM capability when it was retired, but it had been in the works. *We would have had it by now,* Fargo reasoned, *probably with something better than the Phoenix as well! Could-a, should-a, would-a!* he swore viciously to himself, as he flew for their lives.

Both aviators were hawking the threat receiver and doing the 'Linda Blair', craning their necks and looking for visible signs of missiles. Fargo caught sight of a smoke trail at their eight o'clock, coming fast. He broke left, punching out more chaff and flares. The missile took the bait, swerving into a chaff cloud and blowing apart. Fargo came out of burner, cursing some more as the Rhino immediately bled airspeed in the turn, acting like a tired whore. He unloaded the jet for knots and went back into burner, trading altitude for airspeed, but that trick only worked until you ran out of altitude, or gas. The bottom line was that their overall energy state was bleeding down, and they were still spiked according to the threat warning receiver.

Fargo scanned the sky and hollered at Dex to talk to him; he could make out two dark, vaguely vertical looking smears in the sky out to the east, descending and trailing thick black smoke as they fell. Obviously some of their missiles had hit *something,* but there was no knowing whose missiles had hit what or where any surviving bandits were now, unless Dex found them on radar and fast. Under better circumstances he could call Closeout for a clear-eyed assessment of what was what, but the radios were bonkers, and it was apparent from the panicked Vampire calls in the background that their entire force was engaged in a pitched battle. It was then that he noticed that the datalink picture had gone mostly dark—their AWACS support was missing. Without it, all they would see was what their own radar was pointing at. He was too busy to worry about it for now.

"Deedee, check in!" he called.

Nothing.

"Lobo 2-2, check in!" he repeated, desperately scanning the skies out ahead and to their right. "Dex! You got 'em?"

Dexter pulled his head out of his radar and squirmed around to the right, checking their whole right hemisphere. "I don't see 'em," he replied after a moment.

"Lobo, Bulldog, I've got two bandits on radar about fourteen miles east of you and closing. Your wingman is down and y'all bagged two of them. I'm flanking them but still out of Sidewinder range. If you turn southeast it'll help me out!"

"Got 'em!" Dex called. "Twenty left and twelve miles, hot! They're two thousand feet below us!" Fargo unloaded to zero-G, and jettisoned the HARMs—they were nothing but deadweight and drag, now. At that moment he would have traded his left nut for more AMRAAMs instead of those now-worthless HARMs, but life just wasn't fair. Free of all external stores and tanks except for two wingtip mounted Sidewinders, the Super Hornet finally seemed to find some acceptable acceleration as it leapt forward in the pushover. Fargo was caught between a rock and a hard place: his wingman was down, he was outnumbered, and well inside the enemy's range in a jet that *couldn't outrun its pursuers.* Not that he considered it, but running away simply wasn't an option at this point—not when there was a wounded P-3 and a Seahawk somewhere behind him, and Bulldog 412 charging in where angels feared to tread. Even if he could disengage, he wouldn't. Simple self-preservation was no longer a priority—it was just kill or be killed. The best chance for all of them now was for he and Dexter to press into Sidewinder range, fangs out.

Sharp eyes and his HUD picked out all three players. Two more radar missiles came off enemy rails—point blank shots with too much closure. Fargo's defensive canopy roll was more instinctive than necessary as the missiles blew past without even a chance to track him. He'd already selected Sidewinder—it was all he had left—and took an off-boresight shot as the three jets entered the merge. His missile came off the rails and hooked sharply left. It tried, but overshot the target due to high closure and went stupid. Both MiGs pulled vertical with an excess of energy, going into afterburner and accelerating straight up. That helped Swampy, whose own Sidewinder tracked beautifully into the tailpipe of the closest enemy jet and blew off its back end. The MiG wreckage stalled out and tumbled; the ejection seat fired a moment later as its pilot abandoned ship. Fargo realized that the MiGs had no idea the Harrier was there, and it gave him an idea.

"Bulldog, I've got tally on you," he called. "I think the MiG only sees me. I'm the bait."

"Got it!" Swampy called, grunting under heavy-G as he pulled for all he was worth.

Almost as soon as he made the call, he knew it might work out for the Harrier, but not for them. Fargo felt a sense of helplessness as the Fulcrum converted on them, pulling over the top and straight back down. He could have rolled and taken his last off-boresight shot, but Swampy was mixed up with them now and he couldn't risk his own missile tracking the Harrier instead of the MiG. The first IR missile came off the MiG a moment later, followed by another about a second after that. Fargo used up the energy the jet had left in a last-ditch defensive break, firing off the last of his flares.

One missile ate into a flare and exploded. The second tracked in perfectly, hitting the Super Hornet right in the hot nozzles of its twin engines. Missile fragments and shrapnel blew through both engines and the port vertical stabilizer. The jet shuddered so violently that Fargo thought they were going to explode outright, but somehow, miraculously, it kept flying for a few precious moments. Time seemed to compress to a single, infinite moment. Fargo popped the speed brake, pulled straight up and bled the last of his airspeed as the annunciator panel lit up like a Christmas tree decorated in red. Dexter was shouting something at him when their left engine exploded violently, and Lobo 201 departed controlled flight. The fighter cartwheeled toward the sea in flames; in the cockpit, both aviators were slammed sideways almost hard enough to knock them unconscious. Fargo's helmet cracked against the canopy hard enough to star it, and his vision swam. He thought he heard Dexter shouting for them to eject, but maybe he was the one shouting. His hand groped for the yellow-striped handle between his legs, and he instinctively threw his head back and tried to straighten his back up as he pulled it.

The canopy blew off the jet and the seats fired a split second later, punching them both out of the doomed aircraft. Fargo had never ejected from an airplane before; he'd been briefed on what to expect but no description could prepare him for the violence of it. Sharp, searing pain lanced through his right arm, and the slipstream tore at him. He was surprised to feel the jolt of the chute deploying what seemed like only a moment later—he never noticed the seat separation, but then again the parachute riggers always said that if you had enough time to notice the seat wasn't gone, then it had malfunctioned, and you were in deep trouble.

As if he wasn't already.

Fargo was too groggy from hitting his head to perform his post-ejection procedures. Fortunately, his gear was designed to help keep him alive even if he was incapacitated. He managed to release his seat pan, but that was it. He tried to look around and see if he could spot Dexter, but the parachute risers were bunched up around his helmet and he could barely turn his head at all. He thought to look up and check his chute, but when he tried to reach up he found that only his left arm would work; his right arm dangled loosely and felt like it was on fire.

He had no idea how long it took for him to swing down to the water in his chute. He knew they were low when he punched out, but it still seemed an eternity. The seat pan containing Fargo's raft hit the water before he did, and the saltwater activated charges auto-inflated the raft. Then it was Fargo's turn—his first thought hitting the water was that it was *cold,* and it woke him right up for a minute. The impact jarred his arm, and he howled in pain. His harness Koch fittings and life-preserver lobes were also saltwater activated—they fired automatically, releasing the chute from his torso harness, and inflating the buoyant bladders built into his survival vest. The lobes were positioned to keep him on his back with his head out of the water, a feature designed to save the life of an unconscious pilot. Fortunately, there was a slight breeze that carried his parachute canopy clear so that it didn't collapse over him in the water.

His raft was only a few yards away, and he began tugging the tether awkwardly, trying to work it over to him. By the time he reached the raft and got himself into it he was just about exhausted.

Fargo fumbled with his left glove, biting at the fingers until he could work his hand out of it. He stuffed it down his torso harness and sat back, taking a few deep breaths, trying to re-cage his wits. It was then that he thought of Dex. Fargo tried to shout, but his voice came out as little more than a hoarse croak. He struggled to sit up in the raft and look around. He spotted Dexter floating in the water about fifty yards away, bobbing freely in the swells alongside his raft. The dye marker that released into the water made him easy to spot, but he wasn't moving at all as far as Fargo could tell. He found his voice. "Dex!" he called desperately. "DEX?"

Nothing.

"Shit!" Fargo swore frantically. Heedless of the sharp pain in his arm, he flung himself over onto his belly and scootched down so that his lower torso was in the water. He then began a slow, steady, but awkward frog kick. He was panting like an Olympic sprinter and just about at the end of his physical endurance roughly ten minutes later when he finally managed to reach his WSO. It was a hard swim battling his own raft, the weight of his gear, his injuries, and the current. He was tethered to his own raft and not in danger of losing it, so he let himself splash into the water once he was close and stroked the last few feet to LTJG John Wong. Fargo realized he was dead before he even reached him. His neck hung at an angle that was terribly wrong, and there was blood in the water around him as well—a *lot* of it, mixing with the green-yellow dye from the dye marker and staining the water an ominous, vaguely fluorescent brown. For all that, there was a strangely peaceful, almost triumphant look on his face. His eyes were closed, and the handsome, oriental features showing from under his flight helmet made him look even younger than he was.

"Oh no...." Fargo breathed. "Ahh, fuck no. Dex!" he cried. Fargo used the last strength he had to work himself back into his raft, and did his best to pull Dex in with him. He managed to get the WSO's body partially onto his lap, draped over his legs, before his strength gave out. He lay back panting, looking up at a deceptively tranquil sky. Devoid of anything aside from his own senses, it was strange to think that a furious battle was still raging all around them, in the sky and on the sea. His head started to spin dizzily, and that was the last thing he remembered before losing consciousness.

VIII

USS *Boxer*

RADM Brandt was glued to the Flag Tactical Data Display (FTDD) and listening to the Strike frequency when the situation in the strait began to escalate a hundred miles to the northeast of where he was sitting. He'd been here all day, even taking his lunch right in his seat rather than retiring to his mess for his repast. The situation with *Green Bay* on the far side of the strait was bad enough; the large numbers of aircraft getting airborne over Iran was worse still. His stomach twisted itself in knots when the first call had come from the P-3 to report a possible minelayer—a sure sign that fresh trouble was brewing. If he could get his SEALs aboard the Iranian corvette and determine if they were truly laying mines or not, he might be able to contain the situation and prevent it from getting out of hand. If not, things were going to get ugly. The thought that kept repeating in his head was more than half-prayer: *Please God, don't make me have to sink that ship!*

Despite the problem he faced, nobody would have guessed how anxious he was right now. Brandt maintained a world class poker face, presenting the appearance of calm confidence to his officers and sailors. He saw them stealing the occasional glance in his direction, trying to read his mind, and wondering if they were about to get into a full blown shooting match. If that happened, they needed to believe in his ability to carry them through it. *Mind your bearing, admiral!* he told himself.

The real danger was their proximity to the coast of Iran. They needed sea-room, but there was none to be had. Assuming they could detect the launch of a shore-based cruise missile swarm the moment it happened, there was less than a two minute window to classify, intercept, and destroy a supersonic cruise missile before it hit them. As they continued to close the strait, that window would gradually narrow down to mere seconds. Even for a force like his with computer-optimized cooperative engagement capability, there was no guarantee that they could defeat a saturation attack. He considered ordering the entire group to change course and head southwest, at least until things cooled off a bit, but resisted the impulse. He suspected that Fifth Fleet would order them to transit the strait soon, and when the order came he wanted to execute it as quickly as possible.

At least the government of Oman had agreed to play ball, giving U.S. aircraft access to their airspace. If the *Boxer* group was ordered through the strait, it would *not* be under the right of innocent passage: they would transit high speed at Condition I, guns run out and with friendly air cover overhead.

Brandt listened to the calls on Strike, and eventually got on the net himself to pass his direct orders to the P-3 mission commander. He was grateful to the P-3 TACCO for calling him instead of just shooting the minelayer—the mission commander would have been well within his rights based on international law and the current ROE, but the TACCO had displayed some real horse sense by checking fire. Brandt planned on finding out who he was and putting him in for a commendation. He watched the plot tensely for several minutes as the two Seahawks inched their way closer to the Iranian corvette. He'd breathe a lot easier once the first sets of SEAL boots hit the deck of that ship.

***

The Persian Gulf

Six *Ghadir* Class midget submarines slowly surfaced among the small flotilla of fishing boats that casually moved across the wake of the *Boxer* carrier strike group once it passed by them, heading northeast. Of the entire fleet of Iranian submarines that had put to sea over the past week or more, this small wolf pack had the good fortune to find itself in the proper position with respect to the American carrier group. There were others out there, but they would not be part of the coming battle. It was impossible to predict which line of approach the Americans would take toward the strait, but the options were finite, driven by geography and civil shipping traffic. This group of midget submarines had 'won the lottery', in a manner of speaking.

Although small and limited in their capabilities, the miniature subs were well-suited to the shallow waters of the Gulf, and packed a significant punch: each one had two 21-inch torpedo tubes, loaded with wake-homing torpedoes. Although the USN had been testing potential defenses against these weapons, none were currently deployed as standard equipment. Impervious to standard torpedo countermeasures, wake-homing torpedoes detected changes in the water in the wake of a surface ship, then zig-zagged between the wake's edges in a stern chase until finally detonating under the vulnerable stern of their target, where propulsion and steering were located.

The fishing boats were previously identified by patrolling helicopters and tagged as civil craft, even though they *weren't*. With the distractions of the USS *Green Bay* rescue operation and the situation with the potential minelayer in the strait, nobody noticed as the flotilla of boats gradually began spreading out, providing cover to the midget submarines as they maneuvered into position a few miles behind the six ships of the *Boxer* strike group. Those half dozen American vessels represented the strongest naval presence that existed anywhere in this part of the world, but six ships of any kind were nothing but potential targets to a submariner, and far from invulnerable against the weapons they carried.

***

Several miles to the north of the strike group, a second 'fishing fleet' began launching a swarm of small, radio-controlled drone aircraft. These were extremely simple, made of monocoque coatings over light wooden frames, with few metal parts and small radar cross sections. Each one carried a small contact charge, with the destructive power of about half a stick of dynamite. Their operators, located on the decks of the fishing boats, used simple hand-held controls and drone-mounted cameras for guidance. Their electronics were more robust than those used by hobbyists; each drone represented an outlay of about ten thousand U.S. dollars. Considering their intended purpose, it was more than a bargain. Five dozen of them grouped over a fishing fleet looked like a densely-packed flock of sea-birds to a radar operator—at least at the beginning. Expectation bias could be weaponized: one *expected* a fleet of fishing boats to draw flocks of birds.

In the realm of asymmetric warfare, every advantage had to be utilized.

***

Several miles north of the *Boxer* strike group, the crew of an old, rust-bucket cargo ship sprang into action. The ship turned to the northeast, so its starboard beam was facing southeast, and several cargo containers were opened. Makeshift rail systems were run out, until two dozen small, battery-powered catapult launchers were aimed at the American strike group. Each launcher held a flying decoy drone, fabricated with off-the-shelf technology, military grade electronics, and the skull-sweat of Iranian university students dedicated to the twin causes of the Islamic Revolution and Persian nationalism. Each of the drones cost approximately fifty thousand U.S. dollars, for a total investment of less than half the cost of a single American SM-2 standard missile.

***

Over the Persian Gulf

Arkady Kovalev glanced to either side, and saw that his three wingmen were tucked in tight—as tight as any aerial demonstration team. To a distant radar they would paint as a single air target. The four-ship division of Fulcrums was dawdling along at a mere .78 Mach, precisely twenty miles in trail of the airliner ahead of them, with another airliner twenty miles behind them. To the outside world, the flight was nothing but another civil air track gradually making its way along the A453 air corridor over the Gulf, even making regular communication check-ins with civil air traffic control. Kovalev knew that another division of his Red Talon fighters was doing the same thing in another patch of sky a few hundred miles away, and so was Cheng Ye's *Feilong* squadron.

Kovalev wondered if the civil traffic controllers in Iran knew the truth, but only for a moment. In the end, all that mattered was what the American AWACS controllers knew—or believed they knew. When they learned the truth, it would be too late for them.

***

USS *Boxer*

One of the operations specialists monitoring the surface plot pushed her glasses up the bridge of her nose, squinting slightly at the picture in front of her. Track November Sierra 38 was considered a suspect vessel; it was a Liberian flagged cargo ship in the registry, but it had been quite obviously shadowing the strike group for the past several days. It had just maneuvered again, turning to parallel their northeasterly course, and matching their speed. She keyed her mike.

"TAO, we've got another change on November Sierra 38," she reported. "Want to step over here and have a look?"

"Not now," the TAO replied immediately. Alpha Whiskey just reported the appearance of a strange cloud of low-level air contacts hovering around to the north of them, and they were trying to figure out what they were. In addition, there was the situation with a potential minelayer rapidly escalating over the strait, and concerns over four dozen new air contacts over southern Iran in the past thirty minutes.

Okay, she said to herself, stifling a yawn. *I guess I'll just keep an eye on it myself.* While she watched the track to the north, she failed to notice the fishing fleet to the southwest of them gradually spreading out behind the strike group, something it had never done before. Even if she had noticed, there was really nothing there to concern herself with now.

***

When it all went sideways, it happened fast. RADM Brandt heard the P-3 TACCO shout his warning about the MANPAD over the net, and the fight was on. His electronic warfare commander informed him that they were picking up scrambled communications between the gunboat and Iran, and then Strike reported Iranian bogeys moving toward the gunboat's position in the strait. The gunboat's track flickered briefly and died on the display less than a minute later: the Orion had blown her clean out of the water.

Brandt's eyes flickered to another part of the plot, where a cluster of confused air contacts seemed to be moving relatively slowly toward the strike group. He picked up his handset. "Alpha Whiskey from Alpha Bravo. What's that low-slow cloud of contacts to the north of us?"

His relatively new-to-the-job air warfare commander was the commanding officer of one of the strike group's two *Burke* Class destroyer escorts. He was in the CDC aboard his own ship, wondering the same thing, and keenly aware that his predecessor had been fired for letting a threat get through to the group. "Alpha Bravo from Alpha Whiskey, until a minute ago we had classified it as a flock of sea birds over a fishing fleet. Re-classifying now as a possible drone swarm—it's on a direct line towards us."

"Admiral," called his battle watch captain, "we've got Iranian fighters moving to engage our units over the strait. We'd better get that patrol pl—"

"—Deal with it!" Brandt snapped, turning to his chief of staff. "COS, let's get some EW going. Direct full jamming at that drone swarm if that's what it is. Let's see if we can disrupt it. Also, we need to re-identify and classify the surface contacts under the drones. They probably aren't fishing boats."

"Aye aye, sir," his chief of staff replied. "Recommend we take the group to Condition I."

"Do it!"

CAPT Moreno passed the orders. The general alarm sounded shortly thereafter, and the announcement from the bridge came over the 1MC, ordering the *Boxer* to General Quarters. On the bridge, the ship's captain issued orders to turn the gigantic ship into the wind so they could launch the alert fighters that were sitting on the flight deck, ready to go.

"Alpha Bravo from Alpha Whiskey, I've got mass movement south of Iranian air contacts, and breakout air contacts from the civil air corridors. My assessment is that we are under attack, admiral."

At that moment, the sea combat commander reported torpedoes in the water—he had reports of high speed subsurface screw noises closing the strike group from astern.

Torpedoes? Brandt thought incredulously. *What the—?* His eyes roamed over the flag display as symbology began to change in all directions. Too much was happening all at once, and things were suddenly spiraling out of his control. He felt a slight surge of acceleration under his feet as *Boxer's* captain abandoned his turn into the wind and ordered flank speed, trying to outrun the homing torpedoes snaking up their wake.

"Sir…?" his chief of staff prompted him.

"I see it, goddammit!" Brandt snarled. He keyed his command circuit. "Warfare commanders, from Alpha Bravo. Execute plan Delta India, ROE option 2. Execute! Execute! Execute!"

He listened as the Strike controller took point: "99 Alpha Bravo, this is Strike. Starlight! Starlight! Starlight! Air warning red, weapons tight. All India tracks are declared hostile. Repeat, all India tracks are Bandit! Authentication one-romeo-romeo-five!" The verbiage of the order was important: *weapons tight* meant that target tracks had to be declared hostile before they could be engaged. The idea was *to control* the violence, sparing any non-combatants in the battlespace. The next level was *weapons free.* That was authorization to destroy any target *not declared friendly*. To laymen the two sounded like the same thing, but in fact they were worlds apart. One demanded caution and verification, the other resulted in the battlespace turning into a free-fire zone that was lethal to civilians. Usually, a 'weapons free' scenario was a clear indicator that the good guys were losing the battle.

"Alpha Whiskey, Panhead," the Air Force AWACS plane assigned to them called. "Vampire! Vampire! Vampire! Multiple tracks on your north axis, bearing three-five-five!"

"Alpha Whiskey copies," the radio crackled. "99 Alpha Bravo, air action, north. Take all inbound Vampire tracks." At this point, the computerized defense systems in the strike group began to take over the fight. The idea of a cooperative engagement system was that the computer would prioritize every threat to the strike group in the battlespace, determine which platform and weapon was best suited for dealing with it, and then issue the appropriate engagement orders electronically over the net. This would happen on the strike group level; at the unit level, ship self-defense systems would perform the same function for specific threats in close, selecting either ESSM, CIWS, or seaRAM batteries to engage incoming missiles as a last resort. Before this could happen, threats needed to be detected and classified with very little reaction time.

The arc of defending ships around the carrier began losing its cohesion as individual captains accelerated and maneuvered against the torpedoes approaching from behind them. *Boxer*, faster than any of her escorts, was leaving them behind, running at flank speed to the northeast and leaving herself somewhat exposed. The two *Perry* Class frigate captains coordinated their maneuvers over the radio, deliberately crisscrossing their courses over the carrier's wake to try and lure any wake-homing weapons onto themselves and off the carrier they were assigned to protect.

The rest of the strike group went to General Quarters. The VLS systems of the cruiser and destroyers began spitting missiles at a prodigious rate, and there was a sound over the Persian Gulf like crackling thunder as three dozen SM-2 missiles went supersonic in their efforts to close and intercept the first wave of decoy drones coming at the strike group: these were the larger decoys launched from the Liberian flagged cargo ship. The reaction time was too short for any of them to realize that the first wave of incoming 'missiles' wasn't the real thing. They were emitting threat missile radar frequencies, and were mis-classified as a result. The system responded as it was designed to, and dozens of missiles were wasted against harmless non-threats.

Brandt turned to his chief of staff. "Pat, re-designate the neutrals we're sure about as friendlies. If I go weapons free, I want to minimize collateral damage."

The chief of staff nodded grimly. "Aye aye, sir."

***

Over the Persian Gulf

"Break now," Kovalev ordered over the radio. He eased into a turn to the southeast, listening to the vectors being passed by the A-50 controllers and complying with their instructions. His wingman split out into a combat spread, with his second section splitting farther out on his opposite side, going to a spread-four formation. All four aircraft brought up their radars—a deliberate move, because they wanted the USAF fighters on their western CAP station to know they were being flanked by hostiles. Far to the east, a second division of Red Talons was performing the same *maskirovka*, drawing off the eastern CAP and leaving a gap in the U.S. defensive line to the north. In truth, it was more than just a feint—the threat posed by the Red Talons was real, and had to be honored. Fortunately for the Red Talons, there was no jamming in play this far to the west; the entire electronic warfare effort was taking place near the carrier group itself.

On Kovalev's signal, his Red Talons accelerated to supersonic speed. Their opponents were a flight of four American F-16 fighters: worthy opponents. The engagement started with a healthy speed and altitude advantage for Kovalev. Further, the Russian expats were carrying extended-range R-

27EA active guided missiles, with an effective range of about 80 miles, greater than the AMRAAMs carried by the American jets. They fired their first salvo at high altitude, supersonic speed, and from maximum range, knowing it would force their opponents onto the defensive. The Americans played for time, however. Their mission was to defend the E-3 Sentry behind them, and they knew that they were considered expendable in that role. They courageously stayed the course, waiting to go defensive until they were within range to fire their own AMRAAMs in return. Kovalev's flight fired their second salvo at sixty miles, and two American jets were hit by their first salvo just before returning fire. The MiG's immediately broke off and turned back to the northwest, running supersonic as the remaining F-16's finally went defensive. One of the Red Talons was hit by an AMRAAM and went down; the other three, including Kovalev, got away. One more F-16 was hit and destroyed by the second salvo. Kovalev would have liked to turn back and re-engage the lone survivor, but his flight was now out of missiles and fuel-critical. They headed north for home, having completed their assigned mission.

**

Cheng Ye didn't have the datalink capability enjoyed by his American adversaries, but he could see the picture in his head based on the information being passed to him by the A-50 controllers. There were two enemy AWACS aircraft flying. Together, they provided not only the airborne control for American fighter assets, but the look-down early warning capability so vital to American defenses in the case of a saturation cruise missile attack.

Defeating the Air Force AWACS was the simpler of the two battle problems. Not because they were any less capable or proficient—it was just a matter of force disposition. The Americans were not expecting to be attacked en-masse; the E-3 was defended by a meager force of eight fighters forming a rough east-west picket line to the north of the Sentry's track. Two groups of Red Talons succeeded in drawing those fighter pickets east and west, leaving the AWACS relatively undefended from the north. Cheng Ye's division was armed with weapons that the Americans had no idea were in Iranian possession: the KS-172 Novator, designed specifically as an AWACS killer with a range better than 160 NM. Cheng Ye was armed with one of these, and his second section leader with another. For backup, they also carried the same R-27EA long range missiles used by Kovalev's Red Talons. Cheng Ye's flight had also used the civil air corridors for cover, flying a civilian profile. Once he was informed that the Red Talons had engaged, his flight broke to the south in a high supersonic sprint. They fired their Novator missiles from 100 NM and 80 NM away, then followed up with a salvo of two R-27's from 60 NM, and another at 40 NM.

The Sentry never stood a real chance.

Once it realized it was under attack, the E-3 shut down its radar and dove for the deck, but it was easily caught by the Mach 3+ Novators. The first missile blew the left wing off the hapless E-3; the second struck mid-fuselage in a 2500 knot dive. Even without the warhead, the kinetic energy alone was enough to break the remainder of the aircraft in half. The follow-up salvoes were pure overkill: wasted shots.

The E-2C Hawkeye suffered a similar fate. This problem was harder, but not too much harder. By this time the surface ships were fighting decoys, actual cruise missiles, airborne drones, suicide boghammers, and three of them had been hit astern by wake-homing torpedoes. In short, they didn't have anything to spare against incoming fighters. The eastern, outer CAP station (Fargo's) was overwhelmed and shot down by Iranian fighters. The other three CAP stations were similarly engaged by the last of Iran's Persian cats, a mixed bag of F-5's and F-4's, recently acquired MiG-21s, and two squadrons of imported JF-17's. Those were overwhelming odds, and the carrier was never able to launch relief fighters due to her maneuvering torpedo defense. That left the Hawkeye and on-station Prowlers vulnerable to *Feilong* Flankers armed with Novators and other long range missiles, some of which were programmed to home-on-jam. The

Hawkeye was downed shortly after the E-3 Sentry, and both airborne Prowlers were killed as well, removing much of the electronic warfare advantage enjoyed by the strike group.

These were merely the opening moves in preparation for the real knockout punch. When the first *real* swarm of anti-ship missiles came over the horizon, both frigates and their *Ticonderoga* Class escort were already dead in the water, struck by torpedoes and down by the stern with flooding in their engineering spaces. This made them easy targets for *kamikaze* boghammers loaded with explosives. The small patrol boats rammed themselves into the stricken ships and detonated, finishing the job started by the midget submarines. The two smaller frigates were wracked by secondary explosions and sank quickly; the cruiser took longer to die and more of her crew survived, but she eventually went under as well.

Boxer was now well out of position in relation to her surviving two escorts. She'd avoided being hit by any torpedoes, but several small radio-controlled drones struck her flight deck, damaging two of the catapults and hitting a fully armed and fueled ready-alert fighter, resulting in secondary explosions and a large deck fire. Now the captain was maneuvering the ship to fight the fire; flight operations were out of the question. Her two remaining *Burke* Class escorts were maneuvering at high speed, low on anti-air missiles and fighting off boghammers, trying to avoid being rammed.

***

USS *Boxer*

The strike group wasn't limited solely to playing defense. Once the battle was joined, the strike group counterpunched immediately with an efficiency that only technology and tireless training could achieve.

Strike controllers responsible for offensive operations began assigning their own targets by previously established priorities, and issuing attack orders. A large wave of Tomahawk missiles was launched in the opening minutes, and they crossed the Gulf in the opposite direction to strike coastal, island, and platform-based missile launch sites that were already mapped and targeted. This forced the Iranians to finally activate their integrated air defense system for the first time, bringing it into play.

With offensive electronic warfare largely removed due to the loss of the airborne Prowlers, SAM radars found their targets while they still had enough reaction time to fire. Dozens of SA-10 missiles took to the sky over the Iranian coast, smiting the Tomahawks inbound from the sea. Only a handful of the older, subsonic cruise missiles ever reached their targets; the majority were intercepted and destroyed. U.S. cruise missile technology, sadly, was firmly rooted in the 1980's. Tomahawks, Harpoons, and their variants were all frustratingly slow, and electronically 'stupid' compared to more modern missiles.

RADM Brandt exchanged horrified looks with his staff when the E-2C and E-3 tracks vanished from the plot, and the link picture significantly degraded. "What the *fuck* just happened?" he exclaimed out loud—the first slip in his composure since the battle had started. He got on the radio to demand answers from his air warfare commander.

"Closeout and Panhead are down, sir," came the audibly shaken reply. Brandt could suddenly feel the fear starting to permeate flag plot. They were in serious trouble.

Brandt took a deep breath and keyed his radio. "99 Alpha Bravo, this is Actual. Air warning red, weapons free. I say again, *weapons free.* Take all non-friendly inbound air tracks. Out." He sat back in his seat, not even listening to the acknowledgements. A moment later a shudder rocked the ship, feeling like a small earthquake in flag plot. Brandt tore off his headset and picked up the phone to the *Boxer's* bridge.

"We were just hit by some small drones, admiral," the captain explained immediately. "One of the ready alert birds just blew up on deck. I've got a flight deck fire and mass casualties. I'll keep you posted, sir."

"Very well. Head's up, captain: we just lost AWACS. Anything coming over the horizon without friendly IFF is coming to kill us. You are directed to maneuver as necessary to unmask your point defense batteries. Radiate all ship's emitters at your discretion."

"Aye aye, sir."

He turned to CAPT Moreno. "Any news on the *Thach?*" he asked grimly. Lookouts had reported that the frigate was rammed by a boghammer after taking at least two torpedo hits.

The chief of staff shook his head grimly. "Signals officer says the explosion damn near broke her in two. He reported massive secondaries: she's gone."

"*Sweet Jesus*," Brandt breathed.

As soon as the Hawkeye and Sentry were destroyed, more than 70% of the net contacts below 500 FT in altitude dropped out of the datalink. Most of the contact data lost consisted of inbound cruise missiles. The radar picture was seriously degraded, but ESM receivers were warning all fleet units that several waves of anti-ship cruise missiles were inbound. Most were coming at high subsonic speed, but there were some supersonic tracks as well. Without AWACS, the AEGIS system couldn't pick them up until they appeared from below the horizon. The system was originally designed to defend against high speed supersonic missiles launched from waves of medium to high altitude bombers in a blue water environment. It was also designed to be the *second* line of defense, batting cleanup behind the fleet defense capability of an air wing composed largely of F-14 interceptors with Phoenix missiles, fighting an outer-air battle hundreds of miles up the threat-axis.

Not so today.

As a new wave of missiles streaked toward the ships of the strike group, a few began to leak through. Their cruiser escort was taken out of action early by torpedoes and boghammers, with a third of their AEGIS capability going down with her. With the loss of the two frigates, only three ships remained in the strike group. The two destroyers salvoed the remainder of their Standard missiles, and then the seaRAM and Evolved Sea

Sparrow Missile systems came into play, firing missiles at short ranges to intercept incoming cruise missiles.

From there the cold equations—simple mathematics—wrote the outcome. The defenders were completely saturated and lacked enough reaction time and resources to respond effectively. The first of their destroyer escorts were hit by a pair of Silkworm missiles when her missile magazines were emptied. The hits were so sudden and devastating that the ship was essentially blown apart rather than sunk. Her shattered remains went down with all hands—there were no survivors.

The last two ships of the *Boxer* group were subsequently hit and destroyed by a deluge of anti-ship cruise missiles. Iran fired a half-dozen Sunburn missiles in the second wave along with more Silkworms, saving them for when their kill-probabilities were highest. *Boxer* herself took five direct hits. RADM Brandt and his staff were killed instantly when the first missile hit the ship, along with her captain, the bridge crew, and almost everyone stationed in the large 'island' of the carrier. Electronically, the supercarrier went dark immediately—all her radars and emitters were destroyed outright. The second and third missiles both hit the flight deck squarely, one aft, and one just forward of amidships. They penetrated to the hangar deck, and post-explosion fires were instantly raging out of control. Every person working on the flight deck or fighting the original fire was killed instantly. The ship's executive officer, taking command from his battle station post in Damage Control Central, ordered the ship's weapons magazines flooded. This prevented the single devastating explosion which would have all but vaporized the ship, but in hindsight that might have been a better result. There was more ordnance staged on the hangar deck, and as the fires reached these stores they caused secondary explosions that spread more fires and did more damage.

The *coup de grace* for USS *Boxer* came in the form of a final pair of Silkworms—two of the last missiles to be fired. Both hit the carrier low on her port side, almost at the waterline. The devastating damage caused by these missiles fatally hulled the ship and killed most of the remaining crew. It wasn't an easy or painless death for the supercarrier. In fact, the waters of the Gulf were not even deep enough for her to sink completely beneath the waves. The *Boxer* began to list heavily to port as she took on water, and eventually rolled onto her side and sank until she struck bottom in only 80 feet of water—a portion of the ship's flight deck and shredded island structure remained visible above the surface, still on fire. Very few of her crew were able to abandon ship; and most who did would die later due to radiation exposure from her shattered nuclear reactors.

The few surviving U.S. aircraft diverted into Bahrain, Qatar, or the United Arab Emirates. The air battle was fierce, and the losses were heavy on both sides. *Boxer*'s air wing and the USAF CAP stations took a toll on the Iranian Air Force during the battle, but many of the surviving air wing jets were lost due to fuel starvation before they could reach divert fields.

By noon that day, the *Boxer* strike group was destroyed—not a single ship escaped. The dead numbered more than 5,500, with the remainder either missing in action or missing and presumed dead. Less than half a dozen aircrews managed to land or eject onto friendly soil: a grand total of eight men and women. When the battle ended, hundreds of U.S. sailors were alive in the waters of the Gulf. Some would perish, some would be saved by friendly or neutral ships conducting SAR operations, and an unknown number would be taken captive by the Iranians. It was the worst defeat ever suffered by the U.S. Navy, with losses surpassing those taken at both Leyte Gulf and the Naval Battle of Guadalcanal.

The Iranians limited their attack to the *Boxer* group on the western side of the Strait of Hormuz. Not only did they refrain from attacking the stricken *Green Bay* and her escorts, but they also promised safe passage to any ship or aircraft engaged in rescue efforts out of 'humanitarian concern.' It was a form of hostage taking, preventing a massive, knee-jerk retaliation on the part of the United States or anyone else. The implication was clear: any further attacks on Iran would result in the destruction of the *Green Bay* and any other ship in range. Later, they would claim that the battle itself was just a counterattack in response to the unprovoked sinking of one of their own ships. In one morning, the balance of power in the Persian Gulf shifted firmly to the Islamic Republic of Iran.

USS *North Carolina*

Hours had passed since *North Carolina* destroyed the Iranian Kilo. The mood in the control center was grim as the submarine crept along at four knots, proceeding cautiously back towards the strait, listening to multiple distant explosions on sonar. When the captain finally ordered them to mast depth, they couldn't raise any units in the *Boxer* strike group. A query to COMFIFTHFLT had gone unanswered so far, so now they were reduced to listening and waiting.

Another tense, quiet hour passed, and then another, and still no messages from higher authority. Captain Bergstrom was getting impatient for news, and was considering bypassing his chain of command and contacting COMSUBLANT or CENTCOM directly via satellite for some answers. He drank cup after cup of coffee and paced the control center relentlessly, setting everyone on edge. He finally ordered them back to two knots and up to mast depth yet again. When they were shallow enough, they raised the optical mast and took a three-hundred-sixty degree look around them.

All of them were able to see what the optics showed on a TV screen—it was a far cry from the age-old traditional periscopes used by older submarine classes. Something on the surface caught LT Whorley's eye. "Uh, captain, can you go back about forty degrees?" he said quickly. Bergstrom glanced at him and complied, working the small controller. "There!" Whorley said a moment later. Bergstrom saw it too, now. He stopped, centered the object on the screen, and went to full magnification.

"What the hell is that?" Bergstrom muttered.

"Looks like a survival raft . . . it is a raft! There's someone in it! See the helmet?"

"Jesus, I think you're right!" Bergstrom said. "One of ours?"

"Probably. I doubt the Iranians have the sort of water survival equipment we do. I think we've got a downed pilot up there."

"Down mast," Bergstrom ordered crisply. The submarine's photonic mast abruptly vanished below the surface.

The voice of their lead AW broke the silence permeating the control center. "Conn, sonar. New contact, bearing three-three-five. High speed screw on the surface . . . classify contact as probable boghammer. There's almost no bearing rate change and the signal is increasing in strength . . . the contact is headed towards us."

"Speed?"

"I've got his direct up-doppler frequency . . . I'm looking up what his base frequency should be. I'll have his speed figured in a minute, captain."

"Get Reese up here," Bergstrom ordered. "Up mast," he ordered, sending the mast back up. He slewed it to search along the bearing line his sonarman was reporting on the boghammer. At maximum magnification there was still nothing visible, meaning the small craft was still quite a ways off. He ordered the mast down a second time. LT Whorley ordered their UUV off on a course that would give them a cross fix on the boghammer, telling them exactly how far way it was. The sonarman came back and told them the craft was doing fifteen knots based on doppler analysis, and the craft's closest point of approach was going to be practically on top of them.

LT Reese appeared in the control center in less than a minute, not even out of breath. Bergstrom explained the situation to him.

"They're almost certainly going after the pilot—they don't have the equipment to detect us down here. The quickest way to get him aboard would be to surface the boat," Reese suggested, knowing it was going to go over like a lead balloon.

Bergstrom shook his head. "Absolutely not. There's a shooting war going on topside, and I can't afford to expose us. If we broach and some speedboat tears apart the sail with a machine gun or RPG, we could be stuck on the surface and that would be the end of us. I can't risk this boat and her crew for one man. If I hold her at mast depth, can your team go out and retrieve him? Bring him in through the diving lock or the dry deck shed?"

Reese stroked his chin. "Maybe. It depends on what kind of shape he's in."

"Time's wasting, and I think we should at least try. Is your team up for it?"

"Hell yes, sir!"

"What about the boghammer?" Whorley asked.

"We've got it, no worries," Reese said casually. "I'll muster a team in the lock we'll be ready to go on your order. We just need a few minutes to gear up."

"Do it. That'll give me time to maneuver the boat underneath him."

***

Fargo regained consciousness when an odd wave splashed cold water into his face. His head spun for a few moments before settling down a bit, and he groggily wondered if he had a bit of a concussion from his head smacking the side of the canopy right before he ejected. He was soaked to the bone, shivering violently, and his whole right side was nothing but sharp pain. On top of that, he was parched. Dexter's body was a dead weight across his waist and legs, tipping the raft forward and letting in the cold seawater. He wasn't in any danger of sinking, but he realized he might as well be floating in the water instead of lying in his raft, for all the good it was doing him—he was half submerged. What he wanted to do was pull over Dexter's raft and tie them together, and then he could let Dexter go without worrying about losing his body. The problem with that was that he was already borderline hypothermic, exhausted, and his right arm was useless. He literally didn't have the strength to do it. In fact, he was fast coming to the realization that if he didn't get some help soon, he probably wasn't going to make it. He raised his left arm and looked at his watch, amazed to find that it was still working. He'd been in the water for almost six hours now, and it was going to start getting dark soon. As near as he could remember he should be something on the order of seventy or eighty miles from the Boat, near the mouth of the strait. He wondered whether he was in Iranian territorial waters or not, then decided it didn't make much difference right now. A helicopter from the *Boxer* should have been able to reach him in an hour or so; it was possible there was one in the area already, depending on the tactical situation.

Fargo fumbled one-handed at his vest, grunting in pain as he wrestled out the small plastic water bottle in there. With a little more mobility and presence of mind he would have gone after Dexter's first—his WSO was past needing it. Fargo wasn't thinking that clearly, though, and with one good hand and his chattering teeth he managed to get the cap off the bottle without spilling it all. He managed to get about three ounces inside him, and that was it for his water bottle. It wasn't much, but it helped. That done, he fumbled around until he found his strobe light, which was capped with an IR filter so that it would be visible to someone looking with FLIR, but not the Mark I eyeball. He clicked it on, and attached it to the Velcro pad on the forward part of his flight helmet. Finally, he went for his survival radio. He was trying to wiggle it out of the vest pocket when the first sound of a high-speed motor assaulted his hearing.

Fargo froze, his eyes going wide as he listened carefully. The sound was quite distant, but there was no mistaking the fact that it was gradually getting closer. There was no way on Earth the USN was coming after him with a speed boat; the only people using those around here were the Iranians. He quickly checked the water around his raft and noted with relief that the dye markers had long since dissipated. Not that it mattered much; it was still full daylight, and the seas were calm—he wasn't going to be hard to spot.

A sense of despair and resignation gripped him; this was a nightmare made real. The one thing Fargo had taken away from his Survival, Evasion, Resistance, and Escape training was that he probably didn't want to be taken alive by a Middle Eastern enemy. SERE training emphasized a survival mindset, focusing on maintaining the will to live, but there were limits to how far he wanted to carry that. Fargo wasn't sure how widespread the battle had gotten, but he suspected that if the Iranians pulled him alive out of the water, he would never be seen again by his own side. His people had no way of knowing if he was alive or dead, and the Iranians could take steps to make sure they never found out. He'd be listed as missing in action, eventually presumed dead, and the Iranians would have him forever—just like that missing Hornet driver shot down by the Iraqis on the first day of the first Gulf War, way back in '91.

All these thoughts flashed through his head in just a few seconds. He remembered hearing stories about some of the men captured during the first Gulf War and the various ways they'd been beaten and tortured. Some had their jaws wired up to electrodes, and the spasms when they were shocked were bad enough to break their jaws and teeth. He didn't really care to find out what the Iranians would have in store for an infidel U.S. pilot responsible for killing some of their countrymen. Fargo knew he wasn't Superman—*nobody* was. They could exacerbate his injuries, permanently cripple or disfigure him, starve him, and eventually break his spirit. He could resist, he could follow the Code of Conduct, but there would be no going home. The thought of losing himself and betraying his country was too much to bear. Then the Iranians would eventually kill him anyway, to keep their secrets.

Better to die right here.

Fargo fought his own terror as he dropped his radio and dug back into his vest with his good hand, grasping for the handle of the Beretta 9mm pistol they carried on every hop. He had twelve shots; when they got to him, he planned on taking eleven shots at the bad guys and saving the last one for himself. He prayed that he'd have the courage to follow through when the time came, assuming the Iranians didn't ventilate him first. When he got the weapon out, he realized he had a problem: with his broken arm, he couldn't hold the pistol and rack the slide to chamber a round. "Fuck....*fuck!*" he muttered to himself. He glanced down at Dex's body. "Sorry, bud," he croaked. "God, I'm so sorry," he added, bucking his hips slightly and kicking, working Dexter's body free and casting it loose. "I'm sorry," he repeated through chattering teeth—chattering from terror as well as the cold, now. "Gotta finish what we started," he repeated to himself several times, almost making a chant of it. The motor was a lot louder; he figured they had to see him by now. He tried to scootch back into the raft, to get his legs and feet inside to give him some leverage. He placed the grip and trigger housing of the pistol between his knees, clenching them together to hold it as he tried to rack the slide and chamber the first round. Wet fingers, a wet gun, and poor leverage caused him to fail, and the weapon slipped and splashed into the raft—he almost lost it overboard.

He could hear shouting in Farsi now, barely audible over the roar of the boat's engine. He swore some more and was trying to get the pistol back between his knees when the most startling thing happened: a black clad hand reached into his raft from nowhere and calmly relieved him of the weapon. Fargo couldn't have been more surprised if Santa Claus himself had swooped down in his sleigh and laid a Maverick missile right into the offending Iranian gunboat. A voice spoke just loudly enough for him to hear, but strangely calm. "U.S. Navy SEALS, sir. Take your helmet off, *fast.*"

Fargo was too shocked not to do as he was told. He pulled his helmet off, ignoring the agony in his head as he did so. For a moment his vision swam, and he thought he might pass out again. When his eyes re-focused, he was looking at the goggled face of a black-clad diver. There was no sign of his pistol; the SEAL had dropped it and let it sink. The frogman knew there was nothing more dangerous in a rescue than a shocked survivor fiddling with a live weapon. "Not that I'm not glad to see you, dude, but how did you get here and is that your boat coming at us?"

"No, it ain't our boat," the SEAL replied. "HM2 Holly, at your service, sir. I'm the team medic, and we've got us a situation here. Listen fast because there's no time to explain. Are you hurt?"

"Yeah," Fargo grimaced. "I think my right arm is busted pretty bad; maybe my shoulder, too."

"Do you want to live?" the SEAL asked clearly, voicing it as a challenge.

"Yes!"

"Have you ever gone SCUBA diving? Do you know how to clear a regulator?"

"Yeah, I took a dive class in college," Fargo replied.

"Piece of cake then. Here you go, sir," Holly added, Handing Fargo a regulator attached to the tank on the SEALs back. "I'm going to pop your inflation lobes, and roll you into the water." Even as he said it, the SEAL corpsman pulled a diving knife and went to work on Fargo's flotation lobes. One by one they were punctured and went flat, and then Holly severed his raft tether. "When you roll into the water, wrap your left arm around me, under my armpit, hang on, and just relax. I'll do all the swimming. We aren't going to go very deep, but it'll be deep enough that you'll have to pop your ears a few times. Just relax and breathe, hang on to me, stay awake, and I'll do the rest. My buddies are going to take care of the boat. Got it?"

"Got it," Fargo mumbled as he fitted the regulator into his mouth. It had been a while, but he hadn't forgotten how it worked. The boat sounded like it was almost on top of them. Fargo took an experimental breath, and got air. He nodded. "Let's go!" Holly shouted. Fargo fought the urge to groan as he rolled out of the raft and splashed into the water. Holly didn't hesitate, he simply grabbed a handful of the torso harness in the middle of Fargo's back and drove him underwater, kicking powerfully with his fins. Fargo closed his eyes and grimaced against the pain in his shoulder and arm as the SEAL swam them a good twelve to fifteen feet under the surface, and then leveled them off and slowly began swimming away from the raft. Once they were well under water, the pace became almost insultingly leisurely. For Fargo's part, it didn't require any effort. There was the initial shock of getting pushed underwater, and then the pressure on his ears until he cleared them, but after a few breaths through the regulator he calmed down, realizing he was fine, and that made it easier on both. He went limp in Holly's grasp, giving him a pat to signal he was still conscious, and let the SEAL corpsman do his thing. It wasn't long before another bit of hell broke loose on the surface behind them.

***

The boghammer pulled up to the pair of rafts bobbing about ten yards apart on the surface. Two men stood on the bow of the boat, one with an AK-47 aimed at the rafts and the other holding an RPG; the latter was probably overkill, but the Iranians weren't sure what to expect. There was more shouting as they spotted the body of one of the hated Americans floating near one of the rafts; the man was either unconscious or dead. The two men peering over the bot's gunwale looked at each other quizzically—they could have *sworn* there was a man in the other raft, but now it was empty. The sun was getting low on the horizon, and the light could play strange tricks on the eyes. They briefly discussed the possibility that he might have dipped underwater to hide, and one of them suggested that they pull the rafts out of the water in case an American was hiding *underneath* one of them, having created a pocket of air for himself. They could see a second helmet bobbing in the water not far away: confirmation that there were two of them at some point.

The Iranians weren't too concerned about it. They could wait around for a few minutes, longer than a man could hold his breath. If they didn't find him and he lived, he'd be dead before morning of exposure without his raft. The dead pilot floating on the surface would be useful for propaganda purposes if nothing else. Still, it would be better to capture one of them alive. The Iranians scanned the dark waters around their boat intently, waiting to see if the second pilot was going to appear.

While the Iranians fumbled with the rafts and the body of the dead aviator, two SEALS surfaced just behind the boat, swimming up and unceremoniously dropping a pair of live grenades over the gunwale before ducking back underwater and swimming away fast. The grenades set off the fuel lines and tank when they detonated, causing a secondary explosion that blew the boat apart quite brilliantly. What was left of the shattered hulk sank rapidly, with its bottom half-disintegrated. Most of its crew were killed by the secondary blast; a couple flew several yards and hit the water, shocked but alive.

Unlikely as it was, one of the Iranians hit the water relatively unscathed and was still conscious. Not a born swimmer, he struggled in a near-panic to keep his head above the swells as his clothes soaked through and his boots filled with seawater, weighing him down. He screamed and literally peed himself as a dark shape rose out of the water next to him. An instant later he felt a vice-like grip lock around his throat and he was dragged under. Something powerful and terrifying drove him into the depths, as he gurgled helplessly and tried to scream for his mother. Something razor-sharp stabbed deeply into his kidneys, and the pressure on his throat vanished simultaneously. He reflexively drew breath to shriek in pain, and seawater flooded his lungs instead. The anonymous SEAL left the limp body to finish its long fall to the sea bottom, and struck out for the submerged *North Carolina*.

Another SEAL recovered the body of LTJG John Wong; nobody was left behind.

Part II
Desdichado

Brian J. Smith

IX

The White House
Washington D.C.

President James Marsden sat alone at the Resolute Desk with his head buried in his hands. Final confirmation was thirty minutes old, and the story had already broken all over the world. This wasn't a bad dream—*it was happening*. An entire Navy strike group sunk in open battle, with more than 5,000 dead. That was more than twice the casualty count the United States suffered during ten years of fighting in Afghanistan, and all in a *single day*. It was the first aircraft carrier lost since the Second World War, and the first time *ever* that a nuclear-powered warship had been hit in combat.

Marsden lifted his head and looked around the Oval Office. He thought about the history this room had seen, the men who had occupied this chair, and past events that had staggered the nation over the course of its history. America had suffered through worse trials than this and surely would again, but for Marsden it all seemed overwhelming. There were a lot of pundits who claimed from day one that he wasn't ready for this job: not old enough, not experienced enough, and not tough enough. He knew what he was called behind his back: *The accidental president.* America obviously had enemies who felt the same way, and now he was being put to the test. History would turn on the decisions he made now—he *had* to be up to the task. He felt the presence of ghosts in the room, the specter of the Founding Fathers and other leaders from America's past: Washington, Jefferson, Lincoln, FDR, Truman, Kennedy, and most recently, Al Gore after 9/11. They were tested too, and all rose to the occasion and provided steady leadership during the worst of times. For a strange moment it was like he could feel their eyes on him, watching, taking his measure, and expecting him to *act*. He also felt a sense of encouragement, as if their collective spirit willed him forward for the sake of the nation, *wanting* him to succeed.

The President raised his head and blew out a deep breath. *It was time to lead.*

He flipped the page of the legal pad sitting on his desk, and started making notes. Five minutes later there was a discreet knock on the door. "Come in," he called loudly and firmly. The door cracked open, and his chief of staff looked in on him, wondering what he was going to find. The President waved him in, and went back to finishing up the bullet point he'd been writing down before he lost his train of thought. The chief of staff made a quick gesture behind him, and the White House photographer stepped into the oval office and snapped a quick picture of him sitting at his desk—it was a picture that would become iconic in later years: the image of the Commander in Chief sitting straight in his coat and tie, stern and in command as he prepared his briefing notes in response to the Iranian attack.

"Mister President, the cabinet is assembled," his chief of staff informed him.

The President gathered up his notes and stood up. "Let's go," he said.

***

Every man and woman in the situation room came silently and respectfully to their feet when the President swept in. He saw them taking his measure, and their growing realization that he wasn't coming in with his tail between his legs. His stride was purposeful and measured, his face composed, and his hands steady as he took his place at the head of the table. Of all those he needed to lead, those in uniform were the ones whose confidence he needed most. He could not appear weak or indecisive, or he'd lose them permanently. He resolved not to lose his temper or raise his voice at any of them, as he'd often done in the past. He couldn't afford to bluster—he needed to project a demeanor of calm and control. *You've got this,* he told himself yet again. "Please take your seats," he said clearly. The room was dead silent except for the shuffling of chairs as everyone sat down. Marsden let a thunderous silence permeate the room for about twenty seconds while he looked around the table with a steady, unflinching gaze, meeting every pair of eyes. Then he nodded as if in silent approval, and took a deep breath. "Ladies and gentlemen, we're all aware of what's happened. We'll eventually get to the root of why it happened, and how we lost the battle, but believe me when I tell you that we *will* weather this crisis, we *will* answer it, and we *will* recover from it.

"Now, we have a tremendous amount of work to do. We're going to hammer out some things right now, and then tonight, at 7:00 PM Eastern Time, I'm going to address the nation. Tomorrow at 10:00 AM I plan to address a joint session of Congress. We're going to move quickly on this, but let me caveat that as follows: there will be no kneejerk reactions, only calculated ones. Our military and political response *will* be measured, and well thought out beforehand." He looked at ADM Kirkwood. "CNO, do we have a reliable record of events?"

Kirkwood cleared his throat uncomfortably; the chief of naval operations looked ashen, like he might suffer a coronary at any moment. "We do, Mister President. Two destroyers from the *Nassau* expeditionary group were linked in with the *Boxer* carrier strike group, and we have a moment by moment playback of everything that happened." He spent the next few minutes giving them an overview of the battle before drawing his conclusions. "Our initial analysis indicates that this was a deliberate, pre-planned surprise attack, Mister President. It was too well coordinated to be anything else, and required too many players to be correctly pre-positioned to pull it off. There are also indications that the Iranians possess certain weapons systems that we were unaware of before now—a major intelligence failure on our part. The Iranians are trying to paint the incident with their minelayer in the Strait of Hormuz as the flashpoint for the entire battle, but make no mistake: this was a planned surprise attack, and it will be easy to prove."

"And we have the data to support this, correct?" Marsden asked.

"Yes sir."

"What about the rescue operation?"

"Still underway. *Green Bay* is under tow, and the entire *Nassau* group is in the Arabian Sea, out of harm's way for the moment. The *Coral Sea* carrier strike group is in company, covering them. A damage control team is aboard now to determine if *Green Bay* can safely make port or not. If not, we'll abandon and scuttle her in deep water. Right now, it looks like she'll make port. Unless otherwise directed, I'm ordering the amphibious ships home for now and chopping the *Nassau*'s destroyer squadron and support ships over to *Coral Sea,* forming a full carrier battle group."

"That is approved. I want the data on the battle broken down and summarized in an unclassified format that the average American citizen and congressman can understand. The presentation needs to come to about ten minutes worth of material. Pass it to my speechwriter for integration into my address tonight, and it needs to be done no later than 2:00 PM. Throw in some basic visuals, including a bird's-eye overview. Then prepare a more detailed version, twenty to thirty minutes in length, for the office of the Secretary of Defense to present to the American people by week's end. That presentation will happen in prime time, so our press people need to secure the airtime today."

"Yes sir," Admiral Kirkwood replied again, glancing back at one of his flag aides. The lieutenant in question was already on his way out of the room.

"What's the overall situation in the Gulf right now?" Marsden asked.

"Quiet, and tense," the NSA answered. "Iran has stated that they aren't seeking a war, and that the battle was a matter of self-defense. They are holding the position that the Strait of Hormuz remains closed to U.S. and NATO warships, and any such forces passing into the northern Gulf of Oman will be subject to attack. They have also stated that they will soon have an important announcement to make, but we have no idea what that might be."

"What are your opinions on all that?" the President asked the service chiefs in general.

The JCS chairman snorted derisively. "Brilliant political play on their part," he commented. "It continues to paint us as the aggressor, and puts us right into a 'damned if we do, damned if we don't' scenario. Is your intention to ask for a declaration of war from congress?"

"Yes," Marsden said flatly, which brought the table to an immediate uproar. He let them go for a minute, before rapping the desk firmly with his knuckles, bringing the meeting back to order. "As I said before, our response will be carefully measured. It will be war, yes, but not an unrestricted war. We obviously can't invade Iran, nor do we need or want to. We just need the Persian Gulf free and open to trade, with Iran firmly slapped down. How we achieve that will be your job to determine, gentlemen. What about our Gulf State allies?"

Some uncomfortable looks went around the table, and the Secretary of State fielded the question. "Aside from assisting with rescue and recovery efforts, they are cooling towards us. They respect strength, and they're afraid of Iran. As of now Iran is calling the shots inside the Persian Gulf, and we're largely powerless to stop them until we make our move."

"How many survivors have been recovered?" the President asked.

All eyes went back to Admiral Kirkwood. "As of an hour ago, somewhere between three and four hundred. Anyone with a boat has been out scouring the Gulf where our ships went down. We're reasonably sure the Iranians have picked some up as well, but they aren't talking about who or how many, and frankly there is no way to know. Anyone the Iranians recover become potential hostages, of course. We can demand POW status for them, especially after a formal declaration of war, but good luck in enforcing it. We have archival footage of their current president leading U.S. hostages out of our own embassy in Tehran back in '79, to give you an idea of what we're dealing with. Right now, we're compiling three lists: who's dead, who's alive, and who's unaccounted for. Quite frankly, Mister President, that's going to take some time. We have another pressing problem as well."

"What is it?"

"The Persian Gulf isn't very deep where our ships went down. The *Boxer* is sunk, but she isn't completely submerged. We already know from local sources that she's bleeding radiation, and something will need to be done about that quickly. It won't be the ecological disaster the media will try to make it out to be, but it's bad enough, and it'll get worse if no corrective action is taken. I've got people working on the problem," he added. "I hope to have some potential solutions in the next day or two."

"It will have the effect of keeping scavengers away from her," commented General Terry Malone, the Marine Corps Commandant. "There are a lot of weapons and classified gear still locked away in that ship—stuff we can't afford to let anyone get their hands on."

"Use the nuclear angle, then," Marsden ordered. "The world press is going to lambaste us anyway, so we might as well play it up to our advantage. Put the word out that anyone attempting to board the wreck of the carrier is going to be lethally irradiated."

"I'll take care of that," the Press Secretary said.

"Jesus," someone muttered. "This is going to be a public relations nightmare."

Marsden shrugged stoically. "It can't get much worse than it already is, so let's own it, pull no punches, and look out for our interests going forward." This brought nods of agreement from around the table. Marsden was about to speak again, but noticed Kirkwood clearing his throat and looking even more uncomfortable. "Something more, admiral?"

"Yes, Mister President. There's the matter of accountability." The CNO drew himself upright in his chair. He looked like he had aged ten years in the past forty-eight hours, but his eyes were steady and clear. "I take full responsibility for the failure of the Navy in the Persian Gulf. My resignation has already been drafted, along with a short list of recommendations for my replacement. You'll have it by close of business today. Afterward, I would like to take charge of the casualty relief efforts, particularly with regards to next-of-kin notifications. I can't walk away from that responsibility in good conscience, and it's too big a job for my successor to deal with on top of everything else."

The President nodded. "Your resignation is accepted, as is your offer to take charge of casualty relief. That's fitting, I think."

"Thank you, Mister President," ADM Kirkwood replied humbly. The somberness of the moment was interrupted by a staffer hurrying into the room and whispering something in the NSA's ear. He blanched, and turned to face the rest of the cabinet.

"I'm afraid we just got about the worst news imaginable," he said. "We've just had reports that Iran has successfully test-detonated a nuclear weapon in its eastern desert."

The room fell into stunned silence.

***

Northman-Ironworks Aerospace
Century Park, Los Angeles, CA
Arlington, VA

Pat Jackson watched a news report from his office, breaking down what was known about the battle in the Persian Gulf. He knew the vulnerabilities the Navy was operating under far better than most, but it still came as a massive shock. That it *could* happen was no surprise at all; that it *had* happened was almost unbelievable. *Were the Iranians just nuts?* He asked himself. He didn't have any friends or relatives serving out there in the Gulf that he knew of, but he still felt like he'd been gut-punched—the same way he'd felt on 9/11. The news channels didn't have any solid information yet, but the situation was grim.

Jackson headed for the sideboard and poured himself a stiff shot of scotch from the bottle he kept on hand. The glass was halfway to his lips when he realized it was only 10:30 in the morning, then he shrugged and took it all in a deep gulp. The 24-hour networks were already assembling their hordes of subject matter experts, talking heads, and 'contributors' to comment on what had happened. The narratives had already been decided depending on which way a particular network leaned, and the spinning of those narratives would soon begin in earnest. Jackson knew from long experience they'd be getting it all wrong, for the most part. Nevertheless, the news cycle would be locked on these events and their fallout for the foreseeable future.

Jackson's mind was already in overdrive—this was a *disaster* for the navy establishment, not just in terms of combat losses, but for the Navy as an institution. The United States Navy had built its fighting doctrine around the aircraft carrier for the past seventy years. The modern carrier strike group was supposed to be *inviolable*: it was one of those things that was just accepted as gospel by people who didn't know any better. "Everyone" knew that if you went up against a carrier strike group, you got your butt kicked—at least that was the theory until now. Jackson was upset to find just how much he had subconsciously believed it himself. Unfortunately, Big Navy had let some things slip over the past decade, and the broader DOD procurement system had screwed them over just as hard. Jackson knew how it worked all too well: he had been an employee of Ironworks Aerospace for many years prior to the merger with Northman Aerospace. He'd been in the heart of the fight when the Clinton administration chose the Super Hornet program over the Advanced Super Tomcat.

It still galled him: the borderline illegal way the Super Hornet program was pushed through the appropriations process, with claims that the jet was a follow-on to the legacy Hornet, when in fact it was a completely new design that merely resembled the old. Then, the way DOD had turned a blind eye after the Supercat prototype had absolutely smoked the Rhino during the fly-off competition. Now, years later, the procurement system was still flailing with the cancellation of the beleaguered F-35 program, and the late procurement of the F-25 and AV-36 to replace it.

Jackson knew that Big Navy was about to suffer a shitstorm, and there was no getting around it. Regardless of what happened next in the Gulf, the Senate was going to spend the next year or two crawling up the Navy's ass with a borescope, and they weren't going to like what they found, not one little bit. Committees would be formed, reports would be written, and a few heads would roll. In the meantime, the Navy's funding would be in serious jeopardy. If the Senate Armed Services Committee concluded that carrier strike groups were unviable, it would spell the end of the aircraft carrier.

He saw an opportunity here to come to the Navy's rescue, and correct past mistakes. The company had spent a lot of time, money, and effort keeping its partnership with DARPA alive, working on concepts that might help them sell the Navy a high-end 5th Generation airframe. The prototypes out at China Lake were better than anything currently flying off a carrier flight deck, and the means to produce more of them, rapidly, were already in place. Things were going to happen fast—*very* fast. If he wanted to get involved, it had to be *now.* He picked up his phone and dialed a number he knew by heart. A continent away in Arlington, Virginia, an old friend and colleague picked up.

"Dammit Jen, I *told* you to hold my ca—" the voice on the other end growled.

"—Denny, it's Pat Jackson," he interrupted. "I dialed you direct."

"Oh, it's you," Denny Carter replied, his voice sounding odd and flat. The last time Jackson heard that tone from his friend was twelve years ago, on a September morning when a jet airliner smashed into the Pentagon. Carter had been on his way there for a meeting when it happened, spared only by the Beltway traffic that people constantly complained about. "Good Lord are you seeing this?" he asked in a choked voice. "The news actually broke here last night, unofficially."

"That's why I'm calling. What's the read on the hill?" Jackson asked.

"What do you think? The entire establishment is going apeshit," Carter replied. "The Senate Armed Services Committee has been in closed session since early this morning, and Marsden has called a joint session of Congress for tomorrow morning. Word on the street is that he's going to call for a declaration of war against Iran."

"Bullshit!" Jackson snorted reflexively. "The accidental president? I'd bet money against that—he's a dove and everyone knows it! That's why Iran pulled this stunt in the first place! Besides, Congress and the Senate are split right now, so there's no way in hell they'll agree to do it."

"Pat, you haven't seen the mood around here," Carter replied in a subdued voice. "It's ugly, as ugly as 9-11, if not worse. About one third of everyone in government has a friend or relative burned to death or drowned in the Gulf. If we can't be bipartisan about something like this, then there's no hope for this country at all. I guess we'll see, won't we?"

Jackson was taken aback; Carter sounded awfully sure. He knew that his friend was way more wired into the D.C. scene than he was at their corporate headquarters in Los Angeles; they lived in two different worlds these days. Carter was the company's head of corporate and government relations: essentially the company's voice to the defense establishment on Capitol Hill and inside the halls of the Pentagon. "Well, you know what they say: A conservative is nothing but a liberal who's been mugged."

"This is no time for jokes."

"I know," Jackson replied, his voice turning more serious. "If even half of what I'm hearing on the news is true, the Navy is in big trouble."

Carter chuckled bitterly. "Trouble? They're *finished.* The Coast Guard will have a bigger fleet by the time the hill finishes with them. They're already talking about killing funding for all future carrier construction. They threatened the same thing several years ago when the Navy couldn't demonstrate a proper working defense against supersonic cruise missiles, but I think this time they may do it."

"That's why I'm calling: we can't let that happen, Denny. You take the carriers away and we're nothing but a gunboat navy with some submarines. Hell, they know it too, they're just knee jerking right now. I'm calling about a fix."

"A fix for what?"

"The Navy's payload/range problem off their carrier decks. Their strike footprint, or area of influence, if you prefer. The whole reason they've had to put carriers into the Gulf all along, instead of accomplishing the mission from the Gulf of Oman or the Arabian Sea."

Carter was intrigued. "Are you talking about the China Lake project?"

"Yes sir. The Super Hornet is a pig in a poke, and they've known it all along. They're slow, underpowered, and to carry out a long range strike they have to trade off half their ordnance for fuel tanks. Once the S-3s go away they'll be forced to use their strikers as tankers on top of that. If they mean to force a heavily defended naval chokepoint like the Strait of Hormuz, they need something better. This is a chance for us to show off everything we've been working on."

"That's crazy talk, Pat. The AST is a dead program, dead and all but buried. Listen to me, buddy: It'll *never* work. Even if we had a Republican president, House, and Senate, *which we don't*, the appropriations process takes longer than this whole crisis will last. Big Navy made its bed over a decade ago, and now they have to sleep in it."

"If you remember, the Navy *wanted* what we were selling. It was Clinton's people that stomped it, along with those goddamn lobbyists."

"Water under the bridge."

"Look Denny, we've already got half of Flight Deck 21 in prototype, and we're tooled up in the factory to spit out a few more in just a few months. I'm not talking about starting a full blown production run, but maybe enough to finish up a full squadron of Supercats. We've got the missiles for them as well, and the prototype tankers and jammers. Damn, Denny! What was the expenditure for this past decade if it wasn't for something like this?

"Think about it," Jackson went on. "If you're right, we may be in a declared war by this time tomorrow. The Navy is going to have a helluva time forcing the strait with what they have available now. I mean, it's not that they can't do it, but what will it cost them? The last thing the Navy can afford right now is to lose even one more ship. The Advanced Hawkeye and the SM-6 missiles are ready to go, but those are more defensive than offensive tools. The UCAV airwing program is still a good ten to twenty years away from being a reality, and we all know the Block-1 F-25 isn't going to work as a true fleet defense fighter except as a sensor node for the Navy's new integrated counter-air system. With some Supercats backed up by our upgraded Prowlers and long range tankers, a single carrier will be able to almost *double* its strike footprint. We're talking deeper penetration than the Navy had during Vietnam, and we don't have anything even close to Vietnam ranges right now. With Flight Deck 21, the Navy could control the entire Gulf and strike deep into Iran without having to put a single ship through the Strait of Hormuz. Do you think that might interest them?"

There was a long pause. "What's the boss say about it?" Carter asked tentatively.

Jackson grinned on the end of the phone. "You're the first one I called. You're a harder sell than the boss, so . . . "

"You think I'm hard? Try selling this to the Navy!"

"That's going to be *your* job, Denny. If Congress *does* declare war, the funds will be there for this, and a lot more besides."

"You fucker," Denny growled into the phone. "I hate you. You know that don't you? They'll *never* buy it."

"Hey, the worst they can do is say no, right?" Jackson quipped.

"If we can pull this off, it'll be the stuff of legend," Carter mused thoughtfully. "You crazy son of a bitch. Okay, let's do it. I'll see what I can shake loose on this end."

***

WAR WITH IRAN!
First Declared War since WWII.

-Washington Post

WAR!
Congress Declares War on Iran. Here we go again; how much can we tolerate?

-LA Times

U.S. Declares WAR!
Chief of Naval Operations resigns in disgrace following the destruction of the 5th Fleet.

-San Francisco Chronicle

First Declared War Between Nuclear Powers! Iran and the Bomb—what it means for you.

-N.Y. Times

Israel claims that the Iranian nuclear detonation a hoax; IAEA confirms weapons test in Iran, debunking Israeli clams.

-Chicago Sun Times

Duck and Cover? Iran tests nuclear weapons after Gulf battle.

-N.Y. Post

APR 2013
Washington D.C.

The new Chief of Naval Operations, Admiral Darren J. Harris, watched impassively from the back seat of his chauffeured car at the throng of protestors waving anti-war signs and chanting slogans outside the White House. Today was D.J. Harris's first day on the job as CNO, and he felt a little anxious, given the circumstances. The naval establishment was reeling, hurting physically and emotionally. Morale was rock bottom, and it seemed like half the Atlantic Fleet was making casualty assistance calls for the other half. The news media was heralding their defeat in the Gulf as the end of the aircraft carrier as a weapon of war, and the Senate Armed Services Committee was going to be riding him for his entire tenure in the top job.

Suck it up, Harris told himself. *This is what it is to be a wartime CNO.*

The choice of Harris for this post was very calculated. Unlike his submarine service predecessor, Harris was a combat blooded naval aviator. He'd commanded two aircraft squadrons, an aircraft carrier, a carrier strike group, and the United States Atlantic Fleet during a thirty year naval career. Nobody was better suited to understanding the service's current challenges, or was better versed in the various strengths and vulnerabilities of modern carrier forces.

"That didn't take too long, did it, sir?" remarked his driver, referring to the mob of protestors on Pennsylvania Avenue.

"It never does," Harris replied. "That's alright, though. You and I wear the uniform, so those folks are free to walk around in the cold waving their protest signs. We don't have to like it, but that's why we do it. Never forget that."

"I won't, sir."

Harris's first stop this morning was a White House press conference where President Marsden introduced him to the nation. Then it was on to his first meeting with the Joint Chiefs of Staff and the National Security Advisor. None of them were strangers, given his long tenure as a flag officer and time spent in the Pentagon. When they met, there were brief congratulations before getting down to the business at hand.

The pressing priority was the detonation of a nuclear weapon in Iran. This conversation began with a specially prepared brief presented not just by the Defense Intelligence Agency, but by the CIA as well, along with a guest briefer from the Israeli Defense Force. Harris suspected that the Israeli officer was a member of the Israeli Institute for Intelligence and Special Operations, better known as the Mossad. It didn't matter to him either way, only the information he brought. Despite the hard evidence obtained by IAEA inspectors and several covert operations carried out by several nations, the intelligence assessment was that Iran was still a decade or more away from achieving true status as a nuclear power. The Israeli briefer could not be convinced otherwise by any 'what-if' argument put forth by his American peers, and he came equipped with hard-won intelligence data to back it up. No nation on Earth had more reason to fear a nuclear-capable Iran than Israel, and no nation kept a closer watch on their progress towards achieving the Bomb. The Israeli position was that Iran simply wasn't there yet, and that Iran was conducting a moderately successful deception with someone else's aid.

That begged the questions: where had the weapon come from, *and did Iran have any more of them?* That one was harder to answer, although there was only a short list of answers for the first question. Pakistan and North Korea topped the list as suspects, with Russia a close third. The Israelis were presently going to extreme lengths to find out if there were more nuclear weapons in Iranian hands. So far they were not able to find evidence of any, but Iran was a large country. When superimposed on a map of the United States, its borders would touch Mobile, Denver, Dallas, and Chicago, stretching lengthwise from the Gulf Coast all the way into the southeastern corner of Montana. Much of the country was rugged and mountainous, and there were innumerable places where just about anything could be hidden.

When asked if Israel had plans to strike at known Iranian nuclear facilities, the IDF officer grew guarded, indicating that no strikes were being planned because Israel didn't believe Iran had a nuclear capability at present. To his mind, it was a foolish question: *why would Israel strike Iran when the United States had just committed to doing so?* To further that line of thought, he was authorized to turn over all the information Israel had amassed on the Iranian nuclear weapons program. It was *far* more information than U.S. sources had managed to obtain, and some of it was startling in its detail. The Israeli officer also informed them of his nation's renewed willingness to participate in a covert cyber-attack on the Iranian nuclear program using the Stuxnet computer virus previously developed for this purpose. The prior administration had vetoed its use, but President Marsden would almost certainly approve it under the current circumstances. The JCS voted in favor of a cyber-strike, and the NSA informed them he would take it to the president for final NCA approval.

The intelligence briefers were dismissed once the discussion on the nuclear question was finished, and the chiefs addressed the problem of the war itself. Marsden wanted a clear plan of action and a clear definition of victory. Ironically, one of the restrictions of a 'declared war' rather than the more ambiguous actions undertaken by the U.S. military in past decades was the real need for an actual, legal resolution. Nobody was willing to let the situation in Iran become another North Korean armistice, forever unresolved.

D.J. Harris came to the meeting with those answers in hand. It was a contingency plan drawn up by the previous administration for use in a situation like this one. There were two major aspects to the operation: the first was the economic strangling of Iran. Their oil fields and platforms would be targeted, and the U.S. Navy would ensure that no Iranian tanker got any farther than the Arabian Sea before being seized or sunk. The chief sources of Iran's national income would be systemically removed from play, and the U.S. would wage an information warfare campaign directed at the Iranian people, who were already in various stages of unrest over the Ayatollah's regime. The message would be clear: if you want the pain to stop, the poverty to stop, the deprivation to stop, you must take your country back from its ruthless, fanatical overseers.

The matter of the Gulf itself would involve more traditional, kinetic warfare. The plan involved peeling back Iranian defenses from the coastlines, blunting them, destroying the Iranian Air Force and Navy in the process. In addition, their nuclear weapons program would be targeted and destroyed completely. The final phase of the plan involved the amphibious invasions of five Gulf Islands held by Iran: Abu Musa, Farur, Greater and Lesser Tunb, and Sirri. These islands would be taken and used as permanent U.S. bases to ensure freedom of navigation for all nations in the Strait of Hormuz. The native population of these islands would be forcibly relocated back to mainland Iran. Bandar Abbas and Qeshm Island would be subjected to strikes until there was no military presence remaining, likewise Kish and Lavan Islands to the northwest. Militarily speaking, the objective of the war was to de-fang Iran completely. Getting to this point would take some time, because Iran claimed it was mining the northern Gulf of Oman against the advance of any flotilla of naval vessels, leaving only two dedicated corridors for the passage of civilian shipping. They threatened to mine those as well if any warships pressed north towards the Strait of Hormuz. Such an act would effectively close off the Persian Gulf, throwing the entire world into crisis.

Abu Musa and Sirri Islands both had airfield facilities. Once under the U.S. flag, these air bases would be expanded, and a permanent force of USAF fighters put in place to enforce an ongoing no-fly zone over southeastern Iran and ensure freedom of navigation in Gulf airspace. The goal was to reduce reliance on Gulf State allies needed to conduct operations. In essence, the islands would become 'unsinkable' bases from which the U.S. could carry out unfettered air and maritime security operations. The Navy and Marine Corps would seize these objectives, and then they would be held by the Army and Air Force. The declared war would end when Iran sued for peace, but U.S. military operations would effectively cease when the island bases were secured, the Iranian military was destroyed, and the strait permanently re-opened. The problem of Iran 'acting out' in the Persian Gulf had been ever-present since the Shaw's overthrow in 1979. Now, three and a half decades later, it was going to be settled permanently.

Understandably, the plan Harris showed them met with some hesitancy, even resistance. It was bold and ambitious, and evocative of the previous administration's way of doing business. President Powell had learned the harsh lessons of Vietnam firsthand, and his famous doctrine for foreign interventions was in evidence all over this plan; it was only feasible if Powell's criteria were met. In this case they were, all because Iran had inexplicably decided to flex what muscle it had to sink an American task force. In the end, however, the plan Harris presented met with President Marsden's requirements. The JCS adopted it as the initial blueprint for their war plan against Iran, and they began the detailed staff work needed to make it happen.

***

ADM Harris made his way back around to his office, where he found three men waiting for him. One was his Deputy CNO for Warfare Requirements and Programs. The second man was another officer from his staff: the Director of Test and Evaluation and Technology Requirements. The third man was a civilian, dressed in an expensive suit and wearing a visitor's badge. For all that, he looked like no stranger to the Pentagon. "Gentlemen," the CNO said by way of greeting.

His DCNO stepped forward. "Sir, allow me to introduce Mister Denny Carter, chief of corporate and government relations for Northman-Ironworks Aerospace. Mister Carter, Admiral D.J. Harris, the Chief of Naval Operations."

Denny stuck out his hand and a wry grin split his features. "It's an honor, admiral," he said, shaking Harris's hand. Carter's eyes took note of the gold wings the admiral proudly wore, as well as his 'salad bar' of awards and ribbons. Those were a resume of sorts if one knew how to read them, and Carter was emboldened by what he saw. *Thank God the new boss is an air dale!* He thought triumphantly to himself. That was half the battle won already, and he already knew that 'Fang' Harris had started his career in the cockpit of nothing other than the F-14 Tomcat. It was going to matter, *a lot.*

"Honor's all mine," Harris replied affably. He looked between the three men, and saw the nervous hope in the eyes of his two deputies. He let his gaze roam back and forth between the three of them for a long moment. "You three look like you're up to no good," he finally said. "To what do I owe this august gathering?"

"Boss, we need about an hour of your time. Mister Carter comes to us with an . . . *interesting* proposal, to say the least. It may be a *big* help with what's coming up, and ultimately with carrier viability going forward."

Harris was intrigued. He looked at Carter, whose face still wore that wry grin, although there was a strong hint of seriousness to it now. "Northman-Ironworks, eh? Are we talking about airplanes, or weapons, here?"

"Little of both, admiral. I'm you're an aviator—you'll have an innate grasp of what I'm here to show you. I think you're going to like it."

Harris looked over at his DCNO. "Am I going to like it, Josh?" he asked.

"Sir, you are *very much* going to like it."

"So, what's the catch?" Harris asked.

Carter shrugged. "Nothing much, admiral, only taking a small wrecking ball to some well-established empires and shaking up the military-industrial complex a bit. Interested?"

"And money, I take it?"

Carter grinned. "*Always*, admiral. No getting around that, I'm afraid."

Harris's yeoman stepped up and opened the door to his new office, holding it for them. "Well, I just laid a war plan on the joint chiefs that's going to cause some serious hate and miscontent, so I guess I might as well go all-in with the military industrial complex, eh? Yeoman Nash, hold all calls and find a way to MacGyver an hour into my schedule," he ordered. "Better put on a fresh pot of coffee, too."

"Aye aye, sir."

***

Oceana, Virginia

Fargo's return to the United States was radically different than his past deployments. This time there was no 'air wing flyoff' followed by an emotional, triumphant homecoming on the tarmac at NAS Oceana. Getting home had been a different sort of adventure altogether. USS *North Carolina* had carefully transited the Strait of Hormuz through Oman's territorial waters, unseen and untracked by anyone. Once safely into the Gulf of Oman she moved back into international waters, sailing on into the Arabian Sea for a rendezvous with the USS *Coral Sea* carrier battle group. Fargo and the embarked SEALs had all transferred off the submarine at that point, leaving her to steam back to her homeport as the sole surviving vessel of Carrier Strike Group Two. Once aboard *Coral Sea*, message traffic was sent informing the world at large that one LCDR Michael Thorsen was still among the living, and he was finally able to contact his family directly.

Fargo spent a few days aboard *Coral Sea* having his injuries treated. He'd suffered a simple fracture of his right arm during the ejection, and the corpsman aboard the submarine did a fairly good job of setting his arm and getting a cast on it. When he transferred aboard *Coral Sea,* the medical staff aboard the carrier basically went about redoing the work to their satisfaction. By the time he was evaluated by a flight surgeon aboard the carrier his faculties were completely normal, he wasn't suffering any symptoms of a concussion, and so he wasn't diagnosed with one. He debriefed extensively with the admiral and intelligence staff, then was flown off in a Greyhound COD to Fifth Fleet headquarters in Bahrain, where he was debriefed again. At that time, he learned that he was one of only a handful of survivors from the entire strike group. Lurch Leaper had survived along with his pilot, Rackdog Johnson. The only other squadron survivors were three enlisted men who were blown overboard and lived to tell the tale when the first Silkworm hit the carrier's island. One was still in serious condition, and all three had taken enough radiation to cast doubt on their long-term life-expectancy. The rest of their squadron roster, over three hundred men and women, had perished aboard *Boxer* or died in the air, in combat. The Gray Wolves had effectively ceased to exist except on paper.

The time in Bahrain was tense but uneventful. The Iranians were maintaining their political stance of 'self-defense' even following the declaration of war, so there were no attacks on U.S. forces stationed in the Gulf States anywhere along the southern shores of the Persian Gulf. Any such attack would have been an invitation for the Gulf States to unite and declare war on Iran as well, something Iran wanted to avoid at all costs. Oman and Iran were already on the brink of hostilities, mostly over Iran's minelaying actions, but that situation remained a standoff rather than a shooting war, for the moment. All U.S. air traffic in and out of Gulf State bases flew routes that kept them out of Persian Gulf airspace, where Iran had stated they would be engaged and shot down.

Fargo and a handful of other survivors shipped out of Bahrain almost two weeks after the battle in a C-17 transport, making their way to Germany, and then on to Andrews AFB aboard a C-5 transport. Their arrival at Andrews was low key, under a discreet media blackout. There was a frenetic media manhunt on for any survivors from the battle in the Gulf—the networks were desperate to get them on television, secure story rights, and get their opinions on record. Fortunately, *only* the casualty lists had been made public; the media knew the identities of those who had died but the survivors were safely anonymous for the time being. It would only be a matter of time, of course, but that was the last thing on Fargo's mind when they touched down at Andrews.

Once back on U.S. soil he felt emotionally overwhelmed. All he wanted to do was get home and just . . . well, *get home.* More than ever, the lack of a family to come home to just made it harder. He stood alone in the terminal at Andrews, feeling lost and more than a little bleak as he watched Lurch get bowled over by his wife and three kids. All five of them were bawling uncontrollably within moments, glommed together in a tight knot of flesh that nothing would be able to separate for a good long while. Rackdog was met by a shapely, honey-blond woman who bore up stoically enough but was still wiping tears from the corners of her eyes as she collapsed into his arms and covered his face with frantic kisses. Fargo was happy for them—Rackdog and Lurch had fought a good fight over the Gulf and knocked down one of Iran's new JF-17 fighters in the scrum, managing not to get shot down themselves. That was better than he had managed, Fargo reflected bitterly. Dexter was dead, buried at sea with all due ceremony and dignity, and Fargo was going to have to live with that forever. All around him, people were either meeting and greeting friends or family, or heading for the exits.

Fargo thought about asking someone for a ride over to Oceana, then decided against it. Hunched over slightly with hands in his pockets, he turtled into the unmarked Nomex jacket he wore over his scrounged flight suit, found a payphone, and called a cab to take him home. In the end he wound up breaking a back door window to get into his own house; nobody else was home, and his house keys were at the bottom of the Persian Gulf.

***

Fargo rapidly found that his life experience hadn't prepared him for the realities of a sunken aircraft carrier and a lost battle. Aside from the psychological impact, he mentally likened it to having his house burned down. The overarching sense of loss and failure was devastating enough, but it was the little, *piddling* things that made his life a living hell for the first few days he was back. For example: his truck was parked on base at Oceana, and not only were his house and car keys gone forever, but so was his wallet, which contained all his credit cards and driver's license. He was also missing his checkbook, cellphone, most of his uniforms, his flight gear, and the best portion of his civilian wardrobe. He limped back into the United States with little more than the clothes on his back, his military ID card, and a government issued credit card with enough money to keep him fed and in toothpaste until he could see to getting his house back in order. The money wasn't a freebie either, just an advance on his pay, which would also have to be sorted out. His pay record had been in the care of the squadron's personnel department, and the hard copy of that record, his NATOPS jacket, his service record, flight logbooks, and medical record were all burned to cinders along with the sailors who had maintained them. Some of those records had duplicates stored in other places, some didn't. Thinking about any of it brought up a stark reminder of shipmates who weren't coming home, *shipmates he had failed to protect*, in his private view of things.

Both of his housemates were out of town when he got back: one was at sea doing pre-deployment work-ups, and the other was down in Key West on a weapons detachment. Fargo had a spare set of truck keys in his house, and there was a spare house key from which he could get a replacement cut for himself. From there, it was just a matter of tackling a checklist of all the other items that needed to be reproduced or replaced.

It turned out that some of the survivors' needs had been anticipated. Fargo was up early the first morning after getting back, thanks in part to the time-zone change from Europe and the Gulf. He rolled out of bed in something of a fugue, feeling zombified, for lack of a better term. Too much had happened to him in too short a time; the juxtaposition of being at home in Virginia Beach after almost seven months at sea, the battles, and everything in between just didn't seem quite real. He brewed a pot of strong, black coffee, then sat himself down in the living room of his house and turned on Sportscenter, of all things. He wasn't interested in the latest scores, but he just wasn't ready to turn on the 24-hour news channels and re-immerse himself in the media coverage of current events. He leaned back on the couch with his bare feet up on the coffee table, his plaster arm-cast stretching out across the back of the couch, and just emptied his mind. In a very real sense, he wasn't mentally back from the Gulf yet.

The sun had been up for a while, hidden behind a low, dreary overcast when the phone rang. He frowned slightly before setting his coffee mug down and heaving himself up to answer it. "Good morning," the voice on the other end said. "This is Lieutenant Commander Lee Howard over at the FITWING office. I'm looking for Lieutenant Commander Thorsen. Is he there?"

"Speaking."

"Heya shipmate, welcome home," Howard said warmly. "Is this a good time?"

Fargo mentally shrugged. "As good as any, hoss. What can I do for you?"

"I just wanted to let you know what's going on. We're setting up a survivors' center over on the flight line, in your squadron's old pre-deployment spaces. There will be an influx of admin personnel, civil and military, on temporary orders to help air wing survivors get their affairs back on track. By order of COMNAVAIRLANT, all survivors are on limited duty pending a fitness-for-duty evaluation and the completion of thirty days of survivor's leave."

Something jarred inside Fargo at those words. "There's a war on. *I don't need*—"

"—Yes you do, whether you realize it or not," Commander Howard cut him off firmly. "Every one of you guys says the same thing, and it's exactly what the docs said you were going to say. It's okay, man, and we've got a grief counseling center set up as well for anyone who needs it, *including you*. Don't try to play Atlas, here. Take the time, see your friends and family, and decompress. It's hard enough coming back from a normal deployment, much less anything like this." Howard paused. "At least we have the experience of Afghanistan to go on—this is one area the Army knows more about than we do. My guess is that you have some pieces to pick up and personal shit that needs doing today—go do those things, but go easy. Report to the squadron spaces at 0800 Monday morning—or whenever you need to before that—and there will be a transition team there to help you with *whatever* you need."

Fargo's throat was so tight he could barely speak. "Okay."

There was a slight pause on the other end. "Your file says you're divorced. Do you live alone? Share a house with some roommates?"

"I've got a couple roommates," Fargo replied in a low tone, not mentioning the fact that neither of them was currently in Virginia.

"Okay, so you aren't all by yourself, then. Good," Howard said, sounding relieved. "Hey, remember what I said about the counseling! The chaplain's office is available as well. I cannot stress this enough: if you need any help, we're here."

"Thanks," Fargo replied.

"Keep the faith, bro, and we'll see you Monday morning."

"Roger that," Fargo replied. The repressed rage finally bubbled up, a red tide that refused to be held in check any longer, exploding behind his eyes. When the phone went dead in his ear, he smashed the receiver down on the edge of the counter repeatedly, until it shattered. Then he jerked the remainder of the phone off its mount with his good hand and hurled it against the far wall. He made a fist, looking around wildly for the next thing to smash, and then realized what he was doing. He slumped into a chair at the kitchen table, put his head down, and for the first time since the battle, he wept.

X

Oceana, Virginia

Feeling like a midshipman who was in the doghouse for some unknown transgression, Fargo swallowed nervously as he gave three loud raps on the frame of the conference room hatchway. "Lieutenant Commander Thorsen, reporting as ordered, sir!" he announced himself.

RADM Ken Devereaux, Commander, Naval Air Forces, Atlantic was the officer who replied. "Enter!" Fargo briskly stepped into the conference room and found himself with three other officers: the admiral, a captain, and a lieutenant. Fargo had no idea why he'd been summoned; he took two steps to the foot of the rectangular table and stood at attention; his cover tucked formally under his left arm. RADM Devereaux waved his hand dismissively and came out from behind his chair, walking down to Fargo's end of the table to extend his hand. "This isn't that kind of meeting, commander," he said with a disarming smile. "It's 'Fargo', isn't it?" he asked as they shook hands.

"Yes sir."

"I'm Cajun, that's my chief of staff, Captain 'Flash' Gordon, and the lieutenant there is my aide, 'Chopper' Wainright. Have a seat."

"Thank you, sir."

"Chopper, I could use really use a cup of joe. Flash?"

"Always, boss. Thank you."

"Fargo?"

"Yes sir, thank you," he replied, feeling a little better but still ill at ease. The flag aide poured coffee into four traditional, handle-less Corningware watch mugs, and passed them around. He put a small tray on the table containing fresh cream and sugar, for any takers. Fargo took his coffee straight up, as always.

"I won't keep you hanging," the admiral went on. "We've just got a couple questions about your deployment, and your fight over the strait. You were flying as section leader, with Lieutenant Deidre Danforth as your wingman, correct?"

"Yes sir," Fargo replied. He began to relax a little, having a sudden suspicion about what this whole impromptu meeting was for.

Devereaux looked him over closely, trying to read his expression and noticing that Fargo's right arm was in a cast. "I've seen the reconstruction of what happened out there, Fargo. That was a tough one, no doubt about it. How's the arm?"

"It's fine sir, all things considered. The cast will come off in a week or two."

"Excellent. Did anyone tell you that P-3 you were covering made it home? You and your shipmates made a difference out there."

"I was aware, sir, and thank you. I wish we could have done more."

"You did about as well as you could with the odds you were handed. Now, about Danforth: you were her division lead on a previous mission, when she scored three kills in a single engagement, correct?"

"Yes sir, and those kills were undisputed."

"Of course. It's your fight over the strait we're trying to sort out," Devereux explained. "We've been over the data that's available, but it's fragmented, and, frankly, unreliable. We've got your debrief on record, and that of Major Garret, but we wanted to make sure of things before we make matters public. A lot of people are having a hard time believing that one Marine in a Harrier took down a Tomcat and two Fulcrums."

Fargo's eyebrows went up. "His debrief? You mean *he survived*?"

"He did," Captain Gordon replied with a grin. "He may wind up being the hottest thing in the Corps since Joe Foss and Pappy Boyington. You didn't know he made it?"

"No sir! I knew about the P-3, but not about him. That's a bit of good news," Fargo replied, feeling buoyed by it. "If I may, gentlemen, in my estimation he deserves the Medal. His wife must hate riding in the back seat all the time."

"Wait, what?" the admiral's aide chimed in, looking confused.

The admiral spared his aide a slightly condescending look. "That's because his big brass balls are riding shotgun, Chopper." He turned back to Fargo. "As for the Medal, he may get it, but it's Danforth that we're talking about right now. So, you agree that Garret's claims are correct?"

"I saw him get two of the three he claimed. If he survived, he must have gotten the third—he couldn't have gotten away otherwise unless there was a mutual bugout, and he wasn't about to bug out as long as he had a single bullet or drop of gas left."

"Fair enough. Who got the other Persian cat?"

"That was Deedee," Fargo replied without hesitation. "My shots went after Bulldog 412's target, but he'd already hit it. Deedee and I had two more kills between us, but honestly I couldn't say who got what, just distant visual confirmation of two downed targets in the form of vertical smoke trails."

The admiral and chief of staff exchanged looks. "So, the eastern Tomcat was Danforth's kill, and *maybe* one of the MiGs in the second group?"

Fargo looked COMNAVAIRLANT straight in the eye. "Sir, I'd say *at least* one of the MiGs in the second group. Both, if that's how it needs to read."

"One is all she needs," Gordon said, looking excited.

"We're not trying to *invent* the truth, here, Fargo," Devereaux said carefully.

Sure you are, admiral, but in this case I actually believe it myself, Fargo thought. "I understand that sir. What I'm saying is that if the data shows something definitive, there's no argument. If you are relying on my judgement for the determination, then I say give them *both* kills, sir," Fargo said firmly. "Six victories make it definitive—no ambiguity. Deidre Danforth becomes the first American female ace, and the first ace since the Vietnam war. I do have one thing to add if I may."

"What's that?"

"There were two aviators in that jet. Lieutenant Deidre Danforth was one, and Lieutenant Commander Ned Mullen was the other. They were flying together for the first three kills, too.

All I would ask is that any award or recognition bestowed is given to both."

"That goes without saying," Gordon assured him.

Good, Fargo thought, *because until now, I haven't heard Stinky mentioned even once.*

"Alright then," Devereaux said. "You need to be sure about this, Fargo, because once it becomes a matter of record, it won't do for that record to be disputed in the future. If you want to claim one or even both of those MiGs, now's the time. You've got two victories on record already, so two more would put you in striking range of being an ace yourself. Some pilots would say or do just about anything to tip that scale in their favor."

"I'm not that guy, sir, but all I can give you is my word on that. This will be good for the Navy, and God knows we need the shot in the arm right now. Since it's a posthumous honor for Danforth and Mullen, I want it for their families too. And that's all there is to it," he said firmly.

RADM Devereaux looked impressed, but he was obviously from the 'trust but verify' school. He shot a quick glance at this chief of staff.   "Are you willing to put your statement in writing?" Gordon asked. "We can make it an addendum to the official action report."

"If you have a spare computer handy, captain, I'll write it up before I leave this office," Fargo assured him.

"Chopper will set you up," the admiral said with a nod towards his aide. "That's it then, except for the part about congratulations being in order." He paused to gauge Fargo's reaction, but Fargo just looked at him curiously, waiting for him to continue. Devereaux produced a standard ALNAV message from a blue folder on the table. "Judging by your look, I take it you haven't seen this yet. It's the results of the O-5 promotion and command screening boards. You made the cut, commander. Bravo Zulu, and congrats!"

"Hey, congratulations, fella!" the chief of staff added, thumping him on the back. The flag aide added his congratulations as well. Fist bumps went all around since Fargo's right arm was out of commission. "Have you heard anything on your next set of orders yet?" Gordon added, acting for all the world as if Fargo had just rolled back into town from a normal deployment. The question was a bit surreal, under the circumstances.

"Not yet, sir," Fargo replied, wondering why he felt so numb after hearing that he'd achieved a major professional and personal goal. Was it because it didn't matter to him anymore? *No, that's not it,* he decided. *It did matter, maybe more than ever.* Maybe it was because he expected to make it all along, especially with his combat record in Afghanistan and now the Gulf. It just seemed insignificant right now, stacked against present circumstances.

But he had to wonder: how would it have gone if he hadn't played ball over Deedee's status? A promotion board could give, but higher authority could always take away. *Odd that the air boss just happened to have a copy of that ALNAV on hand,* he thought sourly. *Was that going to be the leverage if they needed it?*

Fargo wrote up the addendum to immortalize his dead wingmen. Big Navy had its first female ace, and some good media fodder for a change. He headed back to the hangar feeling hollow inside, despite the good news of his own pending promotion.

***

Fargo didn't know why he spent so much time during the workday at the hangar set up for the survivors; after so many years in the Navy, just staying at home and not doing anything felt strange. There was still a coffee machine in the hangar ready room, so Fargo stopped in to pour himself a fresh round of joe before wandering out in search of something to do.

It was a difficult time, easily the worst in his life. The loss of his ship and squadron still didn't seem real, to say nothing of losing an entire strike group. It was one thing to lose a friend or shipmate due to combat or a mishap, but it was quite another to lose *all* of them in one day. There was grief, the sense of failure—

that he'd somehow let down the country and the Navy—and worst of all, a rotten case of survivor's guilt. It was mentally easy to understand that war didn't play favorites, but emotionally it was harder to accept. On a battlefield, one man would dodge right and another left; one would step on a landmine, and the other would live. There was no fairness to it, just the fortunes of war. Aviators had a term for it: the Golden BB. When the bullet with your name on it was fired, there was no dodging it: your time was up. He was having a hard time accepting that in Dexter's case. He played the final engagement over and over in his head, torturing himself with the choices that might have made for a different outcome. It still ate away at him that he'd lived, and Dexter had died. John Wong had met his Golden BB over the Strait of Hormuz, and that was that. Fargo knew he would learn to live with it eventually, but not just yet.

Not yet.

As the squadron's former maintenance officer, Fargo filled a string of empty days writing letters to the families of his people. That was typically the task of a commanding officer, but Skipper Jefferson was dead, and Fargo would have written letters anyway. Most of the squadron's enlisted personnel were in his department in some form or other—it was just the way a squadron was set up. He ended up adopting something of a form letter, but it was heartfelt and carried his own unique references to the individual in question. Some he had known better than others, but that was always the case. Every unit had its characters, colorful personalities, golden children, problem children, misfits, and the quiet introverts who faded into the background like chameleons, almost nameless. He made the letters as personal as he could, remembering something unique about each sailor, or sharing an anecdote or story that involved them.

The hardest letters to write were to the families of the young sailors who had worked for him directly, like his administrative yeoman. She'd been nineteen years old, a freckle-faced kid from Wyoming who loved horses. It just seemed strange that a girl off the ranch, not even old enough to drink alcohol, was a fighting bluejacket who'd gone down with her ship, but that was the way of it. When he closed his eyes at night he thought about how they died. When a missile warhead exploded in a confined space, there was only one quick way to go and about a thousand ugly ones, most of which involved suffocation or burning. He wouldn't ever know who went quickly and who suffered, who ran scared and who stood fast, trying to fight fires hot enough to melt steel before dying anyway. When writing the letters, Fargo simply lied. He wrote to every family that based on what he knew, he thought their loved one had died instantly, without pain. He wished he could believe it himself.

Each time he started a letter, he meant to write the one he needed to write the most: the letter to Dexter's parents. Each time, he went to the next name on his list and Dexter's letter went unwritten.

He just wasn't ready for that one.

After a few restless nights he considered going to see one of the grief counselors, then decided against it. How could they possibly understand? What could they say that would make him feel any better? One afternoon the base chaplain came around to his house, making a personal call. Fargo talked to him for a while and felt a little better afterwards, but only a little.

Today, on his way back from his meeting with COMNAVAIRLANT, was the first time he'd paused on the ramp and watched a flight of fighters take off. It startled him to think that for the first time in years, he'd gone a couple of weeks without really thinking about flying. It would be a while before he was medically cleared again; he still had a cast on his arm, although he'd modified it by cutting away some of the plaster around his hand so he could type two handed. The flight docs assured him he'd return to flying status once the cast came off and he had a chance to build his arm strength back up.

Fargo wasn't the only one suffering from some post-traumatic stress. He wandered past Lurch's former office, to find the XO inhabiting his old haunt. Like Fargo, he was having a hard time staying away. The door was open, and when he glanced in he saw Lurch sitting at his desk, staring off blankly into space. When

Lurch found out that Fargo was writing letters, he'd started doing the same for all the other departments. Fargo eased his cast back into its sling and took a slurp of coffee to cover his own discomfort after rapping once on the door. Lurch blinked once as if startled and then looked up at him, appearing lost.

"What's on your mind, boss?" Fargo asked.

"What? Oh, nothing. Just thinking." Ron Leaper leaned back in his seat and sighed, rubbing his eyes under his new navy-issue glasses. He waved at a chair. "Have a seat," he said. "How did your meeting with the admiral go?"

"Good, sir," Fargo replied. He went on to explain that their former shipmates were the first navy aces since Vietnam, and Deedee the first American female ace, period. It was good news—it would have been better if they'd lived to enjoy the accolades. He didn't mention the news about his own promotion and command screen; he certainly didn't feel like blowing his own horn.

"Good, good," Lurch replied, still sounding distracted. He looked around the office, eyes welling up, and for a moment the man was on the verge of tears.

"You okay, Lurch?" Fargo asked.

Lurch chuckled bitterly. "Hell of a command tour, huh?" he said. "Congratulations by the way," he added, and Fargo knew he must have seen the ALNAV message with the promotion board results. He understood what was eating Lurch: the XO had eighteen years on active duty, and he would have assumed command of the Gray Wolves shortly after returning from deployment. Now the squadron was wiped out, and Leaper's professional future was a question mark. On the flip side, at least he was *alive.* Fargo wondered if maybe that was eating at him too: nobody had a monopoly on survivor's guilt. Lurch shook his head. "Shit, listen to me," he went on. "Here I am sitting and crying over my fucking career when everyone else is dead. How selfish is that?"

Fargo shook his head. "It's human, sir," he said. "Worrying about the future is a good sign—it means you're alive, and looking forward."

"It's fuckin' *pathetic*." Lurch looked over at him. "What about you? What do you want to do?"

Fargo thought about it for a moment, then then gave him the most honest answer he had: "I want to go back to the Gulf and kill *all* those fuckers." It was the first time he'd voiced that thought, even to himself, and as soon as he did he knew it was God's truth. He *did* want to go back, something awful. He had unfinished business.

"Well, you're in line for your own squadron, but it won't come that fast. You're going to have to pay your dues on a staff, or in the Pentagon or something first. You know how it goes."

Fargo shifted in his seat uncomfortably. "I don't know, Lurch. I want to go back to the Gulf, and I don't really care how. Shit, I'll go as ship's company on the next carrier headed that way, if I have to. I want back into the fight."

"Well, I'll endorse whatever you ask for when you go hunting for orders. You've been top shelf as a Gray Wolf, Fargo. Couldn't ask for any better."

"Thanks, sir. I wish I could've done more." *I wish I could've brought Dex back!*

Lurch looked at his computer monitor, and forced a grin. "Okay, the pity party is adjourned. I've got work to do. Hey," he called after him, "did your roomie make it back from Key West yet?"

Fargo grinned. "Negative. He's been e-mailing me pictures of bimbos in bikinis while we're up here waiting for Spring, the little bitch."

"Why don't you come on over to my house and have supper with the family tonight? You've been at that keyboard so much that you're going burn your eyes out and go WSO if you aren't careful."

"You got cold beer?" Fargo asked.

Lurch chuckled. "You bring the cold beer, and I'll bring the steaks."

"Sounds good," Fargo replied.

***

Fargo and the rest of the survivors were still under orders to take thirty days survivors' leave. He'd been putting it off, but he knew it was finally time to go when the media circus began catching up with the survivors of the *Boxer* strike group. Coming home from the base a few days after his meeting with the admiral, he swore a blue streak when he spotted three media vans camping outside his house, waiting for him. Somehow they had ferreted him out, but he wasn't surprised. There were rules and procedures about talking to the media, but the media didn't know or care about those rules, and they were hard to live by when the subject was ambushed and had a forest of microphones shoved in their face. Some people couldn't wait to talk to the media, hoping to spin fifteen minutes of fame into some sort of lucrative semi-permanent gig as a talking head or 'contributor.' Fargo was *not* one of those people; he slowed his truck to a crawl, unsure about what he wanted to do. He decided he'd just drive through and head back to the base. He could always get a room at the Bachelor Officer's Quarters for a night or two, waiting them out until he had a chance to sneak home, pack a bag, and skedaddle.

Someone in the camera van with the TNN logo made him, and it peeled out to follow him. Fargo watched the van tail him all the way back to the NAS Oceana main gate, where it was denied access to the base. *Suck it, Traitor News Network!* he thought triumphantly.

Two days later he realized there wouldn't be any 'waiting them out'. The vans sitting outside his residence didn't go away: they multiplied instead. In the end, he parked a block away and knocked on the door of the house behind his own to get permission to sneak over his own back fence. He waited until nightfall, feeling like a Navy SEAL as he stole into his own house to grab some personal things, then back out over the fence to make his escape. He put in his leave papers the next day, and struck out for Minnesota.

***

Islamic Republic of Iran

Arkady Kovalev watched from behind the camera as Toma Baranov concluded his interview with the Al Jazeera television crew. The genie was out of the bottle now; *Krasnyye Kogti* had gone mainstream, and the Red Talons were fast becoming minor celebrities in the Islamic Republic. For reasons of their own, the *Feilong* were staying out of the limelight, and their existence wasn't even officially acknowledged, as far as Kovalev knew. Cheng Ye himself was like a ghost, an enigmatic figure that was rarely seen by anyone unless it was in the air in his distinctively marked Sukhoi.

So far, the Red Talons had been victorious against their foes. Kovalev's bank account was fat with bonus money: the equivalent of $7500, paid in Rubles. The Iranians were offering the volunteers a bonus of $10000 for every fighter or support aircraft shot down in their service, and $25000 for the large prize: an AWACS or JSTARS aircraft. On the day the American carrier group was destroyed, Kovalev's flight of four had split the bounty on three American fighters destroyed between them. Since there was no way of knowing who had killed who in the BVR engagement, the three surviving pilots had each taken credit for one kill, but split the pot four ways. The fourth share was sent back to Russia, to the family of the pilot who had been killed. The others had agreed to this without much hesitation—they knew that next time it might be their own families receiving the money.

Things had settled down for the time being, and there was talk of moving the volunteer groups to the southern coast, perhaps Chabahar, although Kovalev felt that location was too exposed and vulnerable. General Abdi had dropped hints that the IRGC was building a series of secret airbases into the mountainsides north of Bandar Abbas, and that seemed like a much better long term proposition. As much as Kovalev had gotten to know and even like Shiraz, he knew they were terribly exposed here. American satellite intelligence had them pinpointed, and now that America had declared war, an attack on this base or any other was a constant threat. Their navy might have been pushed out of the Gulf for now, but the Americans had stealth bombers capable of making the trip all the way from the United States and attacking Iran without ever being detected. Frankly, he was surprised that such attacks hadn't already happened. Apparently, Iran's declaration of nuclear capability was giving her enemies reason to pause, as intended.

As the camera crew began packing up their equipment to leave, Kovalev couldn't help but notice the journalist who conducted the interview. Her name was Tara Shirazi, and she was well known to regular watchers of Al-Jazeera. Aside from being beautiful, one of the things Kovalev liked about her was that she spoke Russian, if not fluently. She was standing slightly apart as her crew did their work, chatting lightly with Baranov, and Kovalev approached them. She was dressed conservatively, in a green, long sleeve blouse with dark slacks and heeled boots. She wore a large, colorful scarf that swirled around her neck and up over the top of her head, covering it but leaving her face visible. What he could see of her hair was a dark, lustrous mass, and her large eyes were a striking hazel color, seeming almost golden. When her eyes met his, Kovalev found his breath catching slightly in his throat. He could understand why half the young men in this country professed an undying love for her.

Baranov covered a smile when he saw the spellbound look on Kovalev's face, knowing the man was lost. He introduced them and they exchanged pleasantries, with Kovalev trying to impress her with his halting few words of Farsi, while she responded in broken, Farsi-accented Russian. She sensed his interest and smiled inwardly; this was nothing new when she met a man. She found Kovalev impressive, however. He was handsome enough, standing about 5'10", with unruly blond hair, pale blue eyes, and a conservative mustache—the latter was nothing like the hairy abomination Baranov boasted. She was just tall enough to match his height when she was in heels, and she liked that; barefoot, she would be just a few inches shorter than he was. She knew from her research that he had already flown in combat against the Americans, and likely would again, things being the way they were. Despite his demonstrated bravery, he came across as easygoing and even self-deprecating. He had sad eyes, or perhaps the eyes of a man who understood he was living on borrowed time.

Shirazi liked him from the first moment they spoke.

She tried not to show her own interest. It wasn't seemly or proper, and she was a well-known figure. That said, Kovalev and his pilots were becoming well-known locally, and would soon be known throughout her country. Perhaps, in time, they would even be known throughout the Islamic world.

Kovalev finally found an opening in the conversation, and asked her how long she would be in Shiraz. Since her current assignment involved reporting on the Red Talons, she replied that it would be 'a while.' Non-committal, as it was, but with a hint of promise.

"I would like to see you again, *Gospozha* Shirazi," he told her. "Perhaps for tea, or a walk in the park? You can teach me about your country, and I can tell you tales of the *Rodina.*"

Tara Shirazi had a nuclear smile: the kind that lit entire rooms and melted hearts. It was just one of the reasons she was so successful as a television personality. She turned it on Kovalev, agreed to the possibility of a meeting, and gave him the number of the hotel where she was staying. Then she departed with her crew, leaving a hint of jasmine fragrance in her wake.

Kovalev was reeling; it took a few moments for him to return to Earth. "*Bozhe moi!*" he muttered after her.

"That is quite a woman," Baranov agreed sagely, grinning from ear to ear. "Good luck with that one, my friend."

"So, *tovarich*, what happens now?" Kovalev asked.

"Abdi says that Iran's posture will move to a defensive one. The Americans will come, and we'll defend against them to the best of our abilities." The two men were outside, in the central courtyard of the building they lived in. By unspoken agreement, they strolled casually outside of it, through the large sword-arch and into the open where they couldn't be overheard by any listening devices.

"Be careful, Baranov. Cheng Ye will spend all our lives if it suits his purpose. It seems matters are already . . . how should I say? . . . *escalating* beyond what the Iranians intended?"

"These Muslim fanatics—"

"—Careful!" Kovalev warned him in a low voice. They were speaking Russian, but that meant nothing. Iran had plenty of Russian-speaking interpreters, and there were others nearby.

Baranov's features darkened. "—These *fanatics* have an agenda of their own. Don't credit all of this to Cheng Ye. The mullahs were very emboldened by their successes in Iraq. They already look toward the Kuwaiti Oil Fields, and those possessed by the Saudis. They've seen Shia Arabs embrace Shia Persians as brothers, and there are many more in the southern Gulf States who also feel that religious kinship. If Iran can keep the United States out of the Gulf, make them irrelevant, they'll have a stranglehold on energy prices and the means to bend the other Gulf nations to their will. The Gulf States have seen Iraq virtually destroyed by Iranian-backed Shiite militias. They fear the same thing happening to them."

"What about the Americans?"

Baranov shrugged. "Look at your history. The Americans will bluster and fight for a time, enriching their own military-industrial complex and politicians, like they always do. When they've fattened themselves and the public outcry is loud enough, they'll proclaim victory and *leave*. Look what is happening in Afghanistan—the Taliban are already retaking control of the country, and the world hardly notices or cares."

Kovalev scowled. "Leaving Afghanistan after killing Bin Laden was the smartest move the Americans have made this century. Our own experience speaks to that. This feels different, though. The Yankees have not formally declared war in over fifty years."

"It will make no difference in the end, my friend. You'll see. America does not have the stomach for a prolonged war, or mass casualties. Look at the protests already happening on their home soil. There is also the matter of Iran's new status as a nuclear power. That will give the western nations even more cause to vacillate."

"Or strike even harder," Kovalev reflected. "This matter of nuclear weapons . . . what has General Abdi said about it? Or Cheng Ye?"

"Abdi has merely confirmed that Iran is building weapons, and I have very little communication with Cheng Ye. Our Chinese friends clearly have their own agenda."

"Do you believe Abdi?" Kovalev asked.

Baranov gave his subordinate a measured look. "Why shouldn't I?" he asked.

"I have a hard time believing that the national government wouldn't be making threats, if they actually had more of them."

"Perhaps they fear inviting a pre-emptive response from the Zionists. Of course, there is little chance of that, now. The Jewish dogs will fully embrace any opportunity to let the Americans solve their problems for them. As for the Yankees, their new president has no military or foreign policy experience. He'll be a sheep among wolves in the coming months. Cheng Ye's people, our own, and the Iranians will savage him terribly on the world stage before this is all over."

Da, but will we survive it? Kovalev asked himself. He decided to call Tara Shirazi soon, and see her again. In times like these, you had to grab what you could with both hands, *today*, because tomorrow was not promised.

***

Red Lake County, Minnesota

Although the Thorsen clan was relatively spread out around the state of Minnesota, Fargo's return from the dead and subsequent visit was occasion enough to prompt a large reunion on the family farm—it was almost five years since his last short visit. When he called home and told them he was coming, the word had gone out to the entire family. The gathering was planned for the first Saturday he was back, and saw the large farmhouse filled with family and friends.

Fargo had three siblings: one older brother, Eric, married with children of his own, and living in another house on family land just down the road. Eric was a farmer like their father, and had gradually taken over during the past several years as their Dad had gotten older. Eric was wed to his high school sweetheart, and two decades plus four kids later they were still going strong. Wayne was Fargo's younger brother, an auto-mechanic and assistant manager at the service department of a car dealership in Minneapolis. Wayne was also married and had two daughters, and they were pregnant with child number three. The youngest sibling was Fargo's sister Kari, a veterinary nurse who lived one town over. She was in a relationship with her veterinarian boss, still unmarried, but she brought him along anyway to show off to the family.

In addition to the immediate family, two pairs of Fargo's aunts and uncles showed up with a slew of his cousins in tow, and several old family friends were invited as well. The saving grace for Fargo was that the gathering was too large for him to remain the central focus, since there were so many people that hadn't seen each other in a long time. Still, he found himself cornered again and again by curious relatives and acquaintances with questions on one hand and strong opinions on the other. It was good to see his family, but by midafternoon Fargo was starting to miss the relative solitude of his house in Oceana.

The cast was finally off his arm, and he was glad to be free of it. The arm was weak and atrophied, but farm work was the perfect cure for that. He'd made a point of rising early and going out to help Eric in the mornings, although he was out of practice when it came to farm chores. His brother was glad for the company, and Fargo had the chance to reacquaint himself with some heavy machinery that didn't fly. Eric was burning with questions about what Fargo's life was like and what happened in the Gulf, but he was wise enough to wait and let him talk when he was ready. Fargo eventually opened up to him a bit, enough to give him the broad outlines, but not the raw details. Eric quickly realized that he wasn't getting anything near the whole story, and the other problem was that Fargo often sounded like he was speaking a foreign language, laced with acronyms and terms Eric didn't understand. Fargo often forgot that people not versed in 'navy speak' were easily confused by that arcane tongue, and when Eric asked for an explanation or a clarification, his brother tended to stop talking.

Overall, Eric determined that his brother seemed to be doing alright, and he reported that to their concerned parents, who weren't having much luck getting any details out of Fargo about what he'd gone through.

When the house full of people with questions got to feel a little stifling, Fargo headed outside into the snow with a pack of his younger nieces and nephews to build snow forts and engage in a snowball fight. While he was outside, he saw an SUV pull up and park behind the long line of cars in the driveway. Two older folks and a youth he didn't recognize got out, along with a vaguely familiar looking woman about his age. Long, blond hair crept out from under her knit hat, and she was bundled up in a bulky jacket that hid most of her. She caught him looking, and gave a friendly wave before hurrying to catch up with her parents and get inside out of the cold. Fargo was trying to place her in his memory when a well-aimed snowball caught him in the back of the head, exploding in a cloud of stinging ice crystals all around him.

"He shoots; he *scores!*" cried one of his nephews, exchanging a high five with his brother.

"Oh, you little hosers are gonna pay for *that,* you betcha!" Fargo shouted, and pitched back into the fight with relish.

***

A little while later, when the long tables were set with food and guests were loading up plates, Fargo reappeared from upstairs in a dry pair of jeans and a blue-plaid flannel shirt. He stood in the doorway near the dining room, taking it all in with a slight smile on his face when his mother came up from behind and wrapped her arms around him, leaning her head on his shoulder. "Dammit all, Mike, it's good to have you back," she said in her usual forward way, her Norski accent standing out starkly to him after all the years away. "How are you doing?" she asked.

Fargo reached up and patted her hand affectionately. "I'm doing fine, Ma," he replied quietly, watching the blond woman he'd seen before ushering a young, towheaded boy in front of her and helping him prepare a plate. Without a hat and coat and close-up, Fargo finally recognized her. "Holy shit," he muttered quietly, so only his mother could hear, "is that Angela Sorensen?"

He grimaced when his mother cuffed him lightly across the back of the head. "Watch your damn language, Mike!" she scolded, the very soul of motherly hypocrisy. "Yah, that's Angie, all right," she added thoughtfully a moment later. Standing behind him as she was, Fargo didn't see the calculating gaze his mother aimed at the back of his head. "You ought to go say hello to her."

"What's she doing here?"

"I'm pretty sure she came with her parents," his mother replied with just a hint of patronization.

Suddenly all the pieces fell into place in his memory, and he realized who the two older folks he'd seen in the driveway were. "Uff da! That was Ollie and Sue, then!"

"You betcha."

"I didn't recognize them—they look a lot older than I remember."

"That happens when you haven't seen someone in almost twenty years, Mike."

"So, who's the kid, then?"

His mother sighed. "That's Angie's son, A.J."

Fargo's budding interest suddenly fled. "Oh," he replied neutrally, then changed the subject. "You gonna grab some chow?"

"You betcha," his mother replied, stepping around and taking his arm. "C'mon," she said, leading him over to the table. He'd had been hanging back out of subconscious habit—at any community feed, he was used to waiting until his enlisted sailors cycled through a chow-line before jumping in himself. Now he found himself waiting on kids and guests. His mother walked them right up behind Angela and A.J. The latter turned around and looked Fargo over boldly and curiously. "Hey there, A.J.," Fargo's mother said.

"Hi, Mrs. Thorsen."

"A.J., this is my son Mike. He went to school with your mom a long time ago."

"Hey, how ya doing', A.J.," Fargo said by way of greeting. Angela turned around when she heard the exchange. She smiled somewhat self-consciously at them as she put a hand on her son's shoulder. "Well, well," Fargo added. "Hi, Angie."

"Mike! Hey, stranger!" she replied, looking at him curiously. "God, how long has it been?" she asked, as though reading his mind. The last time they had seen each other was at Fargo's high school graduation ceremony, going on nineteen years ago, and Fargo said as much. Angie was slightly younger, two years behind him in school.

"Jeez, you look damn near the same, though," he added gallantly, and it was true. Angela had always been fit, and the few pounds that came for free with the onset of middle age were fetchingly distributed on her. Like a lot of local girls, she had clean, Norski good looks, with long blond hair and pale blue eyes. There was just a hint of crow's feet around her eyes now, and she looked a little more careworn, but who didn't? The Thorsens were all towheads as well; Kari and Angie could have been mistaken for sisters if they were out in town together.

Angela blushed slightly at the compliment, pushing a stray strand of hair back behind her ear like a self-conscious schoolgirl. "Thanks," she replied. "So do you!" Fargo knew that wasn't exactly true: time and trouble had left its mark on him in the form of the premature silver-gray streaks that permeated his close-cropped blond hair. His eyes were different as well; they were harder, colder, tempered by experience and combat, holding a clarity of purpose that was foreign to the boy he'd been all those years before.

A.J. was giving Fargo the once over. "Are you the fighter pilot?" he asked.

"Yes sir."

"My grampa says you've been in a lot of battles, including the one where all those ships got sunk. Is that true?"

"A.J.!" Angie said crossly, but Fargo held up a hand.

"No, it's alright," he replied casually. "Yeah, A.J., I was there. What else did your grampa say about it?"

"He said you got shot down, and you got hurt pretty bad. Did you get shot down? You don't look like you're hurt."

"Yah, I broke my arm, but it's all healed up now," he added, holding it up and wiggling his fingers.

"Oh, that *sucks*," A.J. opined. "Did any of your friends die?"

Angie looked absolutely mortified at the question, and Fargo sensed his mother tensing up behind him. He swallowed once before answering, nodding slowly. "A lot of my friends died, kiddo."

"Here you go, A.J.," Angie added, handing the boy a plate loaded down with food. "Go grab a pop and sit with the kids, okay, honey?"

"But I wanna ask—"

"—*Later*," his mother said firmly, turning him by the shoulders and giving him a gentle shove in the direction she wanted him to go. She looked back quickly at Fargo, who was staring thoughtfully after him. "I am *so* sorry—" she began.

"—Nah, it's okay," Fargo replied, cutting her off steadily. Strangely enough, it *was* okay. He let out a guarded chuckle. "Folks have been tip-toeing around it all day, y'know, asking me about everything else under the sun. He was the first one to look me straight in the eye and just ask, y'know? From the mouths of babes, eh? How old is he?"

"He's ten," she replied.

"Well, that explains it, eh? Too bad your husband couldn't make it, I'd have liked to meet him too," Fargo remarked. A distressed look crossed her features, but Fargo had already noticed she was wearing both an engagement and wedding ring.

Fargo's mom stepped around them and put an arm around Angie's shoulders. "A.J.'s dad passed away a few years ago," she said quietly, giving Angela a squeeze.

"Oh shit, I'm sorry!" Fargo said, feeling about two inches tall.

Angie shrugged, her eyes welling up slightly. "How could you know?" she replied. "Excuse me," she added, walking off.

Fargo turned to his mother and put on his best Jack Nicholson impression. "Well, now don't I feel like the fuckin' ass-hole!" he growled at her. "Thanks for the heads up, Ma!" he added sarcastically.

His mother's response was strongly unsympathetic—not what he expected at all. "Her husband died three years ago, in a car accident. That girl's been living at home and crying in her soup way too long if you ask me. She *needs* a little reality jolt. Get some food, Mike. I need to find Eric junior. He and Kelly Larsen vanished about ten minutes ago, and the *last* thing we need is—"

"—I get it. Not ready to be a great-grandmother yet?" Fargo laughed. "Good luck with that," he added, patting her on the back as she went on her way. Fargo looked over the table, impressed at the layout. There was smoked ham, baked *and* smoked turkeys, a beef roast, and every side dish and fixing known to man. He sorted and prioritized his targets, knowing he'd be back for seconds anyway. He loaded up a plate, grabbed a cold beer out of the ice bucket in the kitchen, and found an unoccupied spot in the living room to sit down and tuck in. There were family and friends on all sides, but the conversations sounded alien to his ear: they concerned livestock, weather, the economy, the price of feed, and so on. This was his home and always would be, but he didn't truly fit in anymore.

He hadn't gotten very far into his meal before Angela Sorensen spotted him by himself and made her way over. She seemed fully recovered from the mention of her dead husband. She didn't ask if she could join him, but just pulled over a chair and sat down. "So," she said after a short interval of silence, "what happened to you after high school? You sort of just dropped off the face of the Earth."

"Remember that spring break trip my class took during my senior year?" he asked. That trip had been to Destin, Florida, on the Gulf Coast. It was a wild time in Fargo's young life, at least from the perspective of age seventeen.

Angie grinned. "I heard the stories. I wish our class had done something like that."

"Well, that trip sold me on warm weather, and I thought it would be nice to go to college down there, so I did. Florida State."

"Gawd, wasn't that expensive, going out of state?"

Fargo shrugged. "The Navy paid for it with an NROTC scholarship. I graduated in '98, got commissioned as an officer, went to flight school, and here I am."

Angie nodded wryly. "And what about all the years in between? Did you ever get married? Have any kids?"

"Yes and no," Fargo replied. "I married a gal from school, but that only lasted a couple years. No kids. Other than that, I've spent most of my time flying airplanes and riding around the world in aircraft carriers." He took a swig of beer and shrugged. "I've enjoyed it, for the most part."

Angie smiled wanly. "What about the wars? The fighting? Now we're in another one."

Fargo thought about how to articulate his answer. "I don't really think about it like that," he explained. "That's what the job is about, when you get down to brass tacks. You prepare for war during peacetime, then fight during wartime. Is it exciting? It can be. It can be pretty awful, too, as we've seen lately."

"So, what happens to you next?" she asked.

Fargo shrugged. "I'm not sure yet. I'll find out when I go back. I recently got promoted and am in line to command a fighter squadron, but that's a few years away yet. What happens between now and then is up in the air," he added, with a dramatic raise of his eyebrows.

Angie laughed. "Pun intended?"

"You betcha. Now what about you?" he asked. Angie told him about going to community college after high school, picking up an accounting degree. She'd met her husband while working for a construction company in Duluth—he was the owner's son. They had married after a few years of an on-and-off-again romance, and A.J. was born a couple of years later. Then, three years ago, her husband lost control of his car on an icy bridge one night in winter and went into the water. It was a mystery at first given that he had simply vanished, and it had taken weeks to find him. Listening to her talk, Fargo realized she had loved him deeply. Three years hadn't done much to ease the hurt, but now at least she could talk about it without losing her composure.

Most of her husband's life insurance payout was rolled into a trust fund for her son, and she'd taken him home to live on her parents' farm. She did farm work and part time clerical work, and was thinking about going back to school, but Fargo could sense she was drifting. The economy was rotten, and tuition costs were getting worse every year. He also learned that her last name was Olsen now, not Sorensen, and she didn't mention anything about her current personal life.

Fargo asked her about A.J. and how he had adjusted. He'd been seven when it happened, a tough age for a boy to lose his father, but was there a good one? He had rebounded well enough, living on the Sorensen farm with his grandfather to look up to, along with a couple of uncles who lived in the area. The meal came and went, and one beer had turned into three or four when Fargo finally noticed the house was a lot emptier than earlier, and it was getting dark outside. Ollie and Sue eventually came around with A.J. in tow, ready to hit the road. The pleasant warmth he'd felt the past few hours began fading away.

"You about ready to get on home?" Ollie asked his daughter.

Angie looked a little crestfallen. "Yah, I suppose we should be getting along." The two of them stood up and Fargo stretched, ignoring the residual, aching twinge that ran up and down his right arm.

Sue Sorensen was looking back and forth between her daughter and Fargo. The latter did cut a relatively handsome figure: he was six feet even, ruggedly handsome like his father and brothers, with a square jaw and athletic build. She wondered what he looked like in his uniform. "How long are you home for, Mike?" she asked.

"I'll be around for a couple weeks yet," Fargo replied.

"Well, maybe we'll see you again before you have to leave."

Fargo nodded, resisting the impulse to steal a look at Angie with their mothers staring straight at them. "That'd be nice, you bet."

Only about three people in the county outside of his own family knew it, but Ollie Sorensen was a Vietnam veteran. He stepped forward and stuck out a gnarled paw. "We're glad you made it home safe and sound, Mike. I know it was tough out there. Thanks for everything you do. I mean that."

"Thank you, sir," Fargo replied, shaking his hand. Ollie led his family out, but Angela tarried for a moment. He turned to her. "Thanks for coming. It's good to see you again after all this time."

"Yah, you too," she replied warmly. She hesitated a beat, then stepped in and gave him a quick hug. Fargo returned it easily, sparking at her touch. Her hair was silk soft against his cheek and ear, and she smelled pleasantly female, mixed with some sort of fragrant body wash and a light hint of perfume. Those were things he hadn't experienced at close quarters in the better part of a year, and his body was letting him know. Then she was gone, vanishing into the night outside. Fargo turned around and caught his nephew, nineteen year old Eric Jr, standing in the doorway of the kitchen with his arm draped casually around Kelly Larsen, who was a buxom seventeen. Both were giggling and pointing at him.

Eric Jr. spoke into an imaginary microphone like a documentary narrator. "And now, on Wild Kingdom, we observe the mating rituals of the middle aged," he quipped, before both teenagers broke into peals of laughter.

Fargo had to laugh as well. "Get lost, mister, before I come over there and put my foot in your ass!"

"Yes sir, Red Foreman!" Eric Jr. saluted.

It was good to be home.

XI

Air battle over southern Iran! U.S. forces strike at coastal defenses in Gulf of Oman.

-Washington Post

U.S. suffers new casualties as fighting continues. U.S. Central Command confirms the loss of more aircraft, including a radar plane.

-Chicago Sun Times

B-2 Strike on Iranian Nuclear Facilities! U.S. Air Force confirms unopposed raid deep into Iran.

-L.A. Times

Aircraft Carriers: Is it the end of an Era? CNO Harris testifies before the House Armed Services Committee.

-N.Y. Times

Israel: Ally or Opportunist? Sources report that Israel is providing major intelligence on Iran to the United States.

-N.Y. Post

Red Lake County, Minnesota

Fargo, Eric, and their father were sitting down to the hearty lunch prepared by his mother and sister-in-law when Fargo's mother waved a finger at him. "Oh, Mike, I almost forgot," she mentioned, "you got a phone call earlier from some gentleman named Ron Leaper."

Fargo set down his sandwich, untouched. "Did he say what it was about?"

"No, he said it wasn't anything urgent."

"Thanks," Fargo replied, getting up and heading straight for the phone.

"For God's sake, Mike, he said it wasn't urgent!" his mother scolded. "Sit down and eat!"

"Yah, you told me," he replied, picking up the phone and dialing Lurch in Oceana.

"Hey Fargo," Lurch greeted him.

"Hey, boss. My Ma said you rang earlier."

"Aye-firm. Your orders came through," he said, sounding a little piqued. "Why the hell didn't you tell me you applied to TPS? I would have written you a letter!"

Fargo hadn't even put in for orders yet—he hadn't made a single call to the bureau of naval personnel. "What? Wait a minute," he replied, perplexed. "Test pilot school? I never applied to TPS! Sir," he added almost as an afterthought. "I was going to put in for an air wing staff!" His voice had risen, his face was getting red, and at the kitchen table his family were exchanging concerned looks.

"That's what I thought, too," Lurch replied. "Don't shoot the messenger, ace. I'm just telling you what came across the message boards this morning."

Fargo shook his head. "This must be some kind of screwup, sir. I'll call BUPERS and get it cleared up. I've been in the cockpit my whole career, which makes me an odd duck as it is. Without the green ink from Afghanistan and the Gulf I wouldn't have passed the command screen. I need a staff tour and a graduate degree in the next couple years, or I'm sunk. There's probably some Thorsen out there in the fleet somewhere who put in for TPS and just got orders to a CAG staff."

"Want me to call on it?"

"No sir, I'll take care of it," Fargo replied.

"Well, just keep your temper when you do, Fargo. You catch more flies with honey, and all that good stuff. Kay?"

"Yes sir."

"How's Minnesota?"

"Still waiting for Spring to arrive."

"Having a good visit with the family?"

"Everything's good, sir, and thanks for asking. Did you get any orders yet?"

"Yeah, I'm going to the Black Aces. Their XO was just permanently grounded for a heart murmur or some damn thing, and he had about four months left on his tour. They're slotting me in to replace him, and I'll take command when their current skipper rolls out."

That was *great* career news for Lurch, but Fargo realized that he didn't sound all that thrilled, and suddenly realized why. "Aw Jeez, they're deployed aboard *Coral Sea*, aren't they? You're going right back out to the Gulf!"

"Yeah," Lurch replied quietly. "I mean it's everything I could ask for: saves my career and gets me right back into the fight, but *fuck,* dude, I think Kathy is gonna divorce me. She locked herself in the bedroom and won't come out, and the kids haven't stopped bawling for two straight days."

Fargo had to admit that sometimes there was a definite upside to being a bachelor. "She's *not* gonna divorce you, Lurch," he assured him, knowing nothing of the kind but trying to make him feel better. "She's just gonna hate the Navy for a while, that's all. Either way, congratulations. Shit, I wish I was going with you," he added whole-heartedly.

"Y'know, I checked. I don't know if you've been keeping up with the news, but the battle group out there is taking some losses in the air. When I asked if there was anywhere they might slot you in, I got shut down. Something to do with these orders of yours. It's screwy."

"I'll figure it out, sir, and thanks for the heads-up. Look, Lurch, if I don't see you before you ship out . . . well, good hunting, sir."

"Thanks, brother. We'll give 'em plenty of hell. Later," he added, before hanging up.

Fargo hung up and immediately dialed BUPERS, ignoring the curious looks from the kitchen table. Within moments he had his detailer on the line: the officer responsible for matching other officers on the same career track with their next jobs. Detailers worked within their own warfare communities: pilots detailed pilots, submariners detailed submariners, and so on. 'Kaiser' Franz was a Hornet driver serving a sentence at BUPERS—it was unpopular duty but 'career enhancing', as the saying went.

"Kaiser's up!" LCDR Franz announced, using his fleet callsign. Fargo identified himself and offered up his social security number for good measure. He went on to explain the situation as Lurch had just presented it to him.

"It's no mistake, commander. We've got you headed to Patuxent River for one of the short courses at TPS: the three month version. After that you're penciled into VX-9 at China Lake for a special assignment."

"Special assignment? What's going on?"

"Whatever it is, I'm not cleared for it. You weren't the only one who got these orders, sir," Kaiser told him in a subdued voice. "The only commonality I can see is that everyone on the list started out flying Tomcats, for whatever it's worth. A list of names including yours was handed down from on high, and I cut the orders. As for the TPS part, you've got the requisite engineering degree, and you're fully qualified for it on paper. Special assignment notwithstanding, there is nothing here to interfere with your pending command tour. My advice, sir, would be to keep quiet and play ball. This strikes me as one of those deals where Big Navy is going to look out for you in the long run. Other than that, I have no idea what it's all about. All things being equal, most guys would give their left nut for TPS orders."

"I know," Fargo replied, perplexed. "I guess it's nothing to complain about, but with the war . . ."

"That would be you and everyone else, looking for a ticket to the Big Game," Kaiser replied. "I see here you were out there on the *Boxer,* but there's a whole fleet full of guys with scores to settle, and I'm having to tell most of them to get in line. In the meantime, your 'No Later Than' date for reporting to Pax River is near the end of the month. I don't have the exact date right in front of me."

"Okay, thanks, Kaiser," Fargo replied.

"Sure, no prob, commander," Kaiser said almost absent-mindedly. Fargo recognized the tone: The detailer was already finished with LCDR Thorsen and was mentally engaging the next issue on his busy plate. Fargo hung up the phone, wondering what it all meant. His brother was finishing up his lunch, having listened to both conversations while he ate.

"Everything okay, bro?" he asked. "You sounded a little intense."

Fargo explained the situation as well as he could. The family was duly impressed, and didn't really understand why he wasn't more enthusiastic. TPS would be a challenge, even one of the 'short' courses, but he didn't doubt he could do well there.

He turned around when he heard the unmistakable sound of his mother clearing her throat behind him. There was Angela Olsen, standing in the middle of the living room with a slight smile. Fargo felt his face warming, and hoped like hell he wasn't blushing. "Oh . . . Heya, Angie, what's up?"

"Just returning some dishes from the get-together last weekend, y'know," she said. She was dressed casually but not *too* casually, in a well-fitting pair of designer jeans, heeled boots, and a fuzzy white sweater that was just tight enough to ignite the imagination without being obvious about it. Her long hair spilled freely around her shoulders, and today she wasn't wearing any rings.

Fargo exchanged a split-second look with Eric, noting the familiar way his brother could openly smirk at him with a completely straight face—a form of sibling telepathy. He could almost hear Eric's voice in his head: *You don't have a hair on your ass if you don't ask her out!*

"Doing anything wild this afternoon?" he almost blurted.

"No, no, nothing wild. A.J. gets home from school about 3:30."

"Want to grab some lunch?" he asked, hoping she couldn't see the untouched sandwich on the plate somewhere behind him.

"Good idea," Fargo's mother added. "You should get on out of here for the afternoon."

"Yah, I think that sounds real nice," Angie said, folding her arms self-consciously.

"I'll go grab my jacket—be right back." Fargo vanished upstairs for a moment, pausing to throw on some clothes that didn't smell like farm work, and adding his leather flight jacket over it all. Technically it was a uniform item, but the nearest naval base was about two states away and nobody around here was going to care. The leather jacket never went on deployment with him, so it was spared the fiery fate of most of his gear. His jacket wasn't overdone as patches went: leather nametag with embossed gold wings and a squadron patch velcroed to the front, with a Fighter Weapons School patch sewn on the right shoulder and a generic U.S. Navy patch on the left. Fargo was issued that jacket in flight school fifteen years prior; it was well broken in and fit him like a glove.

The two of them headed out, Fargo feeling as self-conscious as a teenager leaving on his first date with Mom, Dad, and big brother watching from the living room window. "Where should we go?" he asked.

"Oh, wherever you like," Angie replied, tossing him the keys to her truck. "You drive."

"Well, there used to be that little mom and pop diner in town . . . what was it called?"

"Maxie's," Angela supplied. "They closed a while back. There's another place called the Blue Moose not far from there, though, across the street from the bowling alley. You remember the way?"

"You bet," Fargo replied, swinging the truck around the circle drive and heading back out to the main road. They rode in slightly awkward silence for a couple minutes before Angie asked him about test pilot school—she'd overheard the tail end of the conversation.

Fargo explained the assignment to her, at least as well as he was able. He left out any reference to 'special assignments,' since he didn't know what that was about or how classified it might be. Instead, he described what he knew of the TPS course and where it was located, and what little he knew about China Lake. The latter was a remote desert base about a three-hour drive north of Los Angeles, and Fargo didn't know much about it. The prospect of moving to California didn't excite him—he'd been an east coast sailor for his entire career, and he considered Virginia Beach home.

"California, huh?" Angie said. "That's a long way away."

"Land of the fruits and nuts," Fargo chuckled.

"So, what's the deal with 'Fargo'?" she asked playfully, reading the nametag on his jacket.. He started to explain callsigns to her, but she'd seen the movie Top Gun and knew what they were. "But why 'Fargo'?" she asked.

"Four years of college wasn't long enough to change the way I talk, y'know?" he replied.

Angela laughed again. "Oh, I get it! Like Fargo the movie!"

"You betcha," he replied, pulling up outside the Blue Moose. "It's funny y'know," he added, "my family calls me Mike, and half the time I don't even realize they're talking to me." They headed inside and found a cozy little table in the corner, by the front window. Fargo pulled chairs around so they were sitting more side by side than across from each other, close enough so they could lean on each other a bit if the mood took them. Angie didn't seem to mind. They ordered drinks; Fargo ordered a sandwich, mentally lamenting the fact that it wouldn't be half as good as his Ma's, and Angie ordered a small appetizer—he began to suspect she had already eaten before his invite, but that was okay. They were here, now.

They spent a couple hours chatting about everything and nothing. When she felt safe enough, Angela told him more about the accident, and a little bit about what the past three years were like for her. Listening to her talk, Fargo began thinking that maybe his mother had been a little harsh in her assessment; she seemed relatively fine to him. He could sense there was lingering pain, and there probably always would be to some degree. That was something Fargo could freshly relate to, in his own way.

She got him talking in turn, far more than he intended, and drew more out of him than his family had managed in two weeks at home. Fargo's voice was low and quiet when he told her about Dexter, and his death. He didn't tell her the details: Dex's broken neck, and his body riddled through and through with shrapnel from the blown engine. Either one would have killed him, so he'd really had no chance. They had buried Dex at sea aboard the North Carolina, and Captain Bergstrom had conducted the service. His time on the submarine was a secret; Lurch was the only one in his circle who knew, and he couldn't tell anyone else.

Angela was puzzled now. "How were you rescued?" she asked.

Fargo snapped back to the present, realizing he was on the verge of having said too much. "Well, I got lucky," he summarized. "The good guys showed up and got to me first."

Angie reached out and took his hand in hers; it was warm to the touch. "I'm glad you made it, Mike. I'm sorry about your friend, and all the others."

Fargo's eyes stung, and he blinked a couple times and tilted his head back slightly. "Yup. I'm glad I made it too," he replied through a suddenly tight throat. He stood up. "Want another hot chocolate?" he asked.

Angela looked at her watch. "Actually, we should probably get going. A.J. will already be home from school by the time I get back. My parents are there, but he's used to me being there when he gets home."

Fargo nodded. "Sure. Say, does A.J. like to go bowling?" he asked, looking at the sign for the bowling alley across the street. "Maybe we could take him after school tomorrow or the next day."

Angie nodded enthusiastically. "Yah! He'd like that! So would I."

"So, it's a date!"

"You betcha," Angie replied. They headed back out toward the Thorsen farm. Neither one of them said much on the return trip. About halfway there, she wordlessly unbuckled her seat belt and slid over across the cab to snuggle into the crook of his arm. Fargo glanced over at her as she came, silently slipping his arm around her and holding her close, briefly tilting his head down to inhale her fragrance. When they pulled off the main road and onto the farm's long driveway, he stopped a good quarter of a mile short of the house. They kissed, and he felt there was more there than simple animal attraction. When they broke apart they just sat for a long moment, their foreheads touching as they tried to sort through what they were feeling. Fargo kissed her again, and her hands dug into soft leather of his jacket.

"I want to see you again," he said throatily, and she understood he wasn't talking about bowling.

"Tomorrow," she said, looking up at him with promise in her eyes. "The bus picks A.J. up about eight in the morning or so, I can meet you about nine."

"Okay," Fargo replied simply. He put the truck into gear and drove the rest of the way up to the house. He saw his mother watching in the window as they pulled up, and wondered if she'd spotted the truck stopped along the drive. Not that he really cared.

"Gawd, do you think she saw us?" Angie giggled.

"She'll see this one," he grinned, leaning across the seat and kissing her again. They held each other tightly for a long moment before letting go. "See you tomorrow," he added, opening the driver's door.

"Definitely," she replied, sliding over to the driver's seat as he got out. Fargo reached out and stroked her hair once before shutting the door. He stood and watched her get turned around and head out, and didn't go into the house until her truck was out of sight. His mother was waiting inside for him with a hot mug of coffee and the look of the cat that just snacked on the canary. She gave him a one-armed hug as he stepped inside, handing him the mug after he slipped off his jacket and hung it on the coat rack.

"Well, you sure smell good," his mother teased. "Is she a keeper?"

"You planned that, didn't you?" he asked with an easy smile. "Someone invited the Sorensens over on Saturday, and I don't think it was Dad."

She feigned wide-eyed innocence. "I don't know what the hell you're talking about! Drink your coffee before it gets cold, son, and then you can come peel some spuds for me."

Fargo smiled wryly. "Okay, Ma."

***

Islamic Republic of Iran
Arabian Sea

Cheng Ye led his squadron south of the air base at Chabahar at low altitude until they were in international airspace, then turned them almost due east. The *Feilong* were about to spring a trap that was several weeks in the making. There was an Iranian flagged supertanker steaming east out of the Gulf of Oman, hugging the coast in what looked like an attempt to avoid the American naval forces engaged in blockading Iranian shipping. The American blockade had been largely successful so far, and Iran was starting to feel the effects. Several oil platforms and terminals in the Gulf had been destroyed in stealth B-2 raids which had proven impossible to defend against, cutting into Iran's money-making infrastructure. It was time to hit back, and prove once more to the Americans that they were not invulnerable.

If the Battle of Hormuz wasn't enough to teach the Yankees a lesson, they'd learned a few more since. Early on, the *Coral Sea* battle group had stationed itself too far north in the Gulf of Oman, trying to improve the striking reach of its air wing. While the Americans were successful in destroying many SAM sites along the southern Iranian coast, their attempts to lay traps and down the Iranian force of A-50 Mainstay aircraft had all failed. The Mainstays themselves provided a good deal of their own defense, due to the radar coverage they provided. The planes could track surface targets out to about 160 NM, and air targets twice as far away. The Red Talons, led by Arkady Kovalev, had conducted some careful fighter sweeps in advance of another AWACS killing mission led by Cheng Ye. Two more of the precious Novator missiles had been fired, and another E-2C Hawkeye from the *Coral Sea* battle group was destroyed. Immediately after the AWACS aircraft was down, two squadrons of JF-17's and the remainder of Cheng Ye's *Feilong* unit attempted a cruise missile attack against the battle group. It failed to damage a single ship, but forced them to expend large numbers of missiles to defeat it. *Coral Sea* and her escorts had withdrawn south after that, beyond the tracking range of Iranian AWACS assets. Intelligence from Russian and Chinese sources placed the American flotilla some 200 NM south of Chabahar, and about 250 NM from the center of the Gulf of Oman, on a rough line between Sur, Oman and Porbandar, India. This provided some relief to Iranian forces; American strike aircraft now had to fly much farther to hit their targets, and they were spotted by AWACS (or given away by jamming) far sooner.

The Red Talons in their Fulcrums, armed with long range missiles and support from their Mainstays, had done well against encroaching American Super Hornets, downing two in BVR engagements with no losses of their own. What they were finding was that American electronic warfare capabilities were exceptional, often blunting the edge in performance enjoyed by the MiG-29M fighters. The long-range jousting between American fighters and the Russian and Chinese Volunteer Groups tended to result in large numbers of fired missiles, expended fuel and countermeasures, but few victories on either side. Of course, Kovalev's pilots were well trained, far better on average than their Iranian counterparts, and the same was true of the Chinese volunteers. When regular IRIAF units fought the Americans, the results favored the latter.

In the meantime, U.S. surface units and submarines conducted an effective blockading action. Tankers were boarded and captured, their crews removed, and their cargoes of oil shipped to refineries in Texas rather than those in China or North Korea. Cargo and container ships departing Iranian ports were declared legitimate targets, and any entering the Arabian Sea were torpedoed without mercy.

Today, a converted oil tanker was being used as a lure to draw in American boarders. She was the modern version of a Q-ship, but for use against surface units rather than submarines. Her tanks had been flooded with seawater to ballast her, causing her to ride low in the water as though she was carrying a full load of crude. Missile launchers were concealed on her weather decks, and she carried only a skeleton crew of fanatically loyal IRGC members, willing to sacrifice themselves for the opportunity to strike the Americans. Her course mirrored previous attempts by Iranian ships to run the blockade, skirting the coast or Iran and Pakistan, barely in international waters.

Two American surface ships, a *Burke* Class destroyer, and a *Perry* Class frigate, were steaming northeast at high speed on an intercept course. They were being trailed by a Russian AGI, which stood for 'auxiliary, general intelligence'. In layman's terms, it was a spy trawler. The vessel was passing information on the movement of the American vessels to the Iranians via SATCOM, and there wasn't much the U.S. Navy could do about it other than attempt to jam her transmissions. Attacking the AGI would constitute an act of war against Russia—a step the United States was unwilling to take.

Cheng Ye and Kovalev ferried their squadrons to Chabahar, where they landed, refueled, and waited. When the time was right based on the AGI's reports, the Red Talons took off first and pressed south over the Arabian Sea, intent on causing a distraction for the E-2C AWACS aircraft monitoring the coast. Given recent events, the American response to such a probe was to pull their Hawkeye south and send CAP fighters after the intruders; in this case, the Hawkeye's move south served to keep the *Feilong* off American radar screens, at least initially. Cheng Ye and his fighters took off soon after, pressing along the coast towards the American ships.

The powerful AEGIS system on the American destroyer was fully in play. When Cheng Ye signaled his squadron to climb, they were picked up quickly. The Sukhoi fighters salvoed two anti-ship missiles each before turning west and running. Twenty two anti-ship missiles in a single swarm headed for the two American ships, and soon there were white smoke trails over the Arabian Sea as American SM-2 and SM-3 missiles streaked skyward to intercept the threat. As soon as those smoke trails were visible, missile batteries were unmasked aboard the Iranian Q-ship as she turned beam-on to the American force. Another fourteen missiles were launched from relatively close range, giving the American force very little reaction time. The backblast from the missile launches seriously damaged the supertanker, causing deck fires that couldn't be fought, but that was never the plan anyway. A pair of approaching helicopters with SEALs aboard were fired on by two vehicle-mounted SA-6 SAM systems. Each system targeted one helicopter and fired three missiles apiece. With a range of about twelve miles and speeds just under Mach 2, three missiles from each vehicle streaked in and destroyed both helicopters, leaving no survivors from either.

The surface-fired missile salvo resulted in a single hit on the frigate; the Silkworm's thousand pound warhead blew a gigantic hole in her port side, forward of her bridge superstructure. A significant portion of her crew was killed instantly, and the fires were immediately out of control. The destroyer moved in to render aid, but the frigate rolled over and sank less than fifteen minutes after being hit, with only a handful of survivors later being pulled from the water. Within seconds the destroyer launched a salvo of Harpoon and Tomahawk anti-ship missiles at the tanker, but she was firing at a doomed target. The Q-ship had done her job, and the survivors among her crew abandoned ship and fled north towards the coast in inflatable speedboats, leaving her to her fate. American missiles finished the job started by the firing of the tanker's own jury-rigged weapons, and the tanker slipped beneath the waves a short time later. Any fighter cover the surface ships might have hoped for during this engagement was conveniently drawn off by Kovalev's squadron. Both the Red Talons and *Feilong* refueled a second time at Chabahar before returning to their respective bases, having suffered no losses in this battle. Cheng Ye knew this mission was a one-trick pony—the Americans were overconfident to the point of carelessness with their prior tanker captures, but they wouldn't be careless in the future. The Q-ship gambit would only work once, but it *had* worked.

It was a second bloody nose for the U.S. Navy in this war.

The following day, China and North Korea announced that they were re-flagging Iranian tankers under their own colors to ensure their oil shipments passed through the Arabian Sea unmolested.

Part III
Black Tiger

Brian J. Smith

XII

U.S. destroyer collides with Russian Trawler. Navy to investigate Arabian Sea mishap.

-Washington Post

Trawler captain claims collision at sea was a deliberate act. Russian crew rescued after accidental collision and sinking.

-Miami Herald

Iranian people suffering under embargoes. U.N. requests aid program but U.S. refuses, hoping to incite regime change in Iran.

-N.Y. Times

Russian Volunteers Flying for Iran! Are They The 21st Century's 'Flying Tigers?'

-Chicago Sun Times

Introducing the RVG! Russia's Mercenary Aviators: Are they for real?

-N.Y. Post

Did foreign military pilots participate in the sinking of navy carrier group? House Foreign Affairs Committee scheduled to hold hearings on this topic.

-Washington Post

Is Russia engaged in a proxy war with the United States? Questions arise over the extent of Russian involvement in the Persian Gulf War.

-Reuters

Iran's Revolutionary Guard cracks down on protestors as embargoes cause riots and unrest in cities across Iran.

-International Herald Tribune

JUL 2013
China Lake, California

Fargo discovered that his orders to the three month 'short' test pilot course were just a cover for the special assignment to follow. He and several other aviators, some of whom he knew from past association, were put through the barest outline of a test and evaluation course. It consisted of a quick refresher in aerodynamics, and the policies and procedures involved in testing new airframes and weapons systems. Their class lasted a mere four weeks, and they were told from the outset that they were *not* going to be official TPS graduates when it ended. In addition to the classroom work and dedicated physical training time, they did enough flying to exceed currency requirements, making sure everyone was freshly proficient in the air. Most of their flying was done in Super Hornets, although they were also given the opportunity to fly some other types of aircraft as well. All of them were fitted for special helmets, but those weren't issued at Patuxent River.

They were ordered to China Lake once the class ended, where they would finally learn what was going on. Fargo arrived after spending several days driving across the country; he was aware that Friday afternoon was a poor time to check into a new unit, but he was driven by curiosity. He reported to the duty office at the hangar for VX-9, only to be informed that he was in the wrong place. He was a little relieved that he was at least *expected*—the duty officer stamped his orders and informed him he was assigned to Detachment Six, whatever that was. He gave Fargo directions, and twenty minutes later he arrived at a somewhat dilapidated, older hangar with a number '6' and the old Ironworks Aerospace logo painted on its side in flaking, faded black paint.

Fargo recognized some of the cars in the parking lot: two of his classmates had beaten him here, at least. He felt a slight surge of excited anticipation as he grabbed his paperwork and entered the hangar. Most military hangars followed a standard layout; the various maintenance shops and maintenance control center were located along the sides of the hangar at ground level, with all non-maintenance related spaces being in offices on the upper deck. The center of the hangar was an open space, obviously, to accommodate working on aircraft. It was the airplane inside the hangar that brought Fargo up short. He stepped through a metal hatch and found himself face to face with a new version of his first love: the F-14 Tomcat. His face split into a silly grin, and he stepped forward to run a hand lovingly over the nose of the jet. "Oh, you beautiful girl, you!" he breathed. He had to chuckle at the classic irony of it: only on a navy base would he find a state-of-the-art prototype like this, sitting around unguarded in the most beat-up hangar on the flight line.

He took a slow walk around the jet, studying its lines. It was undoubtedly a Tomcat, but a much newer version than the one he was familiar with. The most obvious difference was the enlarged, rounded leading-edge gloves directly behind the engine intakes. These would improve the lift characteristics of the airframe and increase the jet's internal fuel capacity. The flaps and slats had undergone a redesign, and the engines were upgraded as well, with obvious thrust-vectoring capability. The TV camera system under the nose of the jet had been upgraded and combined with a state-of-the-art infrared search and track system, and there were twin targeting and navigation pods mounted behind them at the front end of the 'tunnel' formed by the twin bulges of the engines. The cockpit canopy was redesigned into a single piece, getting rid of the old canopy bow that used to impair forward visibility. There was no HUD anymore either, suggesting some sort of helmet-mounted display instead. These were just the changes he could *see;* he couldn't wait to learn what was under the hood.

A warrant officer stepped out of maintenance control, saw Fargo looking official in his service dress khaki uniform, and sauntered over. After a moment, Fargo realized he recognized the guy. "Senior Chief Lowden?" he asked hesitantly.

Rory Lowden grinned. "Actually, it's chief warrant now, sir," he replied, approaching closely enough that Fargo could clearly see his collar devices. "Welcome to our humble abode. Checking in?"

"That's right," Fargo replied, his gaze wandering back to the jet. "Is this the only one of these, or are there more?"

Lowden grinned. "Almost a squadron's worth, parked outside under flight line shelters. "There was only a half dozen up until a month or so ago, or so I'm told. I've only been here a few days myself. I got called up out of retirement for this gig if you can believe that."

Fargo was shocked to hear that. "Out of *retirement?*" It was one of those things that was possible on paper, but to his knowledge it hadn't happened any time in recent memory.

Lowden nodded. "Shocked the hell out of me too, commander," he replied. "I'm sorry," he added. "You seem to know me, but I'm afraid I don't recognize you."

Fargo grinned and stuck out his hand. "Sorry. I'm Mike Thorsen. You wouldn't know me—I was in the squadron next door when you were the maintenance control chief for VF-4. Nobody at Oceana could touch your mission-capable rates back then—it used to piss off our MO something awful. Are you doing the same job here?"

"That I am."

"So, what's the story?"

"Well, you are looking at the F-14E Advanced Super Tomcat. You'll get a brief on her vital stats, but I can tell you right now you're going to love her."

"I think I already do," Fargo grinned. He thanked Lowden and found the duty office on the second deck, manned by a mildly attractive, middle-aged chief yeoman who introduced herself as Sheryl Reddy.

"Ahh, Lieutenant Commander Thorsen, we've been expecting you," she informed him after introductions. "I'll take all your paperwork, sir. We're still a detachment as opposed to a squadron, and not fully staffed up yet. I'll make sure everything gets where it needs to go."

Fargo handed over the oversize manila envelope containing his paperwork and asked who was in charge. "I am," a stout voice announced from the doorway. Fargo turned and caught sight of a tall, thin man with flame red hair and an erect bearing. He wore a commander's silver oak leaves and gold pilot wings. "Nathaniel Taft, XO of the Vampires. I go by 'Priest.' Welcome to VX-9, Mister Thorsen."

"Nice to meet you, sir," Fargo replied, shaking his hand.

"Pleasure's all mine. Grab a cup of joe, and step into my parlor."

"Aye aye, sir," Fargo replied, responding subconsciously to Taft's no-nonsense manner. He grabbed a Styrofoam cup full of coffee and followed Taft into his office. Taft briefly queried him about how his cross-country trip had gone, but that was the extent of the pleasantries.

"I suppose by now you are wondering what the hell this is all about," Taft said directly.

"I think I see the writing on the wall, sir. I just finished a bit of school with a handful of former Tomcat drivers, and presto, here we've got some brand new Tomcats. Is this going to be an operational evaluation or are we taking them to war?"

"Both, practically at the same time. Before we get down to brass tacks, I need to sort out the pecking order. I'm VX-9's XO and I was handed this when it was transferred from DARPA to the Navy a couple months ago. I've been laying the foundation for what's coming next, getting a head start on the aircraft manuals, maintenance instruction manuals, you know: the administrative groundwork. This detachment is slated to be established as a fleet squadron. Until that happens and you are fully staffed, VX-9 will continue to provide administrative support.

"I'm not going to blow smoke up your ass, Thorsen: if you thought Pax River was demanding of your time and effort, standby to stand by. Your group will be finalizing the NATOPS manual on this jet, doing some final missile test-shoots, and prepping for deployment—including day and night carrier qualifications. The senior aviators all have experience in Tomcats, but the junior folks coming on board do not, which means you'll be your own in-house fleet replacement squadron as well. We both know the Navy isn't set up to operate the way we're going to be operating here—even your supply chain will be bastardized. You'll be dealing directly with the contractors for most of your aircraft-specific equipment rather than the Navy supply system, and you'll need to get up to speed on that as well.

"Which brings me back to this pecking order I was talking about. You are the most senior officer I have checked in so far." Taft raised his right hand and etched the sign of the cross in the air in front of Fargo. "*In Nomine Patre, et Filii, et Spiritus Sancti*. My son, you are christened the detachment operations officer, and my right hand man in all matters regarding Detachment Six. Chief Warrant Officer Lowden has maintenance control well in hand, but we're going to need a maintenance department head, a couple admin officers, a NATOPS officer, a training officer, and various assistants. Get with your classmates, parcel out duties, and get cracking. You deploy in three months with the *Hornet* carrier battle group."

Fargo felt the color draining from his face. "*Three months?*"

"Three months," Taft repeated. "Do you have a family?"

A quick vision of Angela Olsen and A.J. flashed unbidden through his mind; they had spent almost every waking moment together during the last two weeks of his leave, and he and Angie were speaking almost daily over the phone. However, he hadn't seen her in over a month since reporting to Pax River. They'd talked about her and A.J. making a trip out here, maybe doing Disneyland or something like that, but he saw that there wasn't going to be time for anything but work. He shook his head in response to the question. "No sir."

"Well, you can thank your lucky stars for that. Since this all went high order I haven't spent more than a few days with my wife and kids. Shore duty, my dying ass," he added bitterly. Fargo raised a mental eyebrow—there *did* happen to be a war on, and based on what he saw in the news, things could be going a lot better. He tactfully said nothing on that score.

The operational reality he was being saddled with was something else entirely. "Three months," Fargo breathed. "Jeez, that's less time than a regular squadron spends just doing normal deployment work-ups. Do we have the kind of support we need to make this happen?"

"That's the good news," Taft replied. "This is a CNO directed operation—it comes right from the top. Money, resources, and whatever else you need can be had for the asking. Chief Reddy and Warrant Officer Lowden both have phone numbers they can direct-dial for materiel needs, and stuff just starts showing up like magic. There is a small army of civil-service technical writers working on your various manuals and instructions. We're also at an advantage personnel wise. This unit is set up to be staffed with a lot of senior people, both officers and enlisted. We're bringing in some real talent, and you won't be dealing with boot sailors or nugget officers. Now don't go letting it go to your head, but everyone slated for this operation is top shelf, and anyone who turns out to be a non-hacker is going to be *gone*." Taft paused, and Fargo saw the XO's eyes drawn to his salad bar of ribbons. Among lesser awards, it included a Bronze Star for the engagements he'd recently fought in the Gulf, a Purple Heart (almost unheard of among aviators these days), and a fistful of air medals earned over multiple Afghanistan combat deployments. Fargo had seen about as much combat as any naval aviator currently on active status, with two air-to-air kills to his credit as well. "I heard you were at the Battle of Hormuz," Taft remarked.

"Yes sir. It was not a good day."

"You'll do better next time around, I guarantee it. I have a technical brief scheduled for Monday morning. Two pilots and three RIOs checked in yesterday, and we should have everyone else by close of business Monday, except for maybe a straggler or two. How are you fixed for flight gear?"

"I got a complete re-issue at Pax River, sir," Fargo replied.

"Good. Ops is two doors down the hall. Chief Reddy pre-ordered a bunch of gear, and it's all stacked up in there. Give her a list of anything else you need, and she'll jump on it."

"Yes sir."

"Then let's turn to, then. The day is not getting any younger."

Fargo came to his feet. "Aye aye, sir."

Priest stood up as well and stuck out his hand again. "Welcome aboard."

***

The operations office consisted of about a half dozen desks and chairs shoved against one bulkhead, two computers still in their boxes, a couple dry-erase boards, and four telephones that were sitting on the deck, plugged into their wall jacks. Fargo picked up one of the receivers and was rewarded with a solid dial-tone—he cheerfully took that as a good omen. When he checked the ready room, he found five officers and a couple of enlisted ratings loitering about smartly. Two of the officers he recognized from his brief time at Pax River: LCDR Julia 'Jewels' Baxter, and LCDR Rick 'Hawk' Vasquez. The latter was 'Hawk' because of his 20/10 eyesight.

"Hey Fargo," Jewels greeted him. "I see you finally made it in one piece."

Fargo grinned. Even with the daunting load Taft had just laid on his shoulders, he couldn't get his mind off the jet he'd seen in the hangar. "Hey Jewels, hey Hawk," he replied, looking over the others and finding another familiar face from yesteryear. "Snoopy! How'd they pick *you* for this?"

LCDR Greg Schultz grinned and raised his palm for a high-five, which Fargo landed happily. He and Snoopy had checked into their first squadron together as raw nuggets fresh out of the RAG. They hadn't gotten to fly together much, except on September 11th, when they were ordered to fly out to the USS *Intrepid* with a weapons load cobbled together from whatever was readily available at the time. *Intrepid* was steaming at flank speed for New York City, and nobody had any idea what was happening except that airliners were ramming into skyscrapers. A few months later they were dropping bombs on Afghanistan, and Fargo hadn't seen him since that first tour.

"How have you been, you dumb squarehead?" Snoopy asked.

"Well, they haven't kicked my ass out yet," Fargo chuckled. "What about the rest of you?"

The other two officers were both WSO's, although judging by Priest's choice of words, they were going to go back to being called 'Radar Intercept Officers', or RIOs: LCDR Jill Bagley, callsign 'Bagels', and LT Steve 'Tex' Kemper. Tex's height, demeanor, and accent left no illusions as to where his callsign came from. The two enlisted sailors were Yeoman First Class Dennis Johnson and Cryptologic Technician Second Class Amy Rodriguez. Introductions were made all around. "Everyone else a new check-in?" Fargo asked, and received affirmations from everyone. Fargo was the only O-4 in the group who had completed a department head tour; even Snoopy was more than a year junior to him. "Follow me, folks," Fargo ordered, and led them all back to Ops.

Fargo picked up one of the dry-erase boards, hung it on the wall, and found a marker. He brought them up to speed on what lay ahead, watching as their smiles grew a little ragged when they processed the sheer workload they were in for. Fargo began drawing an organizational chart up on the board. Since they were going to stand up as a squadron, he organized them like one right from the start. He assigned Jewels as the maintenance officer, Hawk as the administration officer, and put Bagels in charge of the Safety / NATOPS department. He assigned Tex as the assistant maintenance officer, and chose Snoopy as his own assistant in operations, since he was a well-known quantity. Petty Officer Rodriguez was assigned to ops, and YN1 Johnson went to assist Hawk and Chief Reddy in admin. As others showed up, they would be slotted into assignments as well. Office spaces were assigned to the new departments as appropriate, and nobody made it to the club that night for beers. They worked late into the evening, getting their spaces set up and ready for work the following Monday morning.

Fargo and Snoopy worked through the entire weekend, sweating over a plan of action and milestones that would get them from a cold start to the Arabian Sea in three months, with the goal of flying a new type of aircraft into combat.

***

Monday afternoon, fifteen officers and a handful of civilian technical representatives assembled in their newly designated 'training room': it was simply the one room down at the end of the upper deck passageway big enough to seat everyone. The seating itself looked like cast off high school desks, and the only technical aid was a laptop computer connected to a digital projector, all of which sat on a folding card table in the center of the room. The large whiteboard at the front of the room doubled as their projection screen. Fargo wondered if this building had seen any regular use since the Vietnam War. Snoopy was sitting back by the hatch and he called the room to attention as Priest entered. Taciturn as ever, he kept them at attention until he reached the front of the room and turned to face them. "Seats," he ordered curtly. "This brief is to introduce you to the reason you are here: the F-14E Advanced Super Tomcat, which you will hear referred to around here as simply the 'Supercat.' Now that the first wave of personnel has all arrived, I can give you some background information.

"Even before serious combat operations began against Iran, the Navy quietly recognized that the Super Hornet isn't all we hoped it would be. The upcoming F-25 Cutlass is going to be an improvement over the Super Hornet in many ways, but it still represents the proverbial 'low end' of a mixed high-low naval air force. For anyone who doesn't understand what that means, it means the 'high' end is made up of a fewer number of more expensive, advanced airplanes, while the 'low' end consists of larger numbers of less expensive, less capable aircraft. An example would be the A-6 Intruder and the A-7 Corsair. Both platforms were attack jets in service at the same time, but they were far from equal on the playing field. The A-6 was 'high end', and the A-7 was 'low end.' In our case, the F-14E represents a 'high-end' platform. Any questions on that point?" he asked. There were none.

"To make a long story short, Northman-Ironworks came to the Navy after the Battle of Hormuz with a plan to resurrect the Flight

Deck 21 concept in a limited fashion, to better facilitate our military objectives in the Gulf. This program is an outgrowth of some prototype research jointly conducted between DARPA and Northman-Ironworks, and authorized by the CNO. The goal is to deploy a concept air wing using a squadron of Supercats, a mixed squadron of EA-6E Advanced Super Prowlers and KA-6E tankers, the first operational squadron of Block-1 F-25's, the first E-2D Advanced Hawkeye squadron, rounded out with two squadrons of stock Super Hornets. Understand this: as of right now there is no plan to put the F-14E into mass production, but I'd be lying if I said that the power brokers at NAVAIR weren't watching this experiment quite closely. This is a one shot deal, something special, and a chance to influence future appropriations. We're grinding down Iran in the Gulf, slowly but steadily, but the minefields in the Gulf of Oman are holding us off to the south, and our striking range is limited by the payload/range of the Super Hornet measured against the standoff our battle groups are having to maintain. This air wing will have *substantially* deeper penetration, and longer range weapons to counter the Russian hardware being used by the enemy. Any questions so far?"

Tex raised his hand. "Sir, is the F-25 going to be ready in time for this? I thought they weren't supposed to deploy for another few years."

"Timetable has been moved up," Priest retorted. "Rest assured, the folks in that program are working just as hard as we are here to make it happen. Wartime has a way of accelerating these things, and the Powell administration's changes to our procurement processes have helped things along. Anyone else?"

One of the WSOs raised his hand. "Lieutenant Commander Bozeman, sir. It's obvious we aren't a regular part of VX-9, so what is our chain of command? Who are we accountable to for all this?"

"For now, you are accountable to me. In my absence you will report to Lieutenant Commander Thorsen. Fargo, stand up so everyone can get a look at you." Fargo did as he was told, standing up and turning around with a slight smile and a wave so everyone could see who he was. "If there are no other questions, there will be a short AOM following this presentation and we'll get the last of our organizational kinks sorted out. Now, I want to introduce the man chiefly responsible for the Supercat: Dr. Edward McKenzie. He'll present the technical brief on the jet. Doctor, the floor is yours."

All eyes turned to Dr. McKenzie as the room lights were dimmed and he began his briefing. The first several slides showed side by side comparisons of the retired F-14D and the new F-14E. The original Tomcats were Vietnam-era analog jets, and they were transforming into digital hybrids when they were retired in 2006. The Supercat was a 21st Century product, all digital, with fly-by-wire flight controls. Coupled with thrust vectoring engines and the redesigned flaps and slats, carrier approach speeds had been reduced, and the jet could 'bring back' 16,000 pounds of stores versus the 9,000 pounds of prior models. Internal fuel capacity had increased from 16,000 to just under 21,000 pounds. With external drop tanks, the maximum fuel load exceeded 25,000 pounds. With that much fuel not even impacting stores, the payload/range numbers on the Supercat were ridiculously superior to the Super Hornet.

The Supercat's engines were the same as those used on the F-22. In addition to the thrust vectoring, in most configurations the Supercat was capable of Mach super cruise at military power, well beyond the capabilities of all current aircraft except the F-22. Top speeds were up to Mach 1.6 at sea level, and better than Mach 2.5 at altitude, depending on stores configuration.

The weapons system was centered around the APG-81 AESA radar—the same one chosen for the F-25. The Supercat would carry AIM-152 long range missiles, themselves a prototype design currently unique to the Advanced Super Tomcat, designed specifically for fleet air defense. With a high speed, supersonic shot, the AIM-152 had demonstrated the ability to hit targets up to 160 NM, or almost four times the range of the current generation AMRAAM missiles. The Supercat could carry AMRAAMs as well, AIM-9X Sidewinders, and its arsenal of air-to-ground weapons included everything in the Super Hornet inventory. With its AESA radar, the Supercat could track air and ground targets simultaneously, opening possibilities for the pilot to handle air-to-air threats while the RIO took on ground problems. For self-defense, the aircraft was equipped with MAWS, the missile approach warning system, joint helmet mounted cueing system, an expanded countermeasures capability, and towed fiber-optic decoys.

Lastly, the jet was designed to be a sensor node the same way the F-25 was, with a full-digital electronic warfare suite. This included a self-protection jammer, AESA EW capability, SATCOM, datalink, and full interoperability with the Navy's new integrated fire-control, counter air capability. A Supercat would be able to 'grab' a ship-fired missile and guide it onto targets that the firing platform could not detect, in the same manner as the E-2D Advanced Hawkeye. These were Generation-4++ airplanes, with capabilities falling just short of Gen-5. The F-25 was being touted as the first Gen-5 naval aircraft, but it's Block-1 model would be less capable than a Supercat.

By the time Dr. McKenzie finished his presentation, every aviator in the room was fairly salivating at the possibilities offered by this aircraft. One of the major drawbacks of the original Tomcat, particularly the early models cursed with the TF-30 engines, had been its propensity for getting into flat spins after compressor stalls or engine flameouts. The former Tomcat drivers watched video footage of an F-14E *deliberately* entering a flat spin, only to be recovered effortlessly thanks to the thrust vectoring capability of the engines. Flat spins had killed a lot of Tomcats and more than a few aviators over the years, but for the Supercat they were a non-event. With the power advantage of the new engines, vectored thrust, re-designed high-lift devices and digital flight controls, the high-alpha handling characteristics of the jet were incomparable—it was going to be almost *impossible* to get the aircraft into trouble at the slow end of the flight regime.

Fargo couldn't wait to take it flying.

***

When the presentation was over, the officers stayed for their AOM. Priest turned the floor over to Fargo early on, and he brought everyone up to speed and outlined their immediate priorities. He assigned the last few jobs that needed assigning, and made a few last-minute changes so people were situated to optimize their various skills and talents. The only other officer in the detachment with prior experience as a department head was LCDR Bozeman, who had asked a lot of technical questions during the aircraft brief. Fargo had never met him before, but he was clearly smart as a whip and technically savvy.

The last item on Fargo's agenda was a pure leadership move. He outlawed office coffee services, asking that everyone cycle through the ready room for caffeine reloads. There was a method to his madness, which he explained to them. Although they all had their assigned jobs, a lot of cross-pollination was going to have to happen for it all to come together. No one man or woman was going to complete their job all on their own; it was going to be a group effort, with all hands backing each other up. He wanted them to bump into each other frequently throughout the course of their long workdays, exchanging information and ideas, brainstorming, coordinating, and solving problems. It would also be a way for them to get acquainted and familiar with one another. Lastly, he addressed the issue nearest and dearest to their hearts: the flight schedule. Daily flight operations would commence the next morning, with the first event scheduled for a 0530 brief. The meeting ended on that exciting note.

When it was over, Gary Bozeman followed Priest down to his office. "Can I help you, commander?" Priest asked. "Your callsign is Buzz, right?"

"Yes sir. Do you have a minute?" he asked.

"A *minute*," Priest replied, the implication clear. They swept past Chief Reddy and into his office, and Buzz closed the door behind him. The latter cut an impressive figure: six feet one, broad shouldered and fit, with jet black hair, a square jaw, and brown eyes. Buzz wore a Naval Academy class ring on his left hand, just forward of his wedding band. He was a former Tomcat RIO with combat experience over Afghanistan, an NSAWC graduate, and former SFTI. His service record was filled with a string of 'outstanding' fitness reports, and he had passed the same O-5 promotion and command screening board that Thorsen had. Except for recent combat experience, Buzz and Fargo were almost professional clones.

"Sir, I'm not happy about the job assignments," Bozeman explained, getting straight to the point. "I've got nothing against Fargo—I don't even know the guy. But I'm senior to him and I was the Ops-O in my last squadron, so I'm kind of curious why he's running ops while I'm shoehorned in as his assistant."

Priest spared him a wan smile. "Timing is everything in this man's navy, commander. Thorsen showed up Friday afternoon at knockoff time, and worked through the weekend after I dumped the entire load in his lap. If you had gotten here first, I would have dumped the entire load in your lap. You two are about interchangeable, and Fargo has really gotten the ball rolling in less than forty-eight hours. I'm sorry, Buzz, but I'm not going to jerk the rug out from under him. Now is that all?"

"Sir, it's simple seniority. The senior man should be in charge."

Priest nodded. "I agree. *I'm* the senior man here, *I'm* in charge, and I'm not making any changes. Actually," he added thoughtfully, "I do have an idea for a change. You are right about one thing: your experience as Ops-O is more recent than Fargo's." He picked up the phone and punched the extension for operations. "Fargo? It's the XO. Step on down here for a moment, will ya? Thanks." He hung up the phone. Fargo rapped on the hatch less than a minute later, surprised to find Bozeman in Taft's office. He glanced uncomfortably between them.

"I'm making one change," Priest explained. "Commander Bozeman will take over operations." He paused for a moment, to see how Thorsen would take that. Fargo's face settled into an unreadable mask, and he nodded tightly, waiting. "You are going to serve the role as detachment 'Honcho.' You are now *my* exec, the XO to the XO, in a manner of speaking." He etched the sign of the cross over both men. "*In Nomine Patre, et Filii, et Spiritus Sancti.* Buzz, I hereby christen you operations officer. Fargo, I hereby christen you Honcho, my 'executive exec.' You shall henceforth be known by that title. Detachment Six is yours to run whenever I am not in this hangar, and you speak with my authority. As soon as I can get the paperwork done, you will be officially designated detachment officer in charge." Fargo relaxed slightly, realizing that Priest had just checked an end-run on Bozeman's part.

"Fargo, move your shit into the office across from this one and take up residence with Chief Reddy. Do either of you have any questions concerning your responsibilities?" he asked with a slight air of impatience.

"No sir," the two men replied together.

"Dismissed." The two officers vacated the XO's office.

Fuckin' ring knocker, Priest scowled behind them. *There's one in every crowd.*

***

"Let's have a chat," Fargo said neutrally to Buzz as they left Priest's office. He led the other man down to the empty training room. Fargo wasn't privy to the conversation before Taft called him down, but he could guess easily enough. Fargo glanced out in the passageway before going in; the coast was clear. He turned to face Buzz. "We didn't get properly introduced yesterday," he said, sticking out his hand. "I'm Fargo."

"Buzz Bozeman," the other man replied, sharing a firm handshake.

"Look," Fargo said directly, "we're all crazy busy here, so I'll just ask you straight up: Do we have a problem?" Buzz quickly told him no, but his body language said yes. Fargo sighed. "You and I are going to war together, Buzz. If you've got an issue with me, let's hear it."

Now Bozeman sighed. "It's nothing personal, dude, just the matter of seniority, that's all. I'm senior to you by a bit."

Fargo resisted the urge to scowl. *"That's it?"* he asked. Bozeman nodded. "Academy guy, huh?" he added, noting Buzz's class ring. In turn, he saw Buzz glance over his salad bar. It reminded Fargo of those drunken club arguments over who the best dogfighter was, or who had the best golf swing, or the hottest girlfriend. *God, I hate this dick-measuring bullshit!* he thought, forcing down his rising temper. Academy graduates always ended up senior to their peers in the same year group; the system was set up that way deliberately, hearkening back to the archaic era when almost the entire officer corps was composed of Academy graduates. "This is not unheard of in the annals of naval history, you know," he went on. "And we've both already passed a command screen, so it's not a competition at this point. What's the worry?"

Bozeman nodded. "No real worry, just principle. Plus, I've been an Ops-O before. I've got the experience."

"The job is now yours," Fargo reminded him.

"I'll be honest, Fargo, I still don't like it. I don't think it's right."

"I appreciate that. The question is, can you deal with it?"

"Guess I'm going to have to, eh?"

"You betcha. Let's head over to ops and I'll fill you in on where we're at. We've got shit to do."

"Aye aye, *Honcho,*" Bozeman replied, forcing a sardonic grin.

***

Tehran, Islamic Republic of Iran

Arkady Kovalev sensed trouble brewing when he arrived at the Azadi Square in central Tehran and found hundreds of protestors gathering. He was in the city on a much-needed furlough, and to meet with Tara Shirazi. They had seen a lot of each other during the time she had spent covering the Red Talons, but for her, that assignment had ended. The focus of her reporting now was the civil unrest that gripped the country. Unchecked American attacks into the southeastern part of the country, coupled with the incessant bombing of air bases, oil platforms, and nuclear facilities had demonstrated to the Iranian people that their government's decision to attack American forces in the Gulf had backfired badly. The government and IRGC continued to claim victory, pointing out that the United States and its western military allies remained shut off from the Gulf, but that mattered little when the buses didn't run, there was no fuel for cars, hunger was rampant, and the value of the Rial plummeted.

The Red Talons had suffered losses as well. Of the twelve aircraft and fifteen pilots they started with, they were down to eight jets and ten pilots. Four had died, and one had already left the group and returned home to Russia. Kovalev was unsure what sort of casualties the *Feilong* had suffered, but he'd heard that Cheng Ye was still alive. Toma Baranov looked grim and unsure these days, and Kovalev knew that if not for Tara Shirazi, he himself would be seriously thinking about returning home as well. How the IRGC would react to an announced mass departure of their mercenary volunteers was unclear—they might become hostages themselves. General Abdi was more rabid than ever, and his reaction if the mercenaries wanted to quit wasn't something Kovalev wanted to test. So far, *Krasnyye Kogti* and the *Feilong* were the two most effective air units in the country by far.

Now that the Americans knew of their existence, Kovalev felt like he had a large, red target on his back any time he was in the air. The Yankees had already set traps for them, coming very close to destroying the entire squadron on more than one occasion. All that saved them was the exceptional skill of the Mainstay operators, but now that force was being slowly pared down as well. The three A-50 aircraft were the backbone of Iranian air defensives in the south, and they were the best-protected military assets in Iran. Several auxiliary runways had been built in remote areas, and the Mainstays were constantly shuttling between those and the regular air bases when they weren't flying missions. American stealth bombers were hitting targets in Iran and the Gulf two to three times per week; the

Mainstays were never left in one spot on the ground for more than a few hours without being moved. It made routine maintenance a challenge, but it was better than losing them. One had been lost anyway, caught at random during an airfield strike, and destroyed in its hangar. Two remained, and Kovalev understood that when they were gone, their final defeat in the air would rapidly follow. Four Iranian Tomcats were still flyable, used solely as AWACS aircraft now when the A-50s were not flying. Like the Mainstays, the last of the Persian Cats were among the most jealously guarded assets in the country.

The Red Talons had moved from Shiraz (which had been hit twice now in B-2 raids) to a secret airfield north of Bandar Abbas, literally built into the side of a mountain. The hangar and maintenance facilities were underground, as was the fuel farm. A single, narrow taxiway led out to a single runway , and great pains had been taken to disguise the existence of the runway itself. Again, Kovalev knew it was simply a matter of time before foreign intelligence assets ferreted out the base, and marked it for destruction.

Worse still was the lack of facilities or even a nearby town at their new base. Shiraz had been more than livable by comparison: their quarters had been pleasant, and the city itself offered all manners of recreation when off duty. Tara could come and go from Shiraz as she pleased, but access to their new base was heavily restricted, and closed to journalists of all stripes. Life in their new facility was dreary and miserable, with the pilots living in depressing underground bunkrooms with little in the way of recreational facilities, no alcohol, and limited opportunities to get away. This current furlough was heaven-sent.

Tara had warned him before coming that the situation in the capital was tumultuous. Protests were a daily event now, and some of the crackdowns were violent and bloody. Tempers were wearing thin on both sides and the streets were more dangerous than ever, but her job required her to be there to report on these events. Kovalev wanted to be with her every chance he had, so he had come.

Their plan today was to meet in Azadi Square and tour the Azadi Tower, formerly known as the *Borj-e Sahyad*, or 'Shaw's Tower.' The tower was almost 150 FT tall, dressed in white marble, and was a central landmark in the city. It had a restaurant and also a museum. Tara had told him she was recording a piece that afternoon in the square just south of the tower; they would meet and spend the remainder of the day together when her work was done.

Kovalev spotted Shirazi and her camera crew. She wasn't making a live broadcast, only recording a report for later. The crowd was unaware of that, however. The presence of Shirazi, who was well known, and her Al Jazeera crew stirred-up nearby protestors, who began gathering in a knot behind her to shout angry slogans and wave ragged, homemade banners in protest of the mullahs. He glanced around and saw more people making their way into the square. There were hundreds now, and more seemed to be arriving every minute, coming from the surrounding park and city. Kovalev was jostled a few times as protestors pushed past him, eager to reach what was quickly becoming the focal point of their protest.

Kovalev pushed forward now as well, concerned for his lover's safety. Al Jazeera was an international organization, but local citizens tended to regard journalists as a propaganda arm of the government, since the government could exercise strict controls over what was broadcast. A hundred meters away, he saw Tara nervously wrapping up her piece, signaling quickly to the crew to break down their gear and pack up. The crowd interpreted it as an attempt to silence them—a refusal to air their protests to the outside world. The shouts became uglier, people pressed in on the camera crew, and the situation began to take on mob overtones.

Kovalev struggled to get to her now, elbowing his way through a tightly packed throng of protestors who were bouncing up and down like they were at a rave, chanting loudly in unison, led by a man with a bullhorn. There were women in the crowd, hundreds of them. Most had discarded the traditional, conservative *chador* in favor of sleeveless blouses and skirts, and went with their heads uncovered in direct violation of Islamic law. Kovalev was sweating from his efforts now, feeling a hint of desperation, when he heard the sirens.

Several truckloads of troops, police, and *Basij* militia arrived in Azadi Square. The armed men hadn't even finished spilling out of the trucks before the first tear gas cannisters were fired into the crowd, causing instant mayhem. Several thousand people tried to move sideways at once, and Kovalev gasped as the human wave nearly swept him off his feet. To go down in this crowd would mean serious injury or death: he saw several fallen protestors haphazardly trampled as the mob shifted and moved, still pumping their fists, waving their banners, chanting—and now throwing rocks and whatever else they could find at the troops and militia.

Kovalev saw a flash of Tara's colorful scarf ahead of him, then gritted his teeth and fought with renewed vigor, becoming more aggressive himself as he abandoned civility and simply pushed, shoved, and punched his way to Tara's side. He found her huddled down on the steps leading up to where she'd made her broadcast, unharmed, wild-eyed, and excited as the crowd surged around her. The noise was deafening now; thousands of bitter, angry voices raised in unison. It was the sort of scene that gave strongmen and dictators nightmares. Somewhere behind him, a single gunshot rang out and there was a louder roar as the mob surged again. New voices in Farsi bellowed out of truck-mounted loudspeakers, ordering the protesters to disperse immediately.

It was turning into a full-blown riot, and fast.

She started somewhat violently when he laid a hand on her arm, instinctively beginning to fight him off until she saw his face and realized who it was. She smiled brightly as she saw him, her eyes bright and alive with a near-fanatic frenzy of her own. He shouted at her, asking if she was alright, but she couldn't hear him over the sound of the mob. She shook her head and pointed to one ear, before grabbing his hand and trying to pull him north, towards the tower.

Kovalev stopped her, pulling her arm and shaking his head. There were several thousand people between them and the tower, and it merely led deeper into the fray, not out of it. They coughed and sneezed together as a tendril of tear gas wafted across them, and Kovalev kept a firm grip on her as he pulled her south and west, across the park lawn and away from where the trucks and troops had come in from the south. He led her towards the perimeter of the park, swimming upstream against a human wave headed in the other direction, and the crowd began to thin out rapidly as they neared the edge. Somewhere east of them, they heard hundreds of people screaming in panic following a long burst of machine gun fire. Kovalev saw the color drain from Tara's face, now set with a steely, determined look.

"They're massacring people!" she shouted. "I've got to find Achmed—I need to get over there with the camera!"

Kovalev shook his head wildly. "*Nyet!*" he shouted back. *Are you crazy?* he silently added to himself. "That's impossible! They are lost in the crowd, or overrun. We're getting out of here, now!"

"It's my job!"

"I don't care if it's your job or not," Kovalev retorted, "I'm *not* letting you go back in there!" As if to punctuate his words, there were two more bursts of machine gun fire accompanied by more screaming, and the entire park seemed to be falling under a haze of tear gas. The two of them coughed and choked some more, and their eyes and noses began to run uncontrollably. Kovalev knew they were fortunate—there were *other* gases the IRGC could have used here, the kind that would have left thousands dead on the ground. Saddam Hussein in Iraq wouldn't have hesitated to use them under circumstances like these. As the protests across this country grew larger and more violent, he wondered how long it would be before the mullahs resorted to similar lethal measures against their own people.

Tara would have fought him, but the tear-gas changed the dynamic. It was getting hard to see and breathe, and she knew that setting up a broadcast was impossible under these conditions. She nodded, ignoring the streams of people fleeing the park around them, as she reached up and cupped Kovalev's cheek with one hand. "You came for me," she said simply. "Thank you."

I love you! He wanted to shout, but now was not the time or place for that conversation. He'd always had the sense that they were star-crossed, that their affair would end badly, but in that moment he didn't know or care what the future held. All he knew was that he had to get her away from *here*. "Come!" he shouted over the noise, pulling her to her feet.

"Wait," she said, catching him. She pulled the scarf off her head, wiping her face clean with one end and then his own, before placing her hand behind his head and kissing him passionately in full public view, right on the edge of Azadi Square, in Iran. In that moment Kovalev understood which side she was truly on, and that he was fighting for the wrong one. A black-clad member of the *Ghast-e Ershad,* the morality patrol, wearing a full hood and face covering appeared beside them, pulling them roughly apart and screaming in Farsi that it was forbidden. *Forbidden!*

"Poshel na khuy!" Kovalev shouted in Russian. *Fuck you!* He hauled off and punched the man squarely in the face, feeling his nose break under his knuckles and the face covering. Kovalev worked out every day, lifting weights to improve his G-tolerance, and he knew how to throw a punch. The militiaman clawed at his face, reeling, and fell to one knee as blood gushed from his shattered nose. Kovalev spat on him and shoved him to the ground. The Russian pilot grinned and caught Tara around the waist as she rushed past him, effortlessly hoisting her up and preventing her from planting a vicious kick to the man's head with the toe of her boot.

"No need to kick him while he's down, *milochka*," he chuckled in her ear, relishing the way she squirmed against him. He set her down a few paces away, then took his lover's hand and led her out of the park, to safety.

***

NAS China Lake, California

The base officer's club was an understated affair, but well suited to serve the needs of the weary wardroom of Detachment Six. After going full steam for a month, their Saturday night gathering had become a quick tradition. They had all grown up professionally in the fighter community, and the 'club culture' that went with it had followed them to their present circumstances. It was tough looking at each other for twelve to sixteen hours a day in the hangar, but a little social bonding was the oil that kept the machine running smoothly. For the folks with families, China Lake was an oddball assignment—they would deploy from here, but the expectation was that they would eventually return to an east or west coast master jet base, and nobody wanted to uproot their spouses and children unnecessarily. Some had brought their families anyway, looking for hard-to-be-found short term leases or base housing, while others had just treated it like deployment, accepting the separation from loved ones. It was easier for the single folks; a room at the BOQ was all they needed, and the busy nature of their days was proving profitable for the club restaurant and other food-joints on and around the base.

Despite the pressure they were under, nobody could work all day, every day, and stay efficient. Fargo set some ground rules after the first few two weeks when he noticed the glassy looks in the hangar and potentially dangerous mistakes on the flight line. He set working hours from 0530 Monday morning to 1800 Saturday afternoon. Saturday nights and Sundays were forced time off: nobody was allowed in the hangar or on the flight line except for the duty section, or by rare special dispensation from himself.

Those who brought spouses and families out to China Lake would normally attend the club gathering for half an hour or so on Saturday evenings before heading home, because family time was currently at a premium. That just left the singles to hang out together, eventually breaking off in small groups or individually to go find their entertainment elsewhere. Sometimes someone would sneak back to the hangar, but Fargo discouraged that during designated down-time.

Fargo sat at a table with Buzz and some of the other department heads, enjoying a steak sandwich and an ice-cold beer. The next table over hosted some of the 'younger' crowd, although all the aviators in the unit were salty lieutenants at a bare minimum. To fill out their roster of personnel, Fargo had aggressively stolen as many VX-9 personnel as Priest would let him get away with, since many of them had experience working on or flying the new jets. Beyond that, he had BUPERS comb the east and west coast fighter squadrons for lieutenants finishing their first sea tours, particularly if they were fresh off deployment.

Snake, Tex, and their newest check-in, 'Grape' Kowalski (Grape because of his big, round head), were huddled in a somewhat predatory looking group around Alicia Landry, the new AIO. Landry, a short blond with a dancer's body and model-good looks, had them eating out of the palm of her hand. She liked being the center of attention, and collected beta-orbiters as a hobby. She was an NROTC graduate, a sorority queen with only four years on active duty, and currently the most junior officer in the unit. Fargo had sensed she was trouble from the moment she'd tried working her charms on him during her check-in interview, and he was keeping a close eye on her. Her work as an intel officer so far had been adequate, and nothing more. Fargo never imagined he'd miss Sweater Boy, but reflected that he could use an Aston Chadwick II about now. But Sweater Boy was dead and gone forever, burned up with the rest of the Gray Wolves. The thought was painful, bringing up a sense of loss that he was still learning to live around.

Bagels dragged him back from that moment of post-traumatic reflection. "Hey, Honcho, what about the patch design contest? Have we got a winner yet?" she wanted to know. Buzz looked across the table at Fargo and the two of them shared a knowing grin. Speculation had run wild when they sequestered themselves in the office to look over the five entries that made the final cut. All of them were good, and Fargo was impressed at the effort that went into them. Things like squadron patches and aircraft tail feathers might seem inconsequential in the greater scheme of things, but to a fighter squadron, they were *not.* Nobody wanted to look like a dweeb, or wear a lame squadron patch.

"Yeah, what about it?" Jewels asked, playfully digging her elbow into his ribs.

"Oh, there's a winner, you betcha," Fargo grinned.

"It's *classified;* we could tell ya, but then we'd have to kill ya," Buzz replied smugly, leaning back and sliding an arm around his wife, Lisa. She was a tall brunette with practical, bobbed hair and the air of a dedicated Navy wife who was gratefully free of her kids for an evening.

A table full of hands pointed at Buzz. "That's a bar fine for the Top Gun movie reference," someone said. "Bartender! Another round here!" Buzz just shrugged as his wife playfully hit him for his *faux paus*, snorting in exasperation but still smiling. Seeing them made Fargo think of Angela, and he wished she was here. Buzz hadn't hesitated to bring his family out to China Lake. School was out for the summer, so there was no immediate impact on their three boys.

"We did get some news today," Fargo told them, digging into the pocket of his flight suit and producing a folded up piece of paper. He passed it around. "We finally got our stand-up orders. In four weeks, we go from Detachment Six to Fighting Six. We'll be assigned to Carrier Air Wing Nine, deploying aboard *Hornet*. We go sometime around the end of September, or the first week of October."

"When are we going to get a head shed? Or are you two going to be it?" Jewels asked, looking back and forth between Fargo and Buzz. It was almost a silly question; at this point it was too late for anyone else to come in and take over, as well as get qualified on the Advanced Super Tomcat.

Fargo smiled. "You'll find out Monday morning at Quarters," he told them, knowing *that* news would spread faster than a brushfire in windstorm. "It looks like CAG for the air wing is a Captain Sutter. Does anyone know him?"

"Nope," Buzz replied.

"Is that Ken Sutter?" Tex called across tables—obviously, the junior tables were eavesdropping. Fargo rechecked the message and nodded.

"He was the DCAG during my last deployment." Tex replied.

"Know anything about him?" Fargo asked.

Tex glanced around, before reluctantly giving up his choice seat next to Alicia Landry and pulling up a chair sort of halfway in between Fargo and Jewels. His face had a programmed neutral look that put Fargo on guard. If he was going to call Sutter a 'great guy' he could have done that from next to Landry. "Not much," Tex finally answered, speaking low enough not to broadcast to everyone in the bar. "He's a single seat guy—he only flew legacy Hornets and E-model Rhinos on my last deployment, so we didn't see much of him in our ready room. Our front office never bad-mouthed him in front of us, obviously, but there always this *look* between the CO and XO whenever his name came up. The impression was that he's a politician and a bit of a pain in the ass. Ring knocker type."

"Hey, watch it there, bub!" Buzz growled.

Tex shrugged. "I'm a boat school grad myself, sir, but I don't wear it on my sleeve," he fired back. "I just call 'em like I see 'em. Anyway, he's obviously done well enough to make it this far. That's all I know, Honcho. Sorry."

Fargo shook his head. "Thanks for making my day brighter, Tex," he joked. "Serves me right."

Buzz grinned at him. "That's your own fault, Fargo. If you don't want the answer to a question, don't ask it."

XIII

Fargo extended a hand to his new boss, Captain Ken 'Spigot' Sutter. "I've been looking forward to meeting you, CAG," he said by way of introduction. On first acquaintance, he had no idea what Sutter's callsign referenced, but it didn't matter much. The air wing commander was 'CAG,' and that was that.

"Nice to meet you too, commander," CAG replied. He was a fireplug of a man, 5'8" and thickly built, with dark hair and eyes. He reminded Fargo a little of a scrappy bull terrier. "I'm impressed with your progress, Fargo . . .or is it Honcho? I've heard both around the hangar."

"It's Fargo, sir. The Honcho thing is a bit of an inside joke, with me as Detachment Six OIC. I've been a little worried that it was going to turn into a callsign change, y'know?"

"Could be worse," CAG replied bluntly. "The way you talk, you could have been 'FAG' for 'funny accent guy' instead. Happiness is relative, eh?"

"Absolutely, sir, when you put it like that."

"Your people have accomplished great things down here in a short period of time. I'll be straight up with you, though: a lot of people have misgivings about this whole idea. Now what's this I hear about the new missiles not working properly?" he asked.

There had been a glitch with the new AIM-152 missiles. When fired in salvo by multiple aircraft (the typical outer air battle scenario), they sometimes went rogue, ignoring their programmed target sort and converging on a single contact. They had troubleshot the problem down to a coding error on one of the missile's electronic microchips. Buzz Bozeman had a master's degree in software engineering; he'd gotten together with tech reps from the missile company and found the solution. Getting the solution implemented into their current batch of missiles technically decertified them for combat. Fargo made the decision (on his own authority) to go ahead with the fix but keep the specifics quiet—the sort of omission that could end his career in a heartbeat if the wrong people found out. Right now, the missiles were working as they were meant to work, but he couldn't get a new, properly certified batch before their deployment, so he was stuck with the 'fixed' inventory he had on hand. Some of his ordnance people were in the know as well as the tech reps, and they were following his lead. He was at a crossroads right now, because he wasn't sure if CAG Sutter was someone he could trust, or the type who would stick a knife in his back and crow about it to his own bosses. CAG had just intimated that perhaps he wasn't happy with the make-up of his new air wing. It was new and experimental, and anything experimental implied the risk of failure, which in turn posed a potential threat to his career.

In the end, it wasn't in Fargo to lie about it—that would go totally against his grain as a person and as an officer. Fully aware that he might be shooting himself down in flames, he briefly explained that they had gotten the missiles working by recoding blank chips and replacing the faulty ones. All the work was done 'in house', at the unit level, which was the problem in this case. Based on how they were altering the missiles, technically speaking it wasn't a proper fix. Bozeman and the tech reps repaired the software bug, and the squadron's ordnance techs re-assembled the guidance units under the supervision and tutelage of the tech reps themselves. It was supposed to be a factory job, not squadron-level or even depot-level maintenance. The problem was time: they just didn't have enough of it to go through normal channels. It was an issue that went beyond simply picking up the phone and asking for help.

Fargo was relieved that CAG understood the root of the problem. "We *need* those missiles," CAG said. "Without them, there isn't much advantage to these Supercats." That wasn't true for a myriad of reasons, but Fargo let it go—CAG's response was encouraging. "Between the SAM traps, current missile ranges, and the advanced fighter cover provided by those mercenary squadrons, we haven't been able to bag those Mainstays yet. These missiles are the key to accomplishing that."

"That's it *exactly*, sir," Fargo said firmly.

CAG waved his hand dismissively. "Don't worry about it—have the tech reps get the paperwork going for a certification waiver and shoot it up their company channels. I'll let COMNAVAIRPAC and the CNO's office know from our end, and it'll come back approved. That's been the one *good* thing about this Cactus Air Force we're putting together: anything I've asked for, I've gotten, no questions asked."

Fargo felt an overwhelming sense of relief flood through him—he'd literally been losing sleep over this, and he knew Buzz was even more unhappy about it than he was. He'd begun to worry that Buzz might end-run him again, but it had just been rendered a non-issue with CAG pulling lead for them. *This is why you shouldn't pre-judge people based on what you hear,* he admonished himself. CAG must have read the relief in his expression.

"Worried about that, were you?" he asked.

"Yes sir," Fargo replied. "I had to make a decision, or we weren't going to complete the test program in time."

Sutter nodded curtly. "Welcome to the big leagues, Fargo. If it works, you're a hero; if it fails, you're a bum. Making the hard calls is part of your job description, son. The important thing is that you told me the truth about it." He gave Fargo a curious look. "Did you think I didn't already know?" With a mental start, Fargo realized that his new wing commander had just tested him, and he'd passed the test.

Fargo shook his head. "I had *no idea* you knew, CAG."

Sutter gave him a wry smile. "This is my air wing, and it's *my job* to know. You're a warrior, Fargo, but you've still got a lot to learn. Let's round up Buzz and get on with it," he said.

***

Five minutes later they stepped into the hangar, finding the entire detachment formed up in three groups: upper deck personnel, the officers, and the maintenance department. All enlisted personnel wore summer white crackerjacks, with the officers and chiefs decked out in service dress khaki. Buzz

Bozeman stood out in front of the topside group, Jewels Baxter at the head of the maintenance department, with Hawk Vasquez acting as adjutant. CAG Sutter hung back momentarily as Fargo squared his cover on his head and took position at the forefront of the entire formation, facing them. Hawk called the detachment to attention, took the reports, and then did an about face to salute Fargo and report Detachment Six formed for Quarters. Fargo introduced CAG Sutter, who gave the order to stand easy before addressing the group. Detachment Six was now a squadron in all but name; they had a full roster of personnel, and ten of the twelve aircraft they were slated to deploy with. In another month they would officially stand up as an active squadron. This morning's gathering held a different purpose. CAPT Sutter called Thorsen and Bozeman front and center. They marched up smartly, squaring off with the wing commander and exchanging sharp salutes.

"It is old news by now, but still my pleasure to announce that the results of the latest O-5 promotion and command screening boards have been published. Lieutenant Commanders Thorsen and Bozeman were both selected for promotion to O-5, and have screened for operational command. Normally these two gentlemen would be forced to serve a sentence in Washington D.C. or something similar before moving on to their command tours, but like so many other things around here, circumstances dictate that we do things a little backwards. By order of the Commander, Naval Air Forces Pacific, Commanders Thorsen and Bozeman are frocked to their new rank effective immediately. In a month's time when Detachment 6 becomes Fighting 6, Commander Thorsen will assume command with Commander Bozeman as executive officer. Until that time, Commander Thorsen will remain detachment officer in charge, with Commander Bozeman as his deputy. Mrs. Bozeman, Chief Reddy, will you do the honors please?"

Lisa Bozeman and Chief Reddy approached and unclipped the shoulder boards from their uniform jackets, replacing them with new boards boasting three full gold stripes. When they were finished, Lisa Bozeman kissed her husband warmly on the cheek while Chief Reddy stepped back smartly and traded salutes with Fargo. Then they stepped aside, and each man saluted CAPT Sutter in turn and shook his hand as he congratulated them. The entire detachment applauded then, with a couple of the more spirited among them letting out a few war-whoops and huzzahs. CAG ordered both officers back to their posts in the formation, and the detachment was called back to attention.

"Alright," CAG announced, "we'll have no more of this 'Honcho' crap. Skipper Thorsen, take charge of your squadron and carry out the plan of the day."

"Aye aye, sir!" Fargo replied sharply. The two men saluted each other again, and then CAG withdrew to the side with Mrs. Bozeman, while Chief Reddy resumed her place in the ranks. The change in atmosphere was tangible; although this wasn't a squadron establishment ceremony, CAG had just addressed them as such, and now the 'front office' was firmly established with a pair of O-5's in charge; things were starting to normalize.

And it was now official: Fargo was the commanding officer.

He turned and faced the assembled detachment, ordering them to stand at-ease. He announced the winner of the squadron name and logo design contest, which would be officially unveiled at the squadron's establishment. A murmur of approval rippled through the ranks when he declared the winner, and a hand went up: CWO3 Lowden's. "Skipper, we've all been saying we're going to be 'Fighting 6' when we establish. Is that gonna be *VFA*-6 or *VF*-6?"

"VF, baby, VF," Fargo replied with a toothy grin, along with a sharp clap and rubbing together of his hands in front of him. "Fighter squadrons are *back!*"

"Back in black!" someone hollered spiritedly from the ranks.

"*Fuckin-A!*" another anonymous voice hooted from the crowd, and a big cheer went up.

"That answer your question, Mister Lowden?" Fargo asked.

"CFB, sir!" Lowden roared his approval.

There was a lot of work to do, so Fargo didn't keep it hanging. He dismissed the detachment from quarters, and everyone promptly went to change into working uniforms so they could turn to and get dirty. As the group broke up, Fargo stepped over to where Buzz was standing with his wife, preparing to kiss her goodbye for the morning. Fargo was glad that the matter of command was officially settled. Buzz had all the earmarks of a good XO, and Fargo's generally easygoing manner would suit him well in the skipper's role as the 'good cop.' He felt the weight of that responsibility settling over him—the 'burden of command,' as it were. Everything that happened here was his responsibility now, and the climate he set was the climate he'd get.

"Congratulations, Fargo," Lisa said, leaning in to give him a friendly buss on the cheek. He and Buzz were grinning from ear to ear, and shook hands with one another in congratulations.

"Y'know," Buzz reflected, "I think I like it this way after all," he said. "You being in charge first, I mean."

"How so?"

"If things run their normal course, you'll get your eighteen months. I'll get that as your exec, plus another eighteen after I take over."

Fargo was a little taken aback. "Shit, I hadn't even thought of *that!*"

"I need to get going," Lisa said casually. "Fargo, don't you have a girlfriend who could've pinned your boards on?"

"I sort of do, but it's a long distance thing right now, y'know," he admitted lamely.

"I see," she said, exchanging a quick glance with her husband. They exchanged a quick hug and kiss, and then she left.

"I'm not fuckin' gay, you hoser," Fargo growled at Buzz, causing him to belly laugh.

"Hey, don't ask, don't tell. Seriously though," he said, "I like it this way. That thing with the missiles—you know I *never* would have taken that risk the way you did, and we'd probably be screwed, limited to AMRAAMs and heaters in the Gulf. When you made the call, and the fix worked . . . that's when I became a believer."

"About that," Fargo grinned. "I've got some more good news: that little problem is *solved*. I talked to CAG about it, and he's taking care of it. We're going to get a certification waiver."

Buzz's eyebrows went up, and he blew out a sigh of relief. "That's some damn good news, Skipper."

"You betcha, XO. One problem solved, and only a couple hundred more to go. Now we're cooking with oil!"

***

SEP 2013
Bandar Abbas, Islamic Republic of Iran

Arkady Kovalev relaxed in bed with Tara Shirazi cradled in the crook of his arm. On the other side of the small oceanside hotel room near Dowlat Park, the cheap television blared at medium volume, offering a form of cover from potential eavesdroppers. They had checked into the hotel individually, and then been very careful about her coming to his room. They were unmarried, and thus their being together alone like this was illegal. Kovalev had laid the groundwork before now, having stayed here a few times during his furloughs from their secret base to the north, as had other members of his unit. The innkeeper and the staff knew him, and the presence of Russian foreigners no longer seemed strange. Their money was good—that was the most important thing.

Tara's firm body was pressed in against his own; the mocha color of her skin contrasted with the sheets, and he relished the way she was sinuously intertwined with him, a bare leg cast carelessly across his thighs. She reached up and took the lit cigarette dangling from the corner of his mouth, drawing on it and exhaling a cloud of smoke across the room. She offered the cigarette back, then sat up slightly when he didn't take it back. He was staring through the shroud of the curtains at the Strait of Hormuz beyond, his mind obviously a thousand miles away.

"What are you thinking about?" she asked.

"Nothing. And everything," Kovalev replied. He paused, wondering how best to broach the subject. The war was not going well, there were shortages everywhere now, and the mood of the Iranian people was like a taut cable, stretched to the breaking point. Even in this hotel, the restaurant hours were almost non-existent and only a quarter of the menu was readily available. Prices were unbelievable, by local standards. Those with enough money ate, those without went hungry. For some, the situation was already desperate. The American blockade of this country was proving very effective, even if they weren't stopping the foreign flagged tankers from moving crude oil out of the Gulf.

Toma Baranov had come to him a few days before, and the two men had shared a frank conversation. The work of the *Krasnyye Kogti* had not gone unnoticed in certain circles in Russia, where a large, private mercenary company called the Wagner Group was ramping up to begin a 'green man' operation on the Crimean Peninsula. They were already stirring up local, ethnic Russian nationalists in a campaign to bring the peninsula back under the Russian flag. The matter of territorial disputes between Ukraine and Russia was longstanding, going back as far as the Stalinist days of the Soviet Union, and truthfully farther back than that. Sevastopol and the Crimea's Black Sea ports were the prize—prizes the Russian government meant to have, especially after their successful invasion of Georgia in 2008. That had been a test of western resolve, and the west had barely responded. The same had happened again with the civil war in Syria, and now Russian eyes were turning toward Crimea, and perhaps even the Donbass region of greater eastern Ukraine. The time was ripe, with American attention focused almost solely on Iran and the Persian Gulf.

Baranov had told him that the Wagner Group was interested in developing a small air arm, and that the surviving Red Talons would be perfect additions to the group. The pay would be steady, and they would be back to working among their own countrymen, in conditions much more favorable than they were in Iran in their present circumstances. Baranov had told him that there would be no pushback from the Russian government if the Red Talons quietly made their exit; Russia's aims in the Persian Gulf had been achieved, and everyone understood that Iran would eventually be forced to capitulate.

Kovalev told his superior that he'd give it serious consideration, and began quietly talking it over with the remaining pilots. He knew they were dissatisfied as well, living in terrible underground conditions with poor food, no alcohol, and no women. Not everyone had been as lucky as he was; most of the men were looking nostalgically back to their days in the Russian military—*not* a ringing endorsement of their present circumstances.

But there was the matter of Tara Shirazi. He absently reached down and stroked her lustrous hair, feeling her shift pleasantly against him. "Would you ever consider leaving Iran?" he asked her.

"For a vacation, or permanently?" she asked.

"Permanently. You could some with me, back to Russia. Pskov is beautiful in the autumn," he added almost dreamily, not mentioning that it was downright cold by anyone's standards, much less an Iranian's, and the winters were worse. Even as he floated the idea to her, in the form of hinting and hoping, he knew it would never work. She'd be a fish out of water back home, left alone in a strange country when he was on an assignment, by herself most of the time. "We could be married," he said anyway.

Distressed by this talk, Tara sat up, instinctively clutching the bed sheet over her chest. "What are you talking about?" she asked. "*Are you leaving?*"

"No, no," he said soothingly, reaching out to caress her cheek. Her eyes were wild now, frightened, and perhaps even a little dangerous. "No," he repeated, "I'm not going anywhere, at least not right now. But my people won't be staying here forever. When we *do* leave, would you consider going with me?"

"No!" she replied immediately. "Iran is my *home*, and these are my people! Things are *happening* here, Arkady! Change is coming, and this war won't last forever. You and your people, you are a part of it! How can you even be *thinking* of leaving?"

"It won't be up to me, in the end," he told her truthfully. "When the decision is made, I'll have no choice. I love you, *milochka*. When I go, I don't want to leave you behind."

"Where would we live? What would I do for work? *It would mean abandoning my career!*" she said vehemently, her voice rising.

"Quietly," Kovalev warned her, gesturing to the walls. "That is something else we needn't worry about in the *Rodina*," he added.

"If we were to marry, we wouldn't have to worry about it *here,*" Tara said pointedly. She dropped the sheet and got out of bed; Kovalev's breath caught at her beauty as she began gathering her clothes and getting dressed. She proceeded to rant angrily at him about the life she had built for herself, her career, her celebrity—was she supposed to just give that all up? Abandon her country and her work at a possible cusp point in the country's history? For what? *To be a Russian housewife*?

In the end, Kovalev recognized it for the empty dream that it was. Worse, by bringing it up, he had opened a permanent rift in their relationship. Tara Shirazi strolled over to the bed and kissed him on the cheek. "I'm sorry, best beloved, but what you ask is impossible. Goodbye, Arkady," she said.

When she was gone, Kovalev lit another cigarette and lay back with an arm behind his head, face impassive, as the smoke curled up around him. He thought about his time here, what it all meant, and asked himself what he had accomplished. He remembered the toast he and Baranov had drunk shortly after his arrival.

To long enough.

Maybe he had been here long enough. He certainly didn't want to die for Iran, especially not the likes of Hamed Abdi and his rabid, fanatic leaders. Cheng Ye was even worse: tactically brilliant, but he was a demon walking in the guise of a man. He *certainly* didn't want to die for Cheng Ye and the Chinese.

He resolved to speak to Baranov when he returned to base.

NAS China Lake, California

The United States Navy had specific ceremonial guidelines for things like commissioning or decommissioning ships, establishing and dis-establishing squadrons, and conducting changes of command. The details of the various ceremonies would change slightly on a case-by-case basis, but the overall structure of such ceremonies was steeped in familiar traditions.

Today, A stage lined one wall of the hangar, looking out over two groupings of seats with a large gap in the center. Squadron personnel mustered in the seats on one side, guests on the other, and guests of honor and/or VIP's not in the official party occupied the first few rows on both sides. A Navy band was seated left of the stage, present because of the august rank of their top guest rather than the ceremony itself. Behind the seats in the center of the hangar, a freshly painted and polished F-14E sat resplendently, sporting brand new tailfeathers. This jet was the 'CAG bird', side-number 100, painted in full color. Most of the Tomcat was dark gray, but her tails, a portion of her top planform, and the area around the cockpit were painted black. The profile of a snarling tiger's head adorned her tails in gold, and her gold-on-black stenciled markings read "VF-6" and "USS *Hornet*", respectively. The full-color 'CAG bird' was a tradition followed by every seagoing squadron in the navy. As such, Captain Sutter's name and rank were painted below the cockpit rail under the pilot's seat, with Buzz's name and rank under the WSO's. On an easel set up next to the center podium on stage, there was a large representation of their new squadron emblem glaring out balefully over the crowd, looking suitably angry and fierce.

What was meant to be a smaller, quiet ceremony had blown up with the unexpected arrival of the Chief of Naval Operations. The guest list swelled dramatically at the last moment as west coast VIPs made it a point to attend the establishment ceremony to see and be seen with the service chief. ADM Harris was invited to speak, but kept his remarks brief. Due to twists of scheduling, Fargo didn't have the opportunity to meet him prior to the ceremony, but understood fully that the CNO's decisions were the reason that the Supercat would be deployed as more than a mere prototype. Nobody knew how long this dream would last, but the important thing for Fargo was the career lightning strike: he was in the right place at the right time, and someone thought he was the right man for the job of leading this unit.

Captain Manning, the CO of VX-9, made his brief remarks following the CNO and formally ordered the standdown of Detachment Six and the establishment of Fighter Squadron Six. Orders were given, salutes exchanged, and the shrill whistle of the bosun's pipe echoed eerily through the hangar. The watch was set, with Lieutenant Taro 'Tiki' Katsumi going down as the first squadron duty officer on record. When it was done, Fargo formally reported to CAG Sutter that Fighting 6 was established, and that he was in command. More salutes were exchanged, and then Fargo took the podium to make his remarks.

That was when he got the surprise of his life, and it made one of the best days of his life impossibly better. There in the front row, seated among the VIPs, was one Angela Olson, looking as glamorous as he'd ever seen her. She looked like a movie star in a blue dress and heels, perfectly coifed hair and almost professional cosmetics. A.J. was with her, hair slicked back and combed, wearing a dark blue suit with tennis shoes as if to remind everyone he was still a kid. She smiled beautifully when Fargo caught sight of them, her eyes shining.

Fargo's surprise caused him to stumble a bit over his opening remarks, but he recovered fast. He cut an impressive figure in full dress whites, and what he had to say injected a hard dose of reality into all the pomp and circumstance. "This is a pretty big day for everyone who works in this hangar," he began, after welcoming and thanking the ranking guests. "Together, we've accomplished a near-impossible task in record time, unlike anything attempted since the Second World War. The Black Tigers can take pride in our hard work, and joy in the experience of being plank owners in a new unit. The work of bringing the Tomcat back to fleet service has *definitely* been a labor of love.

"That said, the job is far from finished. Our pride, our joy are tempered by the hard knowledge that we are here for a grim, singular purpose: to carry the fight to an enemy that has killed thousands of our brothers and sisters. Soon, over the skies of the Gulf and Iran, *we will finish what the enemy started*." Fargo turned slightly and looked ADM D.J. Harris straight in the eye. "I *guarantee* it," he added with complete conviction. It was a tremendously bold thing to say, some might argue over the top, but at the CNO's stern, affirming nod, the hangar burst into thunderous applause. The applause grew over time instead of fading, and was soon punctuated with whoops and huzzahs, and someone shouted the old Tomcat war cry 'Anytime, Baby!' from the ranks. When Fargo waved down the applause, Harris and the other senior guests were smiling fiercely. Months of hard work and sacrifice, peppered with the occasional bit of hard play, had forged them into a highly spirited unit.

"In closing," Fargo finished, "let me remark briefly on our avatar. The mascot we have chosen is symbolic of the task ahead of us. The tiger is an uncompromising hunter, bringing tremendous strength and power to the fight. The tiger is aggressive—the word itself was used to describe fighter pilots of old. To be called a 'tiger' was a professional compliment. The tiger evokes traits that we can all strive to emulate, and I know you will." He turned a stern gaze on the assembled members of his new command, and nodded his approval. "Black Tigers, let's go to work!" he cried. Wild applause broke out again. The ceremony ended with the departure of the official party; they were piped and rung out in order of precedence, with the appropriate number of 'side boys' for each according to this rank. The band played 'Anchors Aweigh' as they went, and the ceremony ended on that note.

The Black Tigers were officially in business.

***

At the end of the ceremony, the official party and guests lingered around the hangar for 'bug juice' and cake. 'Bug juice' was navy speak for a drink that was essentially Kool-Aid. In this case, two enormous cakes were decorated with frosted versions of the Black Tigers and 'Back in Black' Tomcat patches. Fargo knew that he was expected to seek out the CNO for a quiet word, but his priority changed as soon as he saw Angela sitting in the audience. It wouldn't do to keep the boss waiting, but he certainly wasn't going to get fired for it—at least not now. Besides, everyone with stars on their shoulders wanted a little face time with the top man; he could pretend like he was merely waiting his turn.

Angela and A.J. stood off to one side, accompanied by Lisa Bozeman, her sons, and Chief Reddy. All of them were grinning from ear to ear at his somewhat shellshocked approach. Lisa pre-empted the foremost question on his mind: "I arranged to have them here for this, Fargo. I hope it's okay," she said with an easy smile. "Surprised?"

"Oh, you betcha!" Fargo said, folding Angela into his embrace and giving her a careful, chaste kiss. After almost four months, having her in his arms set his spirit soaring to new heights. She was careful not to smear makeup on his white chokers, and dabbed self-consciously at her eyes when he finally let her go. Fargo turned to her son.

"How you are doing there, fella?" he asked, reaching out. A.J. didn't hesitate; he stepped in for a quick one-armed hug, giving Fargo a firm pat on the back and saying he was doing fine. His eyes kept straying to the majestic sight of the polished Tomcat sitting in the hangar, and Fargo promised him a chance to sit in the cockpit of the jet, when they had a moment. None of this was anything new to the Bozeman boys. They looked a little restless and bored, if anything, and Buzz had already brought them in a couple of times to see the planes.

They all shifted a little uncomfortably when they saw the CNO and an entourage of senior officers making a beeline for them. Lisa was quick on her feet, instructing the boys to take A.J. and go raid the cake table. They departed somewhat reluctantly, and Fargo saw the CNO eyeballing the kids curiously as they went. Another round of introductions followed.

"Fang Harris," the CNO replied after Fargo was introduced, feeling a renewed sense of nostalgia for his fighter community roots. "Sorry I wasn't able to meet you *before* the ceremony," he added with a slight smile as they shook hands. He glanced casually at Angela, careful not to stare at her the way a couple of his aides were—she was *very* stare-able right now. "The file on you says you're single. Do we have bad or old information on that?"

"Single *for now*, sir," he explained with a shy glance and smile at Angela.

"I see. Ladies, do you mind if I borrow the commander for a minute?" he asked. Lisa nodded, familiar with these rituals, and led Angela after the boys. Fargo introduced Buzz Bozeman, and they were in turn introduced to two civilians, Pat Jackson and Denny Carter. Both were senior Northman-Ironworks executives, and obviously part of the CNO's official party. Harris turned his attention to the F-14E, his eyes lighting up the way any pilot would recognize. "God, that plane looks faster than stink," Harris grinned. "What do you think of her, Skipper?" he asked Fargo.

"Admiral, that is hands down the best jet I've ever flown. This is the one we should have put into production back in the 90's, and I say that without rancor or apology."

"We wanted it back then, but we were overruled," Harris reminded all of them. "We'll see what happens going forward. How have your mission capable rates been, and your maintenance to flight hour ratios?"

Fargo was bluntly honest. "*Much* better than the old Tomcats, not as good as the Super Hornet. In my opinion, the performance and payload/range numbers are well worth the trade-off."

The CNO gave Fargo a frank look. "A lot is riding on this. Is there *anything* I can do for you?"

The question made Fargo's head spin a little. Coming from the four-star chief of naval operations, the question was unprecedented. His appearance at this ceremony with next to no warning had sent people scrambling all over this base, but none of it drove home the seriousness of the upcoming deployment than this question from the top man.

"Two things, admiral," Fargo replied after a moment's hesitation.

"Shoot."

"I want to hand-pick the tech reps who to go to sea with us," he said, deliberately not bringing up the past missile problems with the prototype AIM-152. "The second is a little more general: up until now, we've gotten anything we've asked for in terms of personnel and materiel. It would mean a lot to see that level of support continue as we press into sustained combat operations. We've had to overcome some unique challenges."

Harris glanced back at Denny Carter, raising an inquisitive brow. "Denny?"

"You'll have whoever you need on the tech rep side. I'll make the bonus checks as big as they need to be."

"Fair enough," the CNO replied, fishing a business card out of his pocket and handing it across to Fargo. "This has the email address of my chief of staff. I know you have a couple of other points of contact for materiel needs, but you can use this if they ever fall through. Don't hesitate, and do not consider it an end-run around higher authority. CAG Sutter has the same card and the same orders for the rest of your air wing."

"Thank you, admiral."

Harris nodded. "I've been looking forward to meeting you. You and your senior people are hand-picked, and I'm well read on what you went through over there on that terrible day. You've already seen some interesting times, commander. Every fifty or a hundred years or so, we hit the perfect storm and something like this happens. In every case, there are a handful of men and women who take center stage. This time it will be you and your people. I wish like hell I was going with you." Harris extended his hand again.

Fargo grasped it. "We'll bring home the win, admiral," he promised.

As soon as the CNO departed with his entourage, Fargo went looking for Angela and A.J. They weren't too far away. A.J. was looking over a few of their new squadron patches. The first was a square patch, one of only a few shaped like that in the fighter community. It was black, outlined in gold-braided thread, sporting the same gold-colored, red-eyed, snarling tiger-head in evidence on the tail of the CAG bird. The top line read: 'Black Tigers' in gold lettering, and 'Fighting 6' along the bottom. The second patch was a variation on the old, triangular F-14 patch that Tomcat aviators used to wear on the right shoulder of their flight suits. This one was black with the aircraft in gray, and simply said 'F-14E Supercat' across the bottom. The last was a variation on the old 'Anytime, Baby' Tomcat patch: round, with the familiar looking cartoon tomcat, leaning casually with a six-gun on his hip, offering a play on the old challenge across the bottom banner: 'Back in Black, Baby.' This patch was also presented in black and gold, with lettering on top that read: 'F-14E Advanced Super Tomcat.'

"Can I keep these?" A.J. asked.

"You betcha," Fargo replied. "We'll scare up a couple Black Tigers ballcaps for you, too. Maybe your Ma can sew the patches on a jacket for you."

"That'd be cool!"

Fargo caught sight of the CAG bird's plane captain in the crowd. "Petty Officer Keeler!" he called. A lanky young woman with straight brown hair, sporting the crow of an Aviation Machinist's Mate 2nd Class, came right over. Fargo turned A.J. over to her, asking her to show him around the jet, and let A.J. sit in the cockpit for a spell. The jet was *her* airplane as plane captain. She knew it backwards and forwards, and like all plane captains she spent most of her working days in company with the jet, making sure it was ready to fly when called upon. She'd keep A.J. safe and out of trouble; jet fighters had a way of biting the uninitiated, even when sitting docile in the hangar.

"Can do, Skipper," she replied, turning her attention to A.J. She introduced herself to the boy, and the two of them headed off eagerly, giving Fargo a moment alone with Angela. He resisted the urge to hold her and cover her in kisses, as much as he yearned to. It was just too public here, and he was the CO.

"God, Angie, I've missed you," he breathed. "How and when did you get here?"

"We flew into L.A. yesterday, rented a car, and drove up. Lisa contacted me at home—don't ask me how she figured out how to reach me, but you've got some talented people around you, you betcha. Gary and Lisa sponsored us onto the base for today," she added, gesturing at the visitor's badge attached to her dress."

"You look absolutely beautiful," Fargo told her. "If I'd known you were coming, I could have—"

She reached up and placed her fingers over his mouth, quieting him. "It's alright," she said. "I'm just glad we could come."

"Where are you staying?"

"With the Bozemans. Lisa offered to put us up, and I told her no, at first. I mean, I don't even really *know* her, but she insisted, then she brought up A.J., and her boys, and, well, *y'know*. It'll be like a kid's sleepover for a couple days, for A.J., and give us a little time alone. She told me you're all leaving soon—that you'll just stay on the ship and head west as you finish your carrier quals. I know you're busy," she went on, speaking faster, on the verge of babbling. "We probably shouldn't even have come—"

Fargo gripped her gently around her upper arms. "I'm glad you're here, sweetheart," he said. "Both of you."

Angela smiled. "I've never seen you in your uniform before," she said, tracing a finger down the white twill of his chokers. She leaned in like a conspirator. "What I really want is to see you *out* of it. Is there going to be any time at all for us out here?"

"We'll make some time," Fargo promised.

***

USS *Hornet,* off the California coast

It was early afternoon when the Air Boss set flight quarters; the skies were clear, with a scattered layer at about six thousand, winds at about twelve knots, and a slow-rolling sea state that translated to a relatively level deck. It was a great day for a Case One recovery. If the weather held, there would be a strong waxing crescent moon that evening, rising early and providing a little moonshine for the night operations that followed.

LT Brad 'Dingo' Rawlins was the head Landing Signal Officer, or LSO, for the Black Tigers. Although he wasn't senior enough to have started his career flying Tomcats, he was a TPS graduate who had participated in the carrier suitability trials for the Supercat when it was in prototype at VX-9. His familiarity with the airplane and his qualifications as an LSO were invaluable— he'd been shanghaied into the Black Tigers early in the proceedings, and two more LSO-qualified pilots had come with him. They were the first to complete carrier qualifications, coming early as a two-plane detachment and getting one another signed off with the help of the wing LSO before taking on the task of 'waving' the remainder of the squadron.

It was quite an experience for all of them, getting ready for this final phase of their pre-deployment qualification. Usually, a deploying squadron went through FLCPs, 'field carrier landing practice', as part of their work-up, which led to carrier quals. FCLPs for the Black Tigers had started on day one of their flying back in July, because there was no time to do it separately. An LSO was stationed at the runway for every returning sortie, with the pilots bagging as many touch-and-goes as fuel allowed. Dingo and his team graded them mercilessly, teaching them the finer points of flying the Supercat around the Boat and refining their skills. It was a little easier for the former Tomcat pilots. The Supercat was all digital, and her thrust vectoring coupled with the redesigned high-lift devices made for a slower and more benign approach to the ship than they remembered from years past. The Supercat still wasn't quite as easy to bring aboard as a Rhino or a legacy Hornet, but almost. Those who had only known the Super Hornet had a tougher go of it, but none of them were first-tour nuggets. Everyone had extensive experience around the Boat, well over a hundred traps or more, and Dingo was sure everyone would qualify with little problem.

They'd better, Fargo reflected, *or the show would be off to an embarrassing start, you betcha.*

Dingo and the assistant LSO behind them held their pickle switches in the air, reminding everyone around them that they didn't have a 'green' deck for landing yet. He checked that his writer was near at hand with his trusty notebook, then looked behind them, up and down the length of the flight deck. Given the unique nature of this operation, no chances were being taken. The entire aft portion of the flight deck was clear of other airplanes, giving them a larger margin for error than they'd have during normal operations. The Air Boss finally called 'green deck,' and they were ready to begin.

The flight deck crews had been through an interesting couple of weeks. First, the Navy's brand new replacement for the Hornet, the stealthy F-25 Cutlass, had shown up in squadron strength to complete their own carrier quals. Those were finished up and the jets safely stashed below the flight deck, in the ship's hangar and out of harm's way. Now, looking up, they saw something that nobody had seen in more than half a decade: F-14 Tomcats orbiting in the marshal stack over the port side of the ship. Ten of them, sucking fuel at prodigious rates but with plenty to spare even after flying directly out here all the way from China Lake. At the bottom of the marshal stack, two thousand feet overhead, CDR Mike Thorsen flew side number 100, their colorful CAG bird, with LCDR Greg Schultz in his back seat. Three more Supercats were stacked up on his right wing in parade formation, waiting. On the ship's island, 'Vulture's Row' was packed with spectators eager to watch the arrival of the Black Tigers.

"Tiger 100," marshal called, "green deck. Your signal is Charlie."

Fargo led them around their last orbit in the stack, then dropped them down to 800 FT for the break as his division closed into a nice, tight formation. In traditional Tomcat fashion, they manually swept the wings full aft, to 68-degrees of sweep. They didn't showboat, but flew their pattern entry strictly by the book, breaking at precise intervals into the pattern and dirtying up on downwind, hitting their target AOA. Although he was fully concentrating on the task at hand, Fargo couldn't help but remember Skipper Jefferson and the way that guy could never fly a bad pass. He did his very best to honor him, for the memory of the Gray Wolves and the pride of the Black Tigers. Dingo gave him a couple of good calls, and he flew a solid OK pass to the 3-wire. There were a few busy moments getting clear of the landing area, and as he taxied forward to the bow cats he got a call on the radio from *Hornet*'s commanding officer, Captain Ross. "Tiger One from *Hornet* Actual, BZ on the first pass. I'd like to extend my welcome aboard to the Black Tigers."

"Thanks, captain, with my respects," Fargo transmitted. He only had to do it nine more times, and then five traps at night over the next two days. *But that one was for you, Chill,* he said to Skipper Jefferson's memory.

***

That evening after chow, a tired but pleased Fargo found himself on the hangar deck, looking curiously over the *other* new fighter the Navy was deploying for the first time. The difference was that the F-25 Cutlass was a mainstream program, put through the new and improved appropriations process implemented by the Powell administration after cancelling the F-35. Fargo had to admit that the Cutlass gave the Supercat a run for its money when it came to aesthetics. The plane was roughly the same size as a Super Hornet, perhaps a bit smaller, with large, forward canards that almost looked like horizontal stabilizers at the wrong end of the jet. The main, swept wing sat behind those, well aft of the cockpit, vaguely reminding him of the wing on an Air Force F-15, but with a zig-zag built into its trailing edge. There were twin, outboard-canted vertical stabilizers, between which sat a pair of powerful engines with 'stealth' nozzles that gave the jet a Mach 2 top end speed. Underneath her wings she was just a little fat out to the sides of her side-mounted twin intakes—those were internal weapons storage bays for missions which called for stealth. Unlike the cancelled F-35, however, the Cutlass was not designed as a *true* stealth aircraft in the same vein as the canceled F-35. One of the many issues with the prototype F-35 was its sensitive, expensive outer coating, which blistered and delaminated from the airframe at her top end speed. The Cutlass had stealthy angles built into her design curves, and she had the same gold-coated canopy as the F-22, but her paint was a much more standard looking dark gray scheme, which had *limited* stealth properties. The Black Tigers Supercats had the same gray paint, for all it was worth. True to the new rules surrounding weapons systems procurement, the designers were forced to go with the technologies on hand when the plane was designed and put into production, rather than stopping midstream and doing massive redesigns to incorporate the latest, greatest, and often untested technology.

For stealth(y) missions, mostly those involving suppression of enemy air defenses (SEAD), the Cutlass would rely on internally carried weapons, speed, 'sensible stealth', and the significant electronic warfare capabilities of her radar—the same AESA variant used in the Supercat. With additional EW support from the new EA-6E Advanced Super Prowlers, coupled with their own onboard capabilities, they were anticipating the Cutlass would be instrumental in the fast removal of what remained of Iran's vaunted integrated air defense system.

Due to abandoning a completely stealth design and all the expensive upkeep that went with it, the Cutlass came in at around fifty-five million dollars per copy, perhaps less when the eventual foreign sales kicked in. That was slightly less than eighty percent of what a Super Hornet cost, for a much more capable and survivable aircraft. In short, the Cutlass was such a great deal for the navy that there was a real danger that the defense establishment would abandon the idea of a 'high/low' mix in favor of a single jet straddling the middle ground. In a way, the Super Hornet program was *already* trying to be that sort of compromise. Fargo didn't worry himself about it; those decisions were well above his paygrade, and he was here, now, in command of a squadron of 'high end' Advanced Super Tomcats.

My cup runneth over, he chuckled to himself.

"She's a real doll, ain't she?" someone drawled behind him in a thick southern accent.

Fargo *knew* that voice.

He turned and found himself face to face with a stocky, muscular pilot with a shiny widow's peak and thinning shock of red hair on top. He was clad in an olive green flight suit, and his brown leather nametag was embossed with a pair of naval aviator wings, below which was his callsign in big bold letters: SWAMPY. Below that, in smaller print, it read: XO, VFA-14 Huntsmen. Like Fargo, he wore silver oak leaves stitched on the shoulders of his flight suit.

Fargo's tone was almost accusatory. "Were you flying a Harrier during the Battle of Hormuz, callsign Bulldog 412?" he asked.

Swampy's face broke into a grin as he read Fargo's nametag. "Guilty as charged!" he replied. "Are you Thorsen? I've been looking all over this damn Boat for you! All you squids look the same!"

"Well, I'll be a son of a bitch!" Fargo exclaimed.

"Maybe so, but we'll talk about your breeding later," Swampy joked without missing a beat. "Sean Garret," he added by way of formal introduction. "Don't let anyone fool you: I *am* a Marine. I'm just cross decking over to y'all for this deployment."

"Jeez, it's great to finally get the chance to meet you," Fargo told him, shaking his hand enthusiastically. "I was planning on tracking you down, but then I got caught up in stuff and things and never had the chance. I was stoked to hear you made it, and even more stoked to learn that you bagged that last bandit that shot me. Three in one day—although you *did* sort of snake one of mine," he added with a wry smile.

"Bastard had it coming," Swampy replied seriously. "Bad luck that we both wasted missiles on that first gomer—you sure could have used yours a few minutes later."

"Ain't that the truth. So how is it that you're out here with us?"

"The Corps is going to be taking the F-25, both the single and two-seat variants. I'm here on sort of a 'head start' program, getting a look at them in advance. Of course, any swingin' dick could have done that. Between you and me, I think the commandant wants a 21st Century Marine ace on the books, now that the squids have a couple."

Fargo chuckled; it wasn't the most radical notion he'd ever heard, and neither one of them brought up the fact that Danforth and Mullen were *dead*. "You're a Harrier guy, though. What about the AV-36?"

"It's a few years away yet, and nobody thinks Harriers are going to score any more kills in this war. Say, is it true that they stole our radar for your new Tomcats?"

Fargo grinned. "I'm not sure who had it *first*—the Supercats were in prototype long before the first Cutlass rolled off the line. The thought did occur to me though, that two different aircraft types with the same radar could be used to play hell with the enemy, under the right circumstances."

Swampy nodded. "I tried having that conversation with CAG, but he wasn't hearing me. Guy seems more interested in paperwork and kissing the admiral's ass than talking turkey, you ask me."

"Hmm," Fargo grunted noncommittally. It wasn't good form to badmouth your seniors like that, but people sometimes did it. Swampy was a Marine, and he was currently a superstar in the Corps. Fargo doubted he much cared what CAG thought about him. Fargo was still grateful for CAG bailing him out of that tight spot over the AIM-152 missile certification. "Maybe we can get together between ready rooms, see what some of our strike planners can cook up," Fargo suggested.

"I'll mention it to my skipper. What do you think about these Russian and Chinese mercenaries the Iranians have flying for them?"

"I think we're going to smoke 'em, with extreme prejudice," Fargo said flatly. "I'm looking forward to the admiral's briefing in a few days. The gouge around the ready rooms is that we've got something big planned."

"I've heard the same," Swampy said. The two men shook hands again. "I'm glad we'll be out there together," he confided, mirroring Fargo's own thoughts. "I've wanted back into this thing since the moment the first round ended."

Fargo's eyes were hard, now. "We've all got scores to settle."

"Soon enough, man. Soon enough. Those bastards are going to reap the whirlwind."

XIV

Iran threatens the use of nuclear weapons in the Gulf of Oman! America declares a 'reciprocal response' policy, stating 'the war will continue until Iran surrenders.'

-Washington Post

Calling the Iranian Bluff—Israel debunks claims of Iran's nuclear capability, claiming the April test was an elaborate deception.

-Reuters

Is regime change coming in Iran? Protests enter their third straight month, and are growing in intensity despite crackdowns.

-L.A. Times

North Korean regime denies culpability over Iran's nuclear test. Kim Jong Un declares that North Korean weapons are under 'airtight control.'

-Miami Herald

Ukrainian President Yanukovych backs out of EU deal! Protests erupt in Kiev, and Russia pledges future financial assistance.

-N.Y. Times.

Political unrest in Crimea. Ukrainian nationalists claim Russia is moving forces into the region.

-International Herald Tribune

NOV 2013
USS *Hornet,* in the Arabian Sea

"Attention on deck!"

"Seats," Fargo ordered, striding briskly to the head of the Black Tigers ready room. He looked out over the sea of faces, feeling a strange sense of *déjà vu.* Skipper Jefferson had introduced a briefing similar to this one just before the Battle of Hormuz. All the aviators wore desert khaki flight suits with black jerseys underneath, sporting the unusual, square-shaped Black Tigers squadron patches and matching nametags. They looked back at him, trying to look casual, exuding the cool, carefree aura of a room full of fighter pilots. But Fargo could see the intensity in their eyes, and sense the coiled tension underneath their casual demeanor. In the front row, the XO sat attentively in his seat, occasionally looking back like a sheriff to make sure there were no hijinks going on behind him, but everyone was paying serious attention. The department heads filled out the front row; he spotted Jewels and Snoopy seated next to each other, trading some last-second notes the way he and Stinky used to. Seeing the familiar interaction between his operations and maintenance officers gave him an oddly comforting sense of continuity—that all was as it should be.

"Ladies and gents," Fargo began, "we have arrived. *Coral Sea* is headed home, and *Yorktown* will remain on station with us until they are relieved by *Oriskany* next month. Today is our last no-fly day, and our first sixty day line period begins tomorrow morning, Vietnam style. We are officially chopped to Task Force Fifty, comprised of the *Hornet* and *Yorktown* carrier battle groups. Vice Admiral Patrick, commanding the Fifth Fleet, is flying his flag in the command ship USS *Mount Whitney*, exercising overall tactical command. Our battle group is designated Task Force Fifty point Two, still under the command of Rear Admiral Yellend. That's our chain of command in a nutshell. Now, in the spirit of passing down commander's intent, our AIO is going to brief you on Operation Desert Cactus. Lieutenant Landry," he said without further ado, turning over the floor.

Alicia Landry didn't tone down her appearance by wearing wash khakis or a purloined flight suit. She was dressed in service dress blues *sans* jacket: a dark skirt with regulation pumps, with a form-fitting white blouse and soft shoulder boards. She wore expertly applied cosmetics, and her hair was carefully coifed in an attractive but regulation hairstyle. She looked like a Maxim cover model in uniform, and she knew it. Nobody wolf-whistled or hooted when she took the podium—that had happened exactly *once* back in China Lake, and the XO had come down on the ready room like a ton of bricks afterward. Landry was deliberately provocative, but always very cautious about it on duty, careful not to cross any lines on *her* part. But she clearly prided herself on being the Devil's own temptation, and she was almost always a subtle, teasing flirt. Jewels and Bagels *hated* her, although they were good at concealing their contempt. Fargo figured she'd make a great talking head on TNN or one of the other networks someday when she finally got tired of ionizing male hormones at sea. In the meantime, he was careful never to be in a space alone with her. Whenever there was official business to conduct, he kept Chief Reddy close at hand, and no closed hatches. She hadn't given him a reason to fire her, but her unabashed narcissism was eventually going to work like a slow poison aboard ship. He fervently hoped no scandals or ill-fated love triangles would break out while he commanded the Tigers.

Landry strolled boldly to the front of the ready room, her eyes flashing as she gave them a winning smile. She began her briefing, which Fargo and Buzz had already gotten during meetings with the flag and air wing staff; this version was meant for the squadron aviators. The concept of 'commander's intent' was that they all know and understand the overall objectives of the campaign going forward. That way, if something unexpected happened during a mission, circumstances changed, or senior leadership was killed or cut off from communications, air crews could make informed decisions on scene to advance the overall objectives of the campaign. It was a concept the Marine Corps used with great success, from the flag level all the way down to the corporals leading fire teams.

The first topic on the list was nuclear weapons. Everyone had heard the reports that Iran was threatening to use them, but their intelligence officer nipped that firmly in the bud. The overwhelming assessment of the intelligence agencies was that Iran was *not* a nuclear power, and thanks to the actions taken during the first six months of the war, it never would be. The matter of the first weapon was the subject of heated international debate. Diplomatic fingers were pointed equally at about four different nations, but so far they all maintained plausible deniability. If every western expert was proven wrong and Iran used a nuclear weapon, the United States had made it clear that the gloves would really come off at that point, and nuclear retaliation wouldn't just be an *option*, but a certainty. Iran had stopped with the threats about two weeks before, while *Hornet* was steaming across the Pacific and Indian Oceans.

Landry continued with a summary of what was accomplished so far. *Coral Sea*, and then later *Yorktown* as well, had conducted months of blockading operations, in concert with a campaign to scour the southeastern portion of Iran clean of air defenses and shore-based missile batteries. If progress had seemed sluggish, there was a reason for it: U.S. and British submarine forces were quietly conducting mine detection operations in the Gulf of Oman, all the way up to the Strait of Hormuz itself.

These operations included the extensive use of undersea drones, and naval special warfare. Despite Iranian claims, the conclusion was that there were no minefields present, at least on the eastern side of the strait. Iran wanted to *control* shipping through the strait, not *stop* it completely, despite their threats. Undersea minefields could be ridiculously hard to get rid of, and usually the mere threat of them was sufficient for area denial. It was a strategy that had worked for Iran—until now. The threat and uncertainty over Iranian claims had bought them six months, but their time was finally up.

The way was finally open for Operation Desert Cactus. At present, southeastern Iran was wide open on a rough line from Seerik to Chabahar, scoured clean of threats by continuous air operations conducted from the Arabian Sea. Apart from the loss of one frigate in the disastrous engagement with an Iranian Q-ship, no U.S. surface combatants had been hit since the loss of the *Boxer* strike group. Although Oman and Iran had refrained from coming to blows themselves, Oman had opened almost all their airspace to U.S. operations. Two amphibious expeditionary strike groups were entering the Arabian Sea with most of a Marine division embarked—the Marines had spent the past few months preparing and rehearsing for the upcoming operation. TF 50 was ready to move north into the Gulf of Oman, and the 'Cactus Air Force' aboard *Hornet* would begin conducting the deep interdiction strikes it was capable of, destroying Iranian shore terminals and port facilities. In the end, it wouldn't matter whose flag a tanker operated under if there was no working terminal for it to take on a load of crude. If Iran didn't capitulate soon, there was a real danger that their nation and economy would be severely crippled for *decades,* not just the near-future.

The endgame of the American strategy hadn't changed: the islands of Abu Musa, the Tunbs, Sirri, and Farur would be taken, occupied, and turned into regional U.S. bases. Iran would not be permitted a military presence in the Persian Gulf going forward, period. It was a tall order, but with the scouring of their eastern flank in the Gulf of Oman and the verification that the way was clear of minefields, things were going to start happening at an accelerated pace.

Fargo sat and listened grimly to the AIO's brief, aware of the occasional looks from his people cast his way. They knew on an academic level what he'd been through, and what he'd lost. They'd seen him work as hard as anyone to stand this squadron up and get back out here—a nearly impossible task under normal circumstances, but wartime priorities took on a life of their own. When combat operations commenced tomorrow, they knew their CO would be leading from the front.

***

USS *Hornet,* the Gulf of Oman

The honor of leading *Hornet's* first alpha strike fell to CAG Sutter, flying one of the new F-25's. The Cutlasses were followed by the Advanced Super Prowlers and their tanker variants, the shorter-ranged Super Hornets, and finally the Supercats. Blessed with the longest payload/range (by far) of all the aircraft in the strike, the Black Tigers launched last, and would not need to take fuel from airborne tankers before pushing for the target area.

A four-ship division of Black Tigers would participate in this event, led by Fargo in Tiger 107. Fargo's RIO was LT Mairead 'Freckles' Coogan, a former Super Hornet WSO with half a combat deployment in Afghanistan under her belt. She was a thin redhead with the 'Celtic curse' that caused her callsign to write itself. She had a quiet, determined demeanor, and the hardest work ethic Fargo had ever seen in a junior officer.

Coogan was a Naval Academy alum with a long naval pedigree: her older brother was the XO of an attack submarine, two of her uncles were retired naval aviators, and her father was the rear admiral commanding the *Yorktown* battle group, which would be headed home in the next several weeks. *All* of them were Academy alumni, so Freckles bled Navy blue and gold. She had more than pulled her weight as Snoopy's assistant operations officer and chief schedule writer, and Fargo figured her propensity for maximum effort was her way of proving she was *earning* it, and wasn't just some admiral's kid. She had certainly put in the hours to master the radar and weapons systems on the Supercat; Fargo considered her the pick of the litter among the junior RIOs with no prior Tomcat experience, and claimed her for his back seat.

Freckles checked their division in with Strike and they proceeded to the rendezvous point northwest of the ship, approximately 270 NM southeast of the primary target: the port facilities on Qeshm Island, right in the Strait of Hormuz just south of Bandar Abbas. *Hornet* was currently at the mouth of the Gulf of Oman, almost on a direct line between Sur in Oman, and Chabahar near the Iran-Pakistan border. The latter had seen its airfield and port facilities destroyed by air strikes; most of the civilian population had fled north with their livelihoods wiped out. There was an Air Force tanker waiting at the rendezvous point, and when the half dozen KA-6E tankers arrived they topped off to serve as refueling 'hose multipliers' for the rest of the strike. A section of Advanced Prowlers stacked up next, followed by

CAG's two F-25 divisions with mixed SEAD / AAW loadouts, and two more divisions of Super Hornets armed for ground attack.

The entire strike except for the Supercats took tanker fuel in the same order they launched, with the shortest-ranged aircraft going last. The launch of the Black Tigers was timed for them to super cruise at low supersonic speed to the rendezvous point to arrive near push time, just as the remainder of the jets finished tanking. Then, on CAG's order, the entire strike package pushed northwest, up the center of the Gulf of Oman towards the strait.

***

Oghab 44 Tactical Air Base,
70 NM Northwest of Bandar Abbas

Arkady Kovalev was lounging in their squadron ready room, idly thumbing through a magazine he couldn't read when the alert buzzer sounded. He swore in Russian, startled by the alarm and noticing the lighting shifting to emergency red. The other pilots were surprised as well, since this had never happened before. Their prior missions had all been pre-planned, not an emergency order to scramble.

Kovalev knew he didn't have his full strength available; two of his eight jets were down for maintenance. The remaining six were armed and fueled, just a hundred yards away in their underground mountain hangar. There were eight other pilots available, so Kovalev quickly made his choice, pointing at five of them and signaling them to grab their gear and follow him to the flight line. Toma Baranov met them on the way to their planes.

"What's happening, *tovarich*?" Kovalev asked.

"An American raid, coming straight towards us up the Gulf of Oman. It looks like more than two full squadrons of aircraft. It appears to be headed either for Qeshm or Bandar Abbas."

Kovalev smiled darkly. "We'll be able to engage them almost immediately after takeoff, if they're that close. I'll explain the situation to the men, and we'll strap in and wait. Once the Americans commence their attack and things get muddled, we'll launch practically into the middle of them. We'll strike quickly, then sprint northwest towards Shiraz, under SAM cover. Their Hawkeye will spot us as soon as we break ground, if not before, and this base will be compromised. What about the *Feilong?*"

"They've been ordered to stand down, to maintain the secrecy of their base. We are in the better position to make an effective counterattack."

"Once we go, the base's SAM defenses should be activated, and all the ground personnel should be evacuated. When the Americans pinpoint our location, the counterattack will be swift."

"I concur. I'll give the orders after you scramble," Baranov added.

Kovalev looked thoughtful, and stroked his chin. "This may be our final fight here, general."

Baranov shrugged casually. "Crimea awaits us, my friend. Make your mark, and good hunting."

***

Over the Strait of Hormuz

This was the moment Fargo had spent six long months waiting for. 'Hawk' Vasquez with 'Bagels' Bagley was his Dash-3 and second section leader; their two wingmen were 'Dingo' Rawlins with 'Red' Morel, and 'Snake' Orman with 'Tex' Kemper, respectively. Each jet was configured for long-range anti-air. Their priority on this mission was to end the radar coverage the IRIAF enjoyed from its Mainstays. There was an element of deliberate deception baked into this inaugural strike: the F-25 was something of a known quantity to the world at large, but the presence of the Supercats, while technically not secret, had not been publicized at all. Their establishment at China Lake was kept out of official channels and communications, as were their deployment orders. The Cutlass, at present, could only carry AMRAAM and AIM-9X air-to-air missiles, the same as a Super Hornet. The Supercats, when classified by ESM, were likely to be mis-identified as F-25's due to their identical radars. The

Iranians and their 'Russian Volunteer Group' were in for a nasty surprise, courtesy of the Black Tigers.

Fargo and his flight stayed throttled back, keeping pace with the rest of the strike as it approached the target area. Once north of Bandar-e Jask, they began to get spiked by SAM radars. The self-protection jamming functions of the Supercats and Cutlasses immediately came into play, and this was the signal for the Advanced Prowlers to switch on their jammers and EW pods, and go to work with their HARM missiles. CAG's two divisions of F-25's followed up, launching their own standoff weapons as well. This was not considered a 'stealth' mission for them, so the combat debut of the F-25 was made with external stores as well as internal, and part of the deception with the Supercats was to let the enemy see the F-25's in the mix.

The Americans had good E-2D Advanced Hawkeye radar coverage as far as Qeshm Island, but beyond that the strikers were more dependent on their own radars to aid them. That was fine, because the Supercats and Cutlasses were designed to be network sensor nodes in and of themselves—their radars were so advanced that each jet could serve as its own mini-AWACS when necessary. The Black Tigers broke out their quarry early: an Iranian A-50 some 120 NM northwest of Bandar Abbas, directly between their position and Shiraz. According to the ESM and radar picture the enemy AWACS plane was being screened by two divisions of Iran's new JF-17 Thunders, flying BARCAP. Under normal circumstances the A-50 would be untouchable, sitting well beyond missile range with screening fighters and SAM protection between themselves and the enemy. Today, the Black Tiger Tomcats were armed with six AIM-152 missiles apiece, and a pair of heat-seekers for close-in work. Both the A-50 and their screening fighters were within attack range of their prototype missiles before Fargo's flight even passed over Qeshm Island.

Fargo's gut was tight with excitement and anticipation, adrenalin surging though him as he ordered them into a line abreast, climbing to Angels 30 and accelerating to an easy Mach 1.2 super cruise. All nine Iranian targets were held on their own radars; Freckles called 'Judy' when they committed, and the Tigers were free to hunt. A single Advanced Prowler peeled off and accompanied them from well behind, unable to keep up with the Tomcats as Fargo took them to just under Mach 2 in afterburner for their missile shots. They were passing feet dry over Iran now, pressing into Indian country northwest of Bandar Abaas. The Advanced Prowler provided heavy jamming, HARM, and EW support, suppressing the SAM sites ahead of them, and denying the Russian AWACS controllers a clear radar picture. The RIOs worked on their own defensive tricks, streaming fiber-optic decoys and using the EW suppression functions of their AESA radars in concert with their target tracking. Targets were sorted electronically without much intervention from human RIOs: this was the newest version of the Navy's net-centric warfare and integrated fire control concepts being brought to bear. Hundreds of miles behind them, everyone in their chain of command all way up to COMFIFTHFLT in *Mount Whitney* watched the air battle unfold in real time, on a sensor-fused tactical data display.

When the shoot cues appeared in the helmet-mounted displays of the pilots, Fargo gave the order, and the Great Iranian Turkey Shoot was underway. Each Tomcat salvoed four missiles, and a few minutes later all hell broke loose in the Iranian formation as their brand new fighters started going down, hit by opponents still more than eighty miles away, beyond the range they could see or return fire though the jamming.

Too late, the Russian Volunteer Group Mainstay operators finally understood they were in mortal danger for the first time in the air. They did as they were trained: they shut down their radar, fired countermeasures, and dove for the deck as they turned to go 'zero-doppler' on the missiles. It didn't matter; the AIM-152s homed in at only slightly more than half of their maximum rated range, and four of them were targeted on the AWACS plane just to make sure. Three of the four missiles hit the lumbering target, and the A-50 plunged earthward as flaming wreckage. Seven of the eight defending JF-17's went down as well, with one survivor running for his life to the northwest, low and supersonic. Fargo was tempted to chase him down, but there were a lot of SAM sites out there ahead of them, and he still had a responsibility to cover the strike behind them. Their primary mission objective accomplished, he turned the division back to the southeast, where the main strike on Qeshm was fully underway. As ground based Iranian radars started emitting to compensate for the loss of their Mainstay coverage, they became targets of opportunity for the SEAD strikers as well.

***

Oghab 44 Tactical Air Base

Kovalev glanced thoughtfully to his port side as he taxied onto the east-west runway. The ridgeline formed by the mountains towered slightly more than a thousand feet over them just to the south, and his instruments were clear of ESM from the American AWACS plane he knew was out there somewhere over the Gulf of Oman. Depending on where that aircraft was, and how high, it might or might not see them immediately upon takeoff. Of course, it would undoubtedly pick them up as soon as they climbed high enough to clear the terrain, so any reprieve from detection would be strictly temporary. Still, in the arena of aerial combat, seconds of time were precious jewels, not to be taken lightly or squandered.

Kovalev exchanged hand signals with his pilots rather than using the radios. Again, remaining undetected for as long as possible was the key here. He advanced his throttles into afterburner, relishing the press of acceleration as his Fulcrum roared down the runway and into the air. His wingman took off in formation with him, and the other two sections were right behind them.

Within moments the six Red Talons climbed to clear the terrain, but just barely. Kovalev kept his flight hugging the ground, hoping to stay off enemy radars for as long as possible. They took off with their own radars in standby, hoping for information from the Mainstay orbiting about a hundred miles northwest of them. They knew from hard experience that there would be heavy jamming; American EW capabilities were far and away the biggest overall obstacle they had faced so far during their combat missions. The number of kills they achieved was frustratingly low for the number of missiles they'd fired in the past several months. Today promised to be far more interesting: they were charging into an ongoing attack where the attention of their adversaries would be focused *somewhere else* to begin with, at much closer ranges than any they had seen in months.

Kovalev sensed something was wrong by the time they'd covered about a third of the distance to Qeshm in full afterburner, running their centerline fuel tanks dry. They were supersonic, closing the American force rapidly, but blind to what was ahead. Repeated radio calls to the Mainstay went unanswered, and they had nothing equivalent to the American datalink capability. Then his threat warning receiver chirped, and he saw ESM lines to the northwest, coming from radars his system didn't recognize. *Those must be their new F-25's,* Kovalev thought, desperate to know how far away they were. The only way to find out was to turn right and bring their radars up, but that was a slow turn at Mach 1.4, and they were almost in position to bounce the Americans ahead of him. Kovalev understood he was now in a bad tactical position with bandits on his right flank, especially with his own AWACS support mysteriously absent, but he gritted his teeth and pressed home his attack. Once they were merged, the Americans would have a much harder time targeting and engaging his half dozen jets. On the other hand, the preponderance of American planes would mean a target rich environment for his own flight.

He couldn't afford to wait any longer; the Americans might *already* be targeting them. He broke radio silence and gave the order, and the Red Talons brought up their radar systems. They immediately had jamming to contend with, but they were *close.* Their radars would soon burn through and track nearby targets. He programmed his first shot to home-on-jam, and fired.

***

Tiger 107

The E-2D Hawkeye's callsign was *Banger*. "99 Strike, Banger. Popup gorilla group, bullseye 316 for 42, low, hot, Bandit. Hunters snap 310 for an immediate commit. Tigers snap 070 for an immediate commit. All units call radar contact." Bullseye was Bandar Abbas, just north of the target, giving everyone an easy mental reference to work from. Fargo glanced at the datalink to get a clear picture of what was happening, when several things happened at once.

"Racket, 060," Freckles called. "Bandits are MiG-29s. Ground spike!" she added an instant later. Several SAM radars from hidden sites surrounding *Oghab*-44 suddenly switched on and illuminated them, and the MAWS signaled missile launches at their 7-9'oclock.

"Merlin-Four is ground spiked and engaged defensive!" their Prowler escort called a moment later.

Fuck! SAM trap! Fargo thought. He eased forward on the stick, unloading the jet to zero-G and plugging burner. They were already in Mach super cruise; now the Supercat accelerated like a bullet from a rifle as Freckles called them defensive and punched the external fuel tanks off, further reducing their drag. The other jets in his division made identical calls, except for Dingo. He pressed forward on the offensive and engaged the tail-end Charlie of the enemy MiG formation, firing his last two AIM-152s. The missiles covered the short distance between the planes at better than Mach 3 and blotted one of the MiGs out of sky. At almost the same time, someone in their escorting Super Prowler cried out that they were hit, and nothing more was heard from them.

In the meantime, Fargo and Freckles were 'doing the Linda Blair', straining their necks to look behind them as the smoke trail on a large surface-to-air missile tracked towards them. Countermeasures hadn't worked, and speed was their only salvation now. Fargo glanced ahead, spotting a small ravine that might do the trick. He gripped the stick and flew for his life, ducking the Supercat behind solid terrain at just about the last moment it would have mattered. Freckles was watching their six, and gasped in fear as the missile stooped on them at high Mach in its final stage of pursuit, only to impact the intervening ridgeline. A large explosion behind them shattered rock, sending it sky-high like the eruption of a small volcano. Fargo was concentrating on keeping them out of the dirt; he only knew they'd made it because they were still breathing, and he thanked God for the Supercat—in anything slower they'd be dead.

Then there was no more time to think: only shocked surprise as he caught a glimpse of gray and black camouflage accentuated by blood-colored wingtips. The planform of a MiG-29 flashed almost right over their heads in its own hard right break; if Fargo had pulled out of the small ravine just a little harder, they'd have collided. He couldn't know it, but this was the wingman of the MiG that Dingo had just shot down, turning to engage Dingo. "Jee-suz *Christ! Where'd he come from?!*" Freckles shouted from the back.

Fargo pulled max-G straight into the vertical to bleed airspeed and yanked the throttles to idle. He tilted his head back and padlocked the MiG, old habits and years of training paying off in the heat of the moment; he'd never taken his eyes off it from the first moment it flashed overhead. The MiG was still in its turn; Fargo guessed it hadn't seen them, buried low in the background of the terrain. "Freckles, get a tally on Dingo. He's out there," he grunted under the G-load. He brought them over-the-top as soon as they were subsonic, using the thrust vectoring to flip the jet end-for-end, bringing his nose instantly onto the rapidly receding MiG. Fargo lit the afterburners again, and the Supercat accelerated back through six hundred knots in less than ten seconds—night and day from what he'd have gotten out of a Super Hornet. He saw the closure rate go from negative to positive in record time, indicating that they were now catching the MiG. The brief vertical reversal this close to the ground was like the craziest roller-coaster ride either of them could have imagined. Freckles kept her head in the game—she had the radar in vertical acquisition, locking the MiG as soon as the Tomcat came over the top and Fargo rolled to line up the enemy with his lift vector. At the same moment, he saw a smoke trail as a missile came off the outer rail of the MiG: an off-boresight shot that hooked sharply left and up.

"Dingo, smoke in the air! Break!" he called, even though he couldn't see his wingman. He had a rough idea where he was, though, with the Iranian's missile serving as a guide. He knew he had a clean line of fire ahead of him, and squeezed the trigger. "Fox-3!" he called. The AIM-152 spat from underneath the 'tunnel' between the engines and ignited, going active almost immediately. The MiG's pilot didn't have time to react before the missile closed and sheared off his port wing. The Fulcrum rolled off violently and plowed into the ground, exploding brilliantly.

"Splash!" Freckles called over the radio in a steely voice.

Fargo throttled them out of burner and pulled up again, banking slightly right this time and craning his head skyward. He'd caught an explosion in his peripheral vision, and heaved a sigh of relief when he saw Dingo and Red were still with him. Even better, he wasn't being ground spiked by a SAM radar any longer. "Dingo, I've got tally on you. I'm at your four o'clock low and climbing. You guys alright?"

"We're right," Dingo called in his Aussie accent—his mother was Australian, and he'd spent most of his childhood Down Under, even though he was an American. "The missile hit the bloody fiber optic!" he added a moment later. "That was too bloomin' close!"

"Tigers, check in!" Fargo called.

"Dash-3 is clean," Hawk called. "I'm two miles north of you, Fargo."

"Dash-4, defending SAMs," Snake called, sounding busy.

"Tigers, drag it south away from that SAM trap and rejoin," he called. He kept a sharp visual lookout, knowing there were more MiGs somewhere nearby, and told Freckles to do the same. He called the Hawkeye for bogey dope.

Banger was no help. "Tiger One, Banger, merged plot. You appear to be on the northwest end of the scrum, green vector 210 to separate."

"Tiger copies. Splash two Fulcrums on this end; we're trying to shake off SAMs now. Request SEAD support."

"Tiger, Banger, no SEAD support available. Vector 210 to disengage or 130 to re-commit."

"Dash-4 is clean," Snake finally called, sounding thoroughly winded. Fargo listened to Hawk try to talk him into visual contact so he could form up on his section leader. Dingo had fired two missiles over their initial salvo, and he'd fired one. They were still well-armed, and Hawk's section still had two AIM-152s and two heaters apiece. The only limiting factor now was fuel, but they were still *well* above bingo even with just their remaining internal fuel.

Fargo grinned under his mask; the Supercat was a *beast,* and the Black Tigers were still in the fight. "Banger, Tigers are vectoring 130, ready for another commit."

***

Red Talon One

Kovalev was rewarded with a significant reduction in jamming when his first missile struck the American jamming plane. The remaining Prowlers were turning southeast and running now that there was a proverbial fox in the henhouse. His own radar picture firmed up, and he saw a myriad of targets over Qeshm, finishing up their attack runs and beginning to move southeast, back over the eastern strait.

His Dash-6 called out in a brief panic that he was spiked, and then Dash-5 reported that he was turning west to engage American fighters at his three o'clock. Kovalev faced a moment's indecision, but the decision was taken away from him as his own threat warning receiver suddenly showed new ESM lines at his nine and ten o'clock: more of the new American radar sets, nose on to his flight and bearing down. His squadron was pincered, and now he was seeing the downside of launching straight into the middle of an enemy raid. He realized it might have been better to hook to the east and hit them from one side, making a high-speed attack and then extending northwest into the protection of friendly SAM envelopes. Hindsight would do little for him now, however. He barked orders into the radio, and his division executed a hard tactical turn to the east, dropping their external fuel tanks and going head-to-head with the new threat.

The two divisions of navy F-25s were tasked primarily with SEAD support, assisting the Prowlers, but were assigned as the secondary anti-air linebackers behind the Black Tigers. They were just finishing servicing SAM sites slightly east of Bandar Abbas, near its airfield, when the Hawkeye called the Bandit group inbound. By the time they responded as a group, the supersonic Fulcrums were almost due west of their position, rocketing south towards the Super Hornets bombing Qeshm Island.

Each F-25 carried two AMRAAMs and two AIM-9X missiles in their internal bays; their external hardpoints had been loaded with HARMs and Mavericks, all of which were expended. Swampy Garret led the second division of Cutlasses, with CAG leading the first. CAG and his planes were the first to engage, firing simultaneously with the Red Talons. Smoke trails filled the air as missiles went in both directions, and fighters on both sides immediately went defensive against the opposing shots. One Cutlass was struck; it retreated south out of the battle area, trailing smoke, and losing altitude. The pilot ejected over the southern part of the strait, coming down in Oman's territorial waters to be rescued later. Two Red Talons were splashed and a third damaged; it was trying to limp north when CAG Sutter rolled in behind it and finished the job with a Sidewinder.

'Swampy' Garret and his division entered the engagement unopposed, with the fight almost over. One Red Talon remained: the lead aircraft. It had survived the initial exchange of missile fire, and was aggressively coming around to engage Hunter Two, CAG's wingman. The latter was doing his job, covering CAG's six, and didn't see the danger. Swampy called for him to break; the Cutlass did so immediately as Kovalev fired a heat-seeker. The missile came of the rail and arced left as the evasive Cutlass came out of afterburner and pulled straight into the sun, spitting chaff and flares behind it. The engine exhausts on the stealthy planes were specifically designed to reduce their IR signature; Kovalev's missile was decoyed into a flare, where it detonated harmlessly.

Kovalev didn't give up. He rolled into a hot pursuit, lighting his own afterburners and pitching up after the Cutlass. He was waiting for it to clear the sun either by turning or diving, and then he'd have it. He squinted into the sun, holding his gloved hand in front of his visor, and waiting for the shadow of the enemy jet to appear on either side, telling him which way to go. He was in the throes of target fixation, a dead man looking for one final victory before the numerous enemies behind him finished him off.

His plane suddenly lurched and departed controlled flight as Swampy's AMRAAM blew out his twin motors and shredded his tail. The Fulcrum immediately stalled out, then backslid through its own fireball as it tumbled. A stunned Kovalev reached down and pulled the ejection handle, right over the top of Bandar Abbas.

***

Tiger 107

"Looks like the Huntsmen cleaned them up," Fargo remarked when Banger called a clean air picture. The strike was over now, and the nearby SAM sites had all been neutralized. He glanced out to starboard and saw his second section about two miles abeam, nicely boxed in his helmet-mounted display. Dingo was formed up on his left side now, about five hundred yards abeam.

CAG's division was at the trailing edge of the strike as it moved south towards the 'get well' point, when Fargo saw them make a one-eighty and turn back towards Qeshm and his own flight. "Tigers, this is CAG," Sutter called. "Did anyone see chutes from that downed Prowler?"

"I saw at least two, CAG," Dingo replied. "We've been monitoring Guard and the rescue frequency, but nothing yet."

"Fargo, do you have enough juice to make a pass over the area?"

"Yes sir, but it's thick with SAMs over there. Any SAR effort is going to need some major SEAD support."

"Disregard, then. We'll get a coordinated rescue op going soonest," he said, sounding discouraged. "What got them? A SAM, or one of those MiGs?"

"Unknown, sir," Fargo replied. He suspected that that their link data was probably good enough to sort it, when the mission was deconstructed. In the end, the matter was a little academic—they had aircrew on the ground somewhere northwest of Bandar Abbas. It was likely that the Iranians knew, and were searching for them. It was possible that the enemy had already found them. The mission was a success, but they hadn't gotten away clean.

Fargo was glad he hadn't suffered any losses. Once they were southeast of the combat area and outside any threat envelopes, they closed formation and headed home at an easy Mach 1.4 super cruise now that they had jettisoned their external tanks and fired at least half their missiles. They rapidly overtook the returning strike package, and Fargo felt another surge of almost smug vindication as they bypassed the waiting tankers and proceeded directly to the marshal stack. The jets hit bingo fuel just before they arrived, but by that time they were already home. The Black Tigers would normally have been last to recover, but in this case it was simply expedient to bring them aboard while the rest of the strike took more tanker fuel for recovery and eventually returned overhead at subsonic speed.

Fargo was excited as he led the formation into the break at 400 knots, Blue Angel tight and wings swept fully back. All his pilots were coming home, nobody had any damage (except for a couple missing towed decoys), and the air battle had been a clean sweep with fifteen enemy jets downed in total, including one of the Iranian Mainstays. Eleven of those fifteen were Black Tiger kills: an eleven-zero kill ratio in the Supercat's combat debut.

The four Advanced Super Tomcats looked mighty good as they passed over Hornet and entered the break. Fargo was so excited that he boltered on his first pass, then forced himself to calm down and caught a 4-wire the second time around. A couple days later they would learn that they had downed the last of the *Krasnyye Kogti*, the Red Talons, and that CDR Mike Thorsen was the navy's newest ace, with five kills to his credit: link data showed that he and Freckles had gotten two JF-17s at long range, and then the Red Talon MiG they'd shot off Dingo's back. Three kills in one engagement, matching what Deedee and Swampy had done on different days, although made much easier due to circumstance and the advanced prototype he was flying.

When they were back aboard, Fargo noticed *Hornet*'s deck was already partially spotted to launch a second strike. As soon as the first strike was recovered, the second strike was launched. This one was aimed at the port facilities and airfield at Bandar Abbas.

***

Bandar Abbas

Fortunately, the wreckage of Kovalev's plane didn't hit a populated area of the city; it tumbled down and struck an open area of scrub just north of Bandar Abbas's Suru Beach Park. It exploded and caused a major fire, but there were no civilian casualties or even property damage as a result. Kovalev came down farther north than his plane. Ironically, he landed about one hundred meters away from the IRGC Navy Specialized Hospital, on the south side of Pasdaran Blvd. He was only about a mile and a half away from the north end of the Shahid Bahonar port facility on the western edge of the city. Unharmed except for bruises and contusions, the Russian mercenary gathered up his chute and stumped over to the hospital under the eyes of dozens of stunned onlookers. Minutes before, they had watched the aerial battle unfold right over their heads. When Kovalev looked up, he could see the drifting spaghetti-string furball of smoke trails and contrails left by the dogfight. The distant crackling thunder of explosions had ended for now, and the sky was quiet; the roar of jet engines had faded, and there were no more sonic booms to rattle the buildings and break windows on the ground.

Once he reached the hospital, he politely but firmly declined insistent attempts to treat non-existent injuries while he commandeered a phone and tried to call *Oghab*-44 and Toma Baranov. He was unable to get through; doubtless the base was currently being evacuated. He placed a second call to General Abdi's office, leaving a message, and then finally succumbed to the insistent attention of the hospital staff. In truth, he didn't have anything better to do until the situation sorted itself out. There was no base to go back to, and all that remained of his unit were two grounded jets, a few disgruntled pilots, and the maintenance crews, all of whom were presumably on the road somewhere between *Oghab*-44 and the town of Rostaq. So, he took the offered hospital bed and tightly rationed food, and tried to ignore the thick pall of smoke he could see from his window, hanging over Qeshm Island to the south.

***

Kovalev still hadn't heard from anyone in an official capacity by late afternoon. Feeling stiff and sore now from his ejection, he pulled his flight suit and boots back on, ignoring the protests of the nurses, and seated himself in the hospital waiting area where there was a small, wall-mounted television. He was alone in the room; he turned on the TV and found a live news report on Qeshm, being broadcast by an Al Jazeera crew from the docks at Shahid Bahonar. To get the best view of the distant fires and smoke raging on Qeshm Island, the crew had parked their van in a small parking lot along the eastern breakwater of the port. He was startled to see that it was none other than Tara Shirazi making the report, and his heart ached at the sight of her, even on the grainy black-and-white screen in front of him. He hadn't spoken or heard from her since she walked out of his hotel room right here in Bandar Abbas, and now here she was, less than two miles away!

Kovalev didn't waste any time. He asked the staff if someone could drive him over to the port, where Tara's crew was working. It took a few minutes and an I.O.U. on a bribe, and then one man agreed to drive him over in the rat-trap van that served as the hospital ambulance. They were just halfway there when the driver cursed and began playing with the tuning knob on the van's old AM/FM radio; the station he'd been listening to abruptly cut out, replaced with screeching static. The driver cursed in Farsi, scowling as he smashed at the old radio with the palm of his hand. In the passenger seat, Kovalev's face screwed up in sudden worry. *RF Jamming!*

"Don't worry radio!" he said quickly in his best broken-Farsi. "No radio! Hurry now! Hurry!" he repeated, with accentuated arm gestures. The driver was confused by his urgency, but understood it. He abandoned his attempts to get the radio working and stepped on the gas. A few minutes later the air raid sirens went off, and there was a large explosion and the accompanying cloud of black smoke mushrooming up from the port facility. Overhead, the sounds of jet airplanes could be heard again.

"Americans!" the driver gasped; fear and rage written all over his features. "Americans come!"

"*Da!*" Kovalev shouted. "Now hurry! Hurry to docks!" he ordered. The driver balked, slowing the van to a halt. As if to commend his caution, another explosion not far away rocked the van on its bald tires.

"We go back!" the driver yelled. "Hospital needs us! We go back!" he said, twisting the wheel to turn the van around. Kovalev didn't argue; he bailed out instead, wincing in pain as he ran as fast as he could towards where he knew Tara was. He was still a good three quarters of a mile away from the beach-end of the breakwater, and she was another quarter mile or so beyond that, well out over the water.

The bombs and missiles started coming down like hail, and Kovalev was thrown to the ground. He covered his head and ears with his arms as explosions wracked the entire port, aiming more at destroying infrastructure than sinking ships—those could certainly be hit later, if they survived at all. Several of the blasts were close enough to lift him bodily into the air, tossing him several yards like a ragdoll and threatening to turn his lungs inside out. He never understood how or why he was spared from being shredded by flying shrapnel, but his wounds from the bombing were limited to a few nicks and cuts, and being battered by the bomb-blasts themselves. As sore and beaten up as he already was, every bomb going off felt like he was being hit by a wooden club.

One image dominated his brain as he helplessly endured the barrage: Tara Shirazi's news van, with its large satellite dish sitting on top. He could only imagine what that would look like to an American pilot staring at a grainy FLIR image on a cockpit screen, as that pilot concentrated on staying alive in a hunk of metal moving at just under the speed of sound.

The bomb detonations stopped after a small eternity. Kovalev was up again and running as fast as he could. When he reached the near end of the breakwater he saw that the entire port was on fire; the Americans had smashed every pier and jetty, and bombed every warehouse. Ships and boats were on fire at their moorings, with some of them heeled over and capsized while others rested on the muddy bottom with their weather decks underwater. There was smoke and fire ahead of him, out along the breakwater. It took a while for the heat and flames to subside enough for him to reach her.

It was far too late when he did. It had been too late from the very start.

The breakwater itself was shattered from a bomb hit. The news van was gone—vaporized—and the outbuildings were flattened from the blast overpressure. The jetty that extended west inside the breakwater was gone—destroyed. There were bodies scattered by the bomb blast, burnt and torn beyond recognition. Some bobbed in the Gulf waters to either side of the breakwater, broken shapes dimly lit by the flames. Nobody here survived.

Kovalev stumbled from body to body, tears streaking down his dirt and soot-caked face as he searched for her. Any one of them could have been her, or none of them—there was just no way to know. The only confirmation he found was the tattered shred of a familiar, multicolored scarf. Torn, scorched, and bloody, it had caught around a broken piece of I-beam jutting from a smashed building. He clenched the fabric in his hands, falling to his knees. He buried his face in it as silent, anguished sobs wracked his body.

XV

Oghab-45, Underground *Feilong* Base
85 NM Northeast of Bandar Abbas

"This is a secure line?" Weh Heng asked from hundreds of miles away in Tehran.

"It is," Cheng Ye assured him. Secure by *Chinese* standards, not Iranian standards. Since moving to this base, Cheng Ye and his ground personnel took the necessary steps to facilitate secure communications with their embassy in Tehran, and Beijing as well.

"The situation is beginning to unravel, as we knew it eventually would," Weh Heng informed him. "We did not anticipate the fervor of the uprising among the local population, especially here in the capital. General Abdi went missing yesterday after a riot; there were reports of heavy street fighting between IRGC units and Iranian civilians armed with makeshift and stolen weapons. Most of our dealings with the IRGC were directly through him, and suddenly we find ourselves isolated."

"What of the Russian group?"

"The Red Talons were defeated in combat against the Americans yesterday, and their base abandoned. In addition, the Americans located and destroyed the last of our Mainstay assets. One was destroyed in the air—we're not sure how—and the last was caught on the ground and destroyed by a Predator drone. Those aircraft were large, and difficult to hide, as you know. With most of the remainder of the IRIAF destroyed either in the air or on the ground, yours is the last substantial air unit the Iranians have left. Unfortunately for our Iranian friends, I have been notified by Beijing that the time has come for us to remove ourselves and mask our involvement to the largest degree possible."

"We can still strike the Americans before withdrawing," Cheng Ye insisted with chilling intensity. "One of their aircraft was downed north of Bandar Abbas, in the vicinity of Baranov's base.

I have reports of survivors on the ground, with IRGC forces searching for them. We know how the Americans will respond— no matter the cost or illogic of it, they will expend as many lives and resources as they need to recover their downed airmen. I still have ten flyable aircraft, and plenty of weapons. The area I speak of is not too far away, making it possible to both strike and displace the squadron to another base afterward."

"That is a matter I wished to speak with you about," Weh Heng told him. "Things are confused right now, and the Americans have decimated the Iranian leadership using signals intercepts coupled with precision strikes. Iran's command and control are heavily fragmented, and their flow of information and intelligence is completely disrupted. There is an opportunity for us to take advantage."

"Beijing wants to bring the planes back?" Cheng Ye guessed. It made sense—he'd already considered the possibility on his own.

"Yes, if we can manage it. The People's assets should not be squandered lightly, after all. We have quietly coordinated this with the Pakistani government. Your ground crews are to withdraw over land to Kerman, and arrangements have been made to fly them out of Iran from there. The *Feilong* will fly from your base to Faisal Air Base in Pakistan, and from there we will coordinate your return to China. Not only does this remove direct evidence of our involvement from Iranian soil, but it is also the most expedient way to recover your unit from the war zone. You and your pilots have amassed valuable combat experience against the Americans, and gained great face. We have learned much from this war, and it will give us the advantage in future conflicts."

"I will make the arrangements on this end, and we'll depart today," Cheng Ye informed him. He terminated the call to Weh Heng without mentioning his plan to hit the Americans a final time, knowing it would be forbidden. Clearly, his government did not want the planes or pilots risked any further in what was now a lost cause. He would hit them anyway, since permission had not specifically been *denied.* Cheng Ye's blood lust was not satisfied—it could *never* be satisfied—and delivering a final defeat to the enemy would grant him even greater face among his peers and superiors at home. It would require close coordination, but it was possible. The laser-semaphore communications system was disrupted, but usable. There were still elements active in Bandar Abbas, and they could inform him when American planes arrived to search for their downed pilots. The distance from *Oghab*-45 to Faisal precluded a combined combat action and then transit to Pakistan. They would launch, strike the Americans quickly, and then withdraw here a final time to immediately refuel and re-launch. The ground crews and their transportation would be staged and ready to depart immediately after the second launch, marking the swift abandonment of the base. So far, the Americans had not shown a proclivity for rapid counterstrikes at ground targets other than SAM sites, and their carrier groups were somewhat tied down by their launch-and-recovery deck cycles. He felt confident that he could make one final use of this base before the Americans could destroy it.

He called his operations officers and began issuing orders.

USS *Hornet*, in the Gulf of Oman

"In Vietnam, these situations had a tendency to turn into meeting engagements," CAG remarked as he studied the chart on the table in CVIC. "You start with a downed aircrew on the ground, then the enemy rushes in assets to find them, we rush in assets to save them, they exchange fire, and soon both sides are rushing even more assets to the scene trying for the upper hand. Before you realize it, a simple SAR operation turns into a major battle."

"It may not be that big an issue this time, gentlemen," LT Landry said from behind them, where she was placing red pins into a wall chart to mark known SAM sites around *Oghab*-44. The same data was also entered into their computerized combat network, but visual aids like wall charts were still popular quick-references for strike planners. "There is widespread civil unrest and rioting throughout the country. Both regular military and

IRGC ground units are being redeployed to metropolitan areas to put them down. The Predator we've had snooping around the SAR coordinates shows limited Iranian ground assets searching for our people, and no reinforcements for them within quick-reaction range."

Fargo was standing next to CAG, chewing absently on the tip of his pen as he studied the chart. "Have we heard anything more from our people?"

"We've got three survivors, in fairly rough shape," CAG informed him. "We were able to establish comms for a short time overnight, thanks to the drone. The pilot is alive with severe injuries and a compound leg fracture, and two of the ECMOs survived with cuts, bruises, and maybe one concussion between them. They are together as a group, thank God, holed up in a dry gulch about thirty-five miles north northwest of Bandar Abbas, with no water other than what they had in their survival vests. We staged a couple Seahawks up to Khasab Air Base in northern Oman overnight—the Omani government was kind enough to let us do that. That puts the helos roughly an hour away from the survivors from the time they launch. It's the SAM threat up around that base that makes this sticky, and we need to hit that base as well. How the hell did it sit for so long right under our noses, anyway?" he added irritably, not really expecting an answer.

"The Iranians did an excellent job of disguising the runway between uses, and the rest of it is under the mountain," Landry explained. "Once we had some cueing data showing us where to look, it was a lot easier to find. Plus, they haven't made any attempt to disguise the runway again after launching yesterday, and the Predator shows that the base appears to be abandoned. We have some imagery of a truck convoy running northwest, deeper into Iran. I think they expect us to hit the base. The question is what sort of trap they might have laid in anticipation of that."

"Fargo, what do you think?" CAG asked.

"I think we may have a plan that'll do the trick, you betcha," he replied, turning to Hawk Vasquez. "Hawk is one of my top strike leads," he explained, "and his team came up with this overnight. Hawk?"

Hawk opened his planning folder and began spreading the contents over the chart. "Here's what we came up with, gentlemen . . ." he began.

***

Bandar Abbas

The sound of a disturbance outside brought Arkady Kovalev to the outer gate of the now-fortified IRGC Hospital. An olive-green colored jeep had pulled up to the barbed-wire covered gate, and a small mob of locals was already converging on it, shouting angrily. Fortunately, none of them appeared to be armed. A quick burst of warning machine-gun fire from a fixed position on the hospital's roof scattered them long enough for the gate to be opened, and the jeep admitted to what now resembled an armed compound more than a hospital. There was an Iranian IRGC soldier driving the jeep; the passenger was easily recognized by a shock of unruly red hair.

"Baranov!" Kovalev said, sounding listless. "What are you doing here? I thought you'd be long gone by now!"

"I came looking for you, *tovarich*," Baranov said robustly, frowning slightly at the sight of his comrade. Kovalev looked tired and defeated, his eyes sunk into dark circles, like the eyes of a dead man walking. Baranov looked him over, and saw that Kovalev appeared unwounded except for cuts and scrapes, but he was heavily bruised. The tattered, bloody remnant of a colorful scarf was tied around his head in a makeshift keffiyeh. "I got word that one of our pilots had survived—I hoped it would be you. I'm glad to find you here, my friend."

"You may regret it later," Kovalev said, looking around as if to check on anyone else within earshot. It was more a habit than anything else; he didn't really care who heard them, now. He was trapped here, with no way out and nowhere to go if he had one. The port was a wreck, and anything that moved on water died as soon as the Americans detected it. There was no fuel for an extended overland trek, and what remained of the Iranian military was under siege by its own citizens. Concertina wire walls had been erected around the hospital and other local military outposts to keep the civil population at bay, and every so often a mob showed up anyway, to chant and throw rocks, until they were scattered by tear gas or machine gun fire. The gunners weren't shooting to kill their own countrymen so far, but that time might be coming. Kovalev asked Baranov how he had found him.

"The Iranian's laser-semaphore system," Baranov replied. "I drove as far south as the nearest relay station, they used their equipment to speak directly to the station on the roof of this hospital, and I learned you were here. I was also able to contact *Oghab-45*. Cheng Ye is abandoning the base today and withdrawing his people to Kerman. I think that if we can join up with that ground convoy, we may have a ticket out of this god-forsaken country, my friend.' His comment drew a stark look from the driver, but both Russians turned cold gazes on him, inviting him to tend to his own concerns, not the conversations of his superiors.

"Sami is alright," Baranov added when Kovalev looked like he might just pull his sidearm and shoot the Iranian driver in the head. "We have an arrangement. I supply the authority; he supplies the local language and what muscle he can. Between the two of us, we've made it this far, and I've promised to get him out of Iran, and eventually his family too."

"It's five hundred kilometers to Kerman," Kovalev pointed out. "That's about three tanks of gas for him," he said, rapping his knuckles against the hood of the jeep. "Do you think you have that much authority left?"

"There's still fuel at *Oghab-45*," Baranov said. "The base will be abandoned by the time we arrive, but we can get what we need there to press on to Kerman."

"Let's go, then," Kovalev said, swinging up into the rear seat of the jeep. He had nothing but the flight suit on his back, and a worn pistol belt with a *Zoaf* 19mm pistol that he'd cadged from the revolutionary guard soldiers fortifying the hospital.

"Are you alright, *tovarich*?" Baranov asked, eyeing Kovalev curiously. "Your mood is very dark—not what I'd expect with salvation at hand."

"I am ready to be rid of this country, Toma Andreyovich," he told the general. "The sooner the better."

"Here," Baranov said, passing back a good-sized flask. Kovalev opened it, sniffed the contents, and then drank deeply, closing his eyes in blessed solace. The vodka burned as it went down his parched throat, hitting an almost-empty stomach and going straight to his bloodstream after a long, forced abstinence. He felt a spark of fire surge through him—the resurgence of a will to live that was missing since the scene on the breakwater. He wiped his hand across his mouth, sighing in pleasure as he handed the flask back to Baranov.

"Do you hear that?" their driver asked suddenly.

"Hear what?" Baranov said. "Shut off the engine," he added a moment later. When it was quiet, there was no mistaking it: all three men heard aircraft in the sky to the south, getting closer.

"Another raid?" Kovalev wondered aloud.

"Maybe," Baranov answered. "If they pass overhead to the north, it's probably a search effort. One of their jamming planes was shot down yesterday during your battle, and the Revolutionary Guard is swarming the hills back towards our base, searching for the survivors." He looked thoughtful. "The semaphore station mentioned that *Oghab*-45 left strict instructions that they were to be notified of any Yankee aircraft sighted north of Bandar Abbas today."

Kovalev rapped the driver sharply on the arm with the back of his hand, gesturing for him to hand over his binoculars. He did so, and Kovalev scanned the sky with an expert's eye, until he caught sight of what he was looking for. "It's the Americans, alright. At least a squadron's worth of fighters, with mixed types. They are heading north," he added. "Did you say there is a semaphore station on the roof of the hospital?" he asked; he hadn't been aware of that before now.

"*Da*," Baranov replied, getting out of the jeep. "Let's go up there, and have them send a report to *Oghab*-45. Perhaps Cheng Ye and the *Feilong* can extract a little vengeance for us." Kovalev heartily agreed, and the report was sent to the first relay station within five minutes.

***

Oghab-44, Abandoned Red Talon Base, Northwest of Bandar Abbas

"I guess I can see why this SAR mission turned into a deck strike overnight," Freckles remarked from the rear cockpit. She and Fargo watched on the IRST as a stick of bombs from their wingman cut the runway at *Oghab*-44, rendering it useless for flight operations until it could be repaired. The ways things were going for Iran in the past 48-hours, nobody really thought anyone would be making the effort anytime soon. There were no signs of life down there, which suited Fargo just fine as his division went about the task of wiping the 'secret' Iranian air base off the map. The four Black Tiger jets were armed for air-to-ground, each carrying the weapons needed for their planned piece of the action. Ironically, they could have hit as far inland as *Tehran* with these payloads if the mission profile had called for it—that was the level of deep-interdiction capability the Advanced Super Tomcat brought to the fight. As it stood, they were at less than half of their striking range and had fuel and ordnance to spare.

One jet cratered the runway with a 4-bomb stick; the remaining three jets each carried a pair of two-thousand pound JDAM bunker busters. That gave them a half dozen designated impact points, and the first was right at the mouth of the underground entrance to the base. From there the impact points worked back and in a slight V-shape at hundred yard intervals, designed to collapse the interior of the base. Without an on-site inspection there would be no way to know if they achieved that goal or not, but the underground entrance was collapsed by the bomb blasts and blocked by hundreds of tons of stone rubble and debris. If there was anyone left alive inside that base, they would be trapped until they perished from a lack of air or water.

To the southeast of them, a second division of F-25's armed for SEAD was cleaning up the SAM sites in the area around the base, most of which appeared abandoned along with the base itself. A few of the sites went active early, overflown by air-launched decoys preceding the strike; the Distributed Aperture System (DAS) on the Cutlass was well-suited for identifying an active site as soon as it became a threat, and the integrated combat network would task the most appropriate asset for an immediate counterattack or site-suppression, depending on whether the SAM battery got any missiles off. The F-25 itself was hard to target even for a relatively advanced SAM system like the S-300; most of the active sites were destroyed before the strike was threatened, and the F-25's killed the rest quickly, before cleaning up the abandoned sites. Most of the truck-mounted SAM launchers were abandoned after their fuel was scavenged to evacuate enemy personnel, but there was no way for the Americans to know that—only that the sites were intact but unmanned.

There were two more divisions of fighters in the strike: a four-ship of two-seat Super Hornets tasked with close air support for the rescue mission, and a final division of single-seat Super Hornets flying RESCAP. Even a section of Supercats by itself would have been a far better choice for the RESCAP, but there was only a dozen of them, and the air tasking order had most of them committed to longer-range strikes that same day. Although less capable, it made sense to use the Super Hornets for missions well within their own striking ranges. The air threat from Iran was almost eliminated at this point, so Fargo hadn't argued too hard for the CAP mission. The Supercat had proven itself as an air-to-air juggernaut on day one of their line period. On day two, it would demonstrate its superior capability in the 'Bombcat' role. Still, the payload capacity of the Supercat was such that even with full bomb loads, each plane still carried four air-to-air missiles: two each of AMRAAM and Sidewinder.

Fargo was grateful for that capacity when the first warning calls came in from the E-2D overwatch, callsign 'Banger.'

***

USS *Mount Whitney,* in the Gulf of Oman

The sensor fusion and network capability provided by the E-2D Advanced Hawkeye allowed the Fifth Fleet battle watch captain to view in real time as several air targets were detected going airborne over southern Iran, northeast of Bandar Abbas. ESM detected by the Hawkeye, and shortly thereafter by the strike package working west over and around *Oghab*-44, positively identified the bandits as SU-30MKM Flankers. Based on ongoing intelligence updates, this was almost certainly the *Feilong*, or 'Flying Dragons'. The Chinese volunteer squadron was the last fighting-strength unit of the IRIAF believed to exist, and they had finally shown themselves. Not only that, but now they had revealed the location of their own hidden mountain-base facility as well. This was a contingency TF-50 had planned and waited for, and a chance for the *Yorktown* battle group to get their last licks in before they were relieved by the *Oriskany* battle group. The watch captain picked up the handset giving him a direct line to *Yorktown*'s Strike net, knowing they were receiving the same information he was. This scenario fell well within their current rules of engagement, and he had the authority to order an immediate strike on the base's location.

The orders were issued, and within minutes a swarm of Tomahawk land-attack missiles arced into the air from the VLS systems of the *Yorktown* group's surface combatants. A second wave was on-call and ready to fire should the first wave encounter heavy SAM resistance or otherwise fail to smash the target. A Predator drone in the area was retasked to the target coordinates to provide an immediate battle damage assessment after the missile-strike. Any units on the ground outdoors at the site of the Iranian base were in for a rude shock.

Feilong One

Cheng Ye judged that speed, surprise, and sudden violence of action were the key to success in this engagement. The Americans would detect his squadron as soon as it was airborne, and the response would be near-immediate. The longer it took to acquire targets and engage, the more opportunity the Americans would have to bring their electronic warfare capabilities into play, fouling his chances. Without the advantage offered by their own A-50 AWACS, it would be nearly impossible to get or stay inside the decision loop of his enemies. He had briefed his pilots that their goals were straightforward: get airborne, acquire, engage, disengage, and escape. They would shoot down as many as they could in one salvo, perhaps two at the most, and then run. After that it would be a race against the clock and the enemy to get back to *Oghab*-45, refuel, and relaunch before their base was targeted and hit.

A mere 85 NM separated his flight from the Americans, who were spread-out in squadron strength on a rough north-south line stretching over about a 40 NM front. He detected about half of them on radar immediately as his group turned west and accelerated to supersonic speed in full afterburner, executing a shallow climb as they went. Of the other half, four presented fair radar returns, and four targets were intermittent at best—those were probably the new American F-25's. A division of four American Super Hornets was already positioning itself to defend against the *Feilong*—those would be his first targets. Apparently there were no Prowler jammers among the Americans this time; jamming was mercifully absent, at least at the beginning. He had ten jets, with each one carrying six R-27 active radar missiles with an 80NM range, and two wingtip-mounted heat seekers. He issued the orders, and a salvo of twenty missiles was launched first at the RESCAP Super Hornets, and another salvo of twenty at the second division showing up cleanly on radar. Once the missiles were fired, he slowed his squadron to subsonic speed but held them nose-on, waiting for the timeout of his first strike. It would be almost a minute before they were within range of the

American AMRAAM missiles, so he enjoyed a little buffer. Before his own missiles even closed the gap to the Americans, the AESA radars and self-protection jammers on the American planes began hindering his radar picture and electronics. In the end he decided there was little need to hold back, and ordered a third salvo of missiles launched at the targets over *Oghab*-44, and a second salvo against the nearest flight of Super Hornet RESCAP fighters. All sixty long range missiles carried by the *Feilong* were in play before the Americans were within range to fire a single shot in return. Rather than turning his flight back to base as he'd briefed, Cheng Ye inexplicably pressed onward, eager to see the results of his work.

***

Tiger 102

"We're spiked! We've got enemy missiles inbound, Fargo," Freckles announced with an odd casualness. The first two salvoes of missiles off the Flankers were large enough that even the distant Hawkeye radar had detected them.

Fargo's heart-rate shot up. Having been shot down once, any mental sense of invulnerability he once possessed was long gone. In this case, however, the early detection meant time was on their side. "Okay, then. Tiger flight, this is lead. Snap two-one-zero and Gate. Get low, and try to outrun them. We can circle back to re-engage." The direction he was ordering them was *supposed* to be clear of SAMs, but they were about to find out for sure. He checked to make sure Dingo was still with him, and executed a hard turn to the heading he ordered, then went to full afterburner. They had already dropped their bombs, so their external tanks and missiles were the only drag left on the jets. The Supercats accelerated beautifully, quickly straining to reach Mach 1.6 with distant Mach 4.5 missiles in pursuit. Fargo was reminded of the word problems he used to hate in math class: *If Johnny starts heading west at 40 MPH, and a train starts ten minutes later from the same point going 60 MPH, how long does it take for the train to catch Johnny?* Only this time, the train might run out of propellant and kinetic energy if Johnny's head start was big enough—that was the hope. The altitude and speed from which the missiles were fired was the critical factor: higher and faster meant more energy, and in the end it was *all* about energy management. And countermeasures. And electronics. *And luck.* Always a bit of luck.

"Countermeasures?" Freckles asked, interrupting his train of thought. She had already called the flight defensive, and Fargo didn't envy the RESCAP flight in the Super Hornets as they went head-to-head with an enemy with superior numbers, superior planes, and longer-range missiles. The radios were getting busy now with frantic calls as the fight developed, and the RESCAP flight salvoed two large waves of AMRAAMs against their oncoming opponents before going defensive and allowing the distant Hawkeye to provide mid-course missile guidance thanks to integrated fire control.

"Use your best judgement, but try not to shoot the whole wad—we may run into a SAM envelope out here," Fargo replied. He keyed the radio. "Tigers, stream decoys," he added.

"Way ahead of you, mate! Er, Skipper!" Dingo called over the radio.

"Tigers, bend it south on the defensive and be ready to reform and turn northeast for the commit," he ordered, looking out ahead for terrain suitable to mask themselves with. It wasn't hard, out here where the terrain was so rugged. It was beautiful in its own way, reminding him of the high desert ranges out around northern and central Nevada where he had spent so much time training. He dropped them lower, bringing the jet out of burner and pulling them behind a large mesa when the threat warning receiver finally went off, signaling that a nearby missile seeker had just gone active. He glanced at the SA page for a bearing, then did a quick 'Linda Blair' to his stern quarter, but didn't see anything. He didn't really expect to at this point—the missile would be out of propellant, on inertia, and hopefully low on energy. He turned his attention back forward and flew for the cover offered by the high terrain as Freckles punched out chaff and flares. He was never sure if there was one missile or a pair after him, but in the end the missiles were defeated by the thick air, distance, and countermeasures. The threat receiver went silent, and Freckles announced they were clean.

In the meantime, they'd taken themselves well out of the fight and burned a prodigious amount of fuel, but Fargo glanced at his totalizer, and he still had almost fourteen thousand pounds of internal fuel remaining—more than enough for a scrap and to make it back to the Boat without even needing to tank.

"Tigers, check in," he ordered. Dingo and Hawk called in immediately, but Hawk's wingman did not. "Grape, check in!" Fargo called, an icy pit descending into his stomach.

"Lead, I've got a smoking hole at my four o'clock," Hawk called, sounding devastated. "They may have been hit."

"Banger, Tiger One, do you hold my Dash-4 in the link?" he called.

"Tiger Four is down," Banger called. "Position marked."

"Hawk, any chutes?" Fargo called.

"Negative, Skipper. Not that I can see, anyway." At supersonic speed, Fargo knew they would have been out of the survivable ejection envelope to begin with. A search could be conducted later, but for now they were still in a fight.

"Tiger flight is clean and regrouping to commit northeast," Freckles reported. "Banger, request SITREP."

"Merged plot at north bullseye, forty miles. Hunter flight is engaged. RESCAP flight is down. Juno flight is down. Numerous bandits are down. Tigers vector 040 to commit. Use caution. Hunter flight merged with Bandit gorilla group. Estimate six total contacts, and we have good IFF on three of ours."

Jesus Christ! Fargo thought. *More than half the strike just got splashed!* It wasn't lost on him that almost all the casualties were Super Hornets. Slow jets, less maneuverable, less agile in terms of acceleration and thrust-to-weight. Surprised and outnumbered by modern Flankers flown by professionals, what chance had they had? The experts kept saying these types of engagements were unrealistic to expect, but here they kept finding themselves, time and again.

"Tiger One copies. Tiger flight commit," Freckles called. "Skipper, I've got radar contact."

"I see it—call it," he ordered. He had already switched over from air-to-ground to air-to-air mode, and he thumbed his selector switch to AMRAAM. He was heartsick over the loss of one of his planes and crew, but there was no time for it now. He was about to enter another furball—their second in as many days. Given what they knew of the state of the Iranian Air Force, this *should* be the last hurrah.

"Tiger Two, radar contact," Red called.

Then Bagels: "Tiger Three, radar contact."

Freckles called 'Judy', taking control of the intercept. As they closed the engagement and the radar broke out separate contacts, designation boxes began to appear in Fargo's helmet display. For some unknown reason, the bandits had pressed into visual range after a successful BVR attack. The dogfight had dragged itself almost down to ground level, as they tended to do. Fargo brought them in fast, almost on the deck themselves, to give the radars a clearer picture and keep them masked like big cats in the tall grass, on the stalk and ready to pounce. The bad news was that with the contacts all mixed up and maneuvering against each other, he couldn't just lock a target and fire—either an AMRAAM or Sidewinder might pick up the wrong target and home in on a friendly. Shots would need to be taken very carefully.

"Tigers, punch your tanks," Fargo ordered. His wingmen complied, and six fuel tanks tumbled off three Tomcats. *Here we go, baby, fangs out!* Fargo grinned darkly. "Freckles, find me someone to shoot," he added.

"Working it, boss," came the tight-lipped reply.

"Hunters, Tiger flight is tally on the scrum," Fargo called. "We're in hot from the southwest, low in the weeds."

"Hunter One is offensive, Two covering," the lead F-25 called. "Fox-2!" he added a moment later. Fargo saw a smoke trail appear out there ahead of him, at about his one o'clock, and his situational awareness solidified that much more. He could see Hunter One now, his wingman, and their target. There were three others, and one other bandit was already going down, trailing smoke.

"Hunter Three, splash one! I'm defensive!" the pilot called in the same breath.

Fargo jammed the throttles into afterburner and felt the hand of God jam him back into the ejection seat as the Supercat leapt forward. "Hunter Three, Tiger One, tally. Break right and extend south," he ordered, selecting Sidewinder. He didn't uncage the seeker; he wanted to be *very sure* which heat source the missile was looking at. At the same moment, Freckles locked the bandit and slewed the IRST onto the target. Fargo saw the paint scheme as plain as day: a mono-colored Flanker with a dragon painted gracefully onto the planform. This was the jet that had overflown the *Boxer* and killed the Irish brothers. Fargo heard Skipper Jefferson's voice in his head like it was yesterday: *Ya'll burn that image into your heads, ya got me? Remember it.*

Fargo remembered.

The *Feilong* jet suddenly maneuvered as if prescient, abandoning its attack on Hunter Three and executing an impossibly tight right break, bringing it nose-on to Fargo's flight. It was a turn only made possible with vectored thrust. The F-25 was still pulling clear to the right in Fargo's HUD—he didn't have a clean shot yet, but two smoke trails immediately came off the opposing Flanker's wingtips, one after another.

"*Uff da!*" Fargo yelled, pulling the throttles to idle and breaking hard right as Freckles fired off chaff and flares. Dingo and Hawk were doing the exact same thing, in various directions. One missile went after Dingo, and was partially decoyed by the towed fiber optic trailing behind the fighter. It detonated close aboard, sending shrapnel flying into the back of the jet. It immediately erupted in flames, and both ejection seats fired two heartbeats later. The second missile went after Hawk and exploded nearby, again peppering the jet with shrapnel, but not fatally. Hawk broke off to the south, decelerating and trailing smoke.

"Two good chutes on Dash-2," Freckles called.

Son of a bitch has thrust-vectoring! Fargo thought as he continued his turn, kicking in his own vectored thrust to bring the nose of the jet around. With Dingo down and Hawk separating with damage, he had a clean shot behind him. The Sukhoi was accelerating now, in full burner, but still close. Fargo uncaged the seeker and used his helmet cueing to take an off-axis shot as soon as he was in parameters. The missile came off the rail and hooked immediately right; the Flanker came out of burner and broke hard left across his flight path in what amounted to a flat-scissors, spitting flares behind it. The missile reversed direction and decoyed into a flare, blowing up.

Fargo had one heat-seeker left; he reversed hard and used thrust vectoring to pull the Flanker back into parameters for an off-boresight shot in the other direction. He held off firing at the last moment, realizing the angles were too extreme and the jets too close for a good kill-probability. The Iranian (Chinese?) jet was out of missiles now; the only hope for the pilot was to get nose-on for a guns-shot. If the enemy pilot extended and ran, Fargo could run him down easily and put an AMRAAM up his tailpipes.

The Flanker reversed again, back to the right, almost out of airspeed now as it used super-maneuverability to try and force the overshoot. Fargo still had a little more energy on the Tomcat, and all his opponent had left was guns. He unloaded and went into burner, opening the range slightly, and then pulling into the vertical where the Flanker couldn't follow. He let that percolate for a few moments, watching to see what his opponent would do. The Flanker went wings level and unloaded as soon as Fargo was nose-high, lit its own burners, and made as if to run.

"He's bugging out!" Freckles yelled, charged up with adrenalin.

"No, he's not," Fargo replied. *This motherfucker is* good, *and he knows better,* he thought to himself. "He's trying to sucker us," Fargo told her as he kicked them back over the top, and sure enough, the Flanker immediately abandoned its ploy and spun nose-on again, almost as if by magic with thrust-vectoring in play. The range was long for guns, but the pilot got his nose up and let off a long burst of cannon-fire. Fargo was forced to evade, and returned fire with his last Sidewinder. He thought that would be the end of it, but the enemy pilot pulled power and let his aircraft sink, spitting a long string of flares behind it. Presenting its lowest-profile IR signature from being nose-on, the Flanker beat the odds. The Sidewinder tracked slightly up into the string of flares and exploded. The Flanker bottomed out impossibly close to the ground before it went flying again, pirouetting vaguely eastward and accelerating at an insultingly leisurely pace, dropping the proverbial gauntlet. It didn't run itself straight into Fargo's AMRAAM envelope, but tempted him in closer instead. It was a sucker play: Fargo *should* have gone for separation and an AMRAAM shot, or invited one of the surviving Huntsmen to finish the job for him.

But now it was starting to feel *personal*.

This bastard had killed two, maybe *four* of his shipmates, shot down Dingo, and seriously damaged Hawk. Moving into guns range at this moment was a *serious* tactical error—as a student at TOPGUN it would have earned him an UNSAT grade on the event. Here, now, it felt like a matter of honor.

Fargo didn't spend more than a heartbeat thinking about it; he saw red, gritted his teeth, and rolled directly in on the Flanker, switching to GUNS on the weapons selector. He took command of the radar up front, entering pilot-lock-on mode, and bore sighted the Flanker, locking it up and bringing his computerized gunsight into play. He let a small closure rate build; slight, but not too much, because he knew exactly what was coming. As he passed into firing range he let off a couple quick squirts of cannon-fire as the Flanker jinked in front of him, then abruptly pulled up to force the overshoot, dragging him into a rolling scissors. With vectored thrust, the enemy pilot doubtlessly thought he could force the Tomcat out in front of him, and finish the fight with a nice snapshot on a floundering target.

What Cheng Ye didn't account for was the extremely good high-alpha flight characteristics of the Supercat, which *also* had vectored thrust. The jets made two slow barrel rolls around each other, shedding energy and increasingly relying on high-lift devices and vectored thrust to keep them from stalling out. The wings on Tiger 102 went to full extension, and Fargo expertly used the rudders to roll the jet in the slow-flight regime as he worked the engine nozzles. In the old days he would have manually dropped the flaps to give him a little extra lift; now the digital flight control system did all that for him, helping to keep them flying.

Both pilots were masterful aviators; both flew top-of-the-line fighters. In this case, the Advanced Super Tomcat had the edge on its older counterpart. Cheng Ye felt his jet finally run out of energy, and he was forced to drop his nose and pick up a little speed, or simply stall and depart controlled flight. He knew he had to eject if he wanted to live; pride and face didn't allow it. He was a double ace, the best Chinese fighter pilot in two generations, and a sociopath incapable of accepting defeat, even if it meant his own life.

Fargo felt a pulse-pounding sense of exultation as the Flanker finally appeared in front of his nose. He remembered Dexter, broken and bloody in his arms, Deedee and Stinky, the Irish brothers, Grape and Jinx today, and maybe Dingo and Red, depending on if they'd survived their ejection. *And five thousand others drowned or burned in their ships,* he thought in the space of a heartbeat. Whoever the guy in the Flanker was, he had it coming.

Fargo flew the gun pipper over the helmet of Cheng Ye, the Flying Dragon, held it there with inhuman precision, and paused with his finger on the trigger. He began to squeeze, time frozen in that moment, when he heard Dexter's voice in his head as plainly as if he was sitting in Freckles' seat: *Don't become the monsters you fight.*

He let the pipper slide behind the cockpit over the Flanker's planform, exhaling slightly as he squeezed the trigger. Twenty millimeter cannon shells spat into the Flanker, shredding it from mid-fuselage back, and it erupted in flames and pitched over. Fargo was vaguely aware of Freckles shouting in his ear as he pitched forward as well, working by instinct and muscle memory to get some flying speed back on the jet. The entire time he watched for an ejection seat from his opponent, but it never fired.

He was close enough to see Cheng Ye look up at him, his black eyes cold, mesmerizing, and empty as the burning Flanker plunged into the ground and exploded.

"*FARGO PULL UP!*" Freckles screamed.

"*Uff da!*" Fargo grunted, hauling back on the stick and jamming the throttles into burner. He used thrust vectoring to kick the tail of the jet down and get a climb rate going; the Tomcat kicked up a swirling cloud of dust from the earth as it bottomed out and began a laborious climb back to altitude, accelerating cleanly once Fargo had things back under control. Even in death, Cheng Ye had almost lulled one more victim into his snare.

"*What the hell is wrong with you?!*" Freckles shouted at him from the back seat. "Sir!" she added a moment later, immediately mortified at her outburst towards her CO.

"I'm okay now, y'know?" Fargo replied in a shaken voice. "Bit of target fixation, there," he added lamely. "Thanks, Freckles. And don't call me 'sir' in the jet," he reminded her for the umpteenth time. He was trembling up front, feeling sick from the adrenalin, the intensity of the fight, and mortified by his own bad judgment. *What the hell had come over him?* he thought, feeling cold sweat between his shoulder blades. The only time he remembered feeling like this was after a rare 'night in the barrel,' taking multiple attempts to trap aboard ship on a black night with a heavily pitching deck.

Banger called a clean air picture, and what was left of the shattered strike turned south for home. The downed Prowler airmen were recovered, as were Dingo, Red, and various survivors of the two Super Hornet divisions savaged by the *Feilong*. The crew of Tiger Four was KIA, and the Prowler pilot died of his wounds before making it back to the Boat.

***

Oghab-45

They saw the smoke long before they reached the shattered runway and taxiway of the *Feilong* base. When they pulled up, they saw a field of broken, burning vehicles, a raging fuel-fire, and dead Chinese bodies. Toma Baranov paled slightly and let out a small cry of "*Bozhe moi!*"

Kovalev didn't lose his color, wince, or express any real emotion at all. It was all burned out of him back on the breakwater, the day before. He slipped out of the jeep when it rolled to a stop and walked among the ruins, silently taking stock.

"What about fuel?" Sami whined, looking beseechingly at Baranov.

"This strike was only a surface strike," Kovalev called back to them. "Probably carried out from their ships. They'll be back to collapse the mountain with an air strike, but there's time. We can obtain fuel from inside the base, and maybe some water and rations. We'll be away before the Americans come back in force. Come, there's no time to waste," Kovalev said, pointing upward.

Baranov craned his neck, and saw the dim outline of an unmanned drone, circling overhead. He didn't consider it at the time, but his picture was being taken in high-resolution color, to be disseminated to intelligence agencies throughout the western world. Kovalev's head was covered and he never looked straight up, but he didn't doubt he would eventually be identified as well.

Not that it really mattered. Nothing mattered now, or would for a good long time.

The three men set about the task at hand, finding plenty of steel jerry cans inside the base and using them to refuel the jeep, before refilling them and tying them down in back—enough gas to get them to Kerman International Airport, or even a little farther if they needed to. The question of an airlift to Pakistan was now in doubt; the Chinese maintenance and support crews were all dead, staged outside and ready to step off overland as soon as their returning fighters were refueled and relaunched—fighters that would never appear, now. The three men had seen no sign of the *Feilong* squadron during their drive up here; only several smoke pillars dotting the desert landscape here and there where aircraft had obviously gone down. Whether they were American or *Feilong* was unknown, but Kovalev hoped that Cheng Ye had given a good accounting in the end. It didn't appear that any of the Chinese volunteers had gotten away, although there was the chance they had passed overhead and then flown on, given the current state of the base.

Baranov had the same thoughts. "Maybe we'll find some of them in Kerman," he said thoughtfully. "The Americans couldn't have gotten them all at once, could they?"

"We'll find out," Kovalev replied casually, slinging an AK-47 around his neck, and checking the ammunition loads in the spare magazines he was stuffing into a salvaged combat harness. With his bloodstained, makeshift keffiyeh, a dark tan from the months spent under a desert sun, and jihadi-style weapons load, all he needed was an Iranian flag to drape around his shoulders to be mistaken for a member of the PLO or the Revolutionary Guard.

He accepted another pull of vodka from Baranov's flask and calmly lit the cigar he was offered before swinging into the passenger seat of the jeep, one boot propped stylishly on the doorless frame of the chassis. Baranov took the back seat this time, saying nothing, but noting that Kovalev was a changed man. Sami the driver, no stranger to scenes of carnage, grinned like a bandit around his own cigar as he pulled back onto the road and drove them west, towards the crossroads leading north.

"When I volunteered, I never thought it'd be anything like this," Baranov remarked over the sound of the engine. "That first villa they gave us in Shiraz . . . the swimming pool, the royal treatment . . . *that* was how I imagined it. Not *this*."

Kovalev thought of all he had seen and done in the past year or so. From a dead end post in the frozen north of the *Rodina* to this strange, violent land, where he had lived, fought, and loved like never before in his life. Right now, there was more money in his Swiss account than he had ever had at one time in his entire life. He felt dead inside right now, because of Tara Shirazi, but he knew there would eventually be other lovers. All he had to do was survive *long enough*, and time would work its magic. In the meantime, just getting out of this war-torn, self-destructing country would be an adventure like no other.

"This is the mercenary life, *tovarich*," Kovalev said philosophically. He waited as Baranov passed his flask to Sami, who took a slug of vodka in defiance of all Islamic convention. He then handed it sideways to Kovalev, who turned slightly and raised it in toast to the former Russian general. "We are the last of the *Krasnyye Kogti,*" he shouted to the wind. "To *long enough*, my friend! May we always survive long enough!"

"*Nashe zdorov'ye*" Baranov laughed, taking back the flask and drinking it to the dregs. *Our health!*

XVI

Tehran under Siege! Reports of heavy fighting, government massacres leak from Iranian capital.

-Reuters

Major air battle over Southern Iran! U.S. Navy admits to losses but states that the Iranian Air Force has been completely destroyed.

-N.Y. Times

How far will the United States go? Pentagon spokesman categorically denies rumors that the United States plans to invade mainland Iran.

-L.A. Times

USS *Hornet*

Fargo stood at parade rest in his summer whites, a salty sea breeze tugging at his cover as he glanced over at the row of thirteen wreath-draped easels holding pictures of the fallen. Each of the pictures was of a young, smiling face, dressed smartly in service dress blues with the American flag standing proudly behind them. Two of them were Black Tigers, LT Paul 'Grape' Kowalski and his RIO, LT Danielle 'Jinx' Thomas. Dingo and Red had ejected without major injury, and Hawk had nursed his wounded Tomcat all the way back to the ship and gotten her aboard in one piece, God bless him. Part of Fargo had believed so much in the capabilities of the F-14E that he hadn't thought to lose a single plane in combat, but once again reality had proven the harshest of mistresses. Today, nobody was safe on a modern battlefield—the technologies were just too advanced. The other eleven combat losses included four dead from the Rampagers, one from the Huntsmen, and four from the Fencers. The last two dead were from the Prowler the day prior to that. That was thirteen fatalities in two days of combat, but in those two days both the Russian and Chinese Volunteer Groups were broken. The *Feilong* had done the most damage by far. Discounting the ill-fated *Boxer*, no carrier air wing had suffered losses like this since Vietnam, but they'd shot down twenty-five of Iran's top shelf aircraft in return—the last of their air force. From this point forward, the air wing would be conducting various ground strike missions almost exclusively, with CAP fighters on station purely as a contingency.

All the other speeches, mercifully brief, were given. Now Fargo listened as the chaplain read scripture for the service, a standard passage he'd heard too many times in his almost sixteen-year naval career: "We therefore commend their souls to God, looking for the general Resurrection in the last day, and the life of the world to come, through our Lord Jesus Christ; at whose second coming in glorious majesty to judge the world, the sea shall give up her dead; and the corruptible bodies of those who sleep in him shall be changed, and made like unto his glorious body; according to the mighty working whereby he is able to subdue all things unto himself. Amen."

"Amen," Fargo muttered, blinking away tears.

"Company, *atten-hut!*" the adjutant barked. The large formation—every squadron in the air wing—snapped to attention. "Hand salute!" Off near the LSO platform, seven Marines in dress blue raised their rifles, angling them out to sea, and fired three salvoes in succession. The formation held their salute as a division of Super Hornets appeared behind the ship, coming on fast in a finger-four formation. Just short of the stern, Dash-3 pulled up and away, leaving a three-ship missing-man formation to pass overhead. As soon as the roar of the jets faded beyond the bow, the bugler played taps.

"Rea-dee, to!" the adjutant barked after the last note. The salutes snapped down as one, and the company stood mute as the colors were ceremonially cased and marched off. The bugler sounded 'Retreat' as they went. At the end, the 5MC rang with the two-note 'Carry on' from the Bosun's pipe, echoed verbally by the Air Boss. The formation broke apart, with everyone headed below decks to change back into working uniforms. Beneath their feet, they felt the deck vibrate with power as the captain ordered *Hornet* back underway, and her four nuclear-driven shafts immediately began putting on turns for knots.

Now it was back to the business of war.

***

Seated in the Dirty Shirt for midrats, Fargo looked over an untouched slider at his RIO. Although his 'no rank in the jet' rule was enforced even as the CO of the Black Tigers, they weren't in the air right now. He'd asked her down to midrats for a private word, when the wardroom was far less crowded than usual, and they could find a table to themselves. "Ranks off for a moment," he told Freckles. She nodded in reply, her lips pressed in a thin line. She looked thoroughly depressed, and Fargo understood why: Jinx was one of her roommates, and the loss was weighing heavily on her. He knew the feeling, and knew it well.

"I owe you an apology, Freckles," he told her. "I lost my head in the jet the other day and *majorly* fucked up—I could've gotten us killed."

"Target fixation can happen to any—" she began, trying to make his excuses for him.

"—I'm not talking about that," Fargo interrupted. "I'm talking about taking us into a gunfight when we still had missiles on the rails. We could have shot that guy from ten miles away and he couldn't have done a thing about it. It was a criminally stupid thing to do. I had no right to risk your life like that."

"Or the navy's prototype jet," she added with a sardonic smile.

"Yah, that too, you bet," Fargo nodded. "Anyway, I just wanted you to know: if you don't want to fly with me anymore, I understand, and it won't be held against you. You're a top shelf aviator. I just wanted you to know that. Just say the word to Snoopy if you want, and it's all good."

"Okay, thanks," Freckles said. "Done blowing smoke up my ass, Fargo?"

Fargo blinked. "Yah?"

"Good. Don't turn into a puss on me now. I understand *what* happened, *why* it was fucked up, and *why* you won't ever do anything like that again. You're a goddamn ace and the best fighter pilot in the air wing. Well, maybe *except* for Swampy. I also get the chance to showcase my superior talents to the guy who writes my fitness reports. Now why would I want to pair up with someone else?"

"Okay then, if that's how you feel about it," Fargo replied, a little taken aback at her response. Ranks off or not, he would *never* have spoken to his own commanding officer like that—not in a million years. Dexter had pushed his buttons from time to time, but Freckles sure had a pair of balls on her—he had to give her that. "I, uh, just wanted to make sure. Clear the air, y'know?"

"You betcha, Skipper," she replied. Ranks were back on, just like that. She gestured across the table at his slider. "You gonna eat that, boss?" she asked.

Fargo slid the plate across to her. "All yours, lieutenant."

***

U.S. Marines occupy Persian Gulf Islands, and the U.S. Navy declares the Strait of Hormuz open!

-Washington Post

Markets stabilize as U.S. forces secure the Strait of Hormuz. Oil futures are expected to drop, but when will consumers see it at the pump?

-Financial Times

Abu Musa Island—property of the United States? The United Arab Emirates renews old territorial claims in international court.

-Chicago Sun Times

Ukrainian President Viktor Yanukovich ousted! Crimean citizens hold pro-Russian demonstrations in protest as a new government takes control of Ukraine.

-Reuters

Russia's quiet Crimean invasion. Ukrainian officials warn that "Green Man" Operations involve Russian Special Forces.

-International Herald Tribune

MAR 2014
USS *Hornet,* in the Gulf of Oman

Fargo sat in the small stateroom that doubled as his office, eyeballing the framed picture of Angela Olson that graced his desk over the course of the deployment. Lisa Bozeman had snapped the shot the day of the squadron's establishment ceremony. Fargo and Angie were in the picture together, arm in arm and smiling at the camera, and Angela looked absolutely ravishing in that blue dress she'd worn. One of the advantages of being CO was that Fargo had his own computer he could use to send and receive emails from the outside world; he'd carried on a daily correspondence with Angela the entire time he'd been aboard *Hornet.* It was hard to come up with anything truly relevant to say daily, especially when he was living aboard the big gray Boat and life distilled down to administrative chores, eating, sleeping, and flying. After the first two harrowing days on station, life had settled down into a routine of 'risk-managed' combat flying that reminded him of his first deployments to Afghanistan: lots of ground strikes made with impunity, spiced up by the occasional SAM threat, and no air threat to speak of. Most of it he couldn't discuss with Angela except in the vaguest terms, nor would she have understood the details of it anyway. At least, not the way Buzz's wife would have, who had spent years as a Navy wife and was fully indoctrinated in the lingo and lifestyle.

After their first sixty day line period, *Hornet* briefly withdrew from the Gulf of Oman for a port call in Karwar, India. During the Korean and Vietnam wars, Japan and the Philippines both offered suitable options for the rest and recreation of tired pilots and sailors. The simple truth was that there were few good options in this part of the world. Someone had floated the idea of Masirah, setting up a 'steel beach' pierside where sailors could at least get off the ship and relax a bit, and maybe drink some beers in a strictly confined enclosure. RADM Yellend had vetoed that, stating in no uncertain terms that his sailors deserved a much better respite, especially when they were fighting a declared war and taking losses. He enlisted the help of VADM Patrick and got the wheels turning at the State Department.

It just so happened that there was an ulterior political motive for the U.S. Navy to make a friendly port call in India: it was a subtle way of expressing U.S. displeasure with *both* Pakistan and China, neither of whom were on particularly friendly terms with India. Pakistan was culpable either directly or indirectly for the sale of JF-17 fighters to Iran, and China's underhanded involvement in this war (perhaps even fomenting it) was considered sheer perfidy. The Indian government approved the port call with a bare minimum of diplomatic fuss.

So it was that the *Hornet* battle group visited Karwar, and the sailors were treated to a rare, almost unique opportunity to 'see the world' instead of seeing the Arabian Sea. The crew joked that Perth, Western Australia would have been even better, but 4500 miles was a long way to go for a port call. Karwar was an easy three-day steam from the Gulf of Oman. India was a place Fargo had never expected to visit. He took time to relax, purchasing souvenirs for his family, for Angela and A.J., drank a little fine scotch, and got caught up on sleep. There was a little official business to attend to as well: his new status as an ace came with fifteen minutes of fame—it led to a couple of carefully choreographed media interviews, and he spent one day riding a helicopter back and forth to the Indian Naval Academy to be a guest speaker.

In the tradition of naval aviation, each squadron in the air wing picked a local hotel and booked a large suite to serve as 'the admin,' a *de facto* base of operations where the aviators could congregate, party, and crash. CAG warned his commanding officers to 'keep it down to a dull roar' on the beach—he understood that his people needed to blow off steam, but there were other units that might like to visit India in the future, and it would be nice if the Navy was invited back rather than banned as rowdy, drunken pests. Fargo passed CAG's order down to Buzz Bozeman, and the XO did a fine job in his role as 'sheriff', making sure that the Black Tigers played hard without besmirching the Navy's reputation, or their own. The Indian Navy proved to be gracious hosts all around, sponsoring events and tours of the surrounding areas, and arranging both soccer and cricket matches as a form of cultural cross-pollination. The ten days in Karwar passed quickly and then *Hornet* returned to the line, resuming sustained combat operations.

Now the deployment was winding down, along with the war itself. Nobody felt like it was going to go on much longer, even if Iran refused to formally surrender. Over the past year, Iran had been strangled militarily and economically. The Iranian Navy and Air Force no longer existed, their command and control were shattered, and their leadership, particularly among the IRGC, was decimated from the top down. Air defenses along the coastlines of the Persian Gulf and Gulf of Oman had been peeled back so that the airspace was clean of threats up to 100 NM inland. Their nuclear program, ironically, had suffered terribly due to the Russian-driven *maskirovka* at the beginning of the war. Fearful of what Iran *might* have accomplished, nuclear sites and any sites even *suspected* of having ties to the nuclear program had been leveled, their electronic infrastructure subjected to relentless cyberattacks, and their human resources targeted by both the U.S. military and the Israeli Mossad.

The destruction of Iranian oil terminals and port facilities in the Gulf, coupled with the U.S. blockade of all shipping traffic to and from Iran, had crushed them economically and set the population at odds with its government. There was little food or fuel to be had, and the people were suffering tremendously, inciting them to rise in rebellion. Nationalism was a powerful force, but it placed a distant second to feeding one's children and keeping clothes on their backs. On the one hand, the United States declared that its war was truly against the Iranian government and military rather than its people, but on the other, they refused to aid the Iranian people in any way, and blocked foreign aid from reaching them by means of blockade. Some relief came by air and over land from Russia, but Russia was currently engaged in operations in Crimea, and by their yardstick, Iran had served its purpose in keeping the United States occupied, engaged, and far removed from events taking place in the Black Sea. The Iranian people, starved and desperate, were now proving to be one of the major instruments in the impending U.S. victory.

The Marine Corps successfully occupied its island objectives in the Persian Gulf, forcibly removing the populations to the southern coast of mainland Iran, where the influx of displaced refugees just added to Iran's problems. A large force of Navy SeaBees came in behind the Marines, expanding the airfields and port facilities on Sirri and Abu Musa Islands, while an American integrated air defense system was put in place on all of them. The long term plan was to base Air Force jets on those islands to enforce a military no-fly zone over Iran even after the war ended, but the Marines were politicking for the island bases to remain under their control, with Marine air assets in place to enforce U.S. policies.

The Chinese government in Beijing read their intelligence reports, protested on the world stage, and smiled behind closed doors. The Marsden Administration was committing U.S. forces to a semi-permanent presence in the Persian Gulf, to an even greater extent than the presence maintained among its Gulf State allies. The more money and resources spent in the Gulf, the less there was to be spent in the western Pacific, especially along the first island chain. The Communist Chinese continued to cast a baleful eye on Taiwan, quietly accelerated their naval buildup, and looked to the future.

The impending end of the deployment meant that Fargo had some decisions to make about his own future. The USS *Essex* carrier strike group was due to relieve them in about four weeks. The fact that the *Essex* deployment was downgraded to a strike group rather than a full battle group was a clear signal that the U.S. Navy had achieved its wartime objectives in the Gulf.

Hornet was a west coast asset, and so was Carrier Air Wing Nine. The decision had been made to 'homeport' the Black Tigers at Lemoore Naval Air Station in California along with the rest of the west coast fighter squadrons. Nobody was sure what was going to happen with the Black Tigers or the F-14E; the program was still a bastard stepchild, but the combat statistics stood for themselves, and nobody in the Pentagon was talking about dis-establishing the squadron. Northman-Ironworks had already offered to replace the single jet lost in combat and add two more, bringing the available number of Supercats up to fourteen, and the D.C. rumor mill seemed to indicate that some price-haggling was going on. The AIM-152 long range missile had proven a smashing success, and was under contract to be put into full production. Block upgrades to the Super Hornet and Cutlass would mean that the Advanced Super Tomcat would no longer have a monopoly on long-range fleet air defense, but it was a good decision for the fleet, the Navy, and the nation. Everyone recognized that many of their losses could have been avoided with the AIM-152 in the inventory from the beginning.

When they got home, Fargo would have about ten months left on his tour as commanding officer before turning the squadron over to Buzz. At that point he was going to be forced to pay his dues if he wanted to continue his career in the Navy: it meant spending a few years in that big, five-sided building in Washington D.C. where military policy and appropriations were decided. In this case, Fargo felt he knew where he could make the biggest difference. He'd go to the Pentagon and cash in on every bit of credibility he had as a warfighter to make sure that the Fifth Generation follow-on to the Supercat was the next platform procured for naval aviation. The Super Hornet was already into its second decade, and it was a proven underachiever in combat—after flying the Supercat, Fargo never wanted to strap on a Super Hornet again. The sooner they got it off the carrier decks and replaced it with a high-low mix of Gen-5 fighters, the longer the aircraft carrier would reign as queen of the seas. Without them, he felt that carrier aviation was doomed inside of a generation. *Maybe it was already*, he sometimes reflected, at the rate technology was progressing.

Those career decisions were certain to impact his personal life. Judging by their sugary correspondence, he and Angela were firmly in love and on the fast track to getting married. *But . . .* he continuously reminded himself that they didn't *really* know each other. A couple of weeks spent mostly in bed and a long-distance correspondence was not a sterling foundation to base a marriage on. Fargo had been badly burned in his first go-round with matrimony, and there was also the matter of her son. In this case, with Angie a widow, there were no underlying issues with 'the ex' and his perpetual influence on their lives. A.J. was a terrific kid and he needed a father, but was Fargo the right guy for the job? Was he even the right guy to be a good husband to Angie? He worked rotten hours, and that wouldn't change when he was in the Pentagon, where O-5s were a dime-a-dozen: worker-bee drones as thick as flies in a cow pasture.

When that was over, he'd probably find himself back at sea again in some capacity or other, and then it would be right back on the deployment train, just like right now. If Angie and A.J. came to Lemoore to live with him after deployment, it would be for a year—roughly fifth or sixth grade for A.J., and then he'd uproot them *again* to move back to the east coast. Both Angie and A.J. had spent almost their whole lives in Red Lake County, Minnesota. Was Angela willing to remove her son from all that he'd known, his school and his friends, and turn him into a military-brat nomad? How would A.J. take to that? Fargo sometimes tried to put himself in A.J.'s shoes, then realized there was no way he could. He'd never lost his father, or grown up as a kid in a single-parent household, although he wasn't sure that A.J. living on his grandparents' farm amounted to quite the same thing.

Up until this month, it was easy for Fargo to put those things on the back burner and just concentrate on running his squadron. Now that the war and deployment were ending, he couldn't ignore them any longer.

Fargo switched on his computer and brought up his email, trying to think about what he wanted to write to Angela. He'd wrestled with it all, not even one hundred percent sure what *he* wanted. He wanted a wife and a family, but he wanted them as more than a 'checked box' on life's laundry list as he went about the business of a busy, successful career. He sat with his fingers poised over the keyboard, his eyes glazed over in a thousand-yard stare, when his phone buzzed and gave him the reprieve he needed. "Skipper Thorsen," he answered.

"It's the SDO, Skipper. There's something on the boob tube you might want to see, so just a head's up."

"What is it?"

"They're about to ... uh, *take care* of the *Boxer*."

"I'll be right there," Fargo replied, hanging up.

When Fargo stepped into the Black Tigers ready room a few minutes later, all eyes were on their big screen television. The aviators watched, slightly spellbound, as an Air Force C-130 passed overhead and dropped a massive weapon from its aft cargo ramp. The weapon had been talked about for months, discussed ad-nauseum by talking heads and 'contributors' on the various 24-hour news channels. It was a specialized variation on the MOAB (massive ordnance air-blast), commonly referred to as the 'Mother of All Bombs.' While a regular MOAB was designed to detonate over its target, this specialized version was designed to penetrate the hulk of the USS *Boxer* and detonate with sufficient force and thermal energy to largely vaporize the remains of the ship, including her shattered nuclear reactors. If the remains of the carrier survived the first attempt in any appreciable form, second and even third weapons were on standby to be deployed. This was the best solution the experts had come up with to rid the Gulf of the ship's remains and minimize the radiation hazard she represented. What little radioactive material survived this bomb-blast would be thinly spread underwater, left to dissipate relatively harmlessly over time. It was an imperfect solution, but nobody had devoted much thought to what would happen if a nuclear-powered aircraft carrier was sunk in the shallow waters of the Persian Gulf, until it happened.

Buzz Bozeman glanced around the room as the bomb fell slowly, and saw the ravaged look on Fargo's face. "Black Tigers!" he barked. "Atten-*hut!*" Every man and woman who wasn't already standing came to their feet, and the ready room braced up in respect.

The bomb released from its parachute and fell directly on target guided by GPS. It was the biggest JDAM ever dropped, sent to destroy a target that was already dead. The bomb hit at transonic speed, penetrating deep into the interior of the ship, then detonating according to precise calculations. A pillar of white fire resembling a nuclear blast erupted from the sea, consuming the remains of the ship and her crew. When the smoke cleared, the normally calm waters of the Gulf roiled and frothed as if in a storm. They gradually calmed, resuming the tranquility they had known before, closing over *Boxer*'s resting place with a finality possessed only by the sea.

***

Washington D.C.

The cabinet broke into vigorous applause when President James Marsden stepped into the situation room. His Secretary of State was at the head of the group, grinning from ear to ear. "It's confirmed," he told the president. "The government of Iran has fallen, and a provisional, secular government is in the process of being formed. It's like 1979, but in reverse. Congratulations, sir!"

Who's the 'accidental president' now? Marsden thought to himself. He worked his way around the room, shaking hands and thanking his staff as the applause continued unabated. There was the sound of a cork popping, and soon someone was pressing a flute of champagne into his hand. It was a heady moment indeed, especially with midterm elections a mere six months away, and a presidential election looming in 2016.

Everyone had written him off early, tagging him as a one-termer. He knew the betting lines in Vegas would be swinging the other way as soon as this news broke worldwide.

Even amidst celebration, the situation needed to be managed. "This provisional government, what do we know about it?"

"It's made up principally of the civil leaders who opposed the mullahs and the Ayatollah," Secretary Robard informed him. "They are drafting a parliamentary constitution, and promising free elections within six months. Their leader is a man named Ghorbani, and right now he controls Tehran and claims to be the provisional prime minister of the country. He has contacted us through diplomatic channels in Qatar, and requested an immediate cease-fire. He has stated that his country has no effective military force remaining, and that the previous government is no longer in charge. There are other requests as well, mostly for aid."

"Free elections or not, there's going to be a power struggle over there, and this Ghorbani character will likely be the one we're dealing with for some time, eh?" Marsden asked.

"That's the way these things usually go, assuming he can hold on to power," Robard replied.

"Okay then, we need a dossier on Ghorbani, and those around him. Dig up everything you can find. In the meantime, which of our contingency plans works best here?" Marsden asked.

"Scenario three, for now. We agree to the cease fire and ease the blockade, with conditions previously stated: Iran's future military is to be restricted to a self-defense force like the restrictions placed on Japan after World War Two. No Iranian military presence permitted within fifty miles of the Persian Gulf coastline except along their national land borders, and for now, we retain possession of the islands we've taken in the Gulf. In addition, the non-Omani waters of the Strait of Hormuz are declared international waters all the way to the Iranian coastline. The other plus side is that under scenario three, we can stage humanitarian relief operations from our island bases within the timeframe of a couple weeks, surging food and supplies into southern Iran."

"What about Iran's economy and infrastructure?"

"Ripe for foreign investment," Robard grinned. "Mister President, this is the best outcome we could have hoped for: Iranian capitulation, followed by the establishment of a western-style secular government. It shifts the entire balance of power in the region *completely*. We won't be beholden to the Saudis any longer, or any religious-based government in the region. Not only that, but it also solves a huge number of problems in the Levant—the Ayatollah's regime was largest state sponsor of terrorism in the world. That all goes away, now. Hezbollah, Hamas . . . they're *hamstrung*," Robard almost chortled, pleased at his own play on words. "Backing for the civil war in Syria is already almost non-existent, thanks to our blockade of Iran. That situation has almost stabilized on its own, albeit not in the best way, but a secular Iran is a *huge* worry off Israel's shoulders."

"What about the situation in Crimea?" Marsden asked. His NSA had informed him that the Russian flag was flying over Sevastopol, and the Kremlin had formally reclaimed the Crimean Peninsula as part of the Russian Federation. With the situation in the Gulf, there hadn't been much time to devote to that issue.

The secretary shrugged. "A problem for another day, Mister President. One crisis at a time, eh? This one is just about wrapped up, thanks to your leadership. Markets are going to be booming within the week, and the economy is going to see a huge uptick, just in time for the midterms! I think you'll be riding this wave all the way into 'sixteen!"

Marsden clapped him on the shoulder, nodding and smiling. "That's good news, Mister Robard. Good news indeed. What would make this a win for the ages is a formal surrender from Iran, bringing an official end to the war. I want you to make that our number one priority, and you make sure Mister Ghorbani understands this is the swiftest route to helping his people, and himself politically."

"Yes, Mister President, we'll make it happen," Robard assured him.

***

IRAN SURRENDERS!
Provisional Government agrees to U.S. conditions; Hostilities cease.

-N.Y. Times

TEHRAN FALLS TO CITIZENS REVOLUTION!
Secular Government forms in Tehran as Ghorbani states: "The reign of the mullahs has ended."

-London Times

Ali Ghorbani. Who is he? What are his plans for the future of Iran?

-Time Magazine

Russian Flag raised over Crimea! Amid turmoil in the Gulf, Russian aggression in the Black Sea goes unchallenged.

-Chicago Sun Times

James Marsden—a shoo-in for 2016? Polls indicate record high approval ratings among voters in both parties.

-Washington Post

USS Hornet *battle group headed home from the Gulf. CNO Harris quoted as saying that the viability of carrier battle groups is 'proven beyond a reasonable doubt.'*

-U.S. Naval Institute News

Funding confirmed for new class of aircraft carriers. USS Ranger, CVN-78, to be the class name of next generation flat top.

-Defense News Weekly

Replacing the Super Hornet—the next dogfight on Capitol Hill. What comes next? Northman-Ironworks pitches the AF/X to the Senate Armed Services Committee.

MAY 2014
Tiger 100, NAS Lemoore, California

Fargo thought about his conversation with Buzz over some cold beers during their brief port call in Pearl Harbor, just a few days before the big air wing flyoff. He'd opened up to his XO, asking him for relationship advice. He verbally ran through all his worries and concerns, and was discomfited to find Buzz smirking at him when he finally ran down, somewhere into their third beer.

"Look, Fargo, there's no perfect answer to all this," Buzz told him. "Think about it: in all walks of life: everyone has relationship issues, everyone works too hard and neglects their spouse, everyone's teenager thinks they're smarter than mom and dad, yadda, yadda, yadda. To hear you break it down, it's amazing humans have survived this long."

"You and Lisa seem to have it all locked down."

Buzz laughed. "We've had our moments, believe me! There were two times during our marriage when I was sure divorce papers were coming across the table, but in the end we've stuck it out and made it work, and we're a stronger couple for it. Look, Fargo, you're overthinking it. There are only two real questions to answer. Do you love her?"

"Yes," Fargo replied immediately, and he was surprised how quickly and easily the answer came to his lips. As soon as it did, he began feeling that knot of anxiety easing inside him.

"Does she love you?"

"She says she does," Fargo replied.

"Well, that's it, then," Buzz said. "The rest is details. If you love each other, don't worry about the other shit—that'll work itself out in the wash. Roll the dice and live your life, Skipper. What the hell is it all for if you've got nobody to go home to at the end of the day?"

"Thanks, Buzz," Fargo had said.

"Don't mention it," Buzz replied, and ordered them another round.

Now Fargo glanced out to either side of his jet, feeling a surge of pride as he saw all eleven of his surviving Supercats riding in a nice, tight formation, wings swept aft, looking good for the home crowd. At that moment he just felt a sense of utter gratitude: that time, circumstances, and fate had brought him to this moment the way they had. He was a naval aviator returning victorious from war, the commanding officer of Fighting 6, flying the hottest jet in existence, and there was no place on God's Earth he would rather be than right where he was. Down there on the flight line, several hundred friends and relatives watched in gleeful anticipation. Fargo's heart was full.

"Tower, Tiger One, flight of eleven, initial," Freckles called from the back seat.

"Black Tigers, Reeves Tower, cleared Runway 32L, break at your discretion. Welcome home!"

"Tiger One and flight," Freckles replied. The formation was too large for Fargo to communicate via hand signals; they had rehearsed this a couple of times overwater in anticipation of this moment. Freckles waited until they hit a predetermined point just short of the numbers, and gave an "Execute!" call over the radio. Starting from the outside of the formation, the Black Tigers began to peel off left and right in pairs, timing their breaks, until all eleven Tomcats were spaced out evenly in the pattern. One by one the wings swept forward, gear and flaps were extended, and the jets began graceful approach turns from the '180' position abeam the runway numbers, arcing around to touch down one after another.

Fargo's heart was thumping in his chest as he taxied onto the flight line and saw the crowd of people there: wives, sweethearts, children, parents, siblings, and friends. There were huge smiles, not a few tears as well, and American flags of every size were well represented. Linemen in yellow deck jerseys conducted themselves like they were at an airshow, marshaling the Tomcats into their parking spots and rendering sharp salutes, before standing smartly at parade rest. The Black Tigers executed a coordinated shutdown of their engines, and opened their canopies as one. As soon as the feet of the aviators touched the deck, the crowd broke in a human wave across the ramp, and the joyous reunions began in earnest.

Angela wore the same blue dress she'd worn for the establishment ceremony; she was easy to pick out as she and A.J. bolted across the ramp to meet him. A.J. was faster than his mom, dressed in blue jeans and a kid-size flight jacket sporting Black Tigers patchwork. Fargo knelt and caught him up in a crushing bearhug, tears stinging his eyes as an eleven-year old boy he hardly knew greeted him like he was his old man. Angela was on him a moment later, and after the past six months of combat and life aboard ship, there was no sweeter feeling than the soft press of her lips against his, breathing her breath into his mouth. All his worries and fears fell away in that moment, and the future crystalized in an instant.

Fortunately for Fargo, his official bio read that he was single. The media were present in force, camera crews weaving their way amongst the revelers, eager to find him in the crowd for an interview. He was able to dodge that bullet for the moment thanks to the camouflage that his family gave him. They managed to make it into the hangar without being accosted, where Fargo changed into a non-descript pair of jeans and a comfortable flannel shirt. When he rejoined A.J. and Angie, he folded them both into his embrace and the three of them headed for the parking lot, arm in arm.

"What now?" A.J. asked.

Fargo laughed. "Well, I've been thinking about that, y'know? How about a trip to Six Flags," he said, looking deep into Angie's shining eyes. "We can ride roller coasters till we puke, eat junk food . . . and your Ma and I can talk about a few things. Whaddya think?"

"Yah, that sounds awesome!" A.J. shouted.

"What do you think?" Fargo repeated, this time to Angela.

She stopped them, wrapped her arms around his neck, and her kiss was all the answer he needed.

Appendix A

Presidential Succession

1980-1988	Ronald Reagan
1988-1992	George H. W. Bush
1992-2000	William J. Clinton
2000-2004	Albert Gore
2004-2012	Colin Powell
2012-	James Marsden

USN Carrier Fleet

CVN-68	USS *Nimitz*	
CVN-69	USS *Yorktown*	
CVN-70	USS *Hornet*	
CVN-71	USS *Boxer*	
CVN-72	USS *Oriskany*	
CVN-73	USS *Intrepid*	
CVN-74	USS *Essex*	
CVN-75	USS *Coral Sea*	
CVN-76	USS *Lexington*	
CVN-77	USS *Saratoga*	
CVN-78	USS *Ranger*	(Proposed)
CVN-79	USS *Kitty Hawk*	(Proposed)
CVN-80	USS *Enterprise*	(Proposed)

Appendix B

Common Brevity Codes

Angels | Altitude stated in thousands of feet.

Bandit | Aircraft identified as hostile.

Bird(s) | Friendly surface-to-air missile(s).

Blind | Caller does not have visual contact with the bogey or target in question.

Bogey | Aircraft which is unidentified or has been declared neutral or non-hostile.

Bugout | Disengagement from an air/ground target with no intent to re-engage.

Buster | Directive to fly at maximum speed without afterburner.

Bullseye | A reference point from which position information on other units are based.

Commit | Fighter signaling intent or readiness to engage.

Extend | An aerial maneuver to gain energy (airspeed) or separation.

Gate | Directive to fly at maximum speed using afterburner.

Judy | Intercepting flight has target in radar or visual contact and assumes responsibility for intercept.

Pelican | A maritime patrol aircraft.

Racket | Refers to the detection, tracking, and identification of a radar emitter.

Skunk | A maritime contact whose identity is unknown.

Snap | An immediate vector to the aircraft receiving it.

Spike | Indicates detection of a threat radar in lock, track, or launch mode.

Tally | Caller has visual contact on the bogey or target.

Tiger | Fuel and/or stores sufficient to accept further tasking.

Vampire | Hostile anti-ship missile.

About the Author

Brian J. Smith is a graduate of the University of Southern California, a former naval aviator, and commercial pilot. An empty nester, he currently resides with his wife Andrea and a pair of furry felines in Boise, Idaho.

www.ingramcontent.com/pod-product-compliance
Lightning Source LLC
Chambersburg PA
CBHW072022020726
47501CB00006B/1917